THE FINAL BOW

THE FINAL BOW

A NOVEL

ALAN

DAVID

JUSTICE

THOMAS NELSON PUBLISHERS
Nashville

Published in Nashville, Tennessee, by Thomas Nelson, Inc., Publishers, and distributed in Canada by Word Communications, Ltd., Richmond, British Columbia, and in the United Kingdom by Word (UK), Ltd., Milton Keynes, England.

Scripture quotations are from The Holy Bible, KING JAMES VERSION.

Library of Congress Information

Justice, Alan David.
    The final bow : a novel / Alan David Justice.
       p.   c.
    ISBN 0-8407-3469-7 (pbk.)
    1. Church history—Primitive and early church, ca. 30–600—Fiction. 2. Rome—History—Diocletian, 284–305—Fiction. I. Title.
PS3560.U83F55 1993
813'.54—dc20   93-18231
                                                CIP

Printed in the United States of America

1 2 3 4 5 6 7 - 98 97 96 95 94 93

For Ginnie,
who introduced me to Genesius years ago

T

he time of the story of Genesius is A.D. 303-304, during the late Roman Empire. It is the time of a ruling body known as the tetrarchy, when in practice there were four Roman "emperors." This system was instituted by Diocletian to better govern the vast areas under his control.

The senior emperor was Diocletian himself, who directly ruled the eastern provinces. His co-emperor was Maximian, who ruled Italy and much of Africa. Under Diocletian was his caesar, Galerius, responsible for Greece and the Danubian provinces.

To cement relations between himself and Galerius, Diocletian named the latter his heir, adopted him as a son, and married his daughter Valeria to him.

Diocletian's aim was to stabilize the government of the empire. Not only did he establish a huge bureaucracy, institutionalize the succession, and successfully defend the borders against barbarian invaders, he also sought, at the urging of Galerius, to control the religious beliefs of his subjects. When he tackled the maturing Christian church, though, his reach exceeded his grasp.

Less than a year after beginning the persecution, Diocletian abdicated.

Genesius' legs twitched in an agony of expectation. In a moment he would step in front of the curtain to face the person of the caesar Galerius. From the other side of the backdrop he could hear a competitor running through his act. Sandaled feet scuffled, dancing across the stone of the stage floor, their steady rhythm interrupted irregularly by pratfall and recovery.

One last time Genesius reviewed his audition piece. Behind the *siparium*, he was bathed in sweat. The shade of the back curtain kept him from the worst of the late spring sun, but it also shut out the breeze. The atmosphere was close and stifling.

"That's enough!" The voice that shouted from the seats was bored and made more distant by the intervening curtain. The broken shuffle went on a moment longer, then faltered to a stop.

"Over there," the voice called. "Wait."

Genesius gathered his concentration, still trembling. The arena was silent, save for the diminishing footsteps of the previous auditioner who was moving toward stage left. Genesius stepped into position, just behind the slit in the curtain, his stomach knotted with anxiety. The man ahead reached the seats; the shuffling stopped. On tiptoe now, Genesius leaned forward. He listened for the subtle sounds of breathing and heard the whispered end of a brief, judgmental conference, the intake of air by the official in charge of the auditions and dived through the curtain into a shoulder roll.

Center stage, he heard the official call "Next!" as he leaped to his feet and tumbled off the lip of the stage and rolled into the flat, semicircular orchestra of the Roman theater. The bright sun blinded him, as he had expected, and he stood up, facing the wrong way. Arms waving furiously, feeling for direction, he fumbled and tripped his way stage left. Sensing the edge of the orchestra, he threw a covert glance over his shoulder and saw the caesar and the official at the center of the house, smiling and leaning forward in their seats.

Still appearing to be sun-blind, he stumbled onward, using a drunkard's walk to fall unerringly into the lap of the previous actor and spring the trap.

"Oh!" he exclaimed. "Excuse me, sir. My apologies."

"Get off of me, you fool!" the man cried, pushing at Genesius' sprawling, somehow clinging, arms and legs.

"I've ruined your audition, I know I have," Genesius whined. "Here, I insist. Come back to the stage. I'll go off, and you can finish."

The man, now enraged, stood up, but Genesius still clung to him, hanging horizontally across his body. He tried to shake Genesius off but failed to loosen his grip.

"Don't drop me!" Genesius screamed. "I'm afraid of heights." The man punched him in the ribs; Genesius grunted and increased the pressure of his grip.

"Just put me down—gently!—and I'll let go," Genesius whispered. "I've already beaten you and you know it. You can either cooperate or be humiliated."

The blows continued to fall on Genesius. "You've made your choice."

Genesius twisted, shifting his weight. The man overbalanced; the two of them tumbled backward onto the orchestra floor and rolled to its center. Genesius leaped to his feet in triumph, downstage of the actor but still facing away from the imperial auditor.

The man struggled to his hands and knees, his face contorted in fury.

"You're trying to make a fool of me!" the man hissed.

"No," Genesius whispered, "I've made a fool of myself. You have, however, been quite helpful."

"No!" the man cried, his eyes widening. They focused on the figure of Galerius doubled up with laughter.

Genesius followed his look. His own eyes grew huge as he turned to face caesar. He circled backward around the man, who was still on all fours. Genesius' eyes searched wildly around the theater as if seeking escape from the august presence, afraid of the offense he must have committed against the imperial majesty.

"I . . . I . . . I . . ." Genesis stuttered. He felt the knots return to his stomach and tightened the muscles to make them even worse.

"Go on!" Galerius shouted through his tears. "More!"

"I beg your forgiv—" Genesius began. Then he widened his eyes again, letting a look of alarm pass over his contorted, terrified face. He belched and contracted his stomach. Desperately he searched the theater for a place to hide. Again he belched, looking helplessly to the laughing caesar, feeling his face go white and the sweat spring from his brow.

Genesius fell to his knees behind the defeated actor and vomited on his head.

The actor wiped the flux from his face and roared deep in his throat. Genesius stood up slowly, alarm spreading over his features. He backed away from the enraged actor and jumped on stage toward the *siparium*, the curtain at the back of the stage. The actor followed, slowly at first; Genesius cowered against the curtain, searching furiously and unsuccessfully for the slit through which he had entered. The actor leaped on stage after Genesius, murder in his eye, but Genesius sidestepped and tripped him, simultaneously yanking on the curtain. It fell in folds around the actor. Genesius wrapped him up in it, dragged the struggling bundle downstage center, stood behind it, and took his bow.

The three spectators—Galerius, myself, and Diarius, the manager-to-be of the troupe—applauded enthusiastically.

Nothing on the stage was more pleasing to auditors and spectators than the comic Christian.
—ST. GREGORY OF NAZIANZUS

Freeborn men are forbidden to marry a prostitute, a procuress, a woman set free by a procurer or procuress, one caught in adultery, one convicted in a public action, or one who has been an actress.
—FROM THE LAWS OF THE EMPEROR AUGUSTUS

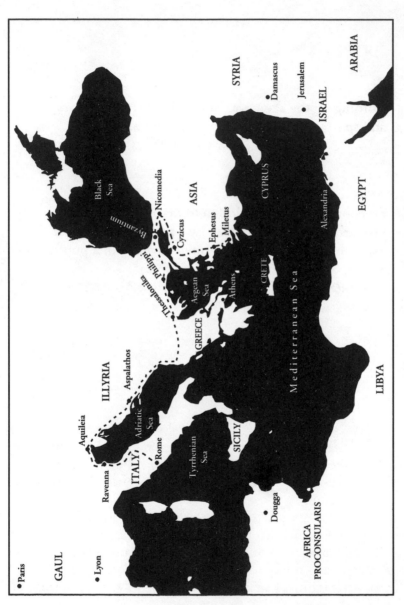

The travels of Genesius, A.D. 303-304

His first journey — ·— ·— ·—

His second journey ·········

M

Y DEAR DONATUS:

Grace to you and peace!

While you stay in prison to learn whether you will remain in the world for a little longer or achieve freedom into the Lord by being released from the clay of your body, I would help you to occupy the waiting hours with the tale of one who just recently achieved the crown of martyrdom.

I begin with his story that I might surprise and amuse you. While my technique may seem unsuited to a work of this kind, my language sometimes rough and uncultured, I want to present to you, and those with you, a true picture of the man—the youth, really—of whom I write. Thus, if sometimes I seem intemperate, it is to show intemperance. Our Lord did not forbid us laughter.

I would not have you dwell on your present troubles. Indeed, you are fortunate in some ways. Your challenge is known to you. In prison, you avoid the mobs of the pagans who cry daily for the blood of the faithful. You are safe from the demands of the magistrates for sacrifice. You have no temptation to visit the lisping players and be distracted from the gaze of the Great Spectator. It is less difficult to focus the mind on God from within the prison's walls than from the bleachers of the amphitheater.

Or so I believe.

For I inhabit a different prison. I live in the belly of the beast that ravages the world, which constantly tries (and constantly fails!) to devour the body of Christ. Encouraged by my bishop, I write to you and to others about the philosophy which our faith preaches and the tales of those who find their way to glory.

In some ways, I even envy you; I, who inhabit the court of the emperor, who never want for splendid foods and graceful comforts, who travel the military roads on an imperial pass to wonderful places, find myself beset with the sin of envy for the clarity of your calling. Forgive me, my brother in Christ; I only tell you of my envy in case that you may lose heart while you lie in prison. As Paul has written, "There are many gifts, but always one Spirit; all sorts of service to be done, but always to the same Lord." He calls us all, but He calls us for different tasks.

The task which He has given me is that of chronicler of these days, and so I am led to live through them, even to the time (may it be soon!) when our sufferings are ended. For now, we must endure these pains and indeed welcome the chance they give us to demonstrate our faith to the world, that all men may be brought to God (some say that even the devil may be forgiven at the end of time; I am not so sure). Lest these struggles be forgotten in later times, I am set to write down and cause to be preserved this record. And lest you and those with you fail in hope, I am set to write down the history of one who gained the crown against all odds and laid down his earthly life to convict of wrongdoing and sin him who held the greatest earthly power, even to the point where he gave up his power, sick of its uses.

For you have heard by now that Diocletian has abdicated the throne of the empire, and in his place rules Galerius, his former lieutenant, one who, when God wills it, will suffer greatly for his crimes against God's people.

But I go before myself in setting the result of my story before the antecedents. See it, then, as a sort of play, a mime. For the leading player is an actor and was indeed one of the foremost of those who parody and ridicule the rites and belief of our church. And yet, even from this source, the Lord finds His followers.

Truly, if even an actor can find forgiveness, then perhaps at the end of time, the devil himself may be saved.

Diocletian, through the counsel of his lieutenant Galerius, had already formed the intention of beginning the persecution. To encourage the citizens to hate the Christians even more, he decided to form a troupe of actors who would use their art to mock the faith. I had my first encounter with the actor Genesius at the occasion of the auditions for this troupe. And truly, his talent was spectacular. Much of my account is written as if from Genesius' point of view, as I had it from him at a later time. When I write of what Genesius saw and heard and felt, I shall try to use his voice and not my own, for his voice indeed was wonderful even before he gained his crown.

Diocletian had sent me to watch the auditions as his representative. The responsibility he gave me was this: that the actors chosen should be the best available. In some sense, I was aiding him in the beginning of the persecution, for the troupe would go among the people and stir their feelings against the Christians. But what was I to do? To refuse the commission of the emperor was not possible.

✦ ✦ ✦

Galerius heaved his bulk from the seat of honor, still laughing at Genesius' antics, and returned to the palace immediately following the auditions. Galerius, the emperor's chief lieutenant, was a huge man, disproportionately large, almost malformed. His size contributed to his power, for it made him personally fearsome. He had strength enough in one of his massive hands to crush a man's skull. I was happy to be out of his presence.

Genesius the actor was a young man, dark-skinned, with curly black hair cut short in the Roman style. He was thin, partly from his natural build, partly from never having quite enough to eat. His manner on the stage mirrored his off-stage behavior—he seemed to revel in the impolite, to delight in irreverence. And there was a sense of opportunism in the youth as well; he knew his goals, and, having no position or fortune to lose, he aimed all of his considerable energy at advancing himself.

The manager, a fat balding little man, took the actor Genesius backstage to the dressing rooms.

✦ ✦ ✦

Alone, I climbed the hill from the theater, a small one built for Diocletian's entertainment, to the church in Nicomedia, which stood on a high hill in those days, overshadowing the imperial palace. Now that hill is bare.

The bishop Anthimus greeted me warmly.

"So," he said, "how goes the new persecution?"

"Galerius gathers his forces," I said. "Even the actors are now enlisted against us."

I told him of the auditions, of the plans of Diocletian and Galerius to use the theater as a place of stirring up the mob. He was calm in the face of this information. He seemed, with his aged face, only to accept knowledge without feeling the pangs which I myself felt at the coming suffering.

Anthimus, bishop of Nicomedia, the city of imperial residence during the reign of Diocletian and the tetrarchy, was an old man. He was born in Ephesus to a family of believers who traced their birth in the faith all the way back to the apostle John. Under Nero, Valerian, Domitian, and Decius, members of his family had been persecuted for their faith. If we are all sinners, then the guilt of Anthimus was borne in the fact that he was a survivor. Raised on the bloody tales of persecutions, he of all his kin was unbloodied. He thought this a fault and hourly prayed to be delivered from it, but still it ate at his vitals like some destroying cancer. Knowing this, I once again questioned him concerning the vocation he had seen for me.

"I am still troubled," I said, "about what you have asked of me. Today I assisted—in a small way, it is true—in arranging the beginnings of the persecution that we all know is coming. Galerius declared himself an enemy to the faith long ago, and he is wearing down Diocletian. It will start soon. I can hear the blacksmiths hammering the swords, the carpenters sawing the wood for crosses. The torches are being set aside for the fires."

"How soon?" Anthimus asked.

I could not see a way to spare him the knowledge. "No one knows the day or the hour, but it is coming closer. Galerius has his plans."

"Let us know," Anthimus said, "when you hear something. The people will need to be prepared." When I returned to the palace, I found that the time was even closer than I had thought.

✦ ✦ ✦

The caesar spoke to his flunky, who came down to the stage floor, then Galerius turned and left for the palace. As he reached the shrine of Venus at the top of the auditorium, his guards closed around him.

"Congratulations!" the official said. "You've earned yourself a job with that one. What's your name?"

"Genesius."

"I am Diarius," the official said, "Diarius of Alexandria."

"You look differently now than you do on stage," Genesius said.

"That's as it should be," Diarius said, "but thank you for the compliment. Where are you from?"

"Here. Nicomedia."

"You're a local?" the little round man asked. "I didn't know such talent grew here."

The bundle of actor at their feet struggled to free itself. Diarius looked down at him.

"Don't worry about him," he said to Genesius. "He'll be well paid. He did a good audition, though it was nothing next to yours. Such audacity! Do you know what the job entails?"

The two walked back through the *siparium*, Diarius making two steps for every one of the lanky Genesius.

"Don't walk so fast," he complained, "I can't keep up with you."

"Sorry." Genesius slowed his steps. Diarius caught up. "What's the job?"

"First," Diarius said, "are you slave or free?"

"Free."

They had reached the stage house now and entered the performers' dressing room.

"Go ahead and change," Diarius said. "I want you to meet the others."

"The others?" Genesius stripped off his stained and torn patchwork tunic and began to sponge off the worst of the sweat and dust.

"Yes," Diarius said. "We're putting together a special mime company. Very special, very important."

"To whom?"

"To Galerius. To Diocletian. To the empire itself," he said. "We already have our ingenue, our old woman, and the leading actor— that's myself—and now we have our fool. If you're interested, that is."

"I want to work," Genesius said, "or else I wouldn't be here."

Diarius handed Genesius a towel. "The rest of the company is still being chosen. We'll have a basic group of six or seven, plus extras for the bit parts.

"The emperor's twentieth anniversary is coming up in about nine months," Diarius went on. "He wants a celebration. No other emperor since Augustus has even lived that long after assuming the purple."

"But why start a mime troupe?" Genesius asked. "He could have the pick of Rome." He threw a clean tunic over his head. In spite of himself, he was beginning to like the little man Diarius. Besides, he had a job. He could be gracious enough to listen to his benefactor.

"Diocletian hates the city, thinks the Roman mob is the most dangerous thing in or out of the empire, except for the Christians and the Manichaeans," Diarius said. "And, he wants quality more than popularity. He figures you'll earn that. Leave your old costume; you'll have better. Aristarchus is our costumer."

"Of Corinth?" Genesius was impressed in spite of himself.

"The same," Diarius grinned. "Now do you see what you've gotten yourself into?"

Genesius grinned back. "He's as good as they come."

"No," said Diarius, "I am. As you will soon find out."

He took from his purse a brooch with the emperor's seal on it and pinned it on Genesius' tunic. "Wear this. You're in. I'll take care of the formalities later."

Genesius' fingers touched the golden brooch in wonder. The risk he had run in the audition had paid off. He was starting a new life.

"Come on," Diarius said. "You can dream later. Let's go meet the others."

As they turned to go, Genesius stopped to look back at the ragged, patched tunic he had left crumpled on the bench of the dressing room. Diarius looked back at him.

"May Bacchus save me from star-struck actors," he moaned. He took Genesius by the arm and led him out into the sunlit streets of Nicomedia.

"After eighteen years of imperial rule here," Diarius said as they walked, "you would think that Nicomedia would finally grow up. It will never be Rome, I know, but still, it could be a bit more cosmopolitan."

"What's the matter with it?" Genesius asked.

"It's a backwater, that's what's wrong with it. You're lucky to be getting out, a young man with your talent. Can you call this—" Diarius waved his arm vaguely at the city as a whole "—a capital?"

"I always have," Genesius said.

"Humph!" Diarius grunted. "It's so commercial! Nothing but bureaucrats and soldiers and the shopkeepers and whores who service them! Where did you ever expect to get work as an artist of the theater?"

Genesius smiled. "Well, I seem to have done so."

"So you have," Diarius admitted. "So you have. It won't be Greek tragedy, I promise you that, but you have found yourself a job."

The stone Jupiter scowled back at Diocletian as he waited for Galerius to return from the city. His attendants, he noticed, shifted nervously on their feet, as if expecting a storm of anger to break from his brow and lash them with hail and lightning. Still he continued to scowl back at the Jupiter on the wall at the far end of the audience chamber.

His wife and empress, Prisca, touched his sleeve. He turned to her.

"Look at them," he said. "They're wondering what's going to happen. As if I knew."

"They're not alone," she said quietly, so that the nearby courtiers would not hear her.

Diocletian turned to look at his wife. She was still, after all this time, the most beautiful woman he knew. And yet there was a secret hidden behind the clear forehead, a secret that he was afraid to uncover. He suspected both her and their daughter Valeria of sedition. He was afraid that they were Christians and that he might have to kill them for it.

It could be worse, he admitted. Prisca might have been tempted by Manichaeism. But that was virtually unthinkable. The followers of the Persian, Mani, were traitors to the empire. He had not, so far, considered the Christ-followers in the same light, but the suspicion was growing in him that tolerance was the wrong road to follow. The allegiance of the Christians was suspect. He hated to compare himself to the dissolute Nero, but the earlier emperor had recognized the dangers to himself and to the empire in the doctrine of the Jewish sect.

His caesar, Galerius, his adopted son, was less temperate than Diocletian. Galerius wanted another persecution. He wanted to eliminate the non-Roman sects from the face of the earth.

Diocletian looked through the window of the hall at the Christian "church" that stood within sight of his palace. The Christians were expanding. There were far more now than there had been in the time of Nero, more than Decius had tried to cleanse from the world. No one knew how many there were, as no one knew how many people were subject to Rome—to him, Augustus of Rome.

Rome—there were plans afoot there too. He would finally be forced to visit the city he detested, the city that was, in theory, the seat of his power.

He slammed his open palm against the arm of his throne. From all over the hall, eyes turned in his direction; the muted buzz of conversation halted. He looked about, and as his eyes caught those of the people staring at him, they turned away, pretending an elaborate unconcern. Like cats they were, his royal subjects, pretending that the startling outburst had not happened, that they were guilty of nothing, that their nervousness was his fault.

He stared them down, group by group, and then looked to Prisca at his side. She wore the same expression he had just seen on the startled faces of the court.

"No," he said, touching her hand, "it's nothing. Just a momentary frustration. Relax. Galerius will be here soon."

No sooner had he spoken than he heard the sound of Galerius' train entering the courtyard. The interrupted conversations of the courtiers resumed. Diocletian knew what they must be saying: although Diocletian held the office of Augustus, Galerius ruled in all but name. What they failed to understand was that the system Diocletian had developed with his co-emperor Maximian and each of the emperors' caesars worked. Diocletian ruled the East, Maximian the West. The empire was too large, too complex for one man to comprehend in any useful detail. While he did not always agree with the decisions of his imperial cohorts, he realized that they each ruled well enough to keep the empire together, and that was an improvement over some of the one-man reigns that had preceded his tetrarchy.

The trumpets sounded. Galerius and Valeria were announced, and all in the hall, save Diocletian and Prisca, knelt at the entry of Caesar. Diocletian rose from his throne and stepped forward to embrace his subordinate partner, who dropped to one knee in obedience.

"Hail, Augustus!" Galerius said and stood.

"And hail, Caesar!" Diocletian answered. "Come, sit with us and tell us what you have found in the city."

Diocletian led Galerius to the dais on which the throne stood. Valeria made her obeisance and joined her mother on a couch to the side of the double throne.

"Information has come in," Galerius said, "that suggests the possibility that there may be Christians among your retinue."

Diocletian stared at his counselor.

"What is the source of your information?" he said coldly. "The reports of paid informers, disaffected slaves, or ambitious courtiers?"

"No, lord," Galerius said. "The Christians keep records of their rites—who participates, the dates of their participation—their church is full of writing. We know, without a doubt. Their own records tell us."

"And how did you find this out?" Diocletian asked. He needed time, for the assault was surely coming. It would strike at his heart—at his wife and daughter—and he needed to deflect it, disprove it somehow.

"An apostate, lord," Galerius said, "who saw the error of his ways and wishes to repent his Christianity and worship you as Jupiter."

"And yourself too?" Diocletian asked.

"In time, perhaps, my lord."

"Tell me, Galerius," Diocletian said, "do you like the idea of being a god?"

"Of course."

"Who is this man?"

"He awaits word from you to enter and confess his error."

"Who is it?" Diocletian demanded.

"His name is John."

"You shouldn't, you know. Gods ought to be more sure of themselves." Diocletian seated himself on the throne. Galerius was younger and did not yet seem to mind standing for long periods of time.

"What are you afraid of?"

"Nothing on this earth, lord," Galerius said.

"Sit down," Diocletian ordered.

"The man will confess!" Galerius said. "And he will implicate others. It's the chance we've been waiting for."

"You've been waiting. I haven't," Diocletian said.

"He is here," Galerius said. "Not only that, he is ready."

"You are certain that he will confess—and repent?"

"I am."

"There will be no surprises?"

"None."

"I will speak with my daughter and my wife," Diocletian said. "Remain here."

He rose, and all in the hall who were seated rose with him. He turned to Prisca and Valeria. "Come."

The three removed themselves through the exit behind the throne, not waiting for the bows of those who stayed in the hall.

Behind the hall, in the small room used for vesting the imperial body before court functions, Diocletian confronted Prisca and Valeria. The former, now in her late forties, seemed to be waiting to be struck; Valeria's younger features mirrored her mother's looks as well as her expression. Valeria had been married to Galerius shortly after Diocletian had assumed the purple, as a way of cementing the relations between the old emperor and his chosen lieutenant. She had never complained, but neither had she thanked her father for the match. Mother and daughter, though, were still close.

Diocletian faced the two. "It's come," he said. "The time when I can no longer protect you from Galerius and from yourselves."

There was no answer from the two women.

"What are you going to do?"

"What can we do?" Prisca said.

"You have a choice," Diocletian said. "You can shake my realm to its foundations, or you can make the sacrifice. You can renounce your Oriental superstitions, or you can break in four the peace of the empire—let Maximian and Constantius wreak havoc on each other in the West, while Galerius and I squabble over the East, and the barbarians come at us from all sides. You can forge a unity that will keep the status quo intact and the savages at bay, or you can sever the empire in four parts. You can bring peace or a sword.

"Make your decision. Make it now," he said. He left the two women, whom he more than suspected of Christianity, in the vesting chamber and returned to his throne. Galerius was waiting, expectant, badly concealing a wolfish look on his face.

"We will proceed," Diocletian said to his lieutenant. "Be careful."

CHAPTER 2

T he actors were herded into line outside the audience hall, behind the bureaucrats and free servants, just in front of the household slaves. No one knew quite what was going on, but they lived their lives at the behest of others at all times. Slaves know how to wait; they passed the time with speculation, some of which, if their masters had known of it, was far more accurate than they would have liked.

After some time, the praetorians opened the carved doors to the audience hall. The stable slaves gawked at the chiseled beauty of the place, the fine clothing of the courtiers and the women. The household slaves pretended that they were unimpressed with all the finery but shot covert glances around the room, trying to read the situation from the relative positions of the members of the court. Genesius, a newcomer to the retinue of the Augustus, acted like a stable hand, eyes lifted to the ceiling, in more than a little awe at his surroundings. Diarius dug an elbow into his ribs and whispered harshly.

"Don't act like a fool!" he said. "Follow my lead."

"What's going on?" Genesius asked.

"Diocletian is in a terrible mood. Look at his face."

"If you ask me," Hysteria whispered, "someone's in deep trouble, and it's someone he likes."

"Who asked you, old woman?" Diarius said.

He spoke to Genesius. "You're playing a role—that of the loyal servant. Play it well." He turned to Hysteria and Atalanta, the inge- nue. "That goes for all of you."

Hysteria smiled coyly. "I hear and obey, O master."

"Is that Diocletian?" Genesius asked. "He looks older than I thought he would."

"When you've been trying to rule the world for twenty years," Diarius said, "see how you look. The wonder of it is that he's alive at all."

"But he doesn't even look like a Roman," Genesius objected.

"He's not," Diarius explained. "I thought everyone knew that he was an Illyrian peasant."

"Illyrian?"

"The area across the Adriatic from Italy. North of Greece."

"And a peasant?"

"He started out as a common soldier," Atalanta put in, "and raised himself up from the ranks."

"And," Hysteria added, "he survived."

"It's all too much for me," Genesius said. He took a small wineskin from beneath his tunic. Before he could raise it to his mouth, Diarius grabbed his wrist, holding it down and out of sight.

"What are you doing with that?"

"I wanted something to drink. What's the harm in that?"

"Drop it," Diarius ordered. "Get rid of it. The guards are jumpy. You're in the presence of the emperor. If they see anything that might hide a weapon, you'll be killed—and us with you."

Genesius nodded. "I didn't know what I was getting into."

"You're in the big time now, boy."

Diarius was distracted as the chatter of the crowd stilled and Prisca and Valeria came into the audience hall from the vesting room to take their places in the front rank of the courtiers. Galerius stepped forward and faced the assembly.

"Bring in the man!" he ordered.

Through the door came two soldiers holding between them a young man in his twenties, scarcely bearded. They marched him through the crowd and deposited him, cowering, in front of Galerius.

No one was watching Genesius. He hid the tiny wineskin beneath his tunic, under his belt. He had used his first pay as a servant of the court to purchase an expensive vintage of white wine. He refused to waste it.

The caesar called for the priest of Jupiter, who came forward followed by two acolytes. Each carried a tripod, one containing incense, the other ready for the fire. In the taller tripod, the priest kindled a fire of small branches and beeswax. Galerius signaled the youth, who reached into the lower tripod, took a pinch of incense, and deposited it in the flame.

"I swear by the sacred name of Jupiter, incarnate in the Emperor Diocletian. I renounce the name of Christ and declare that he and all his kind are false."

Galerius signaled again, and another soldier came forward carrying a golden cross. Galerius took it as if it were tainted and held the cross aloft.

"What is this object?" The question was directed to the youth, Genesius saw, but Galerius' eyes were on Prisca and Valeria.

"It is the symbol of the Christians, lord," the youth said.

His body testified to the fact that he had been thoroughly coached in preparation for this ceremony.

"Wife," Galerius said, turning on her, "how does Rome execute her enemies?"

Valeria, eyes downcast, mumbled unintelligibly.

"Wife, I would have your answer. In the presence of all these subjects of the emperor, I would have your answer."

"Caesar," Prisca said, "the enemies of Rome are crucified, as you well know."

"My thanks, Augusta," he said. "Your daughter seems unable to speak." He turned to the crowd. Genesius saw Diocletian watching Galerius. His expression was troubled but unreadable.

"The enemies of Rome are crucified," Galerius continued, "and this is the symbol of their god, this Christ. It follows, therefore, that this Christ—and his followers—are enemies of Rome."

He lifted the cross into the air so that all could see it. "Who here reveres this sign? Who here is a Christian? Who here declares himself an enemy of Rome?"

There was silence in the hall. Eyes avoided other eyes.

"It is said," Galerius spoke again, "that there are disloyal subjects in the court of our sacred emperor, subjects who secretly obey this criminal, this Christ. It is said that these Christians keep records of the persons belonging to their sect."

Genesius wondered at the Christians' intelligence, keeping files that could be used to hunt down their membership. They had been persecuted several times already; each time, their own writings had been used against them. Galerius, he understood, was reminding all the secret Christians in the court that they could be found out.

"For those of you who are loyal," Galerius continued, "I will explain. These Christians believe that their god is the only god and that he will punish them if they fulfill their duty toward the gods of Rome. Why," Galerius sniffed, "does a god need to be jealous? If he were as powerful as these Christians say he is, he could dissolve us all in a cloud of dust. But he does not."

Galerius handed the cross to a soldier, who placed it on the floor in front of the youth. The youth collected a gob of spittle in his mouth and deposited it on the cross.

At a signal from Galerius the acolytes knelt before Diocletian, then stood, took a pinch of incense from the bowl, and dropped it into the flame.

"As the flame burns this fragrant incense," the acolytes chanted, "so may my heart burn in worship of Diocletian, August Emperor of all Rome, Jupiter Incarnate."

Genesius watched Diocletian, anxious to see what his master was thinking. The emperor's face was impassive, but in his eyes there was the discomfort of a man who knew that he was being flattered. Diocletian was no Jupiter. Perhaps in the old days, there was a chance of the emperor's truly being a god. Why else had the Romans given up their sovereignty to a single man, unless he were something beyond the common run of humanity? But such things, if once possible, were so no longer in Genesius' experience. Maybe there had been miracles once; there were none now. Genesius could see that the man believed himself no god. The emperor was embarrassed as he listened to the fulsome words of the acolytes, then of Galerius, who repeated the formula.

Galerius finished his sacrifice and turned to Prisca and Valeria, who, as wife and daughter to the emperor, were next in precedence for the ceremony.

Prisca hesitated for only a moment (enough to convince Genesius that perhaps she was indeed a Christian, whatever that meant) before stepping in front of the throne. In her hesitation, she seemed to communicate something to her daughter. She knelt and then performed the sacrifice, throwing a large handful of incense on the flame. The fire was nearly smothered. Galerius started forward a step, then halted, almost expectantly. During the sudden, tense silence a cloud of thick, cloying smoke rose from the fire, which hissed for a moment before flaring up again. As it did so, the indrawn breath of all present was released. Prisca then looked to Diocletian.

"Must we also spit on this cross?" she asked. Diocletian nodded.

Prisca cleared her throat and aimed a ball of phlegm at the golden cross. Genesius watched it drop wetly onto the mosaic floor. Prisca looked toward Diocletian, then to Galerius, before starting back to her place.

It was Valeria's turn.

Her mother again caught the daughter's eye as they passed each other. Again the crowd seemed to hold its collective breath to see the outcome of the royal confrontation.

It occurred to Genesius that Galerius must feel very sure of himself to risk humiliating Diocletian publicly. Genesius had, quite literally, jumped at the chance to join the imperial entourage. Now he knew he had reckoned without the danger such advancement could bring. But he had delighted the Caesar Galerius; there was no turning back. He must continue to delight because his life might well depend on keeping his masters entertained.

Valeria passed the test of loyalty, and what had begun as drama declined into empty ceremony as the ministers and servants of the imperial court each declared his loyalty to the sacred person of the emperor. The performance of the rite grew dull in the warm afternoon.

After an hour's time, Galerius, Prisca, and Valeria had seated themselves on their thrones. The air grew smoky as more and more incense was thrown on the fire, which had been rekindled several times. Diocletian still sat erect, but Genesius saw that his thoughts were elsewhere. Galerius was ostentatiously bored, occasionally calling for refreshment. The two women sat stone-faced, apparently waiting for the ritual to end. The young man whose testimony started the whole event swayed from exhaustion.

There was no conversation allowed in the audience hall. But by means of signs and facial expressions, Diarius communicated his intention to entertain the royal audience and the crowd as a whole. Genesius signaled his agreement. In the suspicious atmosphere of the court, this ceremony came as an opportunity from the gods to cement their position as loyal servants of the imperium. The only difficulty would be to discover, in the short time they had left, an act sufficiently outrageous, sufficiently blasphemous to the Christian faith that Diocletian and Galerius would be unable to doubt their loyalty.

As the line moved forward, the actors came closer to the moment when they would make their obeisance. As they came to the fore, Genesius began to tremble, with small tremors at first, which rapidly increased as his time came. Diarius pushed Genesius to the front of the group of actors. Genesius trembled even more, and an expression of panic spread slowly across his features. Some of the panic, as in his audition, was real; some was his own creation. He had no idea how their improvisation would turn out. It was the riskiest kind of acting.

Genesius began a shoving match with Diarius, each trying to maneuver himself behind the other. A praetorian pushed himself toward them; they straightened up and stopped pushing each other. The praetorian returned to his place. The movement of the guard had caught the wandering attention of Diocletian, who glanced in their direction. The two actors looked at each other, grinned simultaneously, and performed a tuck and roll in perfect synchronization, jumping to their feet behind Atalanta and Hysteria. The latter lived up to her name and began to shriek in mock terror. Atalanta, the ingenue, wept with great vigor and greater noise. Several of the praetorians now moved toward the little group. They had no trouble reaching them because the slaves who were near the actors wanted to keep as far away from this attention-getting behavior as possible.

"Come on, you!" ordered a guard as he took Genesius roughly by the arm. Diarius was already in the grasp of another. The two women, shrieking and wailing, attached themselves to the ankles of the praetorians, forcing them to drag them across the floor, while Diarius went limp and Genesius went rigid, forcing the guards to pick them up and carry them forward to the tripod.

Genesius watched Diocletian grow angry for a moment, then saw the look of comprehension that his life depended on. Galerius started to stand up, but Diocletian put a restraining hand on his arm and smiled. Galerius sat back down.

The two praetorians struggled forward, each carrying a man and dragging a woman. Genesius' guard placed him on his feet and turned to disengage himself from Atalanta, who wept even more pitifully—and more loudly. While he attended to her, Genesius, still rigid, toppled over like a felled tree. He landed in front of the spittle-shrouded cross, let his eyes grow wider and wider, and clutched it tightly, kissing it with an almost sexual abandon.

Diarius' guard finally dragged the limp actor-manager's flopping form to the tripod. Atalanta still screamed. The guard released Diarius, who stood rocking confusedly on his heels. He seemed to regain his bearings because his eyes suddenly fell on the figure of the emperor. An expression of utter terror slowly crept across his face as he regarded first Diocletian, then Galerius, and finally the phalanx of praetorians who were beginning to encircle the group of four actors. He aimed a kick that was meant to seem unobtrusive at Hysteria, who went silent in mid-scream. Atalanta, still weeping, looked up to see what was happening. Diarius cuffed her and smiled apologetically at the two rulers on their thrones. Genesius continued to embrace and kiss the phlegmy cross; his face was covered with spittle. He had no idea what would happen next.

"Recant!" Diarius said to Genesius in a stage whisper. "Recant, or we're all in deep trouble."

"I can't recant," Genesius shouted. "You know that. I pledged to follow Christ no matter what happened."

"Please, don't shout!" Diarius whispered loudly. "He'll hear you."

"Let him hear me," Genesius cried. "Let them all hear how Genesius, the actor, is faithful, no matter what happens!"

Diarius knelt by Genesius. "Please?"

"No!" Genesius insisted. "I will not recant. No matter what they do!"

"Well, then," Diarius said. He stood, motioned to Atalanta and Hysteria, took a handful of incense, and with a grand gesture threw it into the flame.

"As the flame burns this fragrant incense," Diarius said, "so may my heart burn in worship of Diocletian, August Emperor of all Rome, Jupiter Incarnate.

"You're on your own now, boy," he said to Genesius.

"I won't recant." Genesius stole a glance at Diocletian. The emperor was intent on their little drama, as were all the inhabitants of the hall.

"They'll punish you."

"I won't recant."

"They'll kill you."

"I won't recant."

"They'll take all your possessions away."

"I won't recant."

"They'll send you to the salt mines."

"I won't recant."

"You'll never get another decent role in this town."

"I won't re—I won't?

"Not a chance."

"Ever?"

"Never."

Genesius stood up shakily, still clutching the cross. "Do you mean that I'd have to work for a living?"

"Indeed, you would," Diarius said.

Genesius looked from the cross to Diarius to Diocletian to the cross. Carefully he set the cross on the floor.

"Why didn't you say so in the first place?"

He straddled the cross, feet apart, and tensed the muscles of his belly. A seam opened in the wineskin.

It was only a small stream, but it was enough.

Led by Diocletian, the crowd exploded. It was the kind of laughter that fed on itself. As soon as it started to die down, one person would catch the eye of another, and it would begin anew. Genesius, at the center of the storm, calmly rearranged his tunic, turned to the crowd, and took his bow. From the corner of his eye, he saw that only two people in the great audience hall were silent—Valeria and Prisca, who left the dais and exited the hall.

He also saw Galerius watch them go and knew that the most dangerous man in the court was not the emperor, but his chief lieutenant.

CHAPTER 3

I am named Lactantius. Under the persecutor Diocletian I was a rhetorician and historian. I became two persons in order to survive the great persecution. One person was court-trained, hypocritical, pragmatic, accommodating. The other, which survives, is Christian. I participated in the official worship of the emperor, watched without objection the persecution of the Christians, and became one of them.

I was with Diocletian through the last ten years of his rule. I saw with my own eyes what his battle against the Christians cost him and the empire.

He set himself against the surge of history unwillingly at first. The real impetus came from his caesar, Galerius, a man cloaked in evil. Diocletian was an Illyrian, born in Salonae, on the coast of Dalmatia. Galerius was rooted on the barbarian side of the Danube, from which he was brought as a child by his mother, a pagan priestess. He grew into a gross, disfigured image of a man; he was misshapen in his height and weight, towering over others, even Diocletian, and swollen in girth. His natural way was to terrorize all around him, even those with whom he had no quarrels. It was he who convinced Diocletian to persecute us. But Diocletian's opposition, once begun, grew furious.

We Christians say that our God is God of history, who chooses the times and places of His revelation according to His will.

Diocletian was in His way.

✦ ✦ ✦

I met with Prisca, as usual, for her instruction in the faith. Neither she nor her daughter Valeria had yet decided to receive baptism. They were still seekers.

We three met in secret at irregular intervals. It was, I suppose, dangerous for all of us. Wife of the Augustus though she might be, Prisca had little of the influence one might expect in her position. Diocletian, though he might have loved her, trusted no one. He had cut Prisca out of his life, except for ceremonial functions.

Our society, like all others, depends on order. The higher ranks rule. Soldiers fight. Slaves work. Philosophers think.

Women have a society all their own, I have learned, cut off, in a sense, from that of men. Noble women, except perhaps in their domestic lives, can do little.

"Read to me," Prisca ordered, like her husband demanding in all things. We were in her private chamber. The attendants were banished on made-up errands. Valeria sat apart from us, veiled.

"I did not bring—"

"Here. From this." She handed me a scroll. "There is a passage marked."

The lady had resources other than myself. I opened the scroll and found the passage. The hand of the scribe was not good, but it was legible.

"'For as many of you were baptized into Christ have put on Christ. There is neither Jew nor Greek, there is neither slave nor free, there is neither male nor female; for you are all one in Christ Jesus.'"

"Explain," Prisca commanded. "Are all distinctions to be wiped away?"

"In a word, yes." There was no other answer.

"I see." Prisca thought for a moment, frowning.

"Then it follows that a slave in the field and I are of equal worth

In the eyes of Jesus."

"It seems so," I answered. I wondered where she was leading me. It seemed to be toward dangerous territory.

"Is that the best you can do, Lactantius? It sounds to me as if Jesus wants to disrupt society, to destroy its order. Who will rule if all are the same? Who will decide who owns which piece of land? This freedom your god offers is dangerous to the order of things."

"It was God who established the order of things," I answered, more boldly than I should to the empress. But it was Valeria, heretofore silent, who answered.

"Was it your god, then, who ordered this?" She stood before me and lifted the veil from her face. She was bruised, both eyes blackened, her jaw swollen, her lips puffy. Her scalp was bloody where a section of hair had been pulled away from it.

"How did this happen?" The brutality of the attack upon the girl shocked me.

"My husband." She hissed the words, overflowing with hurt and hatred. "My husband did this to me. He thought that I did not show sufficient enthusiasm for the sacrifice we made the other day."

"There are other injuries," Prisca said, "that we will not speak of. And this is not the first time. Does Jesus have an answer for this?"

How does one try to justify another's pain? One can only stand at the foot of her cross. Galerius' brutality was known but never discussed in the palace. No one could confront him, except, perhaps, Diocletian himself. I put the question to Prisca.

"My spouse," she said, "deems it politically unwise to interfere between this husband and wife. She must continue to suffer these insults because my husband's political position with Galerius is too weak. It is a woman's place to obey her husband, he says, and he means me to hear the same message. He would not beat me, as Galerius beats our daughter. He is far more civilized than that. But if he believed that I was disloyal, that I was talking to you about the matters we discuss, that I might become a Christian, he would in his civilized way punish me.

"So you see," Prisca went on, pacing now in her anger, "why I want you to explain that passage to me. If there is a way that we can be free of this domination, I want to know it. I want that freedom."

A reply came to mind, but even a Christian may sense when the truth should be delayed. I begged the Augusta's permission to withdraw and gather my thoughts, promising to return when I had put them together.

"You are as bad as my husband," Prisca said. "Go on. Get out."

✦ ✦ ✦

"You're out of your mind!" Genesius said. "After what just happened you want to sneak into their church? You're a sick man, Diarius—self-destructive to a fault."

The four players were alone in their quarters. It was all moving much too fast for Genesius. Scarcely a day before, he had been an out-of-work actor worming his way into an audition. Now he found himself dressed in bright robes, wearing the imperial seal, and trying to discuss calmly an act that could only be described as treason. Actors did not dabble in politics, not since the Greeks, anyway. It was too dangerous a game.

"I tell you," Diarius insisted, "that it's safe enough. Galerius has given me his personal guarantee."

"And you trust him?" Hysteria asked.

"Why not?" Diarius leaned forward on the couch. "I explained to him the reason. If we are to parody the rites of these Christians, we must know what those rites are. Part of our audience will be the Christians themselves. The caesars want this theatrical propaganda we're to perform to be effective. We must go! How else can we know what we are fighting. The whole thing is Galerius' idea—know your enemy, he says."

"I should have saved my old clothes," Genesius said. "They'll never let us in dressed like this."

Hysteria chuckled and opened the chest next to her couch. She tossed the ragged tunic, slightly the worse for wear, across the room. Atalanta caught it as she jumped from Genesius' lap. She held it up against him.

"He hasn't gained that much weight yet," she said. "He can still get into it."

Genesius snatched the tunic from her hands. "Well, it's dirty enough to belong to a Christian," he said. "But I don't see how you can trust Galerius. Why is he so rabid on the subject of the Christians?"

"It's his fury that I trust," Diarius said. "He has a plan, does Galerius, and he's convinced Diocletian that it will work. And we are part of it. We are valuable to both of them—for as long as we are useful.

"Look at it this way—here is our chance to do something of importance in the world. Have you seen the old plays—the plays of Sophocles, Aeschylus, and Euripides?"

"Yes, of course." Genesius lay back on his couch, pulling Atalanta down with him.

"Compare them with our own."

"There is no comparison," Genesius said.

"That's right," Diarius continued. "We perform fluff, farce designed to distract the mind from its troubles."

"So what is the matter with that?" Hysteria said.

"Nothing, my dear, nothing at all. But compare it to the plays of Euripides and what do you find? That where we distract, Euripides attacks. Where we deal in the emotions of the moment, he deals in the philosophy of being. In his day, actors—actors, mind you!—were significant people. They served as diplomats between warring nations. They had safe-conduct all over the world because they served something greater than the mob. The Greeks were philosophers! And we are being offered the same chance."

Genesius' face opened in a parody of dawning comprehension. "A philosopher—me! I can't wait!"

He stood up suddenly, dumping Atalanta to the floor, and stripped off his royal livery.

"Let's go!" he cried, heading naked for the door. Hysteria bent to retrieve the discarded tunic. "Aren't you forgetting something?" Atalanta giggled.

"If I am to be 'reborn,'" Genesius said, "must I not issue from the womb naked?"

"I like you that way," Atalanta said, leering.

"Enough, you young pups," Diarius huffed. "There will be time enough for your lust later on. We have a briefing to attend. Genesius, cover yourself."

The briefing was held by one who called himself Judas. He was not born with the name but took it for himself after one of the disciples who is said to have betrayed the Christ after becoming dissatisfied with His powerlessness against the world.

"You are late," he complained as the group of four actors entered his presence. "You have a lot to learn, and I have very little time in which to teach you."

Judas was a small man but with an abundance of nervous energy that made him move about the small room continuously and rapidly,

darting here and there, making his points by stabbing his fat, stubby
fingers in the faces of his students, sometimes ranting against the
Christians. He was middle-aged, bald, with a fringe of hair stretching
vainly from one ear to the other. He was rude and unpleasant and
had once been a Christian. His nails were dirty, and his breath stank
of cheap wine.

"The Christus was an obscure peasant from a mountainous region
called Galilee in the diocese of Syria. He lived about three hundred
years ago, in the reign of Tiberius. He was a Jew and a fanatic. After
wandering his country for a few years, he was executed by the state
for criminal sedition. Even his fellow Jews became incensed with him;
they brought him before the local prefect and preferred charges of
treason against him. He was crucified."

Atalanta grimaced. "How could anyone worship that?"

"His followers," Judas said, glaring at her for her interruption, "his
followers claimed that he was seen alive after the crucifixion. It was
either a hallucination or an outright lie, of course, but it took hold
of the poorer classes and seems to have fired their imagination. The
superstitious will believe in anything, given only an excuse. This Jesus'
teachings, if you want to give them that much dignity, honored the
poor, and the poor were quick to return the favor."

Judas drew himself up. "I quote from their holy writings. These
are the words attributed to his mother, when she—supposedly—realized she was pregnant with the so-called Son of God: 'He'—meaning,
I surmise, their god—'he has scattered the proud in the imagination
of their hearts. He has put down the mighty from their seats, and
exalted them of low degree. He has filled the hungry with good
things; and the rich he has sent away empty.'

"And this is a theme that carries through with these Christians—
upsetting the natural order of society."

"Can't have that," murmured Genesius, "can we?"

"Do you disapprove of my analysis?"

Diarius' pointed elbow snaked into the small space between
Genesius' eighth and ninth ribs.

"No, no, no!" Genesius exclaimed. "After all, I'm sure that it has
official sanction."

"Indeed. I quote again, this time from the very words of the
Christus: 'I am come to set a man at variance against his father, and
the daughter against her mother, and the daughter-in-law against her
mother-in-law.' He goes on at some length in this vein."

Atalanta giggled and said, "Am I a Christian, then, because I have fought with my mother?"

"Perhaps."

"She was a drooling old whore."

"We shall proceed," Judas said, as if she had not spoken. "You need to know how to behave yourselves at the rituals of the Galileans if you're going to penetrate their community. You women will need a covering for your heads. All of you must dress poorly. . . ."

The actors learned to make the signs of the cross across their breasts and of the fish in the dirt, as a mark to identify themselves as Christians. Judas drilled them in the responses to characteristic phrases and gave them each a cover story to explain their presence in Nicomedia. He taught them how to accept the Eucharistic meal from the priest without arousing suspicion, using a practice that had originated in Antioch in the south. He cautioned them on the things that might give them away as strangers to the cult. Finally, Diarius exploded.

"Enough!" he cried. "We are all actors, masters of improvisation. You overload us with details that not even you could keep straight, let alone ourselves. Are these Christians going to kill us and drink our blood if we are discovered? It is enough!"

The briefing had lasted through the evening meal and into the quiet hours of early morning. Judas turned to the window that overlooked the Christians' church. It was the darkest time of night. The streets below were empty, the city's dogs quiet. Somewhere in the distance, the wheels of a cart grated on the cobbled streets.

"The earth is without form and void," Judas said, "and darkness is upon the face of the deep."

"That's very poetic," Genesius said. "Did you write it?"

"No," Judas answered softly. The lamp guttered out as he answered; the little class was left in darkness. "It is time for you to go."

Chastened by the apostate's seriousness, they made their way through the royal palace, past the concentric rings of praetorians who guarded the person and sanctity of the Augustus. Diarius, following a slave who brandished a pass embossed with the seal of Galerius, led the way. Each actor carried a bundle containing old clothing, including a hooded cloak.

When they reached the outer entrance to the palace, the slave led them to an unused guardhouse. Here, the actors changed from their court finery. The slave placed their clothing in a trunk along with the pass, locked it, and gave Diarius the key. As they set off on the walk to the gathering place of the Christians, Atalanta looked back and saw the slave watching them.

Genesius entertained Hysteria and Diarius with fictional tales of his career as the actors walked the darkening streets. The actor's false buoyancy held out the promise of comfort to the younger actress; she caught up to him and linked her arm in his to listen to his chatter.

As they passed through the streets, others, similarly dressed, joined paths with the actors. Their mood seemed to be an odd combination of elation and caution. The pilgrims of the night streamed happily but carefully through the streets. Greetings were excited but whispered. There was much looking over shoulders. All in all, the atmosphere suggested children on an illicit holiday.

The mood was easy for the actors to catch. To avoid suspicion, Diarius split off from their group; Genesius and Atalanta did the same, leaving Hysteria to walk on alone for a few moments. Soon, Diarius caught up with her and greeted her in the same manner that the midnight Christians did each other. After another few minutes, Genesius and Atalanta caught up again, played the same scene, and were enthusiastically welcomed by Hysteria and Diarius.

They followed the midnight Christians around a corner and into the square on which their building fronted. From all the streets that emptied onto the square there came hesitant, almost surreptitious streams of men and women, converging on the entrance to the church. As they entered, Genesius looked over his shoulder at the assembling crowd. Hundreds, he realized, were making their way into the building.

The throng's movement swept the actors within the old bathhouse, which, except for two torches near the far end, was darkened. The men and women mixed freely. Like a crowd at the beach, each individual or small group found a clear area and staked it out for themselves. But unlike vacationers, each worshiper knelt toward the east, where a large gilt cross stood bathed in the light of two torches. The actors found a spot near the south wall and knelt, imitating the others.

From all around the actors there came a soft murmuring. Atalanta, kneeling by Genesius, leaned toward him and whispered, "What are they saying?"

Genesius' place was next to another group. He shushed Atalanta and listened to the words of the man next to him.

"Our Father, who is in heaven, hallowed by thy name. . . ."

"They're praying," Genesius whispered.

A painful blow caught him over the right kidney.

"Oof!" Genesius barked.

"What do you think you're—"

"I beg your pardon, sir," Diarius said, then whispered, "I suggest that you confine yourselves to prayer. There's no telling what might happen if they realize who we are."

"Sssh!" hissed Hysteria, kneeling at his side. Eyes shining, Genesius redirected his gaze to the brilliant cross, admiring the workmanship, not to mention the price it must have cost. His eyes drifted to the people in prayer before him. They were from all stations in life, but there was a subtle grouping according to status; like stayed generally with like. Off to the right and slightly in front of him the wealthier tradesmen knelt along with their families and servants, but the tradesmen and their wives had cushions between their knees and the mosaic tile floor of the bathhouse. The servants stayed a respectful distance behind their masters, occasionally shifting their weight to take the burden from aching kneecaps.

Beyond this group, further to the north wall, there were the poor. Genesius searched their numbers for a familiar face, only allowing the smallest part of his own face to appear from within his cowl, until he was satisfied that there was no one there who might recognize him. The poor, of course, knelt without cushions.

Separating the poor from the next group, which occupied the couches along the wall, was a line—almost a phalanx—of young, muscular men, each in the livery of one of the noble houses of Nicomedia. The men were unarmed, but there was about them the air of being accustomed to the use of force that was one of the marks of the professional. Like whores, with whom they held much in common, they sold the use of their bodies; self-display was inherent in their character.

The stream of pilgrims had lessened somewhat but not completely, and Genesius watched them come in, surveying the crowd as if looking for someone. He guessed that among the four hundred or so, fully one-third were women, and half of those apparently out at night without accompaniment. There were significant numbers of Greeks, of course, and the expected smattering of Jews, but he also saw Africans, Arabs, Phoenicians—even, here and there, some of the wild tribesmen from Gaul and Britain. For a moment, a blond-haired giant who must have been a Germanic barbarian caught his eye. Bringing his gaze closer, he heard a warning cough from Diarius and turned back around, just in time to see a plainly dressed man extinguish the torches on either side of the cross.

Genesius shivered with a thrill of fear. Were they simply to be killed in the darkness for infiltrating the secret worship of the Christians? He waited for the thrust of the blade, involuntarily tensing his back.

CHAPTER 4

T he murmur of prayer stopped as if all the worshipers' throats had been cut. Even the sound of breathing was suspended. Somewhere in the darkness, the fabric of someone's robe rustled softly. These Christians have a blood sacrifice, Genesius remembered, clutching his hood more securely over his head. Someone touched his right arm, and he shrank away in terror, bumping into his neighbor on the left.

"Please, I beg you . . ." he stammered.

"Don't worry," came a whispered voice, "no harm done. Your first Easter?"

"I . . . yes," Genesius said.

"It will be starting any moment." The voice was calm, soothing. "It affects some people this way. You'll be fine; just wait."

The dark silence stretched until Genesius thought he would break. Then came the scratch of flint on steel. Faint shadows danced indistinctly on the dome of the bathhouse. Genesius turned his head toward the sound, which came from the entrance. There, by the door, a man dressed in ceremonial white blew softly on a handful of tinder. The flame steadied in his hands.

"My brothers and sisters in Christ," he said, "on this night we remember our Lord Christ who passed over from death into life.

"Let us pray," he called. "Father, through Your Son You have given us the brilliance of Your light. Make holy this new fire and grant that in this Paschal festival we may so burn with Your will that we may attain the festival of everlasting light, through Christ our Lord. . . ."

He paused, as if giving the Christians their cue, and they responded with a single voice.

"Amen!"

"Amen," the actors repeated weakly.

The priest then stretched forth his hand and was given a large candle, which he lit from his handful of fire. The latter he passed to an assistant, and then he moved slowly forward through the assembly, stopping occasionally to light the worshipers' smaller candles, which had appeared from nowhere. The effect was a slowly moving but inexorably growing wave of light that traveled from the entry gradually to the altar of the church-bathhouse and threatened to overwhelm Genesius.

Genesius was intoxicated with the ritual. He lost track of where he was for a time, until he saw the surge of flame heading for himself and Atalanta. Neither he nor Atalanta had thought to bring candles; who would have thought that they would be needed? Just before the nearest Christian neighbor turned to him and Atalanta to share his light, Genesius felt a pair of hard objects poking into his back. He turned, and Hysteria thrust two small candles into his hands. He hurriedly took them and handed one to Atalanta just in time, for the neighbor Christian on her side was then turning to her with a beatific smile, a freshly kindled flame, and the phrase "The light of Christ" on his lips. Never one to miss a cue, Atalanta mouthed the correct response as if she had been practicing this strange rite all her life and brought her light in turn to Genesius.

"The light of Christ," she beamed at him aloud. Under her breath she whispered, "The response is to light your candle from mine and say, 'Thanks be to God.' And for all our sakes, smile!"

Genesius lit his own candle. Smiling furiously, he said, "Thanks be to God!" and turned to his left-hand neighbor. The candle in his hand trembled and threatened to go out. The man's hand reached out and steadied Genesius' own.

"The light of Christ," Genesius stuttered. "Thanks be to God!" answered the neighbor. "Steady, lad." Genesius' first task at the Christians' service was completed, but only barely. Judas' instructions had been faulty, and there would be repercussions.

The bathhouse was now a sea of light. The only darkened place was at the altar, where stood another priest quietly waiting for the crowd to finish sharing the light. Their faces full of light, each illuminated by the individual candles, turned up toward the altar in an agony of joyful anticipation. The worshipers leaned forward, waiting for the priest to lead them in the celebration. To Genesius it seemed more like the anticipation of the crowd at the games, but with a purer purpose. There was no blood lust in their straining, but the intensity of feeling was not dissimilar. Something was about to happen, something immense and, to him, frightening. A trap yawned open before him, baited with hope. He struggled back from its edge, trying to find balance in his appointed task of observing the behavior of the worshipers.

"Rejoice now!" cried the second priest, and the Christians cheered. "Rejoice now, heavenly hosts and choirs of angels, and let your trumpets shout salvation for the victory of our mighty King!" The crowd roared enthusiastically.

"They really are traitors," Atalanta whispered to him.

"Galerius was right," Genesius agreed.

After a moment, it was quiet again.

"Rejoice and sing now, all around the earth, for darkness has been vanquished by our eternal King!"

Again the crowd shouted its approval.

"Again, this king business," Genesius said. He felt a blow to his kidney. The voice of Diarius whispered in his ear. "Show some enthusiasm, you fool! You're too quiet for this group."

"Rejoice and be glad now, Mother Church, and let your holy courts, in radiant light, resound with the praises of your people!"

The crowd exploded, exulting in the triumph of their god. They waved their candles high and gave voice to their exultation. Genesius and Atalanta, a beat behind the others around them, joined the wordless cheering.

The second priest held up his hands for silence. Gradually the congregation settled down again.

"The Lord be with you!" he chanted.

"And also with you."

"Let us give thanks to the Lord our God."

"It is right to give Him thanks and praise."

"It is truly right and good, always and everywhere, with heart and mind and voice, to praise You, invisible, almighty, and eternal God. . . ."

The voice of the second priest went on, and the crowd listened attentively to his recital of why they should worship. The audience joined him in his amen, then his voice broke out eagerly.

"Let us hear the record of God's saving deeds in history. Let us hear how He has saved His people in times gone by. And let us pray that our God will bring us each to the fullness of redemption!"

One of the people from the audience moved to the center of the bathhouse and was met by an acolyte carrying a large book. The reader kissed the page as the congregation quieted.

"'In the beginning God created the heaven and the earth. And the earth was without form, and void; and darkness was upon the face of the deep. And the Spirit of God moved upon the face of the waters. And God said, Let there be light: and there was light.'"

The light of all the candles, even Genesius' own, shimmered in tempo with the words of the reader. The reader went on, but Genesius could not hear him; he was fascinated by the warmth, by the light that suffused the faces around him. Overhead there was the darkness of the overarching ceiling, the frescoes lost in blackness. But here, down on his own level, there was light, glowing warmly on all the faces of the people, including his own. He felt the light suffuse his being and knew that the feeling was held in common with the others, who were, somehow, no longer other.

He was enough of an artist to recognize the extended metaphor of light as the source of all things, the first created object not an object at all, but a perceptible intangible, something he could sense and see but never touch. His thoughts drifted to the sometimes cruelty of light, of bringing corruption to light as did Oedipus, and he shuddered at what might come from these Christians. But then, unbidden, came the remembrance that the downfall of Oedipus had meant salvation to Thebes, and he wondered about the destruction of one man for the sake of many.

Genesius came back to himself some time later. The heat in the bathhouse had grown because of the mass of humanity packed into its confines and the hundreds of tiny flames. Another person from the congregation was reading now from the book. The words had filled his ears, without his consciously hearing them.

"'. . . And he said unto me, Son of man, can these bones live? And

I answered, O Lord God, thou knowest. . . . the bones came together.
. . . and the breath came into them, and they lived, and stood up upon
their feet, an exceeding great army.'"

As if the reader had been speaking only to him, Genesius was
nearly toppled over by the sense of the words. An actor, to play a
role, must behave as if he feels the thing presented. All actors of any
quality have known this; only the unconfident and unsure pretend to
try to feel the thing directly. The feeling comes out of the action itself,
as Aristotle so surely knew. And the acting of the thing itself calls
forth the emotion virtually unbidden. This is one of the secrets, one
of the mysteries of the actor. And such was the case with Genesius
the actor while taking part in the Christian mysteries. The mysteries
plumbed his depths. The vision of this prophet Ezekiel took hold of
him. The heat and light surrounding him made him their own.

The priest came forward and prayed as Genesius wondered at his
seeming conversion. The lector stepped aside to make way.

"The catechumens will now come forward!" A hush descended
over the multitude. From the back of the bathhouse, a group of men
and women made their way toward the priest. Some would have run
but for the press of people. Others were more halting, as if having
second thoughts about the rite they were about to pass through. A
few walked with a quiet serenity that Genesius would have sold his
soul for, if he had thought he had one.

"Do you wish to be baptized?"

"I do." A single voice belonging to nearly fifty people answered
the old priest.

"Do you renounce Satan and all the forces of wickedness that rebel
against God?"

"I renounce them," they all answered.

"Do you renounce all sinful desires that draw you from the love of
God?"

"I renounce them." A few voices trickled slowly behind the majority, but all answered.

"Do you turn to Jesus Christ and accept Him as your Savior?"

"I do."

"Do you put your whole trust in His grace and love?"

"I do."

"Do you promise to follow and obey Him as your Lord?"

"I do."

Each question called for a response from a human being who was
trying, with varying levels of success, to change his life. Genesius was

awestruck as he listened to this vow of allegiance to a supernatural power. None of the significance was wasted on him, and he felt he was an outsider, alone amid the throng of true believers.

The priest's attention shifted to the larger congregation. "Do you believe in God the Father?"

The full-throated response, the very sound itself, made all the candles in the bathhouse tremble, and Genesius would have turned and fled but for the restraining hand of Diarius.

"I believe in God, the Father almighty, Creator of heaven and earth."

"Do you believe," the priest continued, "in Jesus Christ, the Son of God?" And the people of this Christ answered His representative, roaring their affirmation, eyes fixed on the cross, on the priest, on their new fellows, on "the resurrection of the body and the life everlasting."

An attendant, one of the lectors, appeared near the priest, carrying a basin of water. He and the priest moved through the catechumens, speaking softly to each, touching each, man or woman, slave or free, rich or poor, briefly and equally, first on the crown of the head, then marking the forehead of each in a small sign of the cross.

Next to Genesius, the man whispered, "I baptize you in the name of the Father, and of the Son, and of the Holy Spirit, Amen." And again, "You are sealed by the Holy Spirit in baptism and marked as Christ's own forever."

The whisper caused Genesius to look at him again, to hear the words that the priest was saying to the catechumens, and his eyes widened in recognition. His neighbor was a man from the court of Diocletian, one of those who had participated in the sacrifice to the emperor only days before. His neighbor was a traitor.

While the priests read from their holy books and moved through the ritual, the two men searched each other's faces. Genesius realized his own danger; he could be denounced in one place or in the other, here or in the palace.

"Lift up your hearts," he heard the priest say in the distance. The common response roared all around Genesius: "We lift them up unto the Lord." And he had a sudden vision of the entire multitude standing, joyously holding dripping bloody hands full of still-beating pumping muscle, outstretched to their Christ, joyful in their muti-lated splendor, thanking this Christ passionately for the opportunity, so graciously given, to rend themselves into pieces for His sake. And above them, grinning demonically down from heaven, from the right hand of a proud and beaming Father, their Christ devouring their sacrifice, the blood still streaming from His own wounds, tasting an especially tempting tidbit of heart, a particularly red and juicy gout of blood.

A snatch of chanting penetrated his fevered brain— "Blessed is He who comes in the name of the Lord!"—and Genesius found himself kneeling, pulled down by hands from either side—by Atalanta, who stared at him from a great distance, a worried look on her face, and by the familiar stranger at his left, whose eyes held a glint of amusement, then flicked away toward the altar, where the priest was instructing them in the proper carrying out of the blood rite.

"Drink this, all of you. This is My blood, which was shed for you and for many for the forgiveness of sins."

They were going to do it. They were going to drink his blood. He had not believed them, but the rumors were true. Someone's blood would be drunk tonight, and who would make a better victim than an outsider, an actor come to spy on them, to learn their rites so that he could mock them? He had heard that Christians sacrificed children for their masses. There was no telling what might happen in the hands of what they believed to be an all-powerful, all-seeing deity. All the new cults to come out of the East were alien, often bloody. Here he was, trapped in the middle of the worst.

He began to look around, searching for an escape. No one moved except for the priest, who raised in his hands a large piece of unleavened bread for all the crowd to see and broke it in half.

"Christ our Passover is sacrificed for us," he said to them. And the crowd answered, "Therefore, let us keep the feast," and stood en masse, without haste forming itself into several lines, peacefully, without shoving, without jostling. A hand took his elbow gently and steered him into one of the files. Looking around, Genesius saw the familiar stranger still at his side. Somehow, Atalanta, Hysteria, and Diarius were separated from him. He could see them at a little distance, moving in one of the great queues, looking about, wondering where he was. But the gentle grip on his arm showed surprising strength when he started in their direction. The familiar stranger held him in the line, which slowly inched forward.

The differences in caste that he had noticed on entering the bathhouse were still visible. The line he was in against his will was made up of a richer group than that of his fellow actors. The clothing around him was of silk from the East and cotton from Egypt, well cut and colorful. The smell of sweat that he had become accustomed to in the close atmosphere was overlaid with perfumes, mixing jaggedly with each other, somehow, like the man who held his arm, both strange and familiar at once.

Before he knew it he had reached nearly the front of the line. A priest, different from the one who had led the ritual, stood in front of Genesius, offering a broken piece of unleavened bread. Genesius stood dumbly. A look of confusion broke across the priest's face, followed by one of understanding. He withdrew the proffered bread and raised his hand over Genesius' head.

"The almighty and merciful Lord, Father, Son, and Holy Spirit, bless you and keep you."

The stranger gently pushed Genesius to one side, held out his hands to the priest, and received the bread. Guiding Genesius ahead of him, he stopped before another, dressed differently from the priests, and took a drink of wine. At first Genesius thought it was indeed blood, but he was near enough to the stranger to catch the smell; it was a rough Falernian wine, the same as he bought after a lucrative morning in the marketplace spent entertaining the shoppers and merchants—nothing supernatural about it. He felt a little safer, knowing that the flesh was bread and the blood was wine. Perhaps they would not, in fact, cut his heart out.

The familiar stranger again took Genesius by the arm, still not speaking, and led him through a door from the main room of the bathhouse into a smaller chamber, not as brightly lit as the gathering they had just left.

When his eyes adjusted to the relative darkness, Genesius fell to his knees: before him stood Prisca, the wife of Diocletian; Valeria, the wife of Galerius; and a young man whose face was terrifyingly familiar. Flanking the trio were two senior officers of the praetorian guard.

CHAPTER 5

I felt sorry for the young man, but there was no question that he had recognized me as a member of Diocletian's entourage. In one way or another, we had to deal with him, to frighten, buy, or otherwise make him keep silent.

If he had seen me, then he might just as well have seen the empress, her daughter Valeria, and perhaps even the prince Constantine, who was at this time being held hostage for the good behavior of his father serving in Britain. In the chaos that was sure to follow when the tetrarchy disintegrated, Constantine might well become a very important man. We thought that a show of royalty might convince the young actor to keep his knowledge to himself.

I had witnessed the lad's performance at court, during the ceremony of obedience where the ladies and I had apostatized ourselves. Let me interject that we did so under the express instructions of our bishop, his belief being that, if a persecution were to occur, our positions were of such influence that we might be able to mitigate its effects. Events have proved his belief wrong, of course, but even a bishop can be forgiven if he makes an error of prescience. In any case I had, as I say, witnessed Genesius' performance, as had the others. We were agreed that he was not so much a devoted pagan as a very frightened young man who was out of his depth but struggling admirably to keep himself afloat in the storm-tossed ocean of court politics.

At this point he was in a state of confusion. The Easter vigil can be quite impressive, even to an initiate. For an outsider, hearing only fictions of blood sacrifice and sexual abandon, the love feast seems to vibrate with dangerous potentials. And with the awareness that he was present as a spy, an informer-to-be so to speak, he had to have felt a sickening fear. We left it to Constantine to begin the interrogation. He enjoys it so.

"Your name," the prince said.

"I am Genesius, the actor."

"Do you know why you have been singled out?"

"No, sir."

"Why do you spy on people who have done you no harm?"

"Spy, sir?"

"You are not a Christian."

"No."

"You serve Diocletian."

"Yes."

"And Diocletian fears the Christians."

"Does he, sir?" the actor asked. "I had thought that the emperor fears nothing."

This Genesius might not have had the experience of those long at court, but he had an instinct that led him unerringly to the right thinking, the right action. I began to think that we had underestimated him—and if him, perhaps his fellows too. Constantine continued his questioning.

"The emperor fears nothing because he knows everything," the prince said. It was a fine, graceful recovery. "He knows that we are here; he knows that you are here. He has declared that such gatherings are seditious. Yet he has arrested neither us nor you—nor any other at this gathering. Do you have an explanation?"

"I?" Genesius temporized.

"You know so much about the emperor," Constantine said. "Surely you know what he is thinking."

"I know," Genesius said, "that he trembled with anxiety that these noble ladies would not make the sacrifice he demanded of them not so long ago."

"And yet," Constantine answered, "they did."

Genesius kept silent in reply to Constantine's statement—wisely, I thought, because there was in fact no answer required. I, however unwisely, often find it difficult to keep silence.

"Actor," I said, "what the prince is saying is that you do not know enough about these things to make a judgment on them. Even if—and I do not say that this is the case—the prince disagrees with the emperor concerning the Christians, the two do agree on the need to maintain the security and integrity of the empire. They—"

"You talk too much, Lactantius," Prisca interrupted. Her blue eyes flashed with anger. "This actor," she said distastefully, "need only know enough to keep his own counsel concerning what, and whom, he has seen tonight."

Prisca was no longer a young woman, but she still had a mature beauty and had not lived so long at court, even as the emperor's wife, without learning how to deal with a delicate situation. Her hair, although showing gray, was still soft and flowing. Valeria, on the other hand, would show more wear if she reached Prisca's age. The daughter took after the emperor, her father, in that her cares showed on her face in small lines and crow's feet. But the mother seemed unruffled by events, untouched by time. The gray in her hair was masked by its blond color; her blue eyes were pure and clear.

"Actor," she said, "understand me well. You have been chosen to act a certain role. As far as we are concerned, you may do so. But you have shown yourself to be overly impulsive. Your patronage protects you, thus far, but do not think that you are invulnerable.

"Do your job. But stay clear of palace intrigue. You will be asked occasionally to come and visit with one of us. If you prove discreet, you will gradually learn much about the fine art of royal survival. If not, you may also learn much."

She turned to leave, flanked by Constantine and Valeria, the interview, in her mind, at an end. But Genesius had another idea.

"Lady," he said, "does the Christian empress threaten her subject, then?"

Prisca stopped so suddenly that the other two went on a step before turning.

"Actor, watch your tongue," Constantine said. Valeria looked to her mother in confusion.

"No," Prisca said, "he has a point." She took the actor by the hand, led him to a couch, sat him down, and then called to me. "Lactantius, join us. I am not sure of my persuasive powers."

I did so, seating myself on Genesius' right. Prisca sat at his left. She waved Valeria and Constantine out of the chamber.

"Genesius," she said, taking his hand in hers, "if I cut off your little finger, would you still be Genesius? The question is not rhetorical."

"Yes, madam," the actor answered.

"And then, if you lost your hand, would you still be Genesius?"

"Yes."

"Of course you would. Now, if this process were continued, what would happen?"

"I would die, eventually."

"Indeed you would."

"Am I to take this as a warning, then, empress?"

"No, Genesius. Bear with me. I am trying to lead you somewhere. You have perceived the restraint under which we must get along. Our faith prevents us from defending ourselves in the usual manner of court politics. I want you at least to understand something of that faith."

"It seems," the actor said, "a weak faith that makes you defenseless before a poor man like me."

"As I said, bear with me." Prisca's eyes flashed angrily. Her Christianity was still new; imperial habits die hard and not without a certain regret. "I was constructing a metaphor."

"You had," grinned Genesius, "just deprived me of my hand and offered to continue the process until I was dead."

"What part," Prisca said, regaining the thread of her argument, "would go just as you died?"

"You've lost me," Genesius said.

"You've lost your finger; that didn't kill you. You've lost your hand, your arm, your leg—are you dead yet?"

"More than likely."

"Why?"

"Loss of blood?"

"No!" Prisca was incensed. "Explain it to this fool of an actor, Lactantius. He refuses to comprehend me!"

"Perhaps, lady," I ventured, "he is not yet capable of understanding."

"And perhaps he never will be!"

She followed through the exit by which the other two had already left. Once she was gone, I regarded the young actor without much hope. Despite his low birth, he looked like a young god. His dark hair, newly curled in the ringlets of those who lived at court, hugged his skull. He had a trace of the Levant in his face; his skin was swarthy. He looked to be only nineteen or twenty, with brown eyes and a darting, suspicious glance. He held himself proudly erect, as if daring the world to hurt him. He had, it appeared, grown to young manhood by sheer force of will. His frame was not large but seemed wiry and tough. He bore the scars of the pox, as did so many of the poor. And like so many of the poor, he was hurt and defensive, no matter how much he tried to shield his pain from others' view. As I think about it now, his defensiveness is characteristic not only of the poor, but of all of us. We have so little; we must protect what little we have. In this meeting, we both proceeded to do exactly that.

"You've had quite a day," I ventured.

He coughed a laugh-like sound of a single syllable. I pressed on.

"My name is Lactantius," I said, "and like you I am in the service of the emperor. You are an actor, I a historian. We have in common the fact that we both make representations. We both, if you will, tell stories—stories to which meanings are attached.

"Come with me. I want to tell you a story."

CHAPTER 6

The people had already gone back to their homes when I, with Genesius in tow, left the bathhouse. The cross loomed over us. The darkened candles seemed to glow dimly, their whiteness barely visible in the gloom. The hall was empty and dark as we made our way to the entrance, illuminated only by a shaft of moonlight that fell on the mosaic tile of the floor. A pale blue glow fell on an image of a slave bathing a man who stood waist-deep in a river. I paused to look before crossing the illuminated area, wondering whether or not I would be able to bring the actor to accept baptism. If I failed, he would, eventually, report our participation in the Christian rites.

We left the hall. Unlike Rome, which bustled with activity and noise through the night, Nicomedia rested during darkness. It was a smaller city, with a smaller need to import grain and other supplies. The emperor had ostensibly chosen it as his seat for strategic reasons; it was closer to the Danube frontier than Rome and had access to the sea for easy transport of troops and supplies. But many said that the

real reason for Diocletian's wish to stay in the East was his distaste
for the Roman mob. Accordingly, Nicomedia was, for a Roman city,
quiet. Praetorian guards enforced the relative peace. Their presence
made for secure sleeping but difficult sneaking about the town. In
Rome the streets were dangerous for honest citizens during the hours
of darkness. In Nicomedia they were dangerous for the dishonest,
for those with something to hide.

Genesius and I were cautious, therefore, when we left the baths.
After I nearly blundered into a pair of guards on turning a corner a
little too quickly, Genesius hauled me into the shadow of a balcony.

"When was the last time," the actor demanded, "that they let you
go out alone at night?"

"It has been some time," I said ruefully.

"You join a revolutionary movement, and you can't even avoid the
emperor's guards." Genesius was disgusted with the inept historian.
"Are all the Christians as stupid as you are?"

"Perhaps," I said, "you should lead the way."

"Perhaps," said Genesius, "I should. Would you care to tell me
where we are going?"

"I think the word you're trying to find is *naive.*"

"What word?"

"Not stupid—*naive,*" I said. "You call me stupid, then you ask me
to tell you where I, a secret Christian, am leading you, a known spy
for the court, illegally, after curfew."

"It doesn't make much sense, does it?" Genesius said.

"No," I agreed. "But it is not much of a secret. We are returning
to the palace, where we belong. I have an arrangement with one of
the guard units."

"Christians—in the army?" Genesius asked.

"Even there."

Genesius turned away from me. "It seems I have much to learn.
You people are everywhere."

The rest of our journey was spent in silence. Genesius and I skulked
to the northwest gate of the palace grounds. He had a native skill for
avoiding the patrols, almost a sixth sense that warned him when to
turn a corner, when to dive into a doorway.

Just before dawn we reached the gate where I had an arrangement
with the sentries, and I took the lead again. In the dust two yards to
the left of the gate, I scratched the sign of the fish. Genesius watched
while I did so, remaining silent, a quizzical look on his face. We drifted
into the shadows again, waiting for the patrol to come by.

Genesius knelt in the shadow, drawing the fish again and again in the dust; each fish he drew had a different expression—smiling, frowning, demonic, laughing, suffering.

A three-man patrol came around from the east wall. The officer called a halt. The two soldiers with him he sent down an alley off to our right. He whistled the signal; I answered. He unlocked the gate and followed his men down the alley. I led Genesius through the heavy door and into the palace.

"And I thought you were stupid," Genesius said.

"Naive," I corrected him. "We are not yet safe. People will be stirring soon. Diocles is an early riser, so all the palace staff rises early."

I turned to lead him to my room. But before I could move, he gripped my arm so that I almost cried out in pain.

"Who?"

"Come!" I whispered. "We must move now!" I shook his hand from my arm and led the way to my room. When we were safely inside, he confronted me again. His eyes were desperate, his face flushed with an emotion that was, for the first time since I had met him, not put on as an act.

"Who is Diocles?" he said.

"The emperor," I answered. "Diocletian." Genesius staggered as if struck. His expression was like that of a gladiator who in the fight has had his weapon knocked from his hand.

"It's true," he said. "It's really true." He then told me a story that I could scarcely credit as he began, but as he went on I found myself marveling at the way in which God's providence works out all things. I have, in the section of my story which follows, joined Genesius' account to what I myself know about the coming to power of Diocletian.

✦ ✦ ✦

It was in the last year of the reign of the emperor Carus. The Persians were once again causing trouble on the eastern frontier, and a detachment of soldiers passed through Nicomedia on their way to reinforce the emperor's forces. Leading them was the general Diocles.

After a long forced march from Salonae in Dalmatia, the troops were exhausted. Nicomedia, as the provincial capital of Bithynia, had plenty of food and billets for the army. For three days Diocles and his troops rested there before pushing on to Melitene In Cappadocia, on the frontier with Armenia where the Persians threatened Carus.

While in Nicomedia, Diocles, as the commander of the Dalmatian troops, was wined and dined by the local garrison. His entertainment included a woman, of course, a slave provided by the local prefect of the praetorian guard. Diocles' tastes were traditional; he was not of the effete Latin nobility but a peasant soldier who had risen through the ranks—something of a stick-in-the-mud, actually, compared to most of the leadership. Because of his traditionalism and his generosity to his soldiers, the troopers loved him with an adulation approaching that reserved for the emperor. The local commanders' provision of a woman for his pleasure was only a courtesy.

The woman was Sarah, a Judean by heritage, though it had been generations since her family had seen Jerusalem. According to family tradition, they had lived in Jerusalem at the time when Vespasian had leveled the city, changed its name to Aelia Capitolina, and forbidden Jews to live there. The family fled, along with the few survivors of the massacre, and gradually, over the generations, made its way north into Asia. All that remained of their Jewish heritage was a dark Semitic beauty and the occasional memory of that heritage marked by the use of a Jewish name.

Sarah slept with Diocles each night of his stay in Nicomedia. She conceived an attachment to the general. Being a realistic woman, she knew that what she had experienced with him would not be rekindled after the three nights. When he left her, riding at the head of his army, she watched without tears. He left her a gold piece as a token thanks.

She discovered later that he had left her pregnant as well. She was not a promiscuous woman; the child she carried was doubtless his.

Sarah listened to the reports from the front. She heard how the Roman forces rallied against the Persians when Diocles arrived. She heard as well how, when the emperor Carus was killed by a thunderbolt, and his son Numerianus became ill, Diocles became his protector. On their return from the front, Numerianus, still gravely ill, traveled in seclusion; Diocles occupied the place of honor. Her belly swollen in the seventh month of her pregnancy, she watched him pass through Nicomedia, heading westward this time. There was a bandage on his upper arm, his shield arm. When the army stopped for the ceremonies, she changed the dirty bandage and bathed the wound. Diocles remembered her, thanked her, and left. She was a realistic woman and expected no more.

Two days later, in Chalcedon, fifty miles to the west of Nicomedia, Numerianus died. A certain praetorian prefect, Aper (the name means wild boar), was suspected of the murder. The legions demanded a court-martial.

A druid priestess had predicted, when Diocles was serving in Gaul, that he would become emperor after killing a wild boar. At the court-martial of Aper, Diocles declared the suspect guilty, drew his sword, and killed him on the spot. The legions proclaimed him emperor and he accepted, changing his name to one more fitting to his new station—Gaius Aurelius Valerius Diocletianus.

Sarah's child was born at about the time when the new emperor's last rival was eliminated from competition.

Diocletian established his capitol in Nicomedia. While Sarah was still recovering from the birth, a messenger, in the uniform of the praetorian guard, came to see her. He bore an order of manumission naming her and any offspring she might have and guaranteeing her freedom for the rest of her life. In addition, there was a small purse, enough to maintain herself and the child for years, along with instructions on how to invest the money safely to achieve that goal. It was not a great deal. The two would not live in luxury, but they would not want. With a certain discretion, she named the child Genesius, at once recalling her own Jewish heritage as she memorialized the beginning of the new emperor's reign, the emperor who had, briefly, loved her.

The child became for her a talisman and a reminder of the brief time when she was loved by the former general, now emperor of all Rome.

Sarah never expected Diocletian to acknowledge her or his son Genesius. In fact, she never again heard from the emperor, who had other problems to occupy his mind. But Sarah built her life around the son and the absent father.

When, in the third year of his reign, Diocletian assumed divine honors as Jupiter, Sarah introduced Genesius to the worship of the god. His life was to be dedicated to the service of his father, Jupiter.

✦ ✦ ✦

"Do you think I am a fool?" Genesius asked. I did not know what to say to the boy.

"Do you think that the emperor is your father?" I asked.

"He could be. My mother always called him Diocles. I didn't even think of the possibility until I heard you use that name for him. She never told me he was the emperor," he said. "She never told me."

The boy's face was flushed with excitement; his breathing came rapidly. I gave him a cup of well-watered wine. The cup that I took had less water.

"She was a wise woman, then," I said. "She saw what the result would be if you approached the Augustus claiming to be his son. Even if he believed you—and from what you say, there is reason to believe that he might—your life would become worthless. Galerius wants to become emperor himself. He would hardly look kindly upon a possible heir to Diocletian."

Genesius remained silent a long while. I thought, in fact, that he might have gone to sleep. We had been awake through a long and rather trying night. I know that I dozed a little myself in the morning sunshine that streamed through my window, for I started awake to see Genesius' face close to mine, his breath brushing my cheek.

"Why are you a traitor to my father, Christian?" Genesius said softly. "Why do you and the others surround him, like a pack of wolves? Are you waiting for him to die? You, the empress, Galerius' wife, and even the prince Constantine—what do you all want?"

I tried to answer him, but the warm sun and the night's exertions had taken their toll. I could not find the energy for explanations.

Nor the words.

CHAPTER 7

T hank the gods, you're back!" Diarius pumped Genesius' hand
up and down in a paroxysm of relief.

Hysteria looked him over skeptically and said, "Humph! You don't
look any the worse for wear. You've had poor Diarius worried sick
about you. We turned around to find you after the mass and you were
gone, vanished into the hands of the Christians. You pick a boy up
out of the gutter, clean the dirt off him, and what thanks do you get?
None. He sees a pretty face and off he goes, with no thanks to the
people who rescued him from a fourth-rate company of rustic clowns
where he was doomed to starva—"

Atalanta cut off the diatribe by enfolding Genesius in a warm, tight
embrace. Genesius hadn't known she thought so highly of him.
Eventually, he found himself released and heard—

"—thinks with his glands, just like all young men. I hope you're
satisfied!"

Genesius waited until she lapsed into silence. "I have an idea for a show," he said. "I'm not sure where it came from, but it's out of the Christians' 'gospel.' We'll need a few extras, some cows, maybe a donkey."

"Not," complained Diarius, "an animal act. Only a fool works with children and animals."

"And cows defecate at inopportune moments," Hysteria said.

"All the better!" Genesius cried. "Now listen, I've been mulling it over. It's just what we need. It'll get a laugh and it will make a point. We do the birth of Christ to a virgin. Imagine the difficulties she'll have. I mean, think about it for a minute!"

The four actors considered the implications in attempted silence.

The silence was soon broken, first by chuckles, then snickers, then by outright belly laughs. Soon, tears ran freely down the faces of Hysteria, Diarius, and Atalanta, as Genesius set forth his scenario.

✦ ✦ ✦

In a few weeks, the new play was ready. Diarius had hired extras, and all the properties and costumes had been made. It was time for the premiere.

As the audience slowly filled the small palace theater, Diarius bustled about backstage.

Genesius, for all his youth, was relatively calm about the troupe's first performance. He had faith in the script the company had developed over the past few weeks. He smiled as they waited for the emperor's arrival. No matter that Diarius had checked every piece of scenery and every prop four or five times. The little man was as nervous as a butterfly and about as effectual. Genesius watched him adjust the placement of his headdress again.

"It will be all right, Diarius," he whispered.

"Are you certain that the extras know their lines?" Diarius said.

"Absolutely."

"I know I'm being a silly old man, but this performance is so important. If we foul up this one, Galerius will have our heads!"

"We won't, old man," Genesius said. He put his arm around Diarius' shoulder.

"Maybe we should cut the bit about—

"We'll cut nothing." Genesius' anger flared brightly in the back-stage darkness. "We have discussed it and decided, all of us."

"You are right," Diarius said. "Of course, you're right. It's just that everything is so important; we must make a good impression."

"And we will," Genesius said.

The trumpet sounded, announcing the arrival of Diocletian.

"Let's go," Genesius said.

The actors, in costume, filed onto the stage just as Diocletian, attended by Galerius and the chamberlain Dorotheus entered. Prisca and Valeria followed behind. Valeria walked unsteadily, as if afraid. Her mother showed greater control but was still grim-faced. Neither looked like someone going to see a play. Genesius' position just right of center stage allowed him to watch the entire audience.

Into the semicircular orchestra came the priests of Bacchus and Venus to give their blessing to the new undertaking. They were followed by the *haruspex*, who would read the entrails of the sacrifice and predict the future of the enterprise.

Diocletian took the seat of honor, at the edge of the orchestra, directly opposite the altar at which the sacrifice would be offered to the gods. Dorotheus stood at his left, Galerius at his right, where he could watch Valeria and Prisca who had seats on the stage-right side of the house.

The *haruspex'* job was to kill the lamb cleanly, cutting its windpipe as he slashed the artery in the throat, so that the animal could not cry out. When all was still, the *haruspex* lifted the lamb to the altar. The crowd—audience, actors, and priests—held its collective breath as the knife flashed, slashing the lamb's throat.

Genesius saw the flicker of movement near the emperor as the knife descended. The *haruspex* must have seen it, too, for he missed the clean kill, and the lamb bleated in agony. Blood spurted over the white robe of the fortune-teller and soaked into the lamb's white fleece. The animal struggled, trying to escape, and the fortune-teller had to hack away at its throat, giving it four or five blows with the knife before it lay still. Covered in blood, he looked doubtfully to Diocletian.

"Continue," the emperor said.

The *haruspex* slit the lamb's belly. Again, he made a bad job of it. Genesius saw the fury contorting his face and his hand trembling with anger and terror. The entrails spilled onto the altar. The *haruspex* again looked helplessly to Diocletian.

"Well?" the emperor said. "What are the omens?"

The *haruspex'* voice trembled. "The beast is diseased. There is a tumor."

The crowd was no longer silent. A murmur of outrage circled the amphitheater.

Genesius stepped from the stage into the orchestra to stand beside the *haruspex*.

"Augustus, may I speak?"

Diocletian nodded.

"There is treason in your household, lord." Genesius pointed to the chamberlain, Dorotheus. "That man made the sign of the Christians just as the sacrifice was made."

Diocletian turned to look where Genesius' finger pointed. His face seemed to collapse in on itself.

Dorotheus, the chamberlain, was one of the few people with direct access to the person of the emperor. As chamberlain he cared for the emperor's personal needs. It was an office of high honor and great intimacy. Now it was revealed that the holder of the honored office was a Christian, a traitor.

Diocletian jumped to his feet and backed away from Dorotheus, into the orchestra of the small theater, near Genesius. He pointed a trembling hand at Dorotheus and screamed a wordless cry. The *haruspex* vanished behind the stage facade.

Galerius confronted the chamberlain across the chair Diocletian had fled.

"Is this accusation true?"

The big lieutenant towered over Dorotheus. His already tall and heavy body seemed to swell with indignation. Genesius half expected to see him burst with anger.

Diocletian backed into Genesius as Dorotheus stepped toward him.

"I am a Christian, Augustus." Dorotheus ignored Galerius, addressing his words to Diocletian. "But I am not a traitor. I have always given you loyal service."

Diocletian turned and spoke directly to Genesius. "I let him touch me; he handled my food; he decided whom I spoke to! He was my friend."

"Out of his own mouth," Galerius said, "he has convicted himself. Take him away."

Two guards stepped forward. Dorotheus shook them off. "Do you," he said to Diocletian, "order my arrest?"

"You betrayed me," Diocletian's voice was hoarse with fear.

"Do you order my arrest?"

"Get him out of here!"

One guard twisted Dorotheus' arm behind his back. The other drew his dagger and held it to the chamberlain's throat.

"Wait!" Diocletian said. He stepped close to the captured officer of his court. "Yes," he said, "I order your arrest."

"I have always been your friend," Dorotheus said. "For whatever may happen to me, I forgive you."

"I don't want your pity," Diocletian shouted. "I wanted your loyalty!"

Galerius nodded to the soldiers. The guard behind Dorotheus twisted his arm up further. Genesius heard the bone snap and saw the chamberlain's face go gray with agony. The man made no sound, but his face reflected the pain. As he inhaled sharply, the second soldier slashed his throat, severing both the windpipe and the artery in his neck. The first guard lowered the body to the floor. At a signal from Galerius, they dragged the body into the orchestra and laid it on the altar before Diocletian.

For a moment, Genesius, standing with the emperor, thought that Diocletian's control would fail. He looked to his wife and daughter, standing to one side, watching. Prisca met his gaze evenly, her face expressionless; Valeria's face was a study in horror, like an actor's tragic mask. She buried her face on her mother's breast. Diocletian snorted and turned away, ashamed, it seemed to me.

The ruler of Rome seemed to gather strength from some invisible source. He stood up straight.

"Where is the misbegotten fortune-teller?" he shouted. The *haruspex* peeked out from behind the siparium. "Here, O Augustus."

"Get out here and get to work." Diocletian strode back to the seat of honor and arranged himself on it. Genesius was still standing over the body. "You!" Diocletian said. "Give us a good—no, an *excellent* performance!"

Genesius resumed his place while the *haruspex* slit the belly of Dorotheus and exposed the man's entrails.

"The sacrifice is clean, Augustus. The omens are favorable."

"Then let the play begin!" the emperor said. The members of the court, still in shock from the killing of Dorotheus, whose mutilated corpse still lay in front of them, slowly settled back into their seats, with the exception of the empress.

Prisca remained standing. Diocletian looked across the seats to her.

"Wife, be seated," he said. "We are about to begin."

"Husband," she said evenly, "Dorotheus was your loyal servant. I go to mourn his death and your betrayal of him."

"Valeria," Galerius said, before Diocletian could reply, "do you share this feeling of your mother's?" His voice was heavy with threat.

Valeria, seated, only shook her head, unable to speak. She leaned away from Prisca, as if to disassociate herself from her mother's stance.

There was silence in the theater as Prisca marched up the aisle, alone, watched by all except Diocletian, who turned his back on her. He nodded to Genesius.

Genesius signaled the musicians to begin playing the pre-show music. After a moment of confusion, they began the music used to celebrate the birth of a male child.

The actors filed backstage. Diarius gathered them for a brief conference.

"You are either the bravest and brightest man I've ever met," he told Genesius, "or the biggest fool the gods ever created. Whatever possessed you?"

"Nothing possessed me," Genesius said. "But once the *haruspex* announced that the sacrifice was diseased, there was nothing for us to lose. Would you rather that all our work be for nothing? That we be tossed back into the world untested?"

"No, but—"

"I just saved us from losing everything. All we have to do now is perform as we have never performed before."

The music from the auditorium halted.

"That's our cue," Genesius said, fixing his headgear. "Let's go."

He pushed Atalanta toward the stage. She entered, crossed down-stage center, tripped, and fell full face flat on the stage. With a distinctly unfeminine grunt, she pulled herself into a sitting position and groaned loudly.

Genesius entered behind her. She raised her arms to him and said, "Joseph, my betrothed, help me up."

"Mary," Genesius said, "my beloved, did you fall down again?" Atalanta nodded and started to sob pitifully. "Was it another of your fits?" Genesius asked solicitously.

"Y-yes," Atalanta sniffled.

"You were thinking about Yahweh again, weren't you?"

"Y-yes."

"I've told you not to do that. You'll hurt yourself."

"I know, but I can't help it. I'm a very prayerful person."

"You'll have to stop this praying business. You have fits, you fall down, you foam at the mouth, you don't watch where you're going, you run into things—you're a mess!"

"I know," Atalanta whimpered.

"You need to settle down, Mary," Genesius said, "and get your mind on real things. All these imaginary conversations with God aren't doing you any good at all. I'll go get the rabbi, and we'll have the wedding now. The sooner you're pregnant and have a baby to worry about instead of God, the better off we'll all be. Now you sit down right here and wait for me. I'll be right back, then we'll go see the rabbi."

"Y-yes, Joseph."

"And whatever you do, don't think about God!" Genesius sat her on the bench and made his exit, looking back at her with great pity and gestures of love.

Atalanta sat quite still for a moment. From overhead, a voice called, echoing her name.

"Mary!"

She stood quickly, lost her footing, and fell facedown across the bench, her back to the audience, her skirt hiked up around her waist.

"Yes, God?"

"Hail, Mary full of grace!" the voice said. "Blessed are you among women, and blessed is the fruit of your womb!"

"What fruit?"

"Behold," the voice said, "you shall conceive a son and you will call his name Jesus. He will be great, and will be called the son of God, and he shall rule over the house of Israel, and he—"

"Now wait a minute," Atalanta interrupted. "I'm a virgin. How is all this going to happen?"

"Um . . . ah, yes," the voice said. "The Holy Ghost will come upon you. The power of God will do it."

"To me?" Atalanta-Mary asked.

"To you," the voice said.

"When?"

"Now."

"But we hardly know each other."

"With God, all things are possible," the voice said.

Atalanta thought it over for a moment, shrugged her shoulders, and made herself more comfortable on the bench.

"Behold, the handmaiden of the Lord," she said.

"It's not easy, you know, being a spiritual being. You'd be surprised at the things you don't get to do in Yahweh's heaven. I had to go through a lot to get this assignment, let me tell you!"

Her frame shook suddenly, then was still.

"Is that all?" she asked, her voice plaintive with disappointment. The rowdy audience howled with delight.

"That's it. Be seeing you." Atalanta sat on the bench, an expression of dissatisfaction on her face. After a few moments the dissatisfaction changed to alarm. She stood, feeling her belly. Her alarm intensified. After a moment, the audience began to see what was happening to her. Their laughter grew as Mary's discovery of her condition proceeded. Her belly grew right before their eyes. In just a few minutes she was nine months pregnant.

Genesius-Joseph returned to the stage.

"Mary! Your father, the rabbi—" In that moment he saw her. "What happened to you?"

"I think I'm . . . pregnant."

"I've always wanted a so—" Genesius-Joseph began. Then his face darkened with suspicion. "Wait a minute."

Genesius was plunged deeply in thought. He counted on his fingers briefly. He looked upward, and said the names of five or six girls in a whisper, then looked sternly at Atalanta.

"I haven't slept with you. How did you get pregnant?"

"I . . . I'm not exactly certain," Atalanta whimpered.

"You're not exactly certain." Genesius mocked her tone, simpering. He strode to the left entrance and called offstage.

"Rabbi!" he shouted. "Would you come here, please? I have something to show you."

Nothing happened.

"Rabbi!"

Diarius entered from the right, his nose buried in a scroll. He walked across the stage until he bumped into Atalanta. "Excuse me, sir," he mumbled, never looking up from his book. His trek continued all the way left, where he bumbled into Genesius. "Excuse me, miss," he said, and exited the stage.

Genesius plunged after him and dragged him back to where Atalanta stood. As her father, the rabbi, approached, Mary hung her head in shame.

Diarius protested as Genesius pulled him along. "I'm reading the holy books," he said. "It's my job. I'm just doing my job."

"Look at her," Genesius demanded. "Just look at her." Diarius looked and shrugged his shoulders. "She looks healthy to me." He buried his nose in the scroll.

Genesius ripped the scroll from his hands. "Look again. What's wrong with her?"

Diarius started at the top of her head and looked her over. "Her hair looks all right. Good clear brow. Her eyebrows are rather beetle-y—she gets that from her mother, but it's not a major fault. Her eyes seem the same as always. There is a blemish on her nose that I haven't seen before, but that's probably just from the excitement of your impending wedding—"

"There won't be any wedding," Genesius bellowed. He failed to interrupt Diarius' catalog.

"—her cheeks are flushed, but that's probably just excitement too; her mother, God rest her soul, was just the same. Couldn't hide her feelings, no matter what the occasion. Always blushing and flushing. Her chin looks like her mother's too. I always said that it was fortunate that little Mary had her mother's looks. Can you imagine if she had taken after me? You wouldn't marry her on a bet!"

"I won't marry her!" Genesius said.

"Good neck," Diarius continued. "Gets her neck from me, I daresay. One of my better features. But the shoulders are her mother's, God rest her soul—I mean her mother's soul, may she rest in peace. Wonderful shoulders that woman had. And feet! Oh, you never saw my Rachel's feet, did you, Joseph? I used to recite to her."

Diarius knelt in front of Atalanta and picked up one of her feet.

"How beautiful are thy feet with shoes, O prince's daughter!" He moved his hand up on her leg.

"The joints of thy thighs are like jewels, the work of the hands of a cunning workman."

He paused, realizing where his hands would go next if he continued. He let go of her leg and stood facing her. Only then did he notice Atalanta's swollen belly. His next words were confused, the rhythm broken.

"Thy navel is like a round goblet, which wanteth not liquor: thy belly is like a heap of wheat set about . . . with lilies—quite a large heap."

Dumbfounded, Diarius paused, staring at his "daughter."

"You little . . . " Words failed him for a moment. "I work until I'm ready to drop, day after day, studying the holy books, giving advice to people who won't follow it, leading the services in the synagogue, doing everything I can to earn enough money to give you a dowry because you're too ugly for any man to want you without one, and what do you do? You go out and get yourself with child without so much as a by-your-leave! I can't believe I fathered you!

"And you!" he wheeled on Genesius. "This is the thanks I get for letting you propose to this beautiful, innocent creature. You set her heart all a-flutter, get her into your bed, and now you want to abandon her because you couldn't wait. Oh no, not you. You just couldn't wait to get into her unmentionables, could you? I ought to beat you silly, you—"

"I didn't do it!" Genesius protested.

"—you misbegotten son of an Egyptian dung beetle!" Diarius said. "What do you mean?"

"I mean, I didn't do it," Genesius said. He turned to Atalanta. "Did I?"

Atalanta hung her head. "No," she whispered.

"Speak up, girl," Diarius ordered. "Did you sleep with him or not?"

"No, Father," she said.

"Then who is responsible for this?"

"I . . . I don't know," Atalanta said.

"There were that many?" Diarius spluttered. Genesius gaped at Atalanta, then hid his head in shame.

"No," she said. "There weren't any! It was the Holy Spirit."

"The what?"

"The Holy Spirit. An angel came and told me that the Holy Spirit was going to . . . you know."

Diarius was a volcano before the eruption. At first he was simply calm, with no outward sign of the boiling fury within. Slowly, he began to quake. Wisps of steam seemed to escape from his nose. His trembling increased to envelop his whole body. The Hebrew robes he wore picked up the movement and began to sway along with his flesh.

His color changed from a healthy pink to deepening scarlet. The redness crept up his neck, filled his face, painted his neck, and finally reached his hairless skull. When all was scarlet, the color deepened and flecks of foam fell from his lips. Veins throbbed in his naked scalp.

Diarius blew up in a cloud of smoke. When the smoke cleared, nothing was left of him but a pile of clothing.

There was a stunned silence in the imperial audience. But Genesius and Atalanta stepped forward to bow. The applause was tentative; the audience did not know what to think. Genesius and Atalanta bowed deeply to Diocletian, then to Galerius. Then Genesius stood and motioned for silence; it did not take long to achieve.

"Ladies and gentlemen, if you will look behind yourselves—"

They did. Diarius stood by the image of Venus, leaning jauntily on her leg, his hand caressing her inner thigh. Diocletian leaped to his feet, cheering. Galerius mimicked his action, and the rest of the audience followed suit.

Diarius left Venus with an affectionate pat on the behind and started down through the seats to the stage, smiling and acknowledging the applause. When he reached the stage, he called for silence and got it.

"Divine Augustus, ladies and gentlemen," he said, "you have just witnessed a miracle. You saw me explode—or think you did. You saw me vanish into the air—or think you did. But who knows what is truth and what is illusion? I stand before you alive and unharmed. How? By the intervention of a supernatural agency?

"Not quite," Diarius continued. "If I were to explain, I would give away a secret of my trade. But we will demonstrate it once more so that you will know that it was no accident. Know that if we, poor actors—I, an inconsequential little man of no influence, hardly worth the notice of humans, let alone of gods—can perform this act, then anyone, anywhere, can be a 'worker of miracles.' Even a Christian. Let his god make Dorotheus reappear—if he can."

The three performers bowed in unison to the assembly. Three small explosions gave forth three puffs of smoke. Three piles of clothing lay empty on the stage.

✦ ✦ ✦

In the dressing room backstage the actors congratulated themselves. Diarius giggled periodically.

"I thought you would have a stroke," Atalanta said, "when you turned your head red."

"Always save something for the performance, my dear," he laughed. "Always hold something back. Speaking of which, Hysteria, have you put the 'magic' out of sight?"

"Yes, dear," the older actress sighed. "Just as I said I would. Don't you have something nice to say for my timing?"

"It was perfection itself." Diarius grinned to his wisdom teeth and wiggled out of his tunic.

Genesius and Atalanta stripped off their costumes. "We need to get these things out of sight. We should be in street clothes in case anyone comes backstage."

As he spoke, someone knocked peremptorily on the door. "Who is it?" Atalanta asked.

I am Lactantius, the orator," I answered. "The emperor wishes to speak with you."

The actors let me into their dressing room while the women were still changing. They were drunk, or seemed to be, but there was no smell of wine on the breath of any of them. I tried to avert my eyes, but both of the women flaunted their nudity; to avoid rudeness, I had no choice but to allow myself to see them. I silently offered the temptation to the Lord, but not, I must admit, instantly.

Diarius and Genesius behaved as if they had just emerged from the rites of one of the mystery cults. Their eyes flashed and flitted from one thing to another, and their thoughts jumped from one idea to the next. They were simply intoxicated by the success of their first performance. But I was sickened by it; their exploitation of the history of the Savior's birth demonstrated all that was wrong with the pagan critique of Christianity. While the achievement of their spectacle had been the stuff of magic, the thinking that lay behind their playlet was obscene. That was, however, exactly what Galerius had wanted. With the martyred body of Dorotheus still warm, their parody was all the more obscene. I kept my silence with difficulty, and when they were dressed, led them to the emperor.

I had been told to take the actors to the private offices of the emperor. Diocletian was huddled in consultation with Galerius, with only a few attendants present. As we entered, a member of the praetorian guard motioned us to wait in silence.

"I agree!" Diocletian said violently. "You were right. The household is riddled with Christians. There is no need for you to convince me further. The question is not to determine whether or not they are present. It is what to do about it. I will not have wholesale killings! We would have civil war throughout the empire."

The persecution was about to begin. Inwardly I trembled for the followers of the Way, partly in fear, partly in joy that we would soon have the opportunity—most of us—to declare our allegiance to the Christ openly and to earn the heavenly crown of martyrdom. Persecution would purify the church, for those who were weak brothers and sisters would join the opposition at the first hint of trouble, as it has happened, while those whose faith, by the grace of God, was strong would inspire new converts among those who were still searching. Thus, it was with thoroughly mixed feelings that I listened to the mutterings of Galerius and Diocletian.

The latter turned away from Galerius and saw us awaiting his attention. He paid the actors an extreme compliment—he rose from his seat and walked over to us. I signaled the actors to kneel in obeisance and prayed that they would not, this time, give forth with any of their outrageous improvisations. My prayers were answered. The actors were awed by their proximity to the emperor.

"Stand up," Diocletian said. "I reward service well performed—and you have done well. I admit to having had my doubts about this program of Galerius', but he was correct in this as in so many things.

"Who leads this troupe of players?"

I introduced Diarius, who quivered with pleasure at the emperor's praise. Diocletian embraced him, and he nearly fainted with pride.

"What is the name of the virgin?" he asked.

"She is Atalanta, divine lord," Diarius said, from within the imperial hug. Diocletian abandoned the actor-manager and strode to take the young actress in his embrace.

"You are talented, young Atalanta. I trust that we shall see more of your work." It was precisely the right thing to say to her. Not for nothing had Diocletian gained the loyalty of the common soldier long ago. He had the common touch; it explained much of his ability to remain on that treacherous throne for twenty years.

Regretfully abandoning his embrace of Atalanta, the emperor stood before Hysteria.

"I did not see you on the stage."

"And yet, lord," she said, "you saw my work too."

"Indeed you did, divine one." Diarius grinned with pride. "For if my wife, Hysteria, had not been behind the scenes, the scenes themselves would have been dull indeed."

Diocletian wheeled on Genesius. The young man had been watching the emperor closely, trying to gauge how he ought to behave in the Augustus' presence. I could not help but think, as he looked upon Diocletian, that he believed that he saw his father, Diocles. I offered a silent prayer that Genesius would curb his impulsiveness.

"You," Diocletian said, "will stay." To the others he again expressed his gratitude, then honoring them beyond their station, he personally ushered them from the room.

"Galerius," Diocletian said from the doorway, "you have done well with your actors. But how is it that this one"—here he indicated Genesius—"can see things that you cannot? You sat by my side when Dorotheus made the Christian sign during the ceremonies, and you said nothing."

"My lord," Galerius said, "it was I who brought the actor into the court. He works for me."

"So." Diocletian strolled to Genesius' side. "You say that in fact *you* discovered Dorotheus' treachery. Through this man." He turned to Genesius. "Did my caesar give you a commission to seek out traitors?"

"No, my lord," Genesius said. "For I have never spoken with him."

Galerius stiffened.

"But when he had me enrolled in the service of the emperor, I was commissioned to do anything that a loyal subject might find to protect your person."

Galerius almost smiled. His huge bulk relaxed. The room held less threat.

Diocletian laughed. "Lactantius!" he said. "What need do I have of your rhetoric when one like this actor has such a golden tongue?"

The question needed no reply. I made none.

"Did you write the mime, Genesius?"

"We all did, my lord."

"Under your direction, I suspect."

"As you say, my lord."

"Yet you did not claim the first place."

"It was in the nature of the script, my lord, that the older actor play the father."

"Still, there are tricks of makeup and costume, are there not?"

"A younger man does not move like an old one without much study."

"You are a serious artist, then?"

"How else?"

Diocletian's attention shifted, in the way for which he was famous. Having gleaned enough information, for the moment, from Genesius, he returned to his conference with Galerius. And while he seemed to ignore the actor and myself, it was only appearance. He knew we were present and listening.

"We will begin tomorrow," he said. "It is the festival of Terminalia, the time of endings and of boundaries."

"With respect, Augustus," Galerius said, "we still need to compose and have copied your proclamation. To have enough copies made will take a day."

Diocletian was impatient. "And if we wait a day, we will miss the most propitious time. Besides, why should we tell them in advance? Do the Christians announce themselves when they enter my service? This actor, except that he denounced Dorotheus today, might be one. Lactantius our orator could be a secret Christian. Even you, my adopted son, my heir, might secretly belong to the cult. I cannot read their hearts, Galerius. Why should I let them read mine?"

They laid their plans for the next day's work. I longed to escape, to warn Anthimus and the brothers, to hide in fear, and at the same time I longed to announce myself to the caesars and declare my allegiance to God.

As usual, I kept silent. Diocletian invited Genesius to remain and dismissed the rest of us. I hurried to warn Anthimus.

✦ ✦ ✦

The emperor was silent for several moments after the others left, lost in thought. Genesius kept quiet as well, content in silence, studying the man-god who had fathered him.

His hair was graying, curled in the style affected by the emperors for generations. His frame was not tall but well proportioned, and fit for a man of fifty. Only a small paunch bulged the fabric of his toga of Tyrian purple. The skin of his legs and arms was leathery, weathered, the hair of his legs gray and grizzled. Clean-shaven, his face was scarred from battles long past. One angry white line meandered from his right ear to his nose. A dozen smaller cuts textured the skin of his face. His forehead was high, only slightly covered by a frieze of curls. Brown eyes shifted watchfully from doorway to doorway, ever alert for the possibility of betrayal, assassination. The eyes never rested for long; they seemed to search ceaselessly for the telltale signs that would herald the beginning of a new emperor's reign—a sudden, silent movement behind a curtain, the meeting of eyes between two or three counselors, the subtle slowness to obey of a servant who has overheard a plot.

The care-filled eyes came to rest on Genesius. He returned the august stare with what he hoped was innocence.

"Who are you?" Diocletian said.

"A survivor, my lord," Genesius said.

"And what do you survive?"

"So far, I have lived through poverty, the death of my mother, and a short life in the theater."

"The higher you rise," Diocletian said, "the less your chances of survival. That is one thing I have learned. What have you learned since you came to the court?"

"That no one is trustworthy."

"Who taught you this?"

"Dorotheus." Genesius sat very still under Diocletian's interrogation. Not knowing how he knew, he sensed that absolute calm was important.

Diocletian was silent, his eyes looking inward into memory, before speaking. "He was a friend, I thought. A man I trusted."

Diocletian's mouth twisted around the word, his eyes brimmed, and he fought for control. Genesius forced himself not to notice the emperor's emotion. The father he had just discovered was in pain, yet he could do nothing.

Diocletian regained control. "You claim to be a survivor," he said. "You remind me of someone."

"Perhaps you have seen me on the stage before."

"I never go to the theaters. The mob is too fickle. How can you stand to go before it day after day?"

"It is my trade, Augustus," Genesius said. "I have to live."

"But how a man lives counts for something, Genesius. The mob is fickle, changeable in its affections. You are no more than a prostitute, perhaps, or a gladiator."

"But my weapon is not trident and net—only laughter. No one ever killed the man they were laughing at."

"And when the laughter stops?"

"Then I hope I am fast on my feet, my lord."

Diocletian laughed with disdain. "You are young!"

"I apologize for my youth, lord. It is a fault that only time will correct."

"If," Diocletian warned, "you are the survivor that you claim to be." He stretched himself, arms extended. "Tomorrow will be a busy day. Get some rest. You'll need to be alert because I have taken a liking to you, and that can be dangerous. I don't quite know why, but I feel"—he laughed harshly—"not that I trust you, but I like you, son."

Genesius almost cried out before he realized that Diocletian meant the word only in the sense that older men use it of younger men for whom they feel affection.

"So I'm going to extend your education. Tomorrow we begin to root out the Christians from the whole empire. It begins there." He pointed out the window, at the former bathhouse that dominated the hill above the imperial palace. "You went there, didn't you, along with the rest of the actors?"

"Research," Genesius said quickly. "It was to spy on them. We had authorization—"

"—from Galerius, I know." Diocletian's expression was wry. "Don't worry. You are not suspected, not after today's performance. You would not be in this room if you had not denounced Dorotheus."

"Trust no one," Genesius said quietly.

"Some evidence is damning," Diocletian said. "One thing I know about the Christians is that they are easy to convict. They joy in confessing themselves."

"Always, my lord?"

"In my experience. None would denounce another. None would do what you did to that cross, no matter what the provocation." Diocletian chuckled at the memory. "That was your first day in the court, wasn't it?"

"Yes, my lord."

"It still makes me laugh." Diocletian turned again to the window. "Tomorrow the troops go to that church. They will arrest the bishop, as he calls himself, and any others they find. They will take the Christians' holy books and burn them. Then they will level the building. One stone will not be left on top of another.

"They are my troops, my officers. But they only obey me; they adore Galerius.

"You will go with them. It will be dangerous for you; Galerius thinks you are his because he hired you. But you will go as my representative. You will be loyal to me, do you understand?"

"Trust no one."

"Not even yourself, son."

The interview seemed to be over. Genesius started to leave the room. Diocletian called after him.

"Wait. I have one more question."

"My lord?"

"Your name is . . . odd. It means 'beginning.' Is it your true name?"

"Yes. My mother was a Jew."

"And you?

"I am an actor, my lord," Genesius said. "It is the only faith I know."

Diocletian turned back to the window. Genesius left his father staring in hunger at the church that loomed above the palace.

A solitary figure labored up the hill, muffled into anonymity against the early spring chill. The weather promised a storm before nightfall.

✦ ✦ ✦

A bitter wind blew down the hill as I ascended to the church. Anthimus must know.

My risk was minimal. While I could be seen from the palace, my cloak was anonymous, my back to the imperium. I wished that I could turn my back on the imperium forever. But even as I felt the wish, I knew what Bishop Anthimus would tell me. While one part of my spirit wanted to rebel against his authority, another recognized the justice of what he required of me.

Someone must leave word for the Christians of the future. Indeed, if there were to be Christians in the future, someone—and I was apparently one—must be left from the coming persecution to teach them.

Many gifts, one spirit. I knew the litany, repeated it over and over as I climbed the hill. But how I wished for a different destiny, for the hope of clarity, to be taken up from the necessity of witnessing this morning's barbarism again and again!

Dorotheus had been a new Christian, baptized only a short time before, a confidant of the emperor, a trusted servant; his corpse lay buried in an unknown place, hidden to keep his brothers and sisters from finding him and venerating his martyrdom.

The wind blew harder. Dead leaves flew in my face; the first drops of rain followed them, stinging like hail.

Genesius dreamed. He was shouting and capering through the streets, struggling to elbow his way through the crowds that kept him from the old man who rode ahead of him, caparisoned in glorious robes and attended by a phalanx of adopted children, fully grown and jealous of their positions of honor. Genesius had the right to his place beside the old man: it had been promised long ago, and he had the proof in his hand, but he could convince no one to pay attention. The more he tried to draw attention to himself, the thicker grew the mob that kept him from the old man. He fought through the stinking mass of humanity with redoubled effort, finally reaching the old man's side. The old man began to turn in Genesius' direction—

A hand shook him roughly. He stared up into the darkness. Where was the old man?

A voice spoke from somewhere above his eyes. "If you're coming, we're going."

The hand released his shoulder. The presence left the room, squeaking faintly.

Leather. Armor. A soldier. Genesius sprang from his bed. He was to accompany the troops to the church, to act as Diocletian's witness among Galerius' men.

He had slept fully dressed, knowing the call would come early. First light was not yet showing in the east. He slipped his sandals on, still half in the world of his dream, and ran groggily down to the palace courtyard where the troops were assembling. The palace was astir with activity unusual for the early hour. Servants gathered in the halls and corners, wondering why the soldiers were out and about. Some talked of a possible coup in the making, but it was only the gossip of the uninformed.

In the courtyard the troops were drawn up in ranks. Three sentries stood at ease, equipped with short swords, shields, and daggers. At their head, a tribune and other officials waited impatiently for the signal to begin.

Genesius skidded into the colonnade that surrounded the courtyard and stopped. He realized that he had no idea how to behave as Diocletian's official observer, but the post surely called for more dignity than he had mustered so far. He paused to survey the situation. The officials kept glancing to the tower in the southwest corner of the palace grounds. Genesius was at the north side of the courtyard, the troops and their leaders to the east. The sky was starting to gray behind them, but no light yet showed in the tower. Genesius waited. The church lay on the hill south of the palace. The tower would be the only vantage from which the operation could be seen in its entirety from the palace. Its entrance, however, was invisible from the east end of the courtyard. The prefect and the tribune, therefore, awaited their signal from the top.

In the predawn darkness two figures moved through the southern colonnade toward the tower. The leader of the two was tall and bulky: Galerius. The smaller figure behind him had to be Diocletian. After giving them time to enter the tower and climb the stairs to the top, Genesius took a deep breath and bellowed a command for attention in his strongest stage voice.

All the soldiers, officers included, braced themselves. Genesius raced through the colonnade, out of their immediate view to the west. With the troops waiting at attention, he took the time to pry a large stone from the pavement. Staggering under its weight, he entered the courtyard.

"Soldiers of Rome!" he yelled. The officers whirled to face him. "The feast of Terminalia marks the beginning of the termination of the treason of the Christians."

There was a murmur of amusement among the troops, some of whom recognized the actor. The officers heard their muffled laughter and whirled again to quiet them. Some of the troops laughed out loud at the officers.

"Open the gates," he shouted. The sentries obeyed; the gates creaked open.

"Soldiers of Rome!" Genesius now staggered under the weight of the stone, as he made his way to the center of the courtyard. "You are the boundary stone of the empire. You incarnate the god Terminus." He raised the boulder over his head. Officers and men stared at him in amazement. His feet danced under him, more and more desperate to maintain balance below the great stone. "As this stone crushes whatever it falls on, may you crush all enemies of the emperor!"

Genesius dropped the paving stone. To all the soldiers, it seemed to land on his foot, for he screamed in pain, grabbed his toes with both hands, and hopped furiously around the courtyard.

Genesius, still holding his foot, hopped to the gate. "Oh, let's go," he said, his voice thinned with pain. He hopped through the gate and started up the hill, still on one foot. Behind, he heard the legionaries start to march, laughing still.

He ran back and forth along the line of march, hectoring the troops and clowning for them, until they were drawn up in ranks before the great wooden door. Awakened by the troops' arrival, residents of the surrounding houses peered cautiously from their doors, many keeping their faces hidden, all anxious to know what was going on.

The tribune at the head of the troops stepped forward, drew his sword, and hammered its butt against the doors. He stood back to wait.

After a moment, the door swung open, revealing an old woman. "What do you want?"

"The bishop Anthimus," the tribune said, "the images of your god, and the books you use here."

"I'll see if he's in," she said. She shut the door in his face.

The tribune was left cooling his heels. Genesius stepped up to him, bowed, borrowed his sword, and pounded on the church door again. The sound boomed hollowly through the neighborhood.

"Open up your doors," Genesius shouted, "that the glory of the emperor may come in!"

There was an audible intake of breath as the doors swung open. Standing in the entrance was Anthimus. The bishop wore his best clothing, as if dressed for his funeral.

"It is the clown," he said. "What is the glory of the emperor next to the glory of God?"

"His soldiers!" Genesius said.

"Stand aside!" the tribune ordered. "Both of you." He ordered his troops forward, and they spilled into the church, sweeping Anthimus and Genesius in with them. A giant of a soldier, a blond German, lifted the bishop and the actor in his massive arms and deposited them out of the way of the armed men.

"Stay here," he said in his heavily accented Latin. "Don't get in the way and you won't get hurt."

He left them by the wall, near to where Genesius had knelt as a spurious Christian on his first visit to the church.

"It seems that they have little respect for either of us," Anthimus said. "What are you?"

"A fool," Genesius said. "A god's fool."

"You could be a fool for God," Anthimus said, fingering the imperial brooch Genesius wore, "instead of for the emperor."

"I am well paid."

"God's pay is better."

"They are destroying your church," Genesius said. "How can you stand here and try to convert me?"

"One does what one can. I cannot stop the soldiers, but I can talk with you while they do their work."

The sounds of search and destruction surrounded the pair. In the square in front of the church, the soldiers were making a pyre of furniture, books, and clothing. Two soldiers came by them, carrying the wooden crucifix that had dominated the service Genesius had attended.

"Do you expect to convince me?"

"Not today," Anthimus said. "Your friend at the court has told me about you. But perhaps, someday, you may remember what is beginning now."

A group of soldiers walked by, bent under the weight of armloads of books. One dropped a scroll and went on without noticing its loss. Genesius bent to retrieve it. He opened the tightly rolled scroll.

"It is one of our scriptures," Anthimus said. "Why don't you keep it?"

Genesius was scanning the closely written script. "'Didn't you know,'" he began derisively, "'that you are the temple of God, and that the spirit of God lives in you? If anyone destroys the temple of God, God will destroy him; for the temple of God is holy, and you are that temple.

"'Let no man deceive himself: if anyone among you seems to be wise in this world, let him become a fool, that he may be wise.'" Genesius became more interested. "'For the wisdom of this world is foolishness with God. For it is written, he takes the wise in their craftiness. Therefore let no man glory in man; for all things are yours, and you are Christ's, and Christ is God's.'"

He threw the scroll to the floor. Anthimus started to pick it up, but Genesius forestalled him.

"Leave it alone. It will be burned with the rest. I liked that part about the fool, though."

Genesius saw that the bishop could barely take his eyes from the discarded scripture. Was it the only thing he hoped to save from the troops?

Two soldiers approached, carrying the basins used in the cleansing ritual, candles, and the silver goblets and dishes with which the priests had fed the midnight multitude with bread and wine. The surface calm of Anthimus broke at the sight of the chalice. He began to tremble with anger. Genesius placed a restraining hand on his arm.

"There is nothing you can do."

Another soldier ordered the old bishop outside. Anthimus stopped to look with longing on the single remaining scroll; the trooper slapped him across the buttocks with the flat of his sword. The old man stumbled out into the light.

Genesius was alone in the desecrated church. The morning cloudiness was starting to break up. Sunlight filtered through the east window. Where the shadow of the mullions crossed on the floor lay the scroll Genesius had read. Glancing to the door, he saw that all the soldiers and officers were outside. He stepped into the trapezoid of light, bent, picked up the scroll, and hid it under his tunic.

Genesius went outside to the square. The crucifix and the books were piled on top of a wooden pyre. Anthimus was under guard to prevent his interference with the destruction.

"You must watch, old man," Genesius said.

"Yes, I know." Anthimus seemed to have mastered his sudden fury, though he still trembled.

The tribune gave an order, and several soldiers applied pitch to the wooden substructure of the bonfire. The silver pieces were missing, probably appropriated by the tribune. Another trooper lit the pitch with a torch. As the flames grew, the scrolls crackled and burst into flame which licked the lifeless figure carved on the cross.

Genesius watched in satisfaction. He would be able to report to Diocletian that his orders had been fulfilled without excessive violence.

The eyes of the wooden figure seemed to turn toward Genesius. He whirled to see what the bishop was doing, but the old man simply stood with his head bowed, his lips moving silently. Genesius slapped him across the face.

"Stop it!" he said.

A cloud of confusion passed over Anthimus' face. "Stop what?"

"Look!" Genesius pointed at the wooden figure. Flame was turning it black. Fingers of fire rose above it, shimmering so that the figure seemed to move. Was it just a trick of the flame, twisting the air so that Jesus' eyes accused Genesius?

"Make it stop!" Genesius hissed at the priest. "They'll all see it. They'll blame me!"

"I am not doing anything," Anthimus said.

"It's your magic," Genesius said, "your Christian magic." A burning fragment of a scroll, lifted by the fire's heat, floated up into the air and drifted in through the open window of one of the houses fronting on the square. A tendril of smoke came from the window. One of the onlookers turned to investigate and cried out that the window of his house was on fire. The tribune dispatched soldiers to help. Genesius still stared at the pyre when the house fire was extinguished. The tribune interrupted his trance.

"You!" the tribune ordered. "Make yourself useful. Go back to the palace."

Genesius turned to leave.

"If we fire this church, the whole neighborhood, maybe the entire city, will burn," the tribune said. "Get us new orders."

Genesius' mind was almost blank, but he welcomed the opportunity to get away from the accusing eyes.

"Do you understand?" the tribune demanded.

"New orders," Genesius said, fighting the numbness.

"And hurry!"

Genesius started to run from the square. He felt the scroll pressing tight between his tunic and his skin. It cut into the flesh of his belly as he ran, seemed to grow hotter and hotter as he approached the palace. His feet thudded against the cobblestones, his breath came hard as he reached the gate. His fine clothing and imperial brooch got him past the guard with a minimum of delay.

Genesius wanted to stop at his quarters to dispose of the scroll. It was contraband. Its presence, if discovered, would ruin everything. But as he cut across the courtyard, still running, Galerius hailed him from the tower. Without stopping, he looked up to the window where Diocletian and Galerius watched, made a wide looping turn around the enclosed area, and ran for the entrance to the tower.

Stumbling at the top of the stairs, he bumped into Galerius, who was waiting for him at the doorway. Genesius felt the scroll start to slip from its hiding place under his tunic. Galerius recoiled from the impact and Genesius clutched his side.

"What do you have there?" Galerius said.

"A pain," Genesius said, more breathlessly than necessary. "I've run all the way from the church!" He doubled over, apparently in agony, to shift the scroll into a position where it would not, he hoped, be visible under his tunic. The only place was between his legs.

The scroll, however, took more room than he thought. When he straightened up, his tunic bulged embarrassingly. He had nothing to do but to brazen it out. He stood to attention, his knees stiff, his thighs locked together, holding the scroll tightly.

"My lord," he addressed Diocletian, "the tribune Lucius Cinna, in command of the troop at the church, requests new orders. Lucius Cinna says that if they burn the church as ordered, it may spread throughout the city. He respectfully requests that you amend his orders."

Diocletian tried to pay attention to what the actor said, but the corners of his mouth crinkled with the beginnings of laughter. Galerius had decided, Genesius noticed, simply to ignore his impropriety. He stared stonily out the window, his face set as stiffly as a marble bust.

Genesius followed the direction of Diocletian's gaze. He grinned helplessly at the emperor, shrugged his shoulders, and then crossed his legs.

"If the emperor will excuse me for a moment—"

"Uh, yes," Diocletian said, smiling. "I think that would be appropriate. When you have taken care of your . . . problem, ask the praetorian prefect to come up here."

Genesius ducked back into the stairwell. He leaned back against the stone, still cool from the night air, and took a deep breath. He took the scroll from between his legs and shifted it behind his back, under the tunic and held in place by his belt, then pushed against the wall, flattening the bulge into the small of his back.

Just as he finished, Diocletian poked his head around the corner of the stairwell. "After you find the prefect, come back up here."

Genesius' face must have registered shock, for Diocletian went on, "When you've taken care of your problem, that is." The emperor returned to his place by the window, chuckling.

Breathing a sigh of relief that the scroll had not been discovered, Genesius hurried down the steps, across the courtyard, and into the palace. He found the prefect, told him of Diocletian's wishes, and dashed toward his room.

On his way through the living quarters, Genesius literally ran into Lactantius, who was yawning on his way to breakfast. He drew the rhetorician into an empty room, lifted his tunic, and pressed the scroll into his hands.

"Take this," Genesius said. "Keep it for me, but don't let anyone know you have it. It's worth both of our lives."

Genesius left Lactantius staring stupidly at the scroll and hurried back to the tower. Diocletian and Galerius were seated side by side, watching the activity on top of the hill. Diocletian heard him come in and invited him to join them. He barely was able to listen to the conversation for thinking about the scroll he had left with Lactantius. If it were discovered, its owner would suffer the same fate as Dorotheus the chamberlain—at best, a swift journey into darkness, at worst—it did not bear thinking of.

"If we destroy their 'churches,' burn their books, and take away their rights as Roman citizens, they will come around," Diocletian said. "I have been their emperor for almost twenty years. I know the people. They can be ruled by fear. But I will not unleash a bloodbath, perhaps a civil war. There must be no mass killings. Look what happened under Decius; for every Christian he had killed, two or three more rose up in his place. Besides, there are more of them now. If we start killing them off, we will rip the fabric of society to pieces."

Genesius knew enough to keep silent. This was no time for the jester to draw attention to himself.

"You don't politely ask rebels to change their ways," Galerius said. "They won't do it. Did the Persians surrender when we asked them to? They gave up only when there weren't enough left to fight. A dead opponent can't fight back."

"No killing." Diocletian was adamant. "Have the edict written and bring it to me. I want to see it myself and read it word for word."

Genesius listened without appearing to pay attention. His eyes rested on the column of troops setting off up the hill to the church. Instead of arms, they carried axes, saws, and picks. The soldiers acted as if they were on a holiday excursion. Even from the tower, he heard their gibes and jokes.

"As you command, Augustus." Galerius bowed, more deeply than the occasion called for, and left the tower to have the edict written.

Diocletian stared from the window, seated by Genesius. Together, they watched the praetorians wind their way up the slope from the palace, the seat of Roman authority in the world, to the church, the physical locus of the only challenge to that power.

Morning wore into afternoon. Diocletian spoke only once, to send Genesius after food and wine. The old emperor and the young actor ate in silence and settled down once more to observe. The soldiers made short work of the wooden church. Starting from the top, the brigade of engineers hacked, sawed, and chopped at the Christians' temple until, by late afternoon, nothing was left but a pile of rubble. Before dark even the debris was hauled away. From the tower Genesius could just see the mosaic on the floor across which he and Lactantius had walked together after the services. Exposed now to the dying light of evening, the slave still bathed his master in the river, although all the protection of the building's outer structure had now been torn away.

The caesar Galerius called on me as the court rhetorician to write out the decree. He was not an educated man. He must have wanted to be certain that the words accomplished their task: to frighten the brethren into rejecting the truth they had struggled to attain. I am still stricken by the irony that I was writing the first edict of the great persecution. I comfort myself, somewhat, with the knowledge that it would have gone forth no matter whose hand wrote the original copy. Still, the ink that stained my fingers that day smelled of blood.

The content of the edict was only a small part of what Galerius desired. Diocletian still held sway over his reason; Galerius was satisfied, but not sated, with what he had achieved as a beginning. The churches were to be torn down, the scriptures surrendered to the authorities and burned, the clergy and those of the faithful who had high positions in society to be tortured. However, no one was to be executed for being a Christian—at least, not yet.

Galerius fairly tore the document from my hands as I finished writing it. I would quote it here, but you already know its import. Indeed, you still suffer under its prescriptions, and an extra copy made now will be one more to destroy when the time of our vindication comes.

Galerius himself took the edict to the scribes to be written out in quantity for distribution to the provincial governors. They in turn would copy and post it in each city of their command. But the first copy was for Nicomedia. Galerius, his face reddened with excitement at the thought of revenge against the faithful, wasted no time in putting the order into effect.

While I wrote, Galerius, between bouts of dictation, ranted, revealing more about himself than perhaps he would have had he known where my true sympathies lay.

Galerius started life as the son of a priestess of the mountain gods among the barbarians north of the Danube. When Carpathian brigands invaded her lands, she fled with her young son to the Alps of Transylvania in Dacia. No one but she knew the boy's father, not even Galerius himself. The common story about his parentage is that he was conceived during the night of a festival sacred to Cybele, the so-called mother of the gods.

Some truth may be in this legend, for Galerius himself was scarred with the marks of self-laceration common to this pagan cult and known for his attachment to Cybele's worship. In his own administrative district, which included then Macedonia and all the Danubian provinces, he maintained a mountain temple to Cybele, complete with demonic women, the Corybants, and neutered men as the goddess's attendants. He thought of himself as the goddess's consort, the one man among many who could keep his manhood among the Corybants. He is still known to use three women in a night, leaving them bruised and broken. This aspect of his character is not spoken aloud.

Galerius formed his hatred of us early in his life. Romula, as his mother was known, almost daily held sacrificial feasts in honor of Cybele. Christians avoided her feasts out of fear for their souls' welfare and gathered to pray and fast while she and her libidinous companions, including her son, indulged all of their appetites in the name of Cybele. Some spark of goodness in Galerius (even such a man as he has an immortal soul, Christ be praised!) recognized his own evil and blamed the Christians for his guilt. Romula urged him on with messages from her temple in Dacia.

At last I finished the fair copy of the proclamation. Galerius took it away, and I was happy to see him leave.

Evening was near; the sky outside my window was darkening into sunset. I wondered what had happened to Anthimus by now. Was he imprisoned, under torture, or dead? While all of the brothers and sisters in Christ are equal in His love, Anthimus was the man whose personal sanctity brought me into the Shepherd's fold. He was my teacher, my confessor, and my friend.

My thoughts drifted back to my early time in Nicomedia. The emperor had sent for me from my home in Africa, where I had gained some measure of fame in the practice of rhetoric. I was a searcher, having rejected the house gods of my family in adolescent rebellion, then passed through my Stoic, Epicurean, and Platonic periods, like many younger men of this age, although I am no longer young.

I heard Anthimus preaching as I wandered the capital, exploring the imperial seat soon after my arrival. There was a great crowd gathered, more to jeer than to listen to his message of salvation. I did not, at the time, know what he meant by salvation, scarcely recogniz-ing my own need. I was celebrated, being newly arrived at court. Nevertheless, I listened to Anthimus through the jeers of the onlook-ers. His words had less effect on me than did his countenance. For all my newfound prosperity and celebrity, I still chafed within, for reasons I could not put into words. Anthimus looked happy.

It was not that I had never heard of Christianity. Christians were everywhere throughout the empire, always preaching their "good news" to anyone who would listen and some who could not escape. But the preachers whom I had heard were sour men who preached sour virtues. The Jesus I had read about had not seemed so pinched in spirit as some of His representatives. They scourged themselves, taking what seemed to me a perverted pleasure in pain and self-denial. In Anthimus, during the time of Diocletian's tolerance, the lively spirit of the gospel breathed life, and I found a brother.

I listened to Anthimus and believed. Now, he was in the hands of the devil. I could do nothing but pray for his deliverance.

Thoughts of Anthimus reminded me of the scroll the actor Genesius had given me—the first letter of Paul to the church at Corinth.

Paul was a persecutor before he became a believer. Did he have doubts about his persecutorial zeal before the journey to Damascus? His letters leave the question unanswered.

Genesius took the tray from the kitchen slave before the servant could enter the emperor's suite. Diocletian was an early riser, used to a simple breakfast before beginning the day's administrative work, even when he had slept little the night before. And when Genesius cracked the door to see if he was awake yet, Diocletian called out to him.

"Bring it here," he said. "I'm awake."

"We had a long night." Genesius brought the tray to the emperor's bedside table. Diocletian sat on the edge of the bed, applying himself to the food.

"Have you eaten?" he asked.

"Hours ago."

"Didn't you sleep?"

"No, my lord."

"Too much excitement." Diocletian chewed noisily. "Get your sleep, lad. When you get to be my age, you'll remember every hour you missed."

Genesius was satisfied that the old man was eating with a good appetite. He felt protective. Diocletian had no friends, no one he could trust. Genesius wanted to be that person for his father.

"What do you think of Galerius?" Diocletian interrupted his reverie.

"A capable and dedicated man," he said, as neutrally as he could.

"Dedicated to what?" Diocletian asked around his bread. Genesius hesitated, uncertain what the emperor wanted from him.

"It's not for me, lord, to judge the doings of the court."

"You've become cautious this morning."

"It wasn't long ago that I was just a poor actor," Genesius said. "Then, I had nothing to lose."

"And what do you have now?"

"Your favor."

Diocletian stood angrily and stalked to the window, where he could look to the hills that rose north of the city. "My favor is a changeable thing these days. I miss Dorotheus. And Peter. And Gorgonius. Members of my household who turned Christian, as perhaps my wife and daughter intend to do. What do you make of that?"

Genesius' memory leaped back to the night in the church, when he had met Valeria and Prisca after the rites. He started to confirm Diocletian's suspicions, then held his tongue. "The emperor knows more than I do."

"Twaddle!" Diocletian said. "I can read the signs and see the distaste on their faces when a sacrifice is called for. I can see that this new religion tempts my wife and our daughter. I can understand it in Valeria's case. She is married to Galerius; living with him would drive anyone to seek whatever salvation she could find. But Prisca knows what price I have paid to hold this thing called Rome together.

"I love my wife. The reason I no longer sleep with her is that I fear her disloyalty. I will not test it again. If she were to fail the test, I would have to kill her."

Genesius had no words to answer the emperor's revelation.

"There was another woman whom I remember," Diocletian said, "one who venerated me, however brief was the affair. When I see you, I am reminded of her."

The door burst open; Galerius filled the room with his furious bulk. "The edict has been torn down! One of the Christians ripped it from the kiosk in the central square and tore it up!"

Diocletian's wistfulness dissolved.

"Do you have the man?"

"Yes."

"Who is he?"

"An official of the municipal government."

"An official, defying imperial law!" Diocletian reddened with anger. A vein on his left temple throbbed dangerously. *"My* law!"

Diocletian paced to the window again. As the emperor turned his back, Genesius saw a smile of satisfaction play briefly on the thin lips of Galerius.

"He says, my lord," Galerius said, "that he obeys a higher law than that of Rome."

"I will show him just how high!" Diocletian spat. "Take him to the courtyard."

Smiling broadly, Galerius dashed from the room.

"Let's go," Diocletian said.

Genesius hesitated. Diocletian stopped in the doorway and spoke to him.

"That is, if you wish to keep my favor."

They descended to the courtyard, where the rising sun had begun to brighten the western colonnade, throwing shadows of the columns against the inner wall like shadows of bars in a jail cell. As they reached the courtyard, a small detachment of the praetorian guard, Galerius at their head, herded their prisoner to the center. Diocletian strode across the open space to meet them. Genesius followed.

Diocletian's wrath swept like a hurricane over the Christian. He berated him, slapped him back and forth across the face, his jeweled fingers slashing the helpless man's face. Genesius stiffened his own face to avoid showing the revulsion he felt as a witness to the anonymous man's pain. It was one thing to denounce a Christian, another to watch him suffer a vicious attack.

"Your name!" Diocletian barked. Genesius heard the fury in his father's throat and silently willed the silent man to answer satisfactorily.

"Your emperor has asked your name," Diocletian said. The man spat in Diocletian's face. The spittle drained down his cheek to drip from his chin. One of the soldiers stepped forward to slap the man down, but the Christian slipped his bonds and drew the soldier's short sword.

The shock of a direct attack upon the person of the emperor, within the boundaries of the palace, was so great that no one moved for a split second. As the prisoner leaped for Diocletian, Genesius threw himself in the way. He grabbed the blade itself in his left hand, immobilizing it as it descended toward Diocletian's head. For a few seconds the actor and the Christian stood locked in struggle, blood dripping down Genesius' arm. The Christian was a big man. Just as his weight and Genesius' wound were about to overcome the actor, Diocletian himself stepped around behind the man and kicked his feet out from under him. As if released from a spell, Galerius' troops piled onto the man.

"Don't kill him!" Diocletian shouted.

Genesius moved to one side, his hand on fire with the wound. The pain forced him to sit in the gravel. Oddly, he noticed that the ground was still cold with the night's chill.

"Leave him alive," Galerius ordered, "but bind him—tightly." Diocletian was breathing hard, unnerved by the close call.

Courtiers appeared from all sides, clucking over the emperor and praising his rapid action. Diocletian swept them out of his way and knelt by Genesius.

"My son," the emperor said, "let me see the wound. Are you all right?"

Genesius let Diocletian take his bleeding left hand. "This will scar,"

Diocletian said, "but you won't bleed to death. It should be cleansed, though, with fire, or it will fester."

"You mean *burn* it?" Genesius asked.

"It is what needs to be done," Diocletian said. "Otherwise—I don't want to lose you. You acted when no one else could." He turned to one of the soldiers.

"Bring fire."

While the coals were transported from the kitchens, Genesius prepared his mind for the ordeal ahead. He deferred to Diocletian's knowledge of battlefield surgery. The wound would have to be cleansed, and fire was the only sure way to do so. The pain would be substantial. But Genesius' pride made him want to bear it well, in honor of his father. "My son," the emperor had said, not knowing that the phrase was literally true. Diocletian had recognized him without knowing it. If Genesius could endure the glowing iron, one more proof of his trustworthiness would be built into the relationship between himself and Diocletian. He cleared his mind as the steel was heated. Diocletian himself bathed the wound as tenderly as any woman could.

"Are you ready?" Diocletian's gentle voice penetrated the great calm within which Genesius had wrapped himself. He nodded.

As if from a great distance, Genesius saw Diocletian take the steel rod, glowing with a dull red color, from the fire. The emperor held the rod's cool handle. Genesius felt its heat on his face.

"Let me do the work," Diocletian said. "Don't grip the rod; let me draw it through the wound. There is no point in burning more than is necessary."

Genesius nodded. He supported his left arm on his knee, holding the wrist with his right hand, his left palm open to the steel. His eyes searched out Diocletian's, and he nodded again to the emperor. Diocletian lowered his eyes to his task.

The point of the glowing steel touched the end of the laceration made by the sword.

The skin hissed. Steam rose from Genesius' hand. He took a sharp breath and held it as the steel moved slowly through the cut, probing down to unhurt tissue.

The point cooled. Diocletian returned the first steel to the flame and took another. Starting where he had left off, he drew the steel through Genesius' hand, cleansing with fire. Through three repetitions Genesius did not move.

Diocletian lay down the last rod.

"That is enough," he said.

Genesius released the breath he was holding. The world swam briefly around his head, then steadied.

"Do you want to lie down for a while?" Diocletian asked.

"No," Genesius said. "There is work to be done. Do it." Diocletian's expression changed from concern to grim determination.

Prisca broke through the mob of soldiers and courtiers to Diocletian. "I heard what happened. Are you hurt?"

Diocletian looked up from tending Genesius' hand. "The Christian failed to murder me, thanks to this actor." His body, his face were tense with the control learned over twenty years of rule.

"The actor," Prisca said. Confusion and shock played over her features. "But you are well, my lord?"

"Build up the fire," Diocletian ordered. "We will interrogate the prisoner."

CHAPTER 11

The emperor himself helped Genesius walk to a dais hurriedly placed at the northern end of the courtyard, out of the direct sunlight. Diocletian placed his actor on a couch where his view of the action would be clear. Another couch was brought for Prisca, whom Diocletian ordered to stay and watch.

The emperor's own physician brought Genesius a draught of poppy while the preparations were made for the interrogation of the Christian. Genesius watched the soldiers pile wood on the fire which had cleansed his wound. Several troopers erected two tripods, one on either side of the fire. Slaves came from the kitchens, carrying bags of salt and jugs of vinegar. An executioner, the armorer of the first unit of praetorian guards, honed his knives to razor sharpness.

Flies buzzed over the blood spilled on the gravel of the courtyard.

The sun groped its way across the open space, warming slave and free alike.

The Christian, bound hand and foot in leather thongs, lay on the ground not far from Genesius, who watched him with a detached curiosity. He had provoked his arrest, then attacked the imperial person. While most of the Christians would never lift a hand against the empire, there were some like this prisoner and like Constantine with real spirit. Perhaps Galerius was right to be so careful of them. Some, at least, posed a real danger.

From within his poppy haze, Genesius watched as the interrogation began. They were using a name now for the man. Someone identified him as Euethius, a member of the council of Nicomedia. He was important, then, and his punishment would be worse than for a lesser man. He would be an example, an object lesson for his cohorts.

At a shouted command from Galerius, the main gate was thrown open and a group of a dozen people was pushed through at the points of soldiers' spears. Two or three fell to their knees, and those behind them were forced either to trip over the fallen ones or to step on them to keep their own footing. They were suspected Christians, brought in to witness the torture of one of their fellows. Galerius would not ask these to sacrifice yet. He wanted them released, to spread the word of Euethius' suffering among the others of their faith. Mass recantations would follow in the natural course of events— or so Genesius hoped. He had no stomach for torture.

The courtyard was filling with people. Some stood silently, repelled by the impending event, drawn to witness almost against their will. Others had a holiday air, chattering, placing bets on the outcome, eating and drinking. Some of the barbarian slaves even brought their children with them.

Galerius looked to Diocletian, who nodded curtly. Galerius signaled the troopers surrounding Euethius; they released him from his bonds. At the same time, other troops surrounded the crowd in the courtyard. Euethius stood unsteadily, trying to unkink his limbs. Some in the crowd laughed at him, as he limped away from the fire.

Euethius was soft, well-clothed, his belly well-paunched. Sweat trickled from his matted hair. His expensive clothing was soiled with the dirt of the courtyard. His legs and arms were pudgy with fat. He was starting to panic.

A whip struck at his ankle, hissing like a snake. The trooper snapped his arm and the corded leather tightened sharply, jerking

Euethius to the ground back first. The soldier walked carelessly to his victim, uncoiled the whip end from his ankles, and walked away apparently unconcerned. Euethius took the bait, the soldier's contempt for his weakness too much for the proud politician to bear.

He rushed the soldier's back. The trooper, whip curled loosely in his hand, heard the footsteps. He whirled, snapped the whip and caught Euethius by the left wrist, pulling him off his feet. He put his foot in the politician's armpit and, bracing himself firmly, heaved on the imprisoned wrist. Genesius heard Euethius' arm pop free of its socket.

Euethius stared stupidly at his useless arm as the soldier once again unwrapped the whip from him. As Genesius observed him, he saw the realization cross the man's pudgy face that his comfortable life was now to end in torture and mutilation. The sun poured early heat into the courtyard, its rays glistening on the sweat of torturer and victim. The soldier called for another whip.

Until this moment, Euethius had hoped for escape. Now, his arm dangling uselessly, he surveyed the crowd, the open space, and the imperial dais, where Genesius lay next to Diocletian and where Galerius stood like a tower of pagan revenge. All exits were barred, all escape cut off. As Euethius came to his senses, he seemed, to Genesius, to grow in dignity, in spite of his tattered finery and soft skin. He stood erect, his dislocated arm hanging longer than the other. His eyes met those of Genesius, not accusing, merely curious to examine the man who had interposed himself between Euethius and his intentions. Those eyes, glowing with understanding, stared into Genesius'.

"Take him!" Galerius ordered. "This has gone on long enough." A squad of soldiers moved forward cautiously to surround Euethius.

"Take me," he said. "You may have my body. I'm nearly finished with it, anyway." Unaccountably, he smiled at them.

The smile became a rictus of pain as the second whip sailed out, this time wrapping itself around Euethius' neck. This new whip had a barbed and weighted tip, which opened a gash on its victim's throat. Blood flowed once more, staining the rich garment.

Genesius sensed each impact in magnified detail. First the lash whistled through the air, the muscles under the skin tensing against the oncoming sound. The weighted barb slowed but did not stop as it contacted flesh and plowed a furrow of skin and muscle.

A hand touched Genesius' shoulder. He jumped in surprise.

"Ask him to recant his treason," Diocletian said. "Perhaps we can stop this cruelty. He must make the sacrifice."

Genesius nodded dumbly, not trusting himself to speak. His stomach threatened to rebel at the twin assaults of his own pain and the whipping of the Christian. He stood with some difficulty and trudged across the hard-packed surface of the courtyard to where Euethius lay. As he approached, the man struggled to his knees. One-handed, Genesius helped him, trying to avoid touching his wounds.

"My hand hurts like hades," Genesius said. Euethius tried to laugh; he produced only a liquid cough.

"It can stop now. If you make the sacrifice, the pain will stop. You'll get an easier death."

Euethius' mouth worked soundlessly. Genesius leaned closer. "Tell the emperor I was wrong," Euethius croaked. "I—should not have tried to kill him. Not the way of Jesus. I confess my evil—repent the act."

"Do you recant, then?" Genesius' whisper was harsh, demanding.

From somewhere, Euethius found his voice.

"No!" he shouted.

Then he looked straight into Genesius' eyes and smiled.

"If I suffer now, here, God will have mercy later, there," he said to Genesius. "Do what you have to do. I forgive you."

Genesius shook off the bureaucrat's soft hand. It left a bloodstain on his tunic. Genesius made his way across the sun-drenched arena to the dais where Diocletian and Galerius waited.

"Kill him, my lord," Genesius said. "He is intractable." Genesius sat down again on the couch. Diocletian's lieutenant announced the verdict to the assembly.

"This man is marked for death. His crimes are treason and impiety. Because he refuses to recant his atheism, he will die slowly. His crime is all the worse because he was a man of some importance. He dies a traitor."

He signaled for the torment to resume.

The soldiers moved to surround Euethius. Surprising them, he stood willingly and walked with quiet, limping dignity to the fire.

"Not yet," a trooper growled. "Over here first." And he led the unprotesting victim to the sack of rock salt.

"Lie down," he ordered. Euethius obeyed and lay with his limbs and eyes open to the sky. He seemed obscenely unworried as the armorer finished honing his blades. One of the soldiers stripped him of his garments, leaving him naked.

The armorer cut open the inner surfaces of Euethius' arms and legs, laying open the flesh down to the bone from armpit to wrist and groin to ankle. He was careful to avoid cutting through the great vessels; there was little blood. The treatment was not meant to kill. He snapped his fingers and a slave stepped forward with a bag. Tenderly, the armorer packed Euethius' new wounds with salt, then bound them with bandages to keep the crystal agony in place. He arranged Euethius' limbs—legs apart as far as possible and arms stretched out to the sides—so that he had free access to the gashes. Taking a jug, he soaked the bandages with vinegar, filling each cut so that the acid would dissolve the salt and carry it deeply into Euethius' tissues. The victim was silent, even cooperative. Genesius bit his tongue to keep his gorge down.

When the armorer was finished, he dropped the jug to the ground. It shattered. He walked away, leaving his tools.

The bonfire had burned down to a glowing bed of coals. Two soldiers laid the trunk of a green sapling lengthwise along Euethius. They tied his hands and feet to it and hoisted him over the fire. Blood-tinged vinegar dripped pale from his frame and hissed as it touched the coals.

Two more soldiers carried buckets of water from the cistern. They sprinkled parts of the fire, with surprising delicacy, leaving only one small section burning actively under Euethius' feet. A fifth soldier laid a pitch-covered torch on the coals. It flamed up instantly. Genesius heard the crackle of searing flesh and smelled its sweet odor.

Galerius and his troopers laughed at him as he ran away, choking back vomit.

CHAPTER 12

I watched with horror as the first official victim of the persecution received his punishment. Against my will, the horror fascinated me. I felt then, and now, as if each detail of each suffering victim was a brand etched forever on my flesh.

I tried to place myself within sight of Euethius, so that he would know that he was not alone. To speak to him would surely have meant joining him in his torment. Galerius watched too closely for signs of sympathy within the crowd. It was clear even then that the persecution would brutalize our society. Even at the beginning, people of all kinds were afraid to be repelled by cruelty, as if it would be an admission of guilt. Those of us who watched the slow death of Euethius either had no sympathy for him or pretended to have none.

If cruelty is mimed, over and over again, the mime becomes the reality. Practice makes perfect, as they say.

Finally, after a full day of torture, Euethius died and his spirit was released from the world.

The troops extinguished the fire. They took his body to the midden heap and left it for the dogs. Under cover of darkness several brave Christians stole the corpse to give it decent burial.

I left the palace and wandered the streets. It was time for the evening meal, but I had no appetite. I walked aimlessly, wondering what was to become of us, how much suffering would be asked of us. I found myself praying wordlessly that the suffering would pass quickly. I was afraid of my weakness, should I be called to face what I had just seen. And yet, I felt a delicious attraction as well. A certain kind of stone pulls iron to itself, with no visible connection between the two. I had been given a reason to resist the pull of martyrdom; what of those who had no such task to perform?

Euethius had no such task. He attacked the persecution in the only way available to him. It brought down Diocletian's wrath and focused the emperor's anger and fears about the Christians. The new martyr drew the imperial lightning down on himself. How many others were to do the same in the coming years? If enough died, perhaps the aims of Diocletian and Galerius would be achieved, for they wanted nothing less than the extermination of the church, which they perceived as a threat to their power. I feared then, and events later proved, that once started the persecution would be difficult to stop. The blood lust of the people, once aroused, would rise higher and higher until past the point of satiation. The people would sicken before they stopped. Families would be split, cities filled with hatred and fear. Old scores would be settled by the mob. Whole towns would be emptied of life.

I found myself atop the hill overlooking the palace, standing on the old mosaic of a young man bathing an older one. It was a pagan work of art, but fitting enough both for the floor of what used to be our church and for the present moment as well, for baptism was a kind of death. Now, instead of being hidden under the roof of the church, the baptismal choice was out in the open air.

"Lactantius?"

The whisper seemed to come from nowhere.

"Lactantius!"

"Who is it?" I answered.

"Here." A shadow detached itself from the alley between two houses, the face a deeper shadow within the darkness.

"Who is it?" I repeated.

Genesius threw back the cowl that shadowed his face. He was haggard, his face marked by sleeplessness, and by something else. I am afraid that I was not patient with him. Neither did I understand what he was talking about.

"I have failed my father today." His remorse was genuine. "He never meant that man—"

"Euethius."

"—to suffer so much." Genesius pulled the cowl over his head again. "It was too much. So much more than was necessary. What are you doing here?"

His sudden change of subject stopped the gesture of comfort I was beginning to make. I tried to see his face, to understand what he was feeling, but without success. He turned away.

"It made me sick," Genesius said. "How can I be his son and get sick when justice is administered? But it was awful. What does he think of me now?"

"Who?" I asked.

"My father!" Genesius shouted. His voice, shrill in the darkness, seemed to make the shutters on the nearby houses tighten against the fearful noises of the night in the shaken city. "Diocletian."

"What about Euethius?" I lost my temper with him. "Nothing happened to Diocletian. He is still alive, his body whole. But Euethius was a brave and truthful man whose corpse was thrown on the garbage heap!"

"He was brave, wasn't he?" Genesius said. "I never saw anyone die so well. How could he endure the torture?"

"And keep his faith."

"And keep his faith. That's what I can't understand. What would it cost him to say the words?"

"They would have killed him anyway," I said. "What did he have to gain?"

"They would have just killed him," Genesius said, "not drawn it out for the whole day. He made it hard on himself. All he had to do was say the words. Your god would understand—wouldn't he?"

An intriguing question, that. Would our God understand the desperation born of pain, of suffering that violated the living flesh? There was my answer: He had set us an example.

"I could denounce you," Genesius said.

"Why don't you?"

"I don't know. You haven't done anything to harm Diocletian."

"What of Dorotheus?" I said. "What did he do?"

"He nearly ruined our performance!"

"And that was worth the man's life?"

Genesius seemed to crumble under my question. "I didn't know he would go that far." His voice was thin, distant, almost childish. I could not let go; I pursued the matter, wanting him to recognize his responsibility.

"You killed him, as surely as if you had swung the sword yourself!" Dorotheus was my friend. I had been his baptismal sponsor. I hid my own guilt from myself by accusing Genesius.

"He was disloyal to my father!" Genesius cried. "He deserved what happened to him."

"He was the most faithful man in the household. Diocletian trusted him."

"And was betrayed."

"Oh, you know about betrayal, don't you?" I lost all restraint. It was as if an angry demon had taken control of my voice, as if I were not the one speaking. Yet I also felt a hot satisfaction in the argument. The control had become a heavy weight; I rejoiced in its absence. "You betrayed me, you betrayed Dorotheus, who was my friend, you will betray anyone or anything for the sake of what you call your art. Your art is nothing but the false posturing of a professional liar. You make me sick. I want to spew you out of my life, vomit you into the sea and watch you sink slowly under the waves. Let the fish chew on your flesh until there is nothing left but crusted bone, lying naked and helpless on the bottom. When you denounced Dorotheus, you betrayed Diocletian!"

The demon raised my hand—*my* hand—to strike the boy. He straightened, preparing to take the blow, and I stopped myself.

"You love him too," Genesius said.

Though my hand was raised against him, it was I who felt the blow.

For Genesius had seen the truth that I had not suspected. I loved Diocletian, the emperor, the persecutor.

The enemy.

My hand was still upraised, though there was no threat left in it. I lowered it, and Genesius took it in his own. My mind was a whirlwind of confusion. Love for Diocletian swirled around with love of Christ and His church. One loyalty threatened to wash over the other, and the maelstrom spun me in its center. I could not speak out of my confusion.

Genesius guided me from the naked ruin of the church back to the palace.

✦ ✦ ✦

"Where have you been?" Diarius demanded.

"What is it to you?" Genesius said.

Well after dark, Genesius had led Lactantius to the gate where they had gotten through before. But he did not use the sign of the fish, not now, not with a persecution underway. Instead he had presented himself and the rhetorician at the gate and simply demanded entrance. The guards now recognized him as the emperor's messenger and new favorite. No questions were asked, no answers volunteered. He put Lactantius to bed with no resistance and no words. Before returning to Diocletian, he went to the actors' quarters to change his clothing. He entered the suite in silence.

"We haven't seen you for days," Diarius said from behind the curtain to his room.

Genesius stripped off the sweat- and blood-stained tunic. Moonlight touched him softly.

"You're staying for a while, then?" Diarius said. Genesius dipped a sponge into the water bucket and washed his body. He scraped his flesh clean. After another rinse, he dried himself and looked for a clean tunic.

"They are being washed." Atalanta spoke for the first time from behind the curtain to her room across the suite from the rooms of Genesius and Diarius. Dressed only in a sleeping gown, she came into the common room, where Genesius still stood unclothed. From Hysteria's room there was only a faint snoring. Diarius remained behind his curtain.

"What happened to you?" Atalanta said. "We saw everything in the courtyard. Everyone was turned out to watch." She saw the bandage on his hand. "How is the wound? Does it hurt?"

Genesius turned to the costume rack. His fool's suit was there; it was as good an outfit to wear as anything else. And it was clean. While he was a fool, he could do anything and not be responsible. He put on the patchwork.

"I have to go now," he said.

"Where?" Atalanta asked.

"To him."

"The emperor?" Diarius said.

"I've been away too long as it is."

"Remember your trade, boy," Diarius said, still behind his curtain.

"You're getting awfully high and mighty."

"I don't understand anything," Genesius said, dangling his mask from his fingers. It was a black felt half-mask, formed to fit his face exactly. The tiny eye-holes seemed to stare up at him, inviting. He put it on, adjusting it over his features. Atalanta stepped behind him to tie the ribbons that held it in place.

"Have another costume made, if you would," he said.

"What for?" Diarius asked.

"I'll need it." Genesius moved to the door. "Nothing else makes any sense at all."

Genesius padded through the halls of the palace, masked and dressed in motley. His costume fluttered as he walked, each triangular flap moving to a rhythm of its own in the breeze of his movement.

The palace was asleep. Even the guards who watched over the sleepers' safety with nervous pacing back and forth among the corridors drifted aimlessly, eyes glazed, arms slack. Genesius was the only one who felt a sense of purpose. He reached Diocletian's quarters. The guards at his door were missing. Genesius posted himself in place of the absent soldiers. One had left his weapon behind; Genesius belted on the short sword and swaggered back and forth in a military mockery before Diocletian's door.

The repetitive stride gave its rhythm to his thoughts. But they were nearly wordless. Images flashed. The silence of Euethius. A wolfish grin on the face of Galerius. The pounding of his heart as he ran from the church to the palace. The pride of place he felt when Diocletian spoke in intimate terms to him. The smell of burning flesh, sweet and sickening in the evening breeze. The itch of his skin under the mask. The throb and crackle of his wound under the bandage each time he forgot it and flexed his hand. The sound of his own skin burning. The crackle of flames when the priest's books burned. Back and forth he paced. After some unmeasured time, he could only sense the burnings of the day, repeated with each exaggerated stride. The remembered smoke stung his eyes under the mask, and tears rolled down the felt, until he felt them on his cheeks, heard them drip onto the stone at his feet. The trickle became a torrent, but he fought the illusion, grimly maintaining his guard at the emperor's door. Someone had to watch over his father, protect him from his enemies.

The night was growing warmer. He thought a change in weather must be approaching from the sound of the wind outside. Twice lightning faintly illuminated his footsteps, followed by the whisper of distant thunder. His eyes teared more and more, until he wept freely.

Through the sheen of tears he glimpsed a brightness at the far end of the hall, as if the palace were on fire, as if they were all going to burn as Euethius had burned. Again he remembered the smell of his flesh as Diocletian himself cauterized the wound. Smoke seemed to drift around him.

Genesius threw himself at the heavy oaken door and bounced off it. Again and again he heaved himself against it, bruising his shoulder and sending arrows of pain through his injured hand.

From within Diocletian called for the guards.

"The guards are gone!" Genesius shouted. "Open up!"

"Never!" came the answering shout behind the massive door.

Genesius panicked. The smoke was growing thicker, the heat rising from the floor below. Again he threw himself against the door.

"I warn you," Diocletian yelled, "I'm armed. Come through that door and die!"

Genesius took a deep breath and coughed on smoke. The spasm left him on his knees, where the air was clearer. Contrary to all expectation, his shouting and banging brought no one to the hallway. The whole wing of the palace must have been deserted, whether by panic or design he did not know.

When the spasm passed, he spoke again.

"Can you hear me?"

"Who is it?"

"Genesius, the actor."

"Are you alone?" Diocletian asked.

"Very." Genesius still knelt by the door. "Can you smell the smoke?"

"Yes. How do I know you're alone out there?"

"You must trust me," Genesius pleaded. "The fire is getting worse."

As he spoke Genesius looked down the corridor. Tongues of flame licked at the hangings on the walls, climbing up from the stairway. A cloud of dense smoke stormed toward him, still crouched by the imperial door. He pounded again.

"Let me in!" he shouted. "I'm trapped here!"

There was silence from the bedroom. Diocletian would leave him to burn to death because he suspected everyone. Panic exploded in Genesius. He scrabbled at the threshold like a rat.

"Father!" he cried. "Help me!"

The door flew open, and Genesius fell into the room. Diocletian stood over him, short sword in hand, poised to strike. His eyes flicked to the smoke and flame moving down the hallway, given new strength by the fresh air from the bedroom. Diocletian hauled Genesius out of the way and slammed the door shut again.

"The door won't hold forever," the disheveled emperor said. "We'll have to go out the window."

From under his bed he took a coil of rope. One end he tied to the bed. He pulled against it with his whole weight, testing the knot's strength. Satisfied, he stepped to Genesius.

"Out you go."

Genesius wobbled to his feet, still dizzy from the smoke. "My hand—I can't hold the rope."

Diocletian touched his hand to the door and snatched it away. "We can't stay here. There's no other way out."

"You go ahead," Genesius said.

"You have one good hand—use it!" Diocletian said. He looped the end of the rope underneath Genesius' arms and knotted it at his chest. "Get up. I'll lower you down myself."

He pushed Genesius to the window. Below, the servants and bureaucrats milled around the courtyard. When the emperor and the actor appeared at the window, a shout went up from the crowd.

"Vultures!" Diocletian said. "To Hades with them. Go." He braced himself, feet against the corner where the wall met the floor, the body of the rope around his back. Genesius climbed onto the windowsill and looked down thirty feet to the floor of the courtyard. "Keep your feet against the wall. Then just walk down, like a fly."

Genesius looked back at the door. Flames licked below the wooden panels, seeking a way into the bedroom. Smoke curled around the edges of the entrance.

"There isn't time."

"There is now," Diocletian said. "But there won't be if you keep talking. Now go!"

With the words Diocletian pushed Genesius from the window. The actor fell the first six feet, until the slack came out of the rope. He heard Diocletian grunt with the effort of holding his weight. Somehow, he twisted in the air and touched his feet to the stone side of the palace wall. The rope tightened cruelly around his chest as his weight pulled it taut. Then he was moving quickly down, feet fending against the wall. A dozen hands grabbed him as he neared the ground.

As his feet touched, he ripped the loop from his chest, looked up, and shouted wordlessly to Diocletian. Smoke poured from the bedroom, obscuring the window. For a hopeless moment he thought that the emperor would never come forth, but then he appeared through the smoke, descending the rope hand over hand with an athletic grace that denied his years. A cheer went up from the crowd.

As Diocletian's feet touched the ground, Galerius was the first to reach out and steady him, elbowing Genesius out of the way.

CHAPTER 13

Where were my guards?" Diocletian demanded of Galerius. The palace stank with the smoke of burned lumber, silk, wool, and linen. A shift in the wind made the stench sweeten suddenly with the odor of cooked flesh. The atmosphere was acrid, dark.

"If it hadn't been for Genesius, I might have been burned to death," Diocletian said. "I want to know why there were no guards!"

Lightning flashed out over the harbor. The storm was moving quickly toward them. Galerius nodded, deep in thought.

"You saw no guards?" he asked Genesius.

"None."

The wind front preceding the storm reached them now, fanning the flames. Genesius' throat was sore.

"Were there any signs of violence?"

Lightning flashed, and through the haze Genesius saw brigades of troops and household servants and, now and then, a bureaucrat or two, passing all sorts of containers, spilling as much water on the ground as on the fire. They were too few; the fire was too widespread.

"No, none. There was no one."

The wind whipped into the courtyard from all directions, buffeting the fire-fighters and onlookers. Even seated, Genesius had difficulty maintaining his balance. First he swayed one way, then the wind would shift without warning, subject to the vagaries of some capricious godling, and what he had been leaning against to the left was at his right and he would nearly fall over. Above him, the bulk of Galerius stood like the Colossus of Rhodes, unmoved by the tempest. He called for the captain of the guard.

Galerius' eyes fell on a young soldier. Unlike most, the soldier was still clean, untouched by ash from the fire. He returned in no time at all with a grimy captain, who saluted Galerius, ignoring Diocletian.

"The Augustus tells me there were no guards at his apartment, Sullus," Galerius said. "Explain!"

"Caesar, they were there when I inspected. All of them."

"When was that?"

"An hour ago."

The wind made it difficult for Genesius to hear the exchange. It whipped the flames higher and higher. At least there was some light between the intermittent flashes of the storm—a red glow that must be what the dead see in the underworld. More and more now the lightning cut through the dim redness with a pale blue image that made them all into corpses suddenly drained of blood and color. Then the hellish red returned, over and over again. Against this setting, Galerius and the captain played out their dialogue. Genesius had missed much of what was said.

"Find them!" Galerius ordered. "Bring them here."

The storm broke with full force over the palace and the courtyard. Thunder crashed. Even through the tempest, they heard the flames hissing as the rain smothered them. Soaked to the skin, Diocletian pounded Genesius on the back with glee.

"We are saved!" he shouted through the whirlwind. "The palace will survive."

The rain was cold, all the more so after the smoke and searing heat of the fire. Genesius felt himself washed and refreshed.

"The fire could have been accidental," Galerius said, "except for this business about your guards. It was intentional." He was shouting through the rain. Genesius watched rivulets of water run down his face. Occasionally he paused to spit water from his mouth. Thunder crashed around them.

"But who?" Diocletian yelled.

The thought occurred to Genesius that Jupiter-on-earth was clearly outclassed by Jupiter-in-the-sky.

"What?" Galerius shouted.

"Who!" Diocletian screamed into the storm. "Who did it?" Galerius shrugged, unable to hear.

Lightning flashed simultaneously with the crash of thunder. The rain ceased, as if a heavenly sluice gate had been closed.

As if his mind were suddenly free of the storm, Diocletian looked around, searching.

"The lady Prisca—where is she? And my daughter."

"Safe," Galerius said, "and unhurt. They were together in the women's quarters. The fire never spread that far."

Genesius wondered whether Galerius seemed disappointed, but then the captain appeared, carrying the body of a guard over his shoulder. He was weeping. He dumped the body in front of them; its throat was cut. Burned into the forehead was a brand—the sign of the fish.

"Where did you find him?" Galerius said.

"In the stables."

"Alone?"

"No. The others are with him. They all have the mark. They're all dead—the emperor's guards, his servants, everyone. Their throats were cut." The captain was pale, even in the darkness. He stood at attention before Diocletian and Galerius, but trembled with anger and grief. "They were my men, sir. Who did this to them?"

Genesius knelt by the dead soldier. He studied the brand on his forehead. The wound was fresh, only hours old, but the fierce rain had washed it clean of blood and debris. The shape of the fish stood out darkly against the man's bloodless, colorless skin.

"This is the thanks you get, my lord," Galerius said, "for your gentleness with the Christians. This sign is their signature on a declaration of rebellion against you and all of Rome. Think how many there must be within your household for them to be able to kill your personal guard right here in the palace! Think of the organization they must have to coordinate their attack even while the fire was being set! The man who attacked you today was an official of the city government. They are everywhere. They must be rooted out before it is too late."

Diocletian shrank away from Galerius, the corpse, Genesius—all of the people who were with him.

"It could be anyone," he said. "How am I to know?"

"There is only one alternative," Galerius said. "Random terror and interrogation."

The rain had stopped. In the courtyard the people were hushed, sensing that trouble faced the emperor, hearing, if not the words, the tenor of the conference taking place around the body of the guard. They saw Diocletian back away from his lieutenant. Tendrils of smoke and steam circled up from the burned palace. Water dripped from the blackened beams to the floor below.

Diocletian leaned forward, using Genesius' shoulder to support his weight. The actor's knees took the added strain. A stone buried under the surface of the mud dug into his right knee painfully. Diocletian leaned over his body to confront Galerius.

"Random terror," Diocletian said, "is the wrong way. For months you have tried to convince me to destroy the empire because of your hatred for the Christians. This corpse is no proof. Anyone can make a branding iron—or have one made."

"Someone who hates the Christians, for instance, might try to implicate them. It's been done before, to hide other purposes."

"You are exhausted," Galerius said. "And frightened. Rightly so. Your servants are dead. Use mine. I will arrange to have guards sent to you. Your apartments, I believe, are useless. Please, use mine. I will find other quarters. You'll feel better after you've slept."

"I won't feel better," Diocletian raged. "Someone has tried to kill me! I want to know who, and I want him killed—after I question him."

"It was a Christian, my lord," Galerius said. "I'm certain of it. But as to who it was—shall we interrogate the entire palace? Whoever killed your guards and servants is gone by now. You are powerless to find out. Take several of my guards, go to my quarters, and rest."

The weight of Diocletian's body came off Genesius' shoulder. He was able to remove his knee from the stone as Diocletian moved around him to face Galerius.

"Your quarters!" Diocletian's face contorted with rage and fear. Water dripped from his hair and ran down his face like tears. "What would happen to me there? Would there be another fire? What do the Christians have to gain by killing me? If I were a Christian, I would want to see *you* dead."

Galerius maintained his calm, behaving as if Diocletian were a temperamental child. Reason oozed from his lips.

"My lord, it has been a trying day. I beg you—"

"Don't patronize me!" Diocletian cried. "I made you what you are, may the gods forgive me. I can unmake you too. Get out of my sight!"

Diocletian helped Genesius to his feet. Galerius caught Sullus' eye, and both of them vanished into the darkness. As Genesius looked around the courtyard, others seemed to follow them into the shadows. Diocletian himself noticed the silent exodus.

"Stop!" he shouted. "All of you!"

Diocletian was obeyed, but grudgingly, haltingly. He was isolated with Genesius in the courtyard of his own half-ruined palace. He glared at them in disgust.

"Go back to bed," he said. "The excitement's over." The onlookers drifted away, looking back at the actor and the emperor, talking softly among themselves.

"You know what they're saying," Diocletian said. "'How the mighty have fallen!' They think they see my power passing to Galerius. My guards are dead; my attendants are dead. Galerius may think he controls the palace, but he doesn't, not while I am Augustus."

Genesius had no reply. He led Diocletian through the mud into the shelter of the unburned section of the palace, to the baths.

"Let's get cleaned up," Genesius said.

The *balneator,* or bath attendant, hurried into the bathhouse just behind Diocletian and Genesius.

"Forgive me, my lord," he said. "With all the excitement, I have neglected the bath fires. If you will give me a few moments— "

"Never mind," Diocletian said. "Lukewarm water is fine." He stretched himself out on the table. The attendant reached for the unguents, but Genesius took them from the *balneator's* hands. "I will attend the emperor."

"As you wish, sir."

"You may withdraw," Genesius said. "Build up the fires for the hot water and steam."

The slave left the *unctuarium.* Genesius removed Diocletian's sleeping gown, which was stained with mud and ashes. He poured fragrant oil on the emperor's back, warming it first in his hand, and began to massage the older man with long, firm movements, following the long muscles of the body. The muscles were as tense as stone. Genesius' good hand massaged slowly and strongly.

Diocletian was silent under his hand. Respecting his wish for quiet, Genesius let his own thoughts drift, trying to relax himself as well.

Genesius imagined that he heard a low buzzing throughout the palace, spreading into the city, and from Nicomedia over the whole map of the empire, like spilled wine. An assassination attempt by the Christians could be the prelude to a coup; Diocletian was right to think of protecting himself from the sect. Word of the nearly successful attempt would already be noising about the city, provoking reaction and gossip. If Euethius had been a member of a political group, more attempts could be expected. In fact, another attempt seemed likely.

But the Christians were not the only group capable of attempting a change in government. The stability of Diocletian's nearly twenty-year reign may have relaxed the empire too much. Even Diocletian himself, he remembered, had come to the purple by killing Aper, the boar, who had himself killed Carinus.

There, perhaps, was the theme of another play—protecting the stability of life in the empire. Rival Roman armies no longer roamed the empire's roads, stripping food and supplies off the land while they searched for a competing "emperor's" forces. Diocletian had ended the period of thirty tyrants. In the hundred or so years between Commodus to the accession of Diocletian, Rome had had dozens of "emperors." Nearly two dozen had been murdered. Diocletian, and only Diocletian, had brought stability. No wonder he was worshiped as a god.

But how to dramatize it? Diocletian must be shown to be the better choice between not only himself and the Christians, but also between himself and Galerius. The Augustus was the only buffer between Galerius and the Christians, between the rabid defensiveness of the old religion and the manic proselytizing of the new. If Diocletian were gone, removed by one force or the other, the conflict would flare to the point where nothing could contain it. One way or the other would be destroyed. Many would suffer.

Diocletian moved under his hand. "That's enough," he said. "Let's get this garbage off our skins."

They moved into the *calidarium*, where the hot water tub was located. Diocletian tested the water. "It's still only lukewarm, but it will have to do. Can't blame the *balneator* because the palace was on fire."

Genesius entered the water first, then helped Diocletian ease himself in. The water was as warm as blood.

---------------— CHAPTER 14 —---------------

G enesius appeared in the actors' quarters just after dawn.
Diocletian was a builder. The rattle of dozens of hammers and the
rhythmic singing of scores of saws echoed through the palace and
into the streets beyond the walls.

Diarius stopped the rehearsal. "We'll have to go elsewhere," he
complained. "I can't work with all this noise."

They were rehearsing in a small audience hall, only fifty feet wide
by one hundred feet long, but it fronted on the courtyard where the
artisans were busily rebuilding the damaged parts of the palace.

"It stinks of smoke anyway," Atalanta said, wrinkling her nose. "I
know I'm having trouble concentrating."

Genesius wandered away from their makeshift playing space and
sat in a corner of the room, away from the other actors.

"So what else is new, dearie?" Hysteria wrinkled her own nose in mimicry of the younger woman. "I really think we need some new material. Some of our best talent is being wasted with this show."

"Because you're not on stage?" Atalanta said, innocence glazing her features.

"Exactly."

"Our last audience seemed to like the show."

"Now, ladies," Diarius said, "there's no use squabbling among ourselves."

"You stay out of this," Atalanta said.

"I want a role!" Hysteria complained. "I'm tired of being hidden away out of sight."

"I want a role!" Atalanta mocked the older woman.

"Shut up!"

"It's all right for you to make fun of me, I guess," Atalanta said, "but you can't take it when the tables are turned."

"Ladies, please!" Diarius pleaded. He turned to Genesius in the corner. "Why don't you help me?"

Genesius did nothing in reply except to stare curiously back into the eyes of Diarius.

"Too high and mighty to spend time with the likes of us?" Hysteria said. "It'll get you in trouble, forgetting your place like that."

Atalanta swung to join the attack.

"It nearly got you burned to death."

Genesius was thinking and barely heard the words of his fellow actors. He was moving further away from them and their concerns in any case. He no longer inhabited a make-believe world. His new world had bite; it had dimension, depth. The deaths were real, the issues immediate. The voices of his fellow actors were no more to him than the rattle of hammers outside, a distracting buzz, no more.

Finally, Diarius shook him. He stared into the manager's face.

"Are you all right?"

"I'm fine."

"We're going to the theater to rehearse," Diarius said. "It's only a few hours."

"You go ahead. I'll be along shortly," Genesius said.

"Are you sure?"

"I'll be there," Genesius said. "It will take the slaves at least an hour to move the equipment and another to set it all up."

"Just make sure you're not late," Diarius warned. "We need a rehearsal. The timing has to be just right. If Hysteria misses by a beat, someone could get hurt."

Genesius waved away the little man. His thoughts were still in the previous night. He had made a difference. If Diocletian had died during the night, Galerius would be climbing onto the throne. He, Genesius the actor, the illegitimate street urchin, had prevented a revolution single-handedly. He had tasted significance, and, like Adam with the fruit of the tree of knowledge, he was forever changed.

He wished that his mother knew.

He opened his eyes to see the empty hall. He must have slept while the crew removed the props and costumes. He glanced at the sun through the window; not much time had passed. The memory of the scroll was suddenly in his mind, as if he had dreamed of reading it. Hungry for meaning, Genesius hurried to find Lactantius.

"Lactantius?"

I looked up. Genesius stood in the doorway, uncertainty written on his face. I moved several scrolls from the extra chair to make room for him.

"Sit down," I said. "I'm sorry about the mess. I was working."

I had left his scroll out where it could be seen. As I reached to pick it up and put it out of sight, he grabbed my hand.

"That is mine!" he said. "What are you doing with it?"

"You gave it to me," I answered.

"I mean now."

"I was studying it."

"What does it mean?" he asked me.

"It is a long document," I said, "and it covers many subjects."

"No!" Genesius shouted. "You don't understand. Why do I have it? Why did I take it? I am not a Christian."

I had no reply. Genesius stood up, looming over me.

"The fire last night—I was wandering. I was out of my head, like a fool. And I was the only one who was there, the only one who could have saved my father's life. And now, this morning, I am a fool again. There was something in the scroll. I want to see it."

I handed him the scroll. He pawed feverishly over it. The edges began to flake away, drifting gently through the morning sunbeams to the floor.

"Be gentle with it," I said. "It's old."

"'Make no mistake about it,'" he read. "'If any one of you thinks of himself as wise, then he must learn to be a fool that he may become wise. For the wisdom of the world is foolishness with God. As the Scripture says'—What does that mean, *Scripture?*"

"The holy writings of the Jews," I answered.

"'As the Scripture says,'" he continued, "'The Lord knows the thoughts of the wise, how useless they are. And again, God is not convinced by the arguments of the wise. He takes them in their own craftiness. Therefore, let no one take glory in the things that are human.'" He tossed the scroll to the floor.

"So," he said, "by your own Scripture, no matter what a human being does, he's a fool."

"Not quite," I said. "You didn't finish the section. 'Paul, Apollo, Cephas, the world, life and death, the present and the future, all are yours. And you are Christ's, and Christ belongs to God.'"

"What is that supposed to mean?" Genesius said.

"That God, through Christ, gives meaning to human life."

"Is that salvation?"

"It might be," I said, "for some. Maybe for you."

"And maybe not." He flung himself into the chair. "Do you know what happened last night?"

"Yes."

"No, I mean to me. I have to tell someone," Genesius said. "But you have to promise that you won't use any of it against him. You're on different sides. You shouldn't be."

I was at a loss as to what to tell the youth. Whatever had happened during the fire had affected him deeply.

"If I were truly his enemy," I ventured, "the first thing I would do would be to assure you that I held no ill will toward Diocletian. But you must know that he threatens me and the people I love. I can't tell you what to do."

"You're a Christian," he said. "He hates them."

"More than that, he kills them—us," I answered. "Decide. I have work to do."

He told me in detail what had happened out in the courtyard, in the palace, in the flames. His face looked haggard and drawn. There was weariness and an incongruous frenzy in his movement, in his speech, in his thoughts, as if he had only a limited time in which to pull all these disparate threads together.

He was desperately seeking Christ, or at least the peace that comes with the acceptance of Christ. I knew the need from my own experience. And I knew that to mention it in so many words to him now would drive him away. He had lost the love of his mother at an early age. He had never known the love of a father.

I told the actor something of my own pilgrimage. My search had been different in detail, but not in design. I was, myself, a latecomer to the faith. Born in Africa of a pagan father and a Christian mother, I was given a scholar's education. The family was of good blood but not, by any means, wealthy. It was a constant struggle for my father to raise the money necessary for my tutoring, but he was determined that he would be the last tradesman in the family line. With me began, he and my mother hoped, a long line of gentlemen-scholars.

I went the route of so many while traveling the road to salvation. Mother took great pains to prepare me for the spiritual side of my life, and therefore tried to inculcate me with the beliefs of the Christians. But Father's influence was the stronger, and I learned to love more the writings of the great authors than the Author of life Himself. From an early age, I admired the elegance of Cicero, and each piece of writing that I attempted was in imitation of that master of the art. I fear that even now, when I have at my fingertips the greatest of subjects, the salvation of the soul through Christ, my poor abilities are no match for those of my earlier idol.

In my youth, I lived in relative quiet, consumed by my studies and the discipline they imposed upon me. But in my twelfth year, having learned to the limits of my tutor's ability to teach, I left my father and mother and journeyed from my home in Dougga, itself a town of some importance, to the capital, the ancient city of Carthage.

Dougga was a Punic town, with narrow winding streets and with an overlay of Romans descended from colonists. My family was of mixed ancestry, more proud of the Roman than the Punic side. But Carthage was all Roman. Leveled in the second Punic War, Roman colonists rebuilt Carthage at the beginning of the empire. It became the center of learning and of leisure in Africa, after only the old great cities of the empire. To this place my father sent me in my twelfth year to grow wise and wealthy in the study of philosophy and rhetoric.

To my discredit, while I reveled in the discourse of the academy, enjoying the thrust and parry of argument, I became enamored of the games. I divided my time between the groves of the academy and the blood-stained sands of the amphitheater. The rapidity of death in the theater, its arbitrary inevitability, seemed to me to mirror the way death came into the lives of everyone I knew.

There was a certain gladiator who fought under the name of Carnivorous and enjoyed a great following with the crowd. Carnivorous, at the beginning of a match, would recite a selection from the *Aeneid*, and then proceed to destroy his opponent in the same manner as that described in his recitation. The crowd, of course, adored his cockiness, but they also longed for the day on which he would meet someone more powerful than himself, the day on which his self confidence would be shattered.

Eventually it happened. I was sitting down front, just above the arena, and looked into Carnivorous' eyes as his nameless opponent's trident pierced his belly. I watched the eyes widen in surprise, as if Carnivorous still believed that because he had always won, he always would win, that he would somehow escape that which came to everyone. The crowd cheered the newcomer's victory, and as he died, Carnivorous heard their cheers for a new champion and knew that he had been abandoned by those who had claimed to love him. Then the master of the arena, infuriated that he had lost his best attraction, unleashed a dozen gladiators on the unfortunate victor. Soon, his blood, too, dribbled into the sand, mixing with that of Carnivorous; the crowd cheered this turn of events as well—myself among them.

I took this as an object lesson. Keeping to my studies in which I was beginning to gain some small degree of fame, I gave myself over to riotous living in my hours outside the academy. By my fifteenth year, I had mastered, so I thought, all the sensual knowledge of which the human body is capable. I learned to cherish intoxication. I, with others, used to roam the city's streets at night, bursting into the houses of the citizens, masked, to terrorize the innocent. There were no bounds on my actions. I thought it only amusing to argue for one cause in the morning and its opposite in the afternoon. No one could overcome my rhetoric, and indeed I became a sort of gladiator of words, my intellect for sale to the highest bidder.

At this point in my history, Genesius stood and left me, without speaking. He was still distraught. There was a struggle in the youth. He stood like a man in an earthquake, with one foot on each side of a widening chasm.

I knew the feeling.

✦ ✦ ✦

The audience was filing into the theater as Genesius made his way backstage. The others were getting into costume. There was the usual tension among the players before the show, exacerbated by Genesius' lateness.

"There he is!" Diarius shouted. "It's about time you graced us with your presence."

"Sorry," Genesius said. "I had some things to take care of."

Diarius smiled up at him, always a dangerous sign. "Oh, well, then—as long as there's a reason. At least you're dressed."

"I said I was sorry."

"Listen," Diarius was saying, "I warned you to be here for the rehearsal. There is no time now. At the end of the show, where the smoke goes off and I drop through the trapdoor into the under-stage—this time, all three of us will do it. Atalanta will go up under the statue of Eros, I'll take Jupiter, you get Venus. You just let yourself fall limply as the trap opens. There's a mattress underneath the stage. Then take the right-hand tunnel and it will lead you to a door that opens behind Venus. Think you can handle that?"

"I think so." Genesius, Diarius thought, seemed to be elsewhere, his concentration not on the task at hand, which was their first performance outside the palace.

"Be sure you do. It's time. The house is full." The little actor called to Hysteria. "Are you all ready?"

"As ever," the older actress said, filing her nails.

"Your turn will come," Diarius promised. "For now, keep your mind on your work. Places!"

"At least I was here for the rehearsal," Hysteria said.

"Quiet!" Diarius hissed. Atalanta and Genesius took their places, each behind one of the doors of the *scaena frons*. The musicians played to their climax and went silent. The crowd hushed in anticipation. Simultaneously, the players stepped forward, and the play began.

Genesius acted with a strange abandon. During his first scene, Diarius listened, then whispered to Hysteria.

"What's he doing out there?"

"I don't know," she said. The audience's laughter roared, and she waited for the muffled voices of Atalanta and Genesius to continue. When there was no sound, both she and Diarius listened worriedly to the pause which had not been a part of the scene.

"Did they go up?" she asked.

"I don't know," Diarius whispered. "I'm going to look."

"No! The crowd will see you."

"I don't care. We can't leave them hung up out there." He moved to the stage-left entrance to peek out. As he reached for the curtain that covered the doorway, the audience whooped with gleeful laughter and cheered. The laughter died down and the dialogue resumed.

Diarius came back to Hysteria.

"What did he do?" she asked.

"I don't know. We never had that business there before. He must have made it up on the spot."

"And whatever you do," Genesius Joseph called, "don't think about God!"

Genesius made his first exit. Diarius watched him wipe the sweat from his forehead. The young actor was trembling, his face pale with fear. Diarius was about to question him when Hysteria punched him in the ribs.

"It's your cue!" she hissed.

Diarius went to work, calling through the speaking tube that carried his voice to three separate megaphones, so that the voice of the "angel" seemed to emanate from all directions around Atalanta-Mary. The strength of voice required by the device demanded his complete concentration.

The show was not going well. The audience responded properly, laughed in the right places, but everything was somehow off-center. The rhythms were only roughly what they had been, and none of the four members of the company knew, with the precision that an actor needs, the exact instant another would speak or move or grunt. Diarius' "slow burn" never managed to reach full intensity; his face never became bright red, only pale pink, because he wondered whether or not Genesius would come in on time. Genesius, distracted by the lack of sleep and the wild emotional ride he had taken in the last three days, was foggy mentally and unsure of his cues. Atalanta was confused by their confusion, while Hysteria, backstage running the machinery, worried about what was happening on stage and at the end of the play missed her timing for the explosive exits. Instead of toggling the trapdoors simultaneously, she missed one of the levers—the one opening Genesius' trap—allowing Diarius and Atalanta to vanish safely as the charges exploded. Realizing her mistake, she almost immediately corrected it by slapping the third lever. But the correction meant that Genesius was still above the stage level when the force of the small explosion reached him. The explosion itself caused no injury, but in protecting his eyes, he moved his hands over his face, disturbing his balance as he belatedly fell through the trap.

His right hand caught the edge of the opening as he fell. He managed to suppress his outcry and hurried to the statue of Venus as arranged, scrabbling through the musty tunnel. Because of his injury, he emerged a few beats later than Diarius and Atalanta. The effect was spoiled, the applause less than it should have been.

After the actors escaped backstage, Diarius cornered Genesius. "What is going on with you?" he demanded. "The whole performance was pitiful. Why didn't you come for the rehearsal? I knew this was going to happen. What do you have to say for yourself?"

"I—" Genesius began.

"Don't interrupt!" Diarius bellowed. "I don't understand you. One moment you are absolutely brilliant. Then the next time around you behave like the rankest amateur."

Genesius swayed, like a sapling in a storm. Days had passed since his last sleep.

Diarius went on, oblivious. "I know you're the favorite of the Augustus, but that's no excuse for what happened out there today. I don't care if you complain to him or not. As long as you're a member of my troupe, you'll tow the line. From now on, no more missed rehearsals. No more vanishing into the night. You keep regular hours like the rest of us. You show up on time at every call. You—"

Genesius, his newly injured hand cradled against his breast, fell forward on the little actor-manager, sound asleep. Struggle as he might, Diarius could not free himself. He shouted for help to Hysteria, who lived up to her name. Atalanta joined her fellow actress.

"It's only a play, Diarius," Hysteria gasped through her laughter. "For the gods' sake, it's only a play. Let the boy sleep."

CHAPTER 15

Genesius was asleep—a deep sleep, dreamless, with a warm sense of dread. Someone shook him without letting up. He swung wildly, but the young actress was ready; she caught his arm and pulled him from the bed.

Eyes still coated with sleep, he stumbled through the corridor after Atalanta, not understanding where she was leading him but sleepily agreeable to follow. He was becoming inured to conspiracy. In his present state, he did not care; if he went along, they might let him sleep again soon.

The two passed through the darkened corridors of the palace, Atalanta holding him up. A distant roar grew louder behind them, punctuated by hisses and crackling sounds of which Genesius could make no sense whatever.

They emerged, thus encumbered with each other, into the hellish brilliance of the courtyard, again surrounded by a corona of flame. The new construction, framed with dry lumber, blazed as if the fires of hell were its kindling. The previously undamaged portion of the imperial residence burned with such ferocity that the very stones themselves seemed to be aflame. Through the corridor from which Atalanta and Genesius had just emerged, a blast of heat and flame exploded, throwing the two away from the entrance toward the middle of the courtyard. They held on to each other in desperation, until rough hands pulled them apart and streams of water extinguished the small fires on their hair and clothing. When they could once again stand, both were hauled without regard for their burns to a group of people waiting for interrogation.

Genesius was now fully awake, the dregs of sleep burned from him along with the hair on the back of his head. Atalanta was separated from him by the crowd. He fought through the confused mass of people toward her, until he was pulled up short by Diarius.

"Whoa, boy!"

"Let me go," Genesius said. "What are they doing to her?"

"We'll find her later. Nothing's going to happen to her that won't happen to us." Diarius tightened his grip on Genesius' arm. "Don't draw unnecessary attention to yourself."

"Where is Diocletian?" Genesius demanded. "This fire is no accident. Where is he?"

Diarius pointed to a knot of praetorian guards. "He is safe enough. He brought in fresh troops after the first fire. His own men. They got him out in time. No thanks to Galerius and his men." Diarius pointed in the opposite direction. Another clump of soldiers surrounded the figure of Diocletian's lieutenant, whose size left him still visible, towering over even the tallest among his troops. Within the ring of soldiers was a smaller group of civilians, the courtiers who followed Galerius' rising star, who maneuvered and plotted to bring him to the purple as soon as Diocletian might be induced, one way or another, to give up his own prior claim.

Above the palace refugees in the courtyard, the clear night sky was obscured by a vault of sparks and flames, streaked with smoke from the dying palace. The fire surrounded the crowd; hundreds of souls were encompassed by the fire, which even burned along the walls that cordoned the palace from the city. Among the myriad of smells, Genesius caught the stink of burning oil. The flame front that raged on the walls burned black smoke.

Even the great wooden doors that had once protected the interior of the courtyard from the city began to smolder. Tongues of flame licked under the cedar beams. A handful of troopers tried to open the gates, but fell back, unable to handle the iron fittings because of the heat. The hundreds of people in the courtyard could do nothing but wait until the fire burned itself out.

Eventually, the doors burned through, and there was a safe opening to the outside. No one, not even the emperor himself, could prevent the destruction.

Both Diocletian and Galerius ignored the conflagration. Instead, each conferred with his advisers, and messengers ran back and forth between the two camps, dodging sparks and threading their ways among the groups of slaves, servants, bureaucrats, and courtiers. As the flames began to die down, troops surrounded each group. When the flames were reduced to random flickers against the predawn sky, Galerius moved out through the ruined gates with his bodyguard. Diocletian and his men, farther from the great doors, went through next. In order of precedence, first the courtiers, then the bureaucrats, then the servants, and last of all the slaves, each class of people went through the gates and into the open field beyond, under guard.

Genesius went with his group across a wide area of blackened earth. Whoever had set the fire had planned well, piling brush against the main gate to prevent anyone from escaping.

✦ ✦ ✦

I touched Genesius' shoulder. He whirled to face me. I led him to the edge of our group. Standing a few yards from anyone in the confused mass of freemen, I importuned Genesius.

"You must go to him," I said. "All this"—I indicated the ruins of the palace—"will be laid at our feet. The persecution will explode all through the empire because of this crime."

"And what am I supposed to do, if I can get to him?"

"We did not do this!"

"Oh?"

"I swear to you," I said. "We had no hand in it. He must come to know that."

We were standing on a small hillock that raised us slightly higher than the milling crowds. Genesius scanned the multitude. Individual faces were becoming visible in the beginnings of the dawn.

"And you want me to tell him?"

"Yes. It must be you. There is no one else he will listen to."

Genesius shivered in the breeze that came down from the mountains. Messengers, envoys, still scurried back and forth between the two royal entourages.

"Who is responsible, then?"

"I think it must be Galerius," I said. "He has the most to gain."

"It's no secret that Galerius wants the throne for himself," Genesius said, "but could it not be someone else? Constantine, for instance, is no great friend of the emperor. And I seem to recall he has strong connections to you Christians."

I reacted with unplanned fury. "No! You mustn't believe that. Why, if that were true, it would mean a betrayal of the worst kind."

"Why couldn't it be true?" Genesius asked. "He has natural allies in Valeria and Prisca. Both of them have good reason to fear Diocletian and better reason to fear Galerius. What better solution to their problems than to throw the blame for this treason onto their most hated enemy? If I were in their place, I would at least examine the thought of eliminating the persecution and the chief persecutor by the use of a piece of flint and steel."

I sighed in exasperation. "You still don't understand the faith."

"You're right," Genesius said. "But I do understand that someone is trying to kill my father. It might be Constantine; it might be your bishop Anthimus. It might be Galerius. It might be you. The only thing I know is that it is not me."

His accusation stunned me momentarily. To believe, even as a hypothesis, that the people of God would do such a thing, seemed almost blasphemous. But from the point of view of an unbeliever, we of the faith would appear as no more, no different, certainly no better, than just another of the factions that multiplied in number every day in every city of the empire.

Galerius and his personal guard mounted their horses and galloped off. In the distance, I saw a baggage train rouse itself like a waking dog, stretch itself, and curve to intersect the course which Galerius was following. The ship of state, Galerius now believed, was sinking. Later, it became known that he had left Bithynia forever. He returned to his own territory on the Danube.

Both Genesius and I became aware of a third presence on our little hillock. It was Diarius, the leader of the actors.

"He is looking for you," the little man said, his face creased with worry. "He sent a special messenger. You are to go to him at once."

Without farewell, Genesius left me to attend the emperor.

✦ ✦ ✦

"The people are leaving, sire!" the centurion reported. "The city people are taking them in. If they mix together, we'll never sort this out."

Diocletian sighed in frustration. "Deploy the garrison troops around the perimeter of the field. No one passes in either direction. Move!"

As the centurion hurried to obey, Diocletian turned to the Praetorian Prefect, the chief officer of the guard detachment. "I want tribunals set up. For each, choose a magistrate from among your best officers. Send each of the magistrates to me to receive their instructions. We will interrogate everyone. We will find out who is responsible for this crime. And then we will eliminate the cause." The prefect hesitated momentarily. "Move, man!"

The officer left. Diocletian stood alone on the hilltop, watching the soldiers sprint to form a perimeter around the fire's refugees. There was a grunt from someone behind him. He whirled, dagger in hand, to face this new danger.

It was Genesius. Diocletian exhaled, the release of breath bringing no release from the fear of treason that seemed to be in the very air he breathed.

"Stand your ground. Don't come any closer." He examined Genesius from head to toe. There was no sign of a weapon.

"Strip," he ordered. Genesius obeyed without hesitation. There was something in the emperor's face that forced him to instant compliance. Diocletian's breathing was ragged, the breath of a man surrounded by enemies, fighting what might be his last fight.

"I must trust someone," Diocletian said. His voice was thinner than normal. "But how to choose? Men whom I lifted up connive against me with each other. Those who preach peace come bearing swords. My own people lie. Rome teeters. My adopted son deserts me. And yet, I must trust someone."

Genesius was naked. He stood silent, waiting for Diocletian to let him know how to be of help.

"Can you handle one of these?" Diocletian reversed the knife and tossed it to Genesius, hilt first. Genesius stepped forward to catch the handle and hefted it in his hand. Diocletian stepped back in momentary fear, until Genesius knelt and offered the knife to the emperor.

"Keep it," Diocletian said. "And put your clothes on. You'll catch your death." Genesius obeyed.

"Stay with me. There is work to be done, and to do it, I need a good hand at my back. You are the only one who has never asked anything of me. The only one."

"I will ask this, lord," Genesius said, still kneeling. "I have no right to ask, but the question nags at me like an unsure wife. May I ask?"

"If it is only a question, yes."

"What is the reason that you struggle so hard against the Christians? It seems to cost you so much, and the benefit to you seems little." Genesius thought that the question might be dangerous but plowed ahead. "Pardon me for asking. It's really none of my business, but I have found that when things seem to be going badly, it is a good idea to try to remember first purposes."

Diocletian stopped his pacing. "I didn't expect so much wisdom from an actor."

"It's not wisdom, just a trick of the trade," Genesius said.

"There is more wisdom in your trade than I realized," Diocletian said. "To try to answer your question: I don't want to eliminate the people, but the belief they hold is hazardous. Look around you!"

Genesius held his breath, then released it in fulfilling Lactantius' request. "If the Christians did this thing—"

"If?" Diocletian demanded. "Not so long ago you intercepted a direct attack on me from a Christian. That man would have killed me if you hadn't intervened." Diocletian knelt facing Genesius. "Let me see the wound."

Genesius gave Diocletian his hand.

"It's healing nicely."

"Thanks to you, it has not festered. Soon it will be no more than a memory," Genesius said.

"See that you don't forget," Diocletian ordered. He rose with difficulty. "Come, stand by me. My knees won't take that kind of thing indefinitely." Side by side, the actor and the emperor looked over the field, the huddled groups of refugees, the circled troops holding them in place, and the ruins of the palace beyond.

"What you see out there," Diocletian said, "is what you will see throughout the empire, if you live long enough. The Christians are by nature rebels. I have made a study of them. They want nothing less than to bring all the peoples of the world under the domination of their god. Their Christ leaves no room for Rome. He wants more than reverence, more than worship. He wants the whole being of every person on this earth. And he will stop at nothing—nothing at all!—to gain it.

"Our gods may or may not exist. Probably they don't, and that is just as well. Even Jupiter, if he were real, would be an abomination. But their Christ is worse than the worst of the Roman gods."

The two men did not look at each other, but at the refugees below.

"I am afraid that he may turn out to exist," Diocletian said. "There is no telling at this point. I have seen such fanaticism on behalf of many causes. People will die for whatever they may believe. And kill. I have spent twenty years stabilizing Rome. I have beaten off the barbarians from the north. I have reduced the Persian threat to nothing. I have taken a disintegrating collection of peoples and returned it to the unity of an empire. A man can farm with the expectation that his crops won't be burned by marauding armies. With just a little luck, when I am gone, the succession will go peacefully, and the next Augustus will not have to rebuild from scratch. I have saved a civilization from chaos, and I will not let it be broken apart by a mob of religious fanatics. If the Roman gods are false, then there is something fundamentally right in worshiping false gods. False gods have a special virtue—they don't interfere. But if this Christ takes over the world, what chance does human reason have against divine will? You see, he is more dangerous if he is real. There will be no standing against him. And if he is false, there is no need to destroy a working system to replace it with something untried."

"Any other man would be afraid." Still neither man looked at the other, only at the vision Diocletian had painted with his words.

"I am afraid," Diocletian said. "I fear each and every person I come near. I fear that I will lose this fight. I fear the hiss of my searing flesh in that ruined palace. I fear the betrayal of those in whom I place my trust. Galerius, for instance, will betray me, is betraying me at this very moment. He takes fear for weakness and believes that his opponents' fears give him the upper hand. I fear that even you, whom I trust with my thoughts, will someday change sides. For an old soldier, fear is the warning that comes, if you're lucky and attentive, in the darkness just before the unseen hand strikes."

A movement in the diminishing darkness caught Genesius' eye. "My lord, someone is coming. Three men—officers."

"It's about time."

The officers arrived. Diocletian briefed them on their duties. They were to interrogate the entire population of the palace about the origin of the fire, both on that night and on the night of the first outbreak. Their interrogations were aimed not at finding the guilty party, although that would be a useful extra benefit, but at establishing once more the power of the emperor in the minds of the people. Diocletian took on the aspect of terrible divinity in his demand for revenge. He specified torture and eventual execution for all those, of whatever rank, who refused to acknowledge his supremacy.

"The Christians have a saying," he thundered, "that I will turn against them. They will believe it on my terms.

"'There is one lord'—the August Diocletian. 'There is one faith'—in my power over their lives. 'There is one baptism'—and it is of the blood of the enemies of Rome. 'There is one god and father of them all'—and they will now feel a father's wrath. Go!"

The officers left to begin their task. Diocletian watched them leave, then turned to Genesius. "Can you write?" he asked.

"Yes, lord," Genesius answered. "It is another trick of the trade."

"Then you will write for me a new edict. If there is to be war, then it will be a war without quarter. Galerius was right to demand it earlier. I only hope that it is not too late to destroy the Christians root and branch."

Diocletian put his fingers to his mouth and whistled loudly. A slave appeared.

"Bring writing implements at once."

The slave scurried away. From some unknown place, he found paper, pen, and ink. Within moments he returned. Genesius took them and sat on the ground.

Diocletian dictated; Genesius wrote. When it was done, he sent Genesius down into the field to read the proclamation to the palace's inhabitants.

With Galerius' departure, Genesius felt lighter in spirit, as if a cloak had been removed from the sky. The rising sun penetrated the dawn's chill; the movement loosened his joints. The confidences shared by Diocletian reassured him of his father's favor. If only he could let Diocletian know of the relationship between them! Of course, he never could; it would make the emperor suspicious of him and threaten the trust that was growing between the older man and the younger. It was almost enough to know it for himself—better in some ways if Diocletian were never to know consciously what drew him to Genesius.

As he descended, the proclamation clutched in his hand, Genesius saw the people and their guards watching him. He felt chosen, singled out, the bearer of the will of the most powerful being alive.

The congregation numbered about three hundred people. The

departure of Galerius and his entourage had thinned their ranks by nearly a third.

Genesius was anxious to perform well.

An officer of one of the magistrates approached him. Genesius explained his errand. While he waited, the officer scurried to his superior. The magistrate listened briefly and turned to his second-in-command. Two decurions left his circle, one heading for each of the circles presided over by the other magistrates. In a few moments, the people and their guards were formed into one group surrounding Genesius, who found himself surrounded by twenty praetorians as a bodyguard. Around the crowd, the soldiers on the perimeter closed in, tightening the circle.

The people stood silently, waiting.

The bodyguard kept them at bay. He could see only the people in the front ranks. His voice needed to include all of them, but he was too low. He moved to the decurion in charge of his bodyguard and explained the problem. The two biggest men of the twenty were pulled out of the circle toward the middle. Genesius jumped up and planted one foot on the shoulder of each. Thus upraised, he could survey the entire crowd. As he did so, he picked out his fellow actors. They were soot-stained and disheveled. Lactantius, hemmed in on all sides by others, tried to keep his eyes on the bishop, Anthimus, who stood with quiet dignity. The crowd seemed to want to reject Anthimus; those who were near him edged toward their other neighbors as if the bishop were an irritant. Satisfied with his perch, Genesius knew that his voice would carry. He began to speak:

> I, Gaius Aurelius Valerius Diocletianus, Augustus of Rome, High Priest of Jupiter, Tribune of the eighteenth term, Consul of the thirteenth year, Emperor of the twentieth year, Supreme Magistrate, and Father of my people, do order and proclaim that from this time hence all the leaders of the so-called Christians are to be considered rebels and outlaws against the public order. The so-called Christians have themselves proclaimed that they follow Christ as a king, owing this Christ a higher loyalty than that owed to the Emperor. The so-called Christians refuse to honor the ancient and true gods of Rome, who have watched over and protected its peoples time out of mind; instead, they honor only this newfound Christ and for his sake deny the ancient and true gods of Rome. They form among themselves secret societies, in which

they practice unspeakable actions that cannot bear the light of knowledge. They refuse to take part in the public ceremonies of the Roman citizenry and thereby foment disunion in the empire. By these and other acts they declare themselves rebels against their rulers, traitors to Rome, and a clear and present danger to society.

Henceforth: the leaders of the so-called Christians are ordered to present themselves to the appropriate authorities for trial and judgment. If any such leader will abjure his place and correct his error, he shall be freed, with no prejudice held against him in any manner whatsoever. If any such leader fails to do so, he shall be subject to the penalties of treason.

Given by me, Gaius Aurelius Valerius Diocletianus, *Imperator*.

The final words soared from Genesius' lips and out over the crowd. Around Anthimus, the gap grew wider, as the people near him tried to avoid even being seen in his presence. A squad of soldiers began to move through the crowd toward the old man, and the crowd parted willingly to let them go by.

The priest offered no resistance. In fact, he raised one hand above his head and stood proudly, so that there would be no mistaking him.

Anthimus was brought into the circle for judgment. Genesius stayed in the circle himself, only ten feet from the bishop. Their eyes met; the priest might bargain his life for Genesius' over the stolen scroll. Genesius came to know guilt as a delicate itch between the shoulder blades, an almost uncontrollable desire to glance behind, a sense of identity with the man who waited just three steps away for his violent death.

Genesius found that he had a soul. He told himself that his possession of the scroll did not mean that he was a practicing Christian, did not mean that he shared the bishop's treasonous belief, did not mean that he was disloyal to Diocletian. But the scroll burned his hands as if he held one of the still-glowing beams of the palace in them. He broke eye contact with Anthimus and stared at his hands. In the left was the scabbed wound earned when he saved the emperor from the blade of Euethius; in the right was the hurt received only yesterday during the abortive performance of the virgin-birth play.

Anthimus said softly, "Only two, thus far. There are more to come." Genesius turned away abruptly.

"Don't speak to me, Christian. Magistrate, the man has identified himself. Carry out your emperor's order."

"I need no actor to remind me of my duty," the officer said.

"Then get on with it," Genesius retorted. He had a new enemy and knew it, but the words had escaped his lips before he had a chance to think. The officer, a veteran of Diocletian's old unit in the Persian war twenty years earlier, now in balding middle age, looked to the hill where Diocletian stood overlooking the proceedings. He started to move toward Genesius, looked back at the hill, and saw Diocletian shake his head. Thus warned, the officer returned his attention to Anthimus and began the interrogation.

"You have heard the decree," he said. "Are you, in fact, a leader of the Christians?"

"I am," Anthimus said.

"You know the penalty for treason."

"I do."

"Are you ready to give up your treason and swear allegiance to the Augustus?" the soldier asked.

"It is no treason to follow the Christ," Anthimus said. "But that is not what you asked. I will not give Him up."

"Then you will die."

"Then I will die," Anthimus said. "If I am now ashamed to acknowledge Christ here among you, will He not be ashamed of me when I go to meet Him? But if I boast of Him now, He will be proud to call me His own to His Father's face, and while you are still suffering here, I will live in the house of the Lord forever."

"Is this your final word?" the magistrate demanded.

"Not quite," Anthimus said. "But it is only a little more. I forgive you, and I will ask Him to forgive you as well."

He looked toward Genesius. "And you." The actor backed away.

Anthimus turned and knelt, his face upturned to the sky. The magistrate, the soldiers, and the crowd looked to Diocletian, solitary on the hill, for a signal. For a long moment, he did not move. Then he raised his fist to shoulder height, extended his thumb, and twisted it to point at the earth. The crowd roared its approval. As the magistrate drew his sword and moved to an arm's length behind Anthimus, silence fell over the onlookers.

"Come, Lord Jesus." Anthimus whispered. "Come now!"

The sword hummed briefly in the chill morning air. Its song ended with a sharp crack as it separated Anthimus' head from his body.

The head tumbled, rolled, and came to rest face up at Genesius' feet—smiling.

---CHAPTER 16---

T he virgin play was a hit throughout Nicomedia. Audiences
flocked to see it. The company played in the public theater, in the
marketplaces, in the temples. The actors began to notice some of the
same faces in the audiences over and over again. It was a smash.

But with success came the necessity to provide something new to
whet the appetite of the public. As time went on, the audiences began
to dwindle. On one occasion, both Genesius and Diarius were
interrupted in the course of the show by members of the audience
chanting the dialogue along with them.

The players needed a new play.

The virgin play parodied one of the Christian myths. The new play
needed a different target—not one of the stories but one of the central
inconsistencies of Christianity. After seemingly endless discussion
they settled on a scenario that would tackle baptism in its most
vulnerable form—deathbed conversion. Here the hypocrisy of "salvation" was most blatant. A man could "sin" throughout his life, from

childhood to old age, and at the point of death, avoid the penalties of his sin merely by suddenly becoming a Christian—or so it was said. Caligula himself—if, on his deathbed, he embraced Christianity— would have died blameless in the eyes of the Christian God and entered into Paradise, while Cicero, one of the best of men by any standard, a noble, upright citizen, would suffer eternal punishment simply because he never professed the Christian God while alive.

It did not seem fair. Worse, it was illogical. The inconsistency was well recognized among the pagans; the Christians themselves pre- ferred not to talk about it. It was an embarrassment to the Christians and thus the perfect subject for parody.

Genesius volunteered to write the scenario. The task suited his own unstated needs, and the others were glad to avoid the research necessary to make the script an accurate parody.

✦ ✦ ✦

"What am I to do?" Prisca asked of me. "Valeria is gone with her obscene husband." The word hissed from Prisca's ravaged face. The tears had finally come with the departure of Valeria. Prisca's daughter had been her confidante, her daughter's suffering her reason to maintain her own composure. "What will happen to her now?"

I had no answer, except the one used by desperate people since time out of mind.

"Let us pray," I said.

✦ ✦ ✦

"Instruct me," Genesius said. "I wish to learn more about what I am to mock."

The ways of the Spirit seem sometimes devious. "Let's go where we can talk without being overheard," I suggested. "Outside."

We left what remained of the palace. Workers were clearing rubble still, while other workers laid stone upon stone to rebuild in the already cleared places. The new palace would rise like a phoenix from the ashes of the old as a demonstration of the superiority of the traditional ways. But even with all the activity, or perhaps because of it, I had to assume that anything said within the palace grounds would be heard and reported. Diocletian's urgency to rebuild mirrored his attitude regarding the Christians—he would try the harder to destroy us.

He had dispatched messengers to all the empire, urging the provincial governors and local authorities to step up their persecution of the Christians, to eliminate us root and branch. He had gone mad with fear; he saw Christians everywhere.

I should have thought it dangerous to talk to Genesius but for the existence of the scroll of Paul's letter to the Corinthians. He knew that I still had it, that I could use it to denounce him. Likewise, he could use my possession of it to denounce me. We each had the means to assure the destruction of the other, and, although I do not pretend to understand it, the situation gave us each a brittle sense of security concerning the other's intentions.

So we walked.

"Your bishop died well," Genesius said.

"It is what we are learning to do best," I answered. I felt an unbecoming but natural anger toward him. He helped to fan the flames. "We have a saying, first spoken during the persecution of Decius, a hundred years ago. 'The blood of the martyrs is the seed of the church.' I think it is true. The more we are persecuted, the stronger we grow."

"Why," Genesius asked, "doesn't your god protect you?"

"He does." I spoke with more certainty than I felt. In some ways, although I truly wished to proclaim myself a Christian to the world and to face down my own fears with faith, as so many others have done, there was a worldly comfort in my assigned role as historian to the church. As long as I remained undiscovered by the authorities, the awful pain of torture and the possibility of failure would not be mine. Which was more difficult?

As we walked I wondered about the seeming solidity of the houses that surrounded us, the very pavement that our sandals slapped against. They seemed real enough, but at any moment, the heavens might open and the world fall away, and I would be called to answer for my sins. The least of them was not envy of those already called to the sacrifice. They had slipped through the false reality of the world; they had gone home. Their names were written in the book of life, sealed for eternity, while for mine the pen was still poised over the page, the judgment not yet made.

"He does?" Genesius said.

"There is a book," I said, "kept in heaven, perhaps in the mind of God, perhaps, somehow, in everything that we are. In it are written the lives and deeds of every soul created. And at the end Christ will judge me according to what I have written in my part of the book.

And He will choose my fate forever according to what I once chose to write in the book. I will have to account for what I have done, for what I have been."

"That hardly seems fair," Genesius said.

As we talked a beggar, seeing that we wore the rich clothing of the court, approached us, his hands outstretched for alms. Genesius tossed him a coin, but I was deep in thought and passed by him unthinking. The actor caught me in my sin.

"Does that count too?"

I realized what I had done and turned around to try to correct my error, but the beggar had vanished.

"It does," I admitted. "Maybe you have more talent for good works than I."

"So," Genesius pounced, "you admit that you Christians are not the only ones who can be virtuous! Goodness is allowed to us heathen too."

"Yes."

"So why should anyone be a Christian? Why take the risk?"

"Who sets himself a goal of virtue in this world?" I asked him. "Is that what you want?"

"I don't know what I want," Genesius said. "But we are not talking about what I want."

"I wonder," I said. And I did. I had the feeling that he was leading me, when I had thought that I was trying to lead him to—something. Did I want to make a Christian out of him? What would happen if I succeeded?

"Why should anyone want to be a Christian?" he repeated. He spoke my thoughts. I stopped walking. I seemed to be unable both to walk and think clearly at the same time.

"It is a truth I cling to," I said, "when the whole world turns upside down." The question he asked me was not unfamiliar, but his asking seemed to set something loose in my mind. The apostolic answers were true—I knew it, then as now!—but the formulae seemed too categorical, too inhuman and distant from the flesh and blood who questioned. How to explain?

"A story," I said. "I started to tell you mine some time ago. You did not have the patience to listen."

✦ ✦ ✦

I was still a student in Carthage, but I was beginning to gain some fame as a rhetorician and advocate in the law courts. I began to gather a following, an audience, who attended my appearances in court. I was something of a sensation, but like the gladiator Carnivorous, I eventually was beaten by another rhetorician. He so thoroughly humiliated me in argument that I felt I had no alternative but to leave Carthage. I decided to return humbled to Dougga to take up my father's trade, but before I could liquidate my property in Carthage and leave, a courier from the court in Nicomedia arrived with orders for me to sail across the sea to the imperial city.

My fame, it seems, had reached Diocletian himself from the lips of a provincial governor who had vacationed in Carthage during the previous year. I was commanded to join the court as imperial rhetorician. There was nothing to do but set sail, humiliated as I had been.

No one came to the dock to see me off. My students, my audience, my public—I had ceased to exist for them on the day I was bested in debate.

I cannot remember what that lawsuit was about, only the losing. I had spoken first. My opponent, a new advocate from the countryside, answered competently but without originality; his argument was lifted straight from the textbooks. I gave my rebuttal almost without thinking, also quoting the traditional response.

And then it happened. He departed from tradition. He cited the ancient writings of the Hebrews. I was helpless because I suddenly found myself in agreement with his point. I simply walked away amidst the applause of the spectators. He had punctured my defenses like so many soap bubbles, and I was left unprotected.

Whether it was my own lapse of thought or his brilliance I have never known, but it was as if my training and my wit had deserted me.

In any case I was publicly beaten. The only way I could see to redeem my self-respect was at the court, and I would need to arrive there before the news of my defeat reached Diocletian. I boarded the ship, and we sailed on the next tide.

The first few days of the voyage were peaceful, the sea calm. I was the only passenger from Carthage, through some stroke of fortune. The crew and the officers knew nothing of my shame, and there was no one else to carry word of it to the emperor; I would have at least a short time to establish myself in Nicomedia before word arrived. I spent the endless shipboard hours composing a greeting to Diocletian, *redemptoris mundi,* the restorer of the world, for his achievements in protecting the borders from the barbarians. If he were sufficiently impressed at my arrival, I reasoned, he might discount as envious rumor the reports of my humiliation that were certain to follow me.

We left the coastline and sailed northeast until in sight of Sicily, then turned eastward to avoid her barren southern coast.

I roughed out the tribute in the first few days of the voyage, then spent each day polishing and sweetening it. To protect the paper from the damp and salt, I kept it in a vase, sealed with wax, when not at work on it. I was fiercely determined to make it the most formidable and polished work I had ever written in order to seal my place in Diocletian's court. Every day I opened the vase, struggled over the writing, and, at dusk, sealed it with hot wax.

Among the crewmen there was a Christian who was treated with grudging tolerance until the afternoon of the storm. We were somewhere north of Crete when the sea began to roughen and the sky to grow dark. Although afflicted by seasickness, I still labored on my ode to Diocletian, unwilling to rest until I had made it perfect. As night came, the storm worsened. The ship rose on the crests and fell into the troughs. I felt more urgency for my manuscript because of the danger and was anxious to seal it in its jar. Part of my urgency was no doubt caused by the prickling I felt; the hair along my arms and on the back of my neck stood up of its own accord. As a precaution I melted extra wax over the flame. As I sealed the bottle a thunderbolt raced down from heaven, struck the mast of the ship, and crackled into the sea. I must have jerked my hand while pouring, for hot wax spilled over the lamp and spread across the deck, burning. The sails were suddenly afire, hissing as the flames ate into the sodden canvas. I had not thought it possible that so wet a fabric could burn, but the violence of the lightning bolt overcame the natural quenching effect of the water. I remember the hissing quite clearly. White steam came from the sails as the flame devoured them. It was an unearthly experience.

We were far along on our journey when the accident took place, somewhere to the north of Crete among the Aegean islands. The spilled wax poured across the deck, spreading farther than imagination would lead one to believe. Flame floated over the planking, swirling in intricate patterns as the ship tossed on the waves.

The crew was in a panic, of course, as was I. We threw ourselves into the sea. The crewman I mentioned earlier, the Christian, stayed aboard, tearing furiously at pieces of the cargo, deck planking, wooden fittings—anything that might float.

He threw these objects into the sea, and we gratefully held onto them to keep ourselves alive. The violence of the storm prevented me from seeing much of his last act of mercy. He must have died, either burned in the flame or swept into the water. "Greater love has no man than this, that he lays down his life for his friends."

As soon as those of us in the water were safe—that is, when we had something to hold onto—the storm ceased as if it had never been. The sky cleared and the waves subsided. We floated on a gentle swell, calling back and forth to each other. One man had abandoned ship with a coil of rope slung over his shoulder, and he managed to tie us together and even, after some little work, to forge our random pieces of flotsam into a raft of sorts so that we could climb out of the sea.

We were soon rescued by a fishing boat from the island of Patmos. When the fishermen heard our story, they insisted that it was a miracle that we had survived and that our survival was due to the intervention of a man they referred to as John the Divine, a Christian—one of the twelve apostles, in fact—who had been exiled on their island during the reign of the emperor Domitian nearly two hundred years earlier. They attributed supernatural powers to this John and cited many other instances of his intervention, even after his death. I was more inclined to credit our survival to the unnamed man who gave up his life for ours, but no matter which explanation one chose, it seemed that the credit for my being alive, not to mention the rest of the crew, belonged in some sense to the God of the Christians.

The fishermen took us to Patmos, a rocky island west of Miletus, off the coast of Asia. It is a small island, supporting a population of no more than a few hundred hardy souls.

From the harbor, on the eastern side of the island, Patmos is imposing—a stony cliff rises hundreds of feet above the water, topped by a fortress known as Saint John's Cave. Here, the local legend says, John composed his Gospel and Apocalypse under the inspiration of the Holy Spirit.

The fishermen brought us into the town where we were welcomed as the witnesses of a miracle. We were given dry clothing, hot food, and rest. Then on the following day, the townspeople took us on a tour of Saint John's Cave. Our hosts were an old man and a young boy, named Peter and James respectively. Peter was descended, he told me, from the original caretaker who had been Saint John's guard during his exile. James was his grandson and would take over his duties when Peter died.

"You're a Jonah!" Peter said.

"I beg your pardon?" I answered. I had no idea what he meant.

"The cause of the shipwreck," he explained. "It was all because of you."

I was, I admit, baffled by his assertion.

From the folds of his clothing, James produced the vase in which I had sealed the ode to Diocletian. "This is yours." He handed it to me. The seal was broken. I pulled the cork to inspect the paper inside; it was undamaged by the sea.

"We had to open it, to know whom it might belong to," James said. "It washed up on the beach during the night."

I stammered my thanks and turned to leave the cave. James barred my way. "We are not finished with you yet."

"Not everyone receives a sign," James said. "You should be honored."

"You have been singled out for a purpose," Peter said. "When you reach Nicomedia, find the bishop, a man named Anthimus. Listen to him. Talk with him. Tell him your story."

Having delivered his message, Peter smiled, settled himself onto his couch, and died. James was matter-of-fact about the event. He arranged Peter's body decorously as he spoke to me.

"He was waiting for you. Now his task is finished. We will give thanks for him and then bury him. But that is our task now. There is a ship leaving on the next tide that will take you to Nicomedia. May God go with you."

I stumbled from the cave into the blinding Aegean sunlight. Down below, the little town gleamed white at the edge of the harbor. One ship lay by the dock, a white banner flying from its mast.

No one spoke to me as I descended the cliff, nor did I try to speak with anyone. Singled out? My thoughts were confused. Had two people died as soon as they completed a task involving me? The sailor who stayed with the ship, flinging shards of wood to save my life, the old man who had waited who knows how long to deliver a cryptic message—were they somehow assigned these tasks involving me?

I went directly to the ship. I hoped no more people would die before I got the message—whatever it was.

The gangplank bounced treacherously as I walked up. Below, fish heads and entrails floated in the water with clots of pitch that exuded a rainbow film on the surface. I stumbled, but before I fell into the miasma, a rough hand grabbed my shoulder and hauled me aboard.

"You'll be the one we were waiting for, then. Can't have you taking another baptism in the sea now, can we? One dunking is enough for any man."

"Are you the captain?" I asked.

He stood six and a half feet tall. Barefoot, his skin browned dark by nature as well as by sun and saltwater, he was dressed in rough clothing of almost the same hue as his skin. He wore a full beard, and it had been months since his hair felt the nip of shears—if ever. It grew in a wild, barbaric profusion, not falling down his back or across his shoulders, but tightly curled, a nimbus of gray and black around his head, joined to his beard, which was likewise undisciplined.

"That I am." With the words spoken, he turned and bellowed to his small crew. "The tide's rising—take us out of here!" He turned back to me as the cries of the men preparing to sail echoed around the harbor. "We've a cabin below set aside for you. It's this way."

He set off without looking to see whether or not I followed. Having little choice, I did.

I was the only passenger. When evening fell, the captain stood out on the deck and called for attention from the crew. Bathed in moonlight, he began to lead them in prayer to Christ. Knowing the Christians' aversion to allowing nonbelievers to share in their worship, I started to go below.

"Stop right there," the captain shouted, interrupting himself. "You'll be wanting to listen to this, as you're going to be baptized soon."

I had no such intention.

"It's not the Eucharist," he said. "It's just a prayer of thanks for bringing us safely through the day, and a hope that we'll all be safe and sound when morning comes." He came toward the hatch where I was standing and handed me a scroll.

"You read for us, sir, if you please. I do it from memory and hold the book so they'll know that it's a true prayer. But you being a rhetor will know better than I how to place the sounds and pitch the words." He held out the scroll to me.

"Please, sir."

"I am not one of you," I said.

"You're on this ship with us," the captain said.

"Yes," I admitted, "but—"

"Then, 'When in Rome . . . ,' if you get my meaning." He still held the scroll in front of me. "The men don't know what I know about you, sir. You're not a believer yet, but you'll only hold out so long. You might as well get some practice in. Read the prayer for us."

I acquiesced.

"O God, the life of all who live," I said, "the light of the faithful, the strength of those who labor, and the repose of the dead: We thank You for the blessings of the day that is past, and ask Your protection through the coming night. Lord Jesus, stay with us; be our companion in the way, and keep watch with those who work, or watch, or weep this night, and give Your angels charge over those who sleep. Look down from Your heavenly throne, and illumine this night with Your celestial brightness, that by night as by day Your people may glorify Your holy name."

With one voice the captain and the crew softly said, "Through Jesus Christ, our Lord. Amen." Their attention had never left their tasks, but they resumed their duties with new assurance, some to sleep, one as a lookout; the helmsman, although he had never taken his eyes from their course, seemed somehow more confident in his control of the ship.

The moon moved out from its veil of clouds and bathed the sea in pale radiance. I handed the scroll back to the captain.

"Keep it," he said. "I have it from memory, and we will all remember this night and your reading of it. You should have it."

I remember his gentle words there in the moonlight. I could not answer. I kept seeing the moonlight that spilled over the ocean, the ship, myself.

✦ ✦ ✦

"The rest of the voyage passed without incident," I said. "I reached Nicomedia with the prayer scroll still with me, along with the manuscript for my ode to Diocletian. But the words 'the redeemer of the world,' *redemptoris mundi,* no longer seemed proper for an earthly ruler. I went to visit the man they wanted me to meet, the bishop, Anthimus. Three years later, I was baptized a Christian."

Genesius, who had remained still during my long recitation, stood up impatiently. "Is that all? You still haven't answered the question."

"Why baptism?"

"Exactly."

"I thought I had," I said. "Very well. When you read for the first time a script you are going to perform, what do you look for?"

"What I as an actor need to do to make it successful."

"And how do you know what will make it successful?" He became irritated with my roundabout questioning.

"What does this have to do with baptism?"

"Everything. Bear with me," I said. "How do you recognize your tasks?"

"By what happens in the play," Genesius said. "The things that the characters do and say. Aristotle pointed that out."

"So he did," I answered.

"He wasn't a Christian, either," Genesius sulked.

"No, but he knew a thing or two. He knew that you could tell what the playwright wanted the actor to portray by the circumstances he put into the play. If he wanted a character to feel sad, he caused something bad to happen to him. If he wanted a character angry, he caused the circumstances to frustrate him. Am I right?"

Genesius nodded, refusing now to meet my eye. His face was stony as he looked off at something only he could see. I persisted.

"Think of our Christian God as a playwright. Think of us as both actors and audience. I have never heard a voice come down from heaven to tell me, 'This is what you must do.' No visions, no burning chariots, no dreams in the night. It has all been disturbingly ordinary. But I know from the circumstances He has placed me in that He longs for me to respond to His hopes.

"Why He should do so, I have no idea. But the evidence—the evidence, mind you—of His hope is all around me and inside of me, built into my being. I know because the capacity to grow toward Him is there. Why this should be so is a mystery I do not presume to understand."

Genesius did not respond; he only looked at me closely.

I had said enough. We returned to the palace.

CHAPTER 17

The new edict went forth into the entire Roman world. From Hadrian's Wall to the temples of Amen-Hotep, from the western ocean to the border with the Persians, the order was given to eliminate Christianity from the minds of the people.

For those who were not Christian leaders—that is, who were not bishops, priests, deacons, exorcists, or acolytes—Diocletian ordered labor camps to be enlarged. The mines in Judea and Carpathia would swallow thousands of dissidents without so much as a polite political belch.

At dawn on the third day after the second fire Diocletian began.

The process of interrogation was slow, even though helped along by torture and execution. Many refused to condemn their friends to pain and mutilation.

Apparently solid citizens suddenly disappeared from their neighborhoods, abandoning houses and land. Diocletian's terror was frustrated by the refusal of the Christians to be terrorized. While many recanted, many more held firm against their pain, trusting in their Christ to save them, and died. Those who escaped seemed to vanish into the earth. It did not seem possible to Diocletian that there were so many. Even his palace staff was riddled with them.

Catching Christians was in one sense easy. Most could be trapped simply by demanding that they sacrifice to the Roman gods. Neither Diocletian nor his advisers understood why someone would willingly embrace a shameful death. The conspirators who had lit the palace fires were never found.

"Who did this to me?" Diocletian asked.

"It was the Christians," his advisers answered.

"But which Christians?"

"We do not know."

"Where are they?"

"They may be anywhere."

"Where is Galerius?"

"In Macedonia, at Thessalonika."

"Am I safe?"

"We think so."

"What is he doing?"

"We do not know."

"What are the Christians doing?"

"We do not know."

Diocletian had reigned for twenty years as the supreme leader of the empire. It was time for celebration.

"Where is Dorotheus?"

"Dead, lord."

"Peter, my chamberlain?"

"Dead."

"Gorgonius?"

"Dead."

"Galerius?"

"Gone."

"Maximian?"

"In Gaul."

"Constantius?"

"Britain."

"Is anyone left?"

"We are, lord."

"Who are you? I don't even know your names."

"You should celebrate your success, my lord, the happy anniversary of your accession to the purple. You should go to Rome."

"Rome!" Diocletian said. "I'd sooner spend my vicennalia in a cesspit."

"The people expect a celebration. With all the troubles going on now, it would be a welcome distraction. It would turn their minds from the loss of so many friends."

"Are the Christians friends, then?" Diocletian said. "Your friends, perhaps? How am I to know? Rome is a trap."

"The forms must be observed, lord. The people must see your rule over them. The trip will do the empire good. A sort of grand tour."

"Before I die, eh?"

"No one spoke of—"

"Dying."

"No, lord. No one would. But Rome is the center. Rome is the hub of the empire, and—"

"Rome is wherever I am!"

"As you say, my lord."

Diocletian stared out the window of his new chambers until the courtiers left him alone. Government was virtually halted. The fire had removed from him his trusted people because they had, at best, failed to prevent the fire that almost took his life. The new ones, hurriedly recruited from the local nobility and the lower levels of the bureaucracy, were inexperienced and useless. Their faces were new, their habits unknown, their loyalty untested.

"Bring me the actor," he said.

"Are you certain that it is wise?"

"Just bring him."

✦ ✦ ✦

Genesius was working on the new play when the supercilious new courtier found him.

"How can you work here?"

Genesius merely interrupted his writing and waited, looking up at the man. His rich clothing still wore the sheen of novelty. "Are you the actor he wants?" The courtier affected effeminacy as his means of showing disdain for those left behind by his sudden political elevation. He held a perfumed cloth to his nose as he spoke to

Genesius. "I suppose there is a certain rough style to your work. Not to my taste, of course, but I can see where some people might like it."

"Who are you?" Genesius asked. "I don't know you."

"Doesn't anyone keep up with the palace gossip anymore?" he said. "I thought just everyone knew me. We'll just have to become better acquainted. My name is Publius Labius. I am the new chamberlain. Come with me, now."

Publius Labius minced off down the corridor. He stopped, glancing over his shoulder. "Aren't you coming?"

Genesius shrugged his shoulders in disbelief, laid aside his pen, and followed. It had been several days since he had last spent time with Diocletian. He had thought little of it, being busy with writing the baptism script and struggling with the ideas that Lactantius had given him. Events in the palace had moved ahead. Galerius was gone, but it was inconceivable that he had left without leaving his own agents in place to keep track of whatever Diocletian might do.

Publius Labius led Genesius to the new imperial apartment and announced him to Diocletian.

"You may go," Diocletian said.

"But excellency," Publius Labius said, "you must make plans for your journey to Rome for the vicennalia. You remember, we discussed it earlier."

"You may go."

"Of course, my lord. I shall return later." Publius Labius closed the door with a flourish. Like everything else in the apartment, it had a sheen of newness. The wood was undarkened with use, the hardware still shining.

"That's the problem," Diocletian said. "He will return. Have you been well?"

"Yes, lord," Genesius said. "Where did he come from?"

"He is a spy from Galerius, given me to replace Dorotheus. Would you care for a cup of wine?"

"Thank you. Let me." Genesius poured the wine into two chalices, added spring water, and handed one to Diocletian.

"If you would?" Diocletian asked. "I hate to use a friend this way, but—"

"Of course, my lord." Genesius took a large swallow from the cup. "It seems all right. A little rough but drinkable. I feel no ill effects." He drank again. "Must you truly worry about poison?"

"I don't know," Diocletian said. "Too many things are happening.

I can't afford to take any chances. What do you think?"

Genesius thought before he spoke. "Is it civil war that you want?"

Diocletian walked to the window to look out over the courtyard. Genesius stood by his side. Both men remained in silent thought before Diocletian answered. Laborers, carpenters, and stonemasons busied themselves below, rebuilding. Troops drilled in the field beyond the wall.

"I don't think that it will come to civil war. The Christians won't fight. No, what I am trying to do is avert a civil war. Galerius is too strong to oppose on this issue, and he is partly right. The Christians are a danger to the empire, perhaps the greatest danger it has ever faced. The other threats—the Persians, the barbarians, the pirates—they are all external. The people can be rallied against them. But these Christians are everywhere." He sipped from the cup. "I am not squeamish. I have shed blood many times, and I will not give in to this threat. But loyalty cannot be divided. Dorotheus made his choice when he announced himself a Christian. He told me where his loyalty lay—with this Christ. How could I trust him thereafter?"

Diocletian poured a fresh chalice for himself. "Are you ready yet?"

"No, not yet," Genesius said, showing Diocletian that he had not yet emptied his cup.

"I know that the Christians as a group will not make war upon me. Not overtly. It is a war that they would be destined to lose, and they know it. Too many of their people would rather die and be with Jesus than fight. But there are extremists in any group; the fires did not start by themselves."

Genesius found himself speaking before he considered his words. "Galerius left conveniently enough."

"Before I could have his people questioned, you mean?"

"As you say."

"I know." Diocletian returned to the window. "He took my daughter with him. The gods know if I shall ever see her alive again; I have my doubts. He is brutal with her, as if he abuses her to show his attitude toward me. Valeria no longer speaks on her own initiative; she answers direct questions with a word or two but nothing more. He has broken her spirit. For that alone I would kill him."

Genesius could make no answer. Diocletian returned to his theme.

"Do you know what it would mean to accuse Galerius of plotting my death? Even worse, do you know how little your own life was worth on the night that you saved mine? I don't understand why he didn't kill you. He must have been furious. The second fire was almost an accident. I think that some of his followers decided to try again, but the attempt was doomed to failure; we were already alerted.

"My choice, then, is to accuse Galerius or to accuse the Christians. I hate them both; one or the other is guilty of treason. But Galerius is too strong to fight, even if Constantius and Maximian sided with me. The struggle would destroy twenty years of stability. The northern tribes would seize the advantage. Every petty little princeling of a client state would grab at the chance to declare its independence. Even the provincial governors would end up taking sides.

"I will not let that happen," Diocletian said. "Therefore, the Christians are guilty of this attack on me. And treason must be punished."

Diocletian shuddered. "I have dreams, Genesius. Dreams where their Jesus appears to me, bathed in the blood that flows from his wounds, standing among the clouds. And the blood spurts down from the clouds onto the land. The rivers run red with it. The people drink from the rivers and irrigate their fields with it. I stand showered in it."

"They have a saying, these Christians," Genesius said. "It is 'washed in the blood of the lamb.' It means cleansed from the defilement of sin."

"The blood pours over me," Diocletian remembered. "It chokes me and sickens me. I vomit, and it is blood. Cleansed? I am defiled, then, by their lights. I suspect that it is impossible to govern without defilement. If they ever win out and take over the government, they will discover its trials. But in the meantime, I am the government, and I intend to keep my defilement. That is why we are going to Rome. We will show ourself unhurt by the attempt on our life. We will celebrate a vicennalia with all the pomp and ritual that the city can provide."

Night fell slowly as they talked.

"But first you will go to visit the shrine of Apollo at Didymus. You will consult the sacred oracle and listen carefully to its message, which you will write down precisely as I give it to you. It will say that I am the ruler all the gods have chosen for Rome and that I am to visit Rome to give its citizens the opportunity to reaffirm their loyalty to me. No matter what those filthy priests make the oracle say, this is the message you will bring back. Is that understood?"

"It is, my lord."

CHAPTER 18

G enesius and I rode out at dawn two days later with a detachment of ten guardsmen commanded by Martius, the centurion. Martius was short-tempered, displeased to be saddled with civilians. He lectured us on road discipline before we set out on our hurried journey.

"We have about three hundred and fifty miles to travel," he told us. "Relays are waiting for us every fifty miles or thereabouts. That means that we'll be traveling quickly, but not so fast that you can afford to abuse your mounts. It should take us three and a half days to get to Miletus, if all goes as it should. It's my job to see that you get there in one piece. And back. While we are on the roads, if I say jump, you jump. If I say stop, you stop. If I say slow down, you slow down. Now mount up!"

We mounted up.

The soldiers were lightly armed with short sword, round shield, leather armor, helmet, and spear. So close to the imperial seat, organized bandits were not expected. Nevertheless it only made sense to have some kind of protection for travelers on a political journey. Genesius and I were likewise, at the insistence of Martius, in leather armor, although we were armed only with daggers; Martius worried that we might hurt ourselves.

The small troop carried only small water bags and what little food could be kept in our saddlebags. We would victual ourselves when we stopped to change mounts.

The horses we rode were bred from those used by the fierce tribesmen of the Arabian desert. Small but hardy, Genesius' mount stood just under fifteen hands.

"What's his name?" Genesius asked.

"His name?" Martius was confused.

"His name. How am I to talk to this fine beast if I don't know his name?"

"You won't know him for more than half a day," Martius said. "Let's move out!"

The soldiers wheeled smartly in the courtyard; Genesius and I hurried to keep our place in the middle of the troop, thereby causing confusion which the experienced soldiers quickly sorted out. A wink of understanding passed between Genesius and one of the soldiers riding behind him. Martius, at the head of the small column, would never know of the small gaffe.

Our horses' shoes clicked loudly on the pavement; the detachment rode southward through the palace gates.

"I haven't ridden a horse in years," I said to Genesius. "How I ever let you talk me into this I'll never know."

"You'll be safer out in the wilds," Genesius said. "Or didn't you notice that you were going to miss the interrogations?"

"I'm not afraid."

"You should be."

"I'm too old for gallivanting around on horseback!" I complained, feeling an odd stretching sensation that would all too soon become pain.

"Nonsense!"

"I'm already saddle sore."

"Think of it as a ritual purification," Genesius advised, grinning.

"I'll purify you." I grumbled, smiling. Being outside the poisonous atmosphere of the court was like breathing fresh air. We worked our way through the city, and our route took us past the bare site of the Nicomedian church. The tiled mosaic was still open to the sky.

"Purification," Genesius murmured.

"What?"

"Here we are, both in service to the emperor," Genesius said. He glanced around, making sure that the soldiers were not paying attention to their conversation. "You, who are secretly a Christian, occupy a place of honor in society—"

"Must you speak so loudly?"

"They're not listening," Genesius said. "As I was saying, you have an honorable position in society, whatever that means. But I, who am more loyal than any of his advisers, am by law an outcast, cast in the comedy of the imperial court as a buffoon, classed with whores and pimps and cutpurses."

We had passed the ruins of the church now and were on the highway leading out of town. Martius, at the head of the patrol, increased our walking gait to a trot as we passed through the southern gate.

The road looped around the eastern shore of the Bay of Astacus, an arm of the Propontic Sea. The city of Astacus was only a few miles to the south of Nicomedia, and we passed through it quickly. Our horses were still fresh, the day young.

After clearing Astacus, the road straightened out as it entered the foothills between Nicomedia and Nicaea. Roman engineers of old did not deign to curve their proud highways around obstacles unless it was absolutely necessary. When a Roman road turned, it was because its builders wanted it to turn. Mere nature was not permitted to interfere with Roman commerce, communication, or military might. Hills, mountains, and rivers had been thought too insignificant to deflect Roman travel. Further inland, the mountains of Galatia and Cappadocia surrendered to the Roman road builders. Here, in the coastal lowlands of western Bithynia, the roads were wide and straight. The river Ascania at Nicaea was bridged almost as if the task were an afterthought. There was no change in the width, texture, or direction of the road.

We descended the foothills east of the city of Prusa, back down to the coastal lowlands, without incident. To the south, a lens-shaped cloud hung over Mount Olympus, the only cloud in sight. The sun rose high in the sky; we had made good time over the sixty miles from Nicomedia, but our horses were tired from the constant pace. Still east of the settlement, we reached the staging station, where, two days before, a messenger from the court had warned the stationmaster that there would be need for a dozen fresh mounts and refreshment for as many travelers. Martius called a half-hour break for a meal and personal relief.

Genesius stepped off the road, away from the station, and struggled with the leather armor. His need to relieve himself had grown desperate. Martius was a harsh taskmaster and would allow none but the most extremely necessary stops along the way.

The forest was still. Noontime sunlight filtered through the branches of oak and olive. It was unseasonably cool for early summer. Genesius thanked whatever gods might or might not exist.

Finishing, Genesius stepped over the fouled spot. His foot fell on something that seemed to yield; it was the upper arm of a Roman soldier. The pressure of his foot on the arm caused the hand to rise. It seemed to clutch at Genesius' leg. At its touch, he looked down.

Involuntarily, he screamed.

The soldiers assigned to his protection came running, followed by the stationmaster and myself. Martius was in the lead, sword already drawn, fixing his shield over his left arm. When he saw Genesius alone in the forest but for his bristling escort, he was somewhat less than pleased.

"What is the matter with you?"

Genesius pushed aside a bush with his foot, exposing the corpse of a Roman trooper. Martius allowed himself a quick look at the body, then barked orders.

"Surround us," he said. Each man took up a position a sword's length from his neighbor, forming a rough circle around us civilians.

"Back to the road, march!" Martius ordered. Wary against an attack, the formation slipped through the trees, back to the road and the way station. Martius ordered eight men to stand guard over the travelers and sent the remaining two on a reconnaissance patrol into the forest. He turned to the stationmaster.

"What do you know about this?"

"Nothing, sir," the man said. He held the job as a sinecure from his brother-in-law, who was on the town council in Prusa. "By the gods of Olympus, I am as shocked as you are."

The way station consisted of a corral for the horses and a small hut, into which the four men were crowded. Genesius sat on a table in the center of the single room. Martius and the stationmaster watched the outside from the doorway. Martius still held his sword in his hand, although he had slung his shield on his back.

The stationmaster was a short man, given to overindulgence. In youth, one could see he had been heavily muscled, but gluttony and sloth had turned the strength to greasy fat. Now, in his fear, sweat streamed down the few hairs left on his balding head and lost itself in the creases of his neck.

The two troopers emerged from the forest, carrying the head of a Roman soldier. The stationmaster shrank back from the door of the hut. Martius tensed, watching not his two men, but the forest behind them for signs of other watchers. The eight men left on guard redoubled their alertness, their attention likewise on the surroundings. These troops were blooded professionals and recognized their vulnerability in an ambush.

Martius stepped out from the hut to examine the head. He took it in his hands. Genesius pushed past the trembling stationmaster to Martius' side.

A rude brand was burned into the forehead of the dead soldier, a crude fish. Cut in the unburned flesh within the boundary of the fish shape were the letters ICTHYS. On each of the corpse's cheeks was cut a cross.

"This was done while he was alive," Martius said.

"I know that fish sign," Genesius offered. "It is the signal that the Christians use to identify each other."

"Centurion." One of the soldiers spoke, the same one who had winked to Genesius earlier in the day.

"Report."

"We found forty-six bodies in an area about ten yards square. We removed the head of this one ourselves. Each body had similar markings. They were all Roman soldiers. There was also the remains of a medium-sized fire. No sign of a battle. No other bodies. None of the bodies wore weapons. Even their daggers were gone."

Martius walked away from the little group and stared for a long moment into the forest.

"The stationmaster is beside himself with terror. He thinks he will be blamed," I said.

Genesius put a hand on my shoulder. I fell silent.

"How many men did you find?" Martius asked.

"Forty-six, centurion."

Martius returned, still carrying the head. "There may be a few more. You," he called to the stationmaster, "in the hut!"

The fat man scurried out.

"Did a cohort of troops pass here?"

"Yesterday, centurion."

"Was there anything strange about them?"

"Strange?"

"How did they behave?" Martius demanded. "What was their attitude?"

"They were very quiet."

"They were marching out to be decimated," Martius said. His voice was low, but there was no softness in it. "One-tenth of the men were branded, mutilated, and killed by their comrades in arms, at the order of their commander."

"Why?" Genesius asked.

"Treason," Martius said. "They were Christians." As if the matter were now resolved, Martius ordered them to mount their new horses. "There is no danger here. We have a mission to complete."

"What about burial?" I asked.

"They were traitors," Martius said. "Let them rot."

He threw the head over the stationmaster's hut and into the trees. We heard it bounce against a trunk and fall to the ground. He ordered the troop to mount up and move out. As we departed, the stationmaster called after us, "What am I supposed to do now?"

✦ ✦ ✦

Genesius wished he had eaten at the stop near Prusa. Dusk was falling as we came back in sight of the Propontis just outside the town of Cyzicus. Our going would have been easy, if Martius had not insisted on a rapid pace. Riders and horses were lathered with sweat from the sustained canter. Genesius seemed to be in pain; his jaw was set grimly, just like those of his fellow travelers.

Martius had insisted on doing the distance, some fifty miles or more, without interruption for rest, relief, or repast.

Cyzicus came into view. Genesius spurred his horse forward.

"There it is!" he called to Martius.

"I have eyes," the centurion said. "Back to your place." Chagrined, Genesius let his horse drop back to the middle of the party until he was again at my side.

"That officious, self-important clod," he muttered. "I'd like to get him on stage. We'd see how he handled himself there!"

"That officious, self-important clod, as you put it, came running when you screamed in the woods," I pointed out. "He's just doing his job."

"Why do you always have to be right?" Genesius grunted. "My buttocks are sore."

"Be quiet," I said. "Some things are better endured in silence."

"I'm tired, hungry, sore, and I need to go. I'm entitled to complain."

"We are all tired, hungry, sore, and need to go. If you must talk, talk about something else."

Genesius rode for a while in silence, his buttocks thumping regularly against the saddle. "Diocletian is not the only one who is afraid of the Christians, is he?"

I glanced at the flanking soldiers. Each seemed submerged in his own misery. Dutifully, each had his eyes pointed outward, watching the surroundings for signs of an ambush. The clop of the horses' shoes prevented close conversation from being heard. I reined my horse closer to Genesius.

"I was afraid before."

"Of what?"

"Of moving off into an uncharted darkness. Of abandoning tradition. Your whole way of thinking changes. All the old ways are lost to you. You see things differently. Every decision, every single thing you used to do, glows with the potential for evil."

"Evil?" Genesius said. "I thought you prided yourselves on doing good."

"Before the goodness can come, you must recognize the evil. It is a sobering experience. That's why some of us are dour and overly concerned with sin. They have seen the evil and fear it. The fear catches at them and they fail to trust the promise. I think that the whole world knows the fear now. Every person who can think and see knows evil now. You can see it in the rigidity of the sculpture and the tension in the court, in the stasis that has gripped the empire. It no longer grows; it only defends. Keep what you have, that's Rome's motto now.

"And you pagans know the untruth of the old ways. This oracle we are going to consult, for instance. Diocletian told you what answer to bring back. If necessary, he will bribe the priests of Apollo to make certain that he gets the right answer, the politically correct answer. If he believed in Apollo, would he find such a course necessary?"

"I don't believe in Apollo," Genesius said. "I believe in myself."

"Did you believe in yourself when you screamed in the forest?"

"That doesn't count. I was taken by surprise."

"God always takes you by surprise, my friend." I grunted as I shifted slightly in the saddle, trying vainly to find a comfortable position. "When, in my ignorance, I pretend to myself that God is just a man like me, like Apollo, He takes me by surprise. You are one of His startling events, for me. Did you know that?"

"Me?" Genesius said.

"You, indeed," I affirmed. "You have performed every task that Diocletian has asked of you, either directly or by implication. You have put on that wretched piece of blasphemy all over Nicomedia; you denounced Dorotheus and caused his death; you presided over the destruction of our church; you proclaimed for him the new edict of persecution. What haven't you done for him and against us?

"I'll tell you," I continued. I could not seem to stop myself. What is this foolish human need to talk and talk? "What you have not done for him is to denounce me as a Christian."

I tried to look into Genesius but failed. I could only ask the question. "Why?"

Without noticing, we had come up to the gates of Cyzicus, barely in time. Martius kicked his horse into a gallop and rode ahead to prevent the city guards from closing the gates in our faces and barely succeeded. It was dark now, and we needed shelter from the night.

✦ ✦ ✦

After spending the night in Cyzicus, we set out early the following morning for Pergamum, some ninety miles to the south. The road took us inland again, this time through the valley of the river Tarsius. The river meandered, but the road led straight. We forded the river three times in the morning's travel of fifty miles. Martius maintained the pace he had set on the previous day. The escort was alert, for the mountain valley was well suited for ambush.

We reached the next way station at the third ford of the river without incident. We were, Martius told us, within forty miles of the next night's stopping place, Pergamum, but we had a range of high ground to climb and descend before we could rest. Our break at the unnamed rest stop was all too brief.

"You're on a mission for the emperor," he told us when Genesius complained about the pace. "You can rest all you want when it is accomplished. Mount up."

And so we climbed. The road ignored obstacles and lifted us without distraction up to the ridge line, then followed the crest for

another twenty miles. By the time we began the descent into Pergamum, Genesius was too tired to marvel over the sight. I, however,
was ecstatic; worse, I grew garrulous.

"This is history, my lad," I said. "St. Paul's third missionary journey
stopped here in Pergamum. Or at least passed through it; the records
are unclear. But he was here. He came north from Ephesus. John
knew this place too. He had a vision and heard a voice. 'I am the
Alpha and the Omega. What thou seest, write in a book, and send it
unto the seven churches which are in Asia; unto Ephesus, and
Smyrna, and Pergamum, Thyatira, Sardis, Philadelphia, and
Laodicea.' And the vision was of the end of the world and the coming
of the Kingdom. Impressive, eh?"

Genesius tumbled from his horse, sound asleep.

✦ ✦ ✦

Ephesus found me still explaining Paul's journeys and John's
revelations to Genesius. The towns and cities were close together on
the western coast of Asia—Cyme, Smyrna, Ephesus, and dozens of
smaller settlements clustered between the mountains and the sea.

Thanks to Martius' constant hurrying, we arrived in Ephesus well
before dark. The centurion turned us loose in the city with strict
instructions to be ready to leave at first light to continue the journey.

Ephesus was both a center of Christian devotion—as the site of
some of Paul's preaching, John's long residence there, and its fame
as one of the seven churches of the apocalypse—and a powerful
supporter of the pagan point of view.

Genesius and I made our way from the inn to the great theater
that overlooked the harbor of Ephesus.

"Where is everyone?" I wondered. The theater was deserted, silent.

"Look at this!" Genesius exulted. We were standing at the top of
the auditorium under the evening sky. At our backs was the shrine
to Artemis, the patron goddess of the city. "There must be more than
twenty thousand seats. And the acoustics! I'll bet they're perfect. Go
down into the orchestra and talk to me. Don't shout. Just a whisper
ought to do it."

I went way down through the stone seats to the semicircular
orchestra.

"I can hear you puffing," Genesius called. "Say something."

"This was the place where the silversmiths of Ephesus rioted
against Paul. He barely escaped with his life."

"What did the silversmiths have against the Christians?" Genesius asked.

"Look behind you," I said. "Ephesus is a place of pilgrimage. From all over the world people come to worship Artemis the many-breasted." Genesius looked at the statue of Artemis, or Diana as the Romans called her, a human female encumbered with ripened breasts all over her body. He had passed by the statue without noticing her, so great was his hurry to see a really large classical theater.

"She's grotesque."

"Don't let the silversmiths hear you say that," I said. "They worship Artemis and with good reason. Almost every tourist who comes here buys three or four little silver statues of her to take home as gifts for his friends."

"But what did the silversmiths have against Paul?"

"He claimed that Artemis wasn't a real goddess," I answered, "that the only true god was the Christ. They thought they would lose their livelihood if the Christians grew dominant. Does that remind you of anyone we know?"

Before Genesius could answer, there was a rumbling sound in the distance behind him. He ran to the top of the hill on which the theater was built. I struggled up through the seats to watch with him. Thousands of chanting devotees of Artemis were marching toward the theater. The women were bare-chested. The men carried torches, which in the twilight threw confusing shadows on the moving masses.

As they approached, their chant became clear: "Great is Artemis of the Ephesians!"

"I think I know where everyone is," Genesius said. "There seems to be a riot headed this way."

"Let's get out of here!"

Genesius dashed down to the orchestra. "If this is anything like the other theaters I've worked in, there should be an exit out this way." He led me through the stage left *parodos,* or entryway, to the orches-tra. It saved us from having to mount the stage and lose ourselves in the scene building. We paused for breath to watch the Artemisian mob pour over the top of the auditorium bearing images of the goddess. Above the procession hung a pall of black smoke from the hundreds of torches. Their chant thundered through the theater's perfect acoustics until I feared that the very stones themselves would give way under the pressure of the reverberations. A hand gripped my arm; I whirled to see an unfamiliar face.

"Come with me," the stranger said. "This place is dangerous now."

I started to throw off the hand, fearing the stranger, but he spoke in a harsh whisper, "This is the Way." He moved his right hand in a small pattern of a cross in front of his breast. I did the same and we knew that we could trust each other. I followed the stranger without hesitation. We had only gone a few steps when I realized that Genesius was not following.

"It's all right," I said. "Come along. He'll see us safely out of here."

"He's not one of us?" the stranger asked.

"He is a seeker," I answered.

"He must be blindfolded then." The stranger produced a dark cloth.

"Please," I begged Genesius, "there is no time to waste." Genesius allowed himself to be blindfolded, and I took him by the hand. We followed the stranger, and I led Genesius through a labyrinth of alleys and courtyards.

Blinded, Genesius slowed our progress, but the stranger did not seem impatient. He waited as necessary when Genesius, with my aid, had to feel his way carefully over an obstacle. The stranger simply paused, keeping watch over our trail, until Genesius was once more on solid footing.

Finally, we stopped. The stranger rapped a soft, coded knock on a wooden door. An answering code was given from inside, the sound more muffled and distant. A third knock from the outside sounded, different in rhythm. The door was opened; the stranger herded us inside.

My sea captain greeted us.

"Peace be with you, old friend."

"And also with you," I said. "What are you doing here?"

"A seaman goes where he must," the sailor said. "Who is your friend?"

I introduced Genesius to the sea captain who had taken me, years before, from the island of Patmos. "He is not one of us, but I will vouch for him. He has had many opportunities to betray me and has refused them all."

"Remove the blindfold," the captain ordered. Someone obeyed, and Genesius could see again. The room was lit only by one small candle. Its shadows flickered on the domestic mosaics that covered the walls. People stood or sat in small groups, talking softly, occasionally glancing his way. No one seemed inclined to ask for names, nor to give them.

"You were nearly caught up in the monthly riot," the captain said. "The Ephesians like a good excuse for a celebration. With the persecution their lunar get-togethers have become dangerous to us. So we have taken to gathering quietly, and secretly as you noticed, away from the main thoroughfares."

The captain led us to a small table. "We have food and drink. It is likely to be a long night. These 'celebrations' usually turn into orgies."

As we ate and drank, one of the group read from Scripture. The reading was from the Beatitudes; the last had special meaning, given the occasion: "Blessed are you when men revile you and persecute you, for great is your reward in heaven; for so they persecuted the prophets which were before you." The reader, a young woman whose soft voice nevertheless rang with clarity, paused at that point, but a young man said, "Go on. Read the next part." She looked to the captain, who nodded.

"You are the salt of the earth: but if the salt has lost its savor it is good for nothing but to be cast out, and trodden under the foot of men. You are the light of the world. A city set on a hill cannot be hidden. Neither do men light a candle, and put it under a bushel, but on a candlestick; and it gives light to the whole house. Let your light so shine before men that they may see your good works, and glorify your Father which is in heaven."

"Amen," the small assembly murmured. There were, we found out, scattered throughout Ephesus, many such groups of Christians bound together by the common faith and the persecution. They were *collegia* of a sort, having in common their beliefs and a recognized need for mutual support. The young woman who had read explained that the house they were in belonged to a sympathizing nonbeliever. The food they ate came from the larder of a wealthy member, but one could never tell by the group's behavior who was the wealthy member. While gift-giving was encouraged, they considered it bad form to aggrandize the giver, since all gifts, she said, came from God. She herself claimed not to know who provided the feast.

✦ ✦ ✦

"How can you feast," Genesius asked, "knowing that the mob outside would kill you if it found you?"

"We are safe in Jesus' love," she answered. Pitched low for private conversation, her voice still enthralled him. By her dress and demeanor she was unmarried; her age might have been anywhere from seventeen to thirty. She wore her hair long; it framed the olive skin of her face with a black cloud shot through with highlights picked up from the candle's flickering light. Her eyes were likewise dark and liquid. They held the answers to questions he had not yet thought to ask.

Her statement only confused him. And Lactantius, he saw, was away in the far corner of the room, huddled in conversation with the captain.

"Safe?" he echoed. "You are in hiding."

"Only because that is where I am supposed to be," she said. "Do you care for more to eat? A cup of wine?"

She reached across Genesius to pour from the flagon. He inhaled the scent of her hair, a soft muskiness. Her flesh grazed his as she leaned in front of him, reaching again for the flagon. As if she knew his thoughts she smiled as she handed him the full goblet and settled back to her sitting position.

"Whenever you drink wine after tonight," she said softly, "think of me." Genesius accepted the cup and drank, unable to speak, unable to break away from the unreadable depth of her eyes.

Without warning there came a terrible pounding on the front door. Outside, the cries of a mob resounded against the stone walls of the surrounding houses.

"We know you're in there! Open up!"

From outside there came the impact of bodies against the stout wooden door. The noise snatched Genesius' eyes from the young woman. When he recovered and looked back, she was gone. He stood up to search for her, unavailingly. Most of the people were queued at another exit, a door which, under the mosaic, had been invisible in the poor light. Even as he tried to make sense of what was happening, they disappeared through the hidey-hole.

Genesius felt himself lifted up and passed overhead on the hands of the Christians. They fed him through the hidey-hole which led down, below street level. He regained his feet; still they followed a tunnel cut by ancient hands into the bedrock of the city. The young woman was nowhere to be seen in his portion of the line of escapees. He pressed himself against the wall of the tunnel, forcing the others to squeeze by him.

"Keep moving," the sailor ordered. There was nothing conciliatory, nothing "Christian" in his demeanor. "Two people stayed behind so that we could escape the mob. Don't waste their sacrifice."

"Who?"

"A man and a young woman."

Genesius wanted to question him further, but the captain just shoved him forward.

✦ ✦ ✦

Martius dressed us down as if we were raw recruits returned late from leave.

"That's it!" he ordered. "From now on you don't leave my sight. You could have been killed in that mob. Two people were found dead in the street—torn to pieces. You have a mission from the emperor; I personally will see that you accomplish it."

Genesius wanted to question him. I sensed his anxiety and laid a calming hand on his shoulder. "We will be more careful, centurion. I promise it. We were naive."

"*Stupid* was the word I had in mind," Martius said. "We are leaving right away for Miletus. Didyma is just outside of the town. We should be at the shrine this afternoon. Let's go."

We passed through Prienne and Heraclea without stopping. Miletus lay on the southern shore of the Latmic gulf; we turned southwest from the harbor to follow the Via Didymi, a road lined with the tombs of the people of Miletus and Didyma, wide and arrow-straight, out through the Milesian wall at the Didyma Gate. In the distance, the Didymeum, about a mile distant, awaited Genesius. The temple to Apollo Didymeus stood two stories tall. The tombs that lined the street gave way to olive trees.

To break the ominous silence of our approach, I explained the symbolism to Genesius. "The priests here are called Branchidae because they claim descent from Branchus, a young man whom Apollo loved. Because of his love Apollo is said to have bestowed the gift of prophecy on Branchus. When their affair ended, Branchus began the dynasty of priests that to this day prophesy in Apollo's name."

I droned on about the architecture, mentioning the evaluations of the temple's style written by Strabo and Pliny, but Genesius was mesmerized by the statue of Apollo that guarded the seven-stepped entrance to the temple. Its eyes seemed to focus on him as we came nearer, and it towered ever higher over him. As we passed by its feet, my lecture petered out to awed silence.

Beyond the statue, the temple rose in antique splendor. Its columns were more than three times the height of a man.

We dismounted and began to climb the steps. A voice, amplified by the acoustics of stone but impressive still, ordered us to stop.

"Only the messenger may enter," it commanded. "The oracle is for his ears alone."

"I don't like it," I said.

"Do you have any other suggestions?" Genesius asked.

"It could be dangerous."

"I don't think so," Genesius said. "Besides, I rather like their special effects. I wonder how they do that trick."

On hearing the amplified voice, the soldiers stopped in their tracks.

"You'll have to go ahead on your own," Martius said. "None of my men will disobey the god."

Genesius turned again to enter the Didymeum.

"Be careful, my friend," I said. "I will pray for your safety."

"To whom?" Genesius asked. "This is Apollo's territory. Don't make him angry with the wrong prayers." He turned toward the temple, hesitated, then turned back to me.

"That was uncalled for," he said. "Forgive me."

✦ ✦ ✦

Genesius finished climbing the seven steps and walked slowly across the raised stone platform of the *prodomos*. He went under the overhang of the temple's second story and continued in shadow, his bravado now faded with the sunlight. The twenty-foot-high columns flanked his approach, which he made along a walkway of gold filigree inlaid in the stone. At intervals robed priests waited for him. As he passed, each fell in line behind him. Each of the priests seemed identical, as if there had been a single mold from which they were all poured from bronze, all tall, all muscular.

By the time he reached the stairs that led up to the labyrinth, he had an entourage of five men robed in white and gold. At the entrance to the second-story maze they stopped as one.

"Enter," they chorused. The effect was more chilling than comic.

The door was unexceptional—oak, with ordinary iron hinges, rusting from the sea air—and its very ordinariness startled him. One of the priests, he could not tell which, held it open for him. The others crowded at his back, in case he had second thoughts about going through with the ritual.

Before he was quite ready, Genesius found himself propelled

through the door into the blackened labyrinth. He tried to orient himself by locating the door through which he had just been pushed, but all the walls were of rough wood. He hammered on them with his hands but no response came. If he were ever to escape, he would have to complete his mission and hear the message of the oracle, which he already knew. It seemed a stupid situation to be in, risking his sanity, if not his life, to receive a message that was prearranged. But the gods were sneaky. And there was no arguing with them once they settled on a course of action. The only thing a mere human could do was ride it out.

Once he calmed down, he stepped to his left. His foot hovered in empty air and he pulled back reflexively. Left was a trap—just like a trap in a stage floor, and only his acrobat's training saved him from tumbling feet-first into an abyss. More cautiously, he slid his foot along the invisible floor to his right. The floorboards felt somehow wrong; there was too much give in them. He paused in indecision. How wide was the chasm to his left? Could he span it?

He knelt and tried to reach his hand across the gap. It waved in the cool air without touching anything. He stripped off his tunic, stretched out on the floor, head and torso hanging over nothing, and swung the garment forward. It hit the far floor with a satisfying slap. The gap, then, was no more than about six feet wide. Call it eight for good luck. He stood up, threw the tunic over himself, and considered the leap. It would have to be from a standing start; there was no room on the weakened floor behind him to run up to the gap, and besides, he had no way of knowing when he would have to start the jump.

Briefly, Genesius wondered what awaited him on the other side of the gap, whether there would be room to roll when he landed or another trap, of whatever kind. But there was no telling without going there to see. Or feel.

He tucked the hem of his tunic into his belt so that it would not foul his legs. He flooded his lungs with air, willing the muscles in his legs to ready themselves for the effort. A standing jump of eight feet was not a trivial matter. He squatted twice to loosen the muscles and concentrated.

He leaped, legs bent to take the shock of impact—and missed. The ledge caught him squarely in the chest, knocking the air from his lungs. He scrabbled for a handhold as he slid quickly into the empty space. His fingers gripped the edge of the floor. Momentarily, he hung, feet dangling below, kicking wildly for purchase.

Something nibbled his toes.

Without awareness of any transition, he found himself sitting on the ledge he had just been holding with his fingertips. He hated rats; his reflex had saved him. After a few deep breaths to calm his thundering heart, Genesius stood up carefully and went on, moving slowly.

There were no more deadfalls. There were many twistings and turnings to the labyrinth, but it seemed to Genesius that its purpose was more to confuse and humble the seeker than, except for that first trick, to lose him forever. His confidence grew as he traversed the maze.

He bumped into the end of a blind alley. The wall gave way and spilled him down a chute into a place of brilliant light. He picked himself up, squinting against the glare from a burnished ball of gold. He was in the oracular chamber.

"Kneel, mortal, and hear the wisdom of Apollo Didymeus." The voice reverberated through the chamber, echoing from one metallic wall to the other.

The brightness suddenly increased. The whole space glowed with light that pierced his closed eyelids. For Genesius, the world was a brilliant red-gold, nothing but the blood in his tissues keeping him from lucent blindness. With his hands covering his face he opened his eyes. He saw the bones of his hands, suffused with blinding gilt. His eyes began to adjust.

"Mortal," the voice echoed, "prostrate yourself!" Genesius surveyed the chamber. He found the brightest part of the general glow and walked toward it.

"Stop!" the voice echoed. "Kneel before the god!"

Genesius kept walking. The brilliance grew.

"Your blasphemy will be punished."

He could feel the light on his skin, penetrating him to the core. His flesh grew hot.

"Stop! Stop now!" The voice slid up an octave as he kept moving further into the brightness. "If you don't stop, I'll—"

The room fell into relative darkness. Genesius opened his eyes. The great sphere was no longer gold but the color of tarnished brass. The walls were mirrors, with dozens of images of the brass ball. He pushed against the mirror where the voice had come from, without sacrificing his position where he blocked the initial entry of sunlight into the mirrored hall. The panel swung silently on its hinges. Behind it, one of the Branchidae sat, still shouting into his megaphone. The voice still echoed around the chamber's hard surfaces.

"Shall I tell you what you are to tell me?" Genesius asked.

The priest whirled to face him, then cowered in his cubicle. "You can't come in here," he stuttered. "This is blasphemy!"

"You have quite a show here," Genesius said. "If I didn't know a thing or two about the theater, I think it would have taken me in. May I try your megaphone?"

He advanced on the frightened priest, who gave way before him. Genesius put his lips to the megaphone. It was the largest he had ever seen. The sound-carrying tubes must have been run throughout the oracular chamber to produce the rumbling voice of the god.

"Priests of Apollo," he called.

Both Genesius and the priest winced under the waterfall of sound.

"There's no need to shout," the priest said. "It works better if you speak in normal tones."

"Priests of Apollo," Genesius said more softly. He was rewarded with recognizable speech. "Oracles of the god: Your secret has been penetrated by Genesius the actor. If you still have a message for the Emperor Diocletian, now is the time to pass it on to him through me. I shall wait—briefly."

The priest was no longer afraid; the first shock of discovery had passed. He was irritated with Genesius. "You already know the message. Diocletian must go to Rome."

"Why?" Genesius asked.

"The god wills it."

"What god?" Genesius demanded. "Am I to believe that you are Apollo?"

"I speak for him."

"Ox droppings."

"There is a practical reason for Diocletian's journey, as well," the priest said. "He will agree with it, if you report this interview fairly."

"I'm waiting."

"It is political," the priest said. "The trip to Rome is traditional. He has to reaffirm the traditional ways, the traditional beliefs and rites, against the novelties of the Christians. He has to reclaim his place as Pontifex Maximus and make the people believe in him. He must make them follow the Roman gods for the sake of the Roman way, or we will all be lost in mass conversions to the god of the Christians."

"Especially you, priest," Genesius said. "You'll lose your nice little job here and have to work for a living, won't you?"

"Tell him!"

"Oh, I'll tell him," Genesius said. "Everything."

"Tell him this—that Apollo and the other gods will choose a new emperor, if need be one who will show the proper respect to the traditional gods."

"Galerius?" Genesius asked.

"Only if necessary," the priest confirmed. "So you see, while you may have penetrated Apollo's secret, he and his friends still have a few powers."

Genesius left. The pagan gods still had a few surprises for Diocletian.

CHAPTER 19

W e arrived at the palace late in the evening, dirty and worn out by the hard ride. Publius Labius greeted us.

"What did Apollo say?" the eunuch simpered, before we had even had time to dismount our sweating horses. "I so want to see Rome again."

Genesius regarded the greasy little chamberlain from atop his exhausted horse. His buttocks were beyond pain, if the condition of my own was any indication. The ache was a familiar companion, whose presence constantly reminded me that I was still, unfortunately, alive. He swung his leg over the side. "About what was expected," he said.

"But are we going?"

"You'll find out when he wants to tell you," Genesius said. "Where is he?"

"Follow me," Publius Labius said and minced in the direction of the imperial apartments.

Genesius left me and the soldiers to our own devices and followed. I jumped down as fast as my older bones would allow after undergoing the punishment of our hard-pressed journey. They protested but obeyed.

I should explain my antipathy to Publius Labius. He was a character who constantly uncovered his breast to the sword of verbal abuse. I am not proud of my attitude toward the eunuch; he had not chosen his condition, but I was put off by his parody of gender. It was neither an accurate satire of femininity nor a particularly telling comment on masculine behavior. Rather, it was self-demeaning, an invitation to the spectator to abuse him. Most people, both within the court and without, accepted the invitation gleefully. He thought himself smart and witty; most, myself included, saw him as inviting derision and were only too happy to comply. His mask was a useful one, in that it allowed him to be thought harmless and ineffectual, when he was neither.

I followed them to Diocletian's private chamber. Publius Labius was miffed with Diocletian's attempt to dismiss him before hearing Genesius' report.

"But, sire," the eunuch demanded, "if I am to arrange your train for the journey, I must know now whether or not to prepare."

Diocletian grinned wolfishly. "It was decided before their journey, chamberlain. We leave in three days."

"Three days?" Publius Labius exclaimed. "I can never have everything ready in three days. It will take a week just to get the provisions ready. Not to mention the decorations, the imperial banners, new clothing for yourself and the court, the order of the march, and a thousand and one other details. Why, some of the people who must accompany you are out of town—on journeys you yourself sent them on, and—"

"Sire," I said, "the Jewish god—Yahweh is His name—was said to have created the entire world in six days. Surely such an accomplished arranger of things as your new chamberlain can put together a proper entourage for a journey in three."

"It's not poss—"

"I agree, Lactantius," Diocletian said. He turned to Publius Labius. "We leave at dawn, three days from now. We will keep a pace of twenty-five miles per day. The route will be across the Bosporus into

Thrace, thence to Philippi, where we will pick up the Via Egnatia across the Greek peninsula. Once at the Adriatic Sea, we will travel up the coast to Aspalathos, near Salonae, to visit my birthplace. I have a palace under construction there; I want to see how it's coming. From Salonae we shall cross the Adriatic by ship to Ariminum. We shall enter Rome on the Via Flaminia, in the manner of the ancient emperors. We shall give the Romans a show that they will remember forever."

"But I shall never be able to get everything and everyone ready in so short a time, majesty," Publius Labius protested again.

"It will be a military trip," Diocletian said, "not a political journey. The army is always ready to travel. Anyone else you can drum up in three days is welcome to come along." He turned to speak to Genesius, then turned back to Publius Labius. "I shall want all the priests you can come up with, of course."

"Of course."

"Now go," Diocletian said. "If time is so pressing, you must have something else to do than eavesdrop."

"Yes, sire," Labius said. His eyes met Genesius'. "I'll be seeing you later."

"Get out of here!" Diocletian ordered.

Publius Labius scurried from the room.

"Rest yourselves," Diocletian said. "You must be tired after your journey." He poured wine from a golden chalice for both of us. "Sit down. Drink. Then tell me about it."

We reclined on three couches that surrounded the table. Genesius did most of the talking. As we spoke, recounting the journey, Diocletian kept our cups full. Looking back, I see the expert politician at work, setting us at ease, flattering us with personal service by his own hand, but at the time, I accepted it as if it were my due. I was overtired, but Genesius was more alert. He had reached the point in the journey where the Ephesians rioted in the theater. Genesius paused to refill his cup.

I picked up the narrative unthinkingly, describing how we were testing the acoustics in the theater at Ephesus when the mob roared into the auditorium.

"But how did you escape?" Diocletian asked. I realized my error and stuttered meaninglessly. Genesius smoothly intervened.

"We were really in no danger, sire," he said. "No matter where, a theater is a theater. We went underground."

"Underground?"

"Into the passages, below the altar at the center of the orchestra."

"But how did you know they were there?" Diocletian asked.

"Every theater has them," Genesius said, "so that the Furies in Aeschylus' *Eumenides* can appear as if out of the earth. It was simple enough to wait until the Artemisians were through with their worship. I understand that they took a couple of Christians, though. It couldn't have been a pretty sight. Martius was quite furious with us when we showed up hours later."

"I can imagine he was," Diocletian said. "He is a good soldier. Then what?"

"Then we went straight to Didyma."

"And?"

"It's a fake." Genesius poured himself another flagon. "Cunningly enough set up. They blind you with reflected sunlight and magnify the voice in the same way that the Greek actors used to do." He looked closely at Diocletian. "They wanted to impress me with their gadgets, but their message was quite impressive enough, shorn of the special effects. They threatened to have the gods themselves rise against you if you fail to exterminate the Christians."

"How?"

"I am sure that the Branchidae are in communication with the hierarchies of the other major gods. I believe that they will, if you fail, denounce you as a traitor and an atheist and name Galerius as the legitimate emperor in your place."

"That ungrateful son of a she-wolf!" Diocletian said. "I know he wants my throne—he'd be useless if he weren't aggressive—but to plot against me with the priests, when I am Pontifex Maximus!" Diocletian threw his golden cup against the wall, but it hit a thick tapestry, and the effect was spoiled—a muffled thud and a gush of red against the fabric were all that his rage produced.

"I am being forced into an untenable position," Diocletian said, "where they think they have me trapped. But twenty years of this"—he gripped his purple robe—"have left me still in possession of a trick or two."

Genesius stripped off his leather armor. Underneath, he wore the battle underwear of a Roman soldier. He removed it as well and used it to mop up the wine that dripped from the tapestry.

"Stand up!" Diocletian ordered. Genesius continued to mop. "Please, friend, do not do this for me," Diocletian said. "It is not fitting."

What possessed me, I do not even now know. It was as if the Lord

Christ tapped me on the shoulder and showed me the verse from His gospel: *Love your enemies, do good to them that hate you.* I put my arm around the shoulders of Diocletian as if he were a hurt boy. He started to shake me off angrily, then our eyes met, and I saw his fill to overflowing with tears. They tracked down his face, diverted from their straight course by the wrinkles of his age. He gave a shuddering wordless cry and buried his face in my shoulder. I encircled him with my arms and held him close as he sobbed out the acknowledgment of yet another betrayal.

He had grown old.

✦ ✦ ✦

"I thought that I would take a part in your play. After all, if an unlettered street urchin can do it, I thought to myself, so can I! And here I am."

Diarius had pleaded with Genesius not to object to the addition of Publius Labius to the troupe or at least not to object out loud.

"What a pleasant surprise," Genesius said. "This must be what you were hinting at."

"You're so perceptive."

"It's a gift, but thank you," Genesius said. "What about your duties as chamberlain? Will you have time for all the many items you must tend to?"

Publius Labius smiled and waved a hand, as if to say that if one were sufficiently accomplished and organized, one could do anything one pleased. Seeing the gesture, and the smile that accompanied it, Genesius grudgingly admitted to himself that the man could handle his role well enough. He bowed ever so slightly to Publius Labius, then pointedly turned away.

"Don't trouble yourselves on my account," Labius said. "I quite understand. My position here is somewhat anomalous. I am the outsider, and I have forced my way into your little group by virtue of my rank in the emperor's household. Naturally, resentment arises."

Publius Labius was dangerous. He had insinuated himself into the acting company, which had been, until now, safe ground for Genesius, a haven peopled by colleagues whose minds and habits had been shaped, as had his own, by the craft of acting, who shared the common bond of the performer. Acting was, for Genesius, more than the means by which he earned his daily bread; it was the way in which he came to understand the world and make a rough sort of sense out of it. To have his haven breached by an outsider, in all likelihood an informer, was intolerably painful. His weapons were few, only the tools of his craft. Given Publius Labius' position, he could not simply be ordered out, nor could Genesius harass him until he broke. He already knew that behind the mask of false femininity lay in wait a carnivorous beast whose preferred food was the human being. Publius Labius could not be broken—not by humiliation nor by failure. He would have to be understood.

Diarius introduced the new actors. The first was a young boy, barely into his teens, blonde and blue-eyed, who carried the name of Riotamus and would play the acolyte in the baptism play. He shrank away from Publius Labius, who stared at him with libidinous fascination.

The other was a middle-aged hack who used the name Janus, whose work Genesius knew. They had already acted together, though in the past it was Janus who had played the leading parts and Genesius who played the spear carrier. Now their roles were reversed. Janus was politely distant at the introduction, as if he himself were the principal actor still.

Janus had never been kind to those who worked under him. He was a perfectionist in his demands on others, though not on himself, and he blamed others for his failures. Genesius remembered one incident in which Janus had gone up on his lines during a performance of Euripides' *Ion*, before the provincial governor. Janus had thundered about the stage, ad-libbing lines from *The Bacchae*, from *Medea*, even from Plautus' comedy *The Menaechmi*, before another actor had brought the play back on track by giving Janus' proper speech, until he recognized it himself and picked up the action. After the performance Janus had raged at the actor who had helped him, making accusations of upstaging and stealing focus. The helpful actor now worked as a property man, building fake daggers and wheeled beds and such, happy still to be allowed to work near the stage, although Janus' influence was enough to keep him from ever again obtaining a role.

"Nice to work with you again, my boy," Janus said. His tone was arch, superior, as if he were the star. Genesius nodded, then looked back to Publius Labius. These two would get along well together, he thought.

"Now, the first order of business is to get everyone measured for the new costumes," Diarius said. "We have less than six weeks to have everything ready for the vicennalia performance. We want it to look just right, so we have to give Aristarchus plenty of time."

Hysteria bubbled forward with a measuring tape. "Aristarchus is working on the designs right now. Everything is going to be made brand new. He asked me to get your sizes. Who's first?"

Publius Labius stepped to her. "To the ministrations of this fair lady, I submit myself—if I may be allowed to assist her after my own measure is taken."

Riotamus saw what was coming. He must not have been quite as young, quite as guileless, as he looked.

Diocletian had ordered a purely military expedition for the journey to Rome. But bureaucracies are not biddable; they have their own ways of doing things, their own sense of direction. Publius Labius constructed a logistical miracle in three days.

The court was a flurry of activity. Within three hours, Publius Labius sent out riders along the proposed route to arrange for caches of supplies and proper welcomes at each of the cities the imperial entourage would pass through. In Nicomedia and its environs for fifty miles around, wagons and draft animals were commandeered by the praetorian guard for the use of the emperor's train. Those who would be going along—the list was prepared by Publius Labius and updated daily for the three days before the journey began—found themselves battling each other and the troops for the choicest supplies and bits of jewelry and festive clothing for the trip. Blacksmiths' hammers clanged throughout the city; before the three days were through, three men had been hanged by the authorities for theft of strategic materials—nails and horseshoes. Shopkeepers doubled their prices on the day the news of the trip came out, then tripled and finally quadrupled them, and those who were going along gladly paid. It was as if the city, recognizing that it was losing the emperor and all the trade that followed in his wake, were storing up for a long, cold winter. If the emperor left, he might never return.

I had no duties during the period of preparation. As an official of the court I had only to bring my tools, myself, and what few clothes I owned. My packing was the desultory task of an hour. When it was done, I escaped the frenzied activity of the palace. I knew that the actors would be in like condition. Their packing, while more substantial than my own, would be attended to by slaves. Genesius would be free.

The fall air was chill, but it did nothing to lessen the cacophony of the city's preparations. Nicomedia buzzed with speculation, speculation on two issues. The first concerned the politics of the journey; the second was financial. Rumor afflicted both. As we walked I felt a palpable tension in the very air that surrounded us. Through it, I led Genesius to the former site of the church, where we had first met at Easter. I was anxious to know his state of mind, especially concerning the hope I had of bringing him to knowledge of the faith. In his position as confidant to Diocletian, his possible conversion was of strategic importance. I felt some shame at so brazen a manipulation but not enough to stop my intention, merely sufficient to make me a little uncomfortable. The baptismal mosaic seemed a useful setting for my purpose.

"We are not here by accident," Genesius said. "For all the time you have spent in the court, old man, you lack subtlety."

"It may be that you have learned it," I retorted, ashamed to have been seen through so easily.

He paced the circular border of the mosaic, staring into its center, twining around the bench where I sat. "I know what you want, in any case," he said.

My pretense was innocence. I should have known better than to attempt to out-act him, but foolishness is incurable. "What do I want?"

"You want me to become a Christian," he said.

"There are worse things you could be."

"You see before you," Genesius said, "an actor. You know what your own apologist, Tertullian, said of my trade."

I was taken aback. Genesius had done some reading on his own. I wondered what else he had done without my knowledge.

"Tertullian had no love for the theaters," I admitted.

"He hated them." Genesius' pacing became more rapid. "He would burn them down, tear them apart. He was a pleasure-hating old fool, a fanatic. If Tertullian were emperor of Rome, he would persecute the pagans as surely as Diocletian persecutes the Christians. So I ask myself—why trade one persecution for another?"

Genesius had, I saw, come up against the ascetic side of the faith. As an actor he was repelled, of course. He spent his life to bring pleasure, and to the ascetics, like Tertullian, pleasure was a snare of the devil. Tertullian became an extreme ascetic during the course of his life, even to the point of joining the Montanists, a sect now known to be heretical in its renunciation of the world. Did not God Himself say, at the conclusion of each of the days of creation, "It is good"? And if God's created world is good in His eyes, is it not a sin to renounce what He made, to refuse the good things He gave us?

"Your fear is out of date," I said. "That was a heresy, and it was put down a century ago."

"Is that what happens to people who disagree with Holy Mother Church?" Genesius said. "What will happen if you ever come into political power?"

As I understood the faith then I did not think such a thing possible, and I said so. "The best we hope for is toleration, an end to the persecutions forever."

Genesius traced the frozen drops of water in the mosaic with his forefinger. "I have been reading," he said, teasing me with hope.

Like a fish, instead of a fisher of men, I took the bait. "In the Scripture?"

"Yes," he said. "And I find things that don't fit together. Jesus is supposed to have said that he was going to establish the kingdom of God. When and where? 'Before this generation passes away' is what he said. Where is it?"

I could not answer him. His questions were logical and reasonable, but faith is not a matter of logic and reason, not in its core. Reason is a tool to explore the workings of God in the world, but it cannot convince the skeptic in and of itself. And yet, his questions were themselves signs that I should not give up on him. He was interested enough to read and to question, but he was not asking to be convinced. Even Saint Paul did not reason his way to God. Only a Plato, I suspect, might manage that.

"Let's walk," I suggested. "It's too cold to sit still." We walked for some minutes before Genesius spoke again. We wrapped our cloaks against a chill and damp wind that had blown in from the north. Our steps took us into the face of the wind until we reached the docks. There, looking out to the sea, Genesius stopped.

"Where is she?"

"Who?"

"The woman I spoke to in Ephesus," he said. "What happened to her?"

"I do not know."

He hunched his head into the folds of the cloak's hood. "She is a Christian, isn't she?"

"I'm sure of it," I answered.

"'Not a single sparrow falls.'"

"No, not one."

"Would he take care of her? As he says he would?"

"Yes."

"But two died. Martius said so."

"Two died."

"Did he stop caring for them?" Still his voice came from within the cloak's hood. I could not see his face. "They were torn limb from limb by that mob."

At last he had raised an objection that I could answer! More, it came not from his intellect but from his heart.

"He was with them," I said. "He, too, died after torture and humiliation. He cared for those two beyond the end."

"Then I want no part of your Christ!" Genesius said. His face was distorted in pain. "He stands by with idle hands while his followers are hurt. Even Galerius, as barbaric as he is, repays his supporters fairly. He doesn't abandon them to death. What kind of leader is your Christ?"

"They are with Him now," I said. But I knew that nothing I could say now would convince him. He was afraid for the young woman, who had seemed to care for him.

"And they are all dead." The raw wind ripped the words from his throat. He was convinced that the young woman in Ephesus was one of the two who had died.

If she were dead, how could I tell him that she was still alive in Christ? I can only bring myself to hope that is the truth; I cannot know it in the way I know that the sun will rise tomorrow. And, not knowing, how could I, in all honesty, claim the authority to tell him?

I know that I must believe otherwise for the sake of my immortal soul. But when Genesius called them dead, all I felt was absence, a chill void that took all the warmth from me. I believe in Jesus' promises, but sometimes, I confess, their reality seems distant, almost hypothetical. I would pay a great price to know, rather than simply to believe.

I hoped that if they met again she would be kind to him, but the wind was cold.

+ + +

The three days were accomplished; the imperial journey was about to begin.

Before dawn, all of the sojourners were contained in the courtyard.

The actors would travel in the middle of the vast procession, which numbered over two thousand people, including servants, soldiers, bureaucrats, scribes, cooks, accountants, acrobats, musicians, cobblers, armorers, officials, members of noble families, advisers, physicians, jewelers, merchants, souvenir vendors (for the crowds that were sure to gather along the route of march), priests of a dozen gods (among them several of the Branchidae who were to monitor the emperor's actions in the name of all the old gods—bronzed, blonde, youthful creatures who strutted among the people of the entourage with Apollonian arrogance), dealers in wines and sweetmeats, grooms for the horses, wheelwrights, blacksmiths, masseurs, gamblers, whores, porters, parasites, poor relations, couriers, pets, caged fowl, cattle, goats, sheep, hogs, hairdressers, cosmeticians, spies for a dozen factions involved in the empire's ongoing intrigues, washerwomen, the odd sorcerer here and there, astrologers, fortune-tellers, mistresses, gigolos following obediently behind their matrons, personal bodyguards. The social and political lives of the travelers would scarcely be interrupted by their travel.

The field on which they were marshalled smelled of dozens of different varieties of perfume, sweat, and dung.

The actors waded through their fellow travelers until they reached their wagon. It carried most of the properties they would need for the production of the baptism play, even though the script was not yet finished. Genesius was again assigned to write the scenario and much of the dialogue, but had had to delay the actual writing because of his trip to see the oracle at Didyma and the preparations for the journey. The wagon also carried the tents, cots, clothing, food supplies, and makeup to be used in the production and on the road. Diarius had designed the cart, making it as much like that of the inventor of acting, Thespis, as possible from the fragmentary records left of ancient Greece. Horace claimed that Thespis went from town to town in old Attica, riding in his cart, and at each town where he stopped trained a chorus for the production of a tragedy. There were others, though, who believed that Thespis was a comic actor, who rode in his cart through each town he visited hurling scurrilous verses at the inhabitants. The actors preferred the latter story.

Somehow the confused mass of humanity and animality found its form. With the sounding of trumpets, the creak of straining lumber, the rumble of ironclad wheels on stone cobbles, the neighing of horses, the bleating of sheep and goats, the chatter of travelers, the clatter of armor and weapons, the barked orders of officers, and the lowing of the cattle, the head of the procession, the first cohort of the praetorian guard, bearing the eagles of the empire on their standards, set foot on the road to Rome.

Prisca had kept to herself for months, barely venturing from her chamber, coming out into the open air only to escape the flames from the palace's near-destruction. Galerius' hurried departure on the night of the second fire had swept Valeria away from her mother's side. Prisca worried incessantly about her daughter's safety with Galerius but was powerless to affect matters; Diocletian refused to see her. But her presence was a ceremonial necessity during all the events connected with her husband's vicennalia. Therefore, she rode in her own carriage, immediately behind that of Diocletian. No messengers passed between them. But, like a proper Roman matron, she was present for the sake of her husband's honor.

The sun split the horizon just as the standard-bearer's foot touched pavement. Applause swept back into the field, the travelers congratulating themselves on the auspicious beginning of the journey. The cheer swelled around the wagon in which Diocletian rode, itself surrounded by a full cohort of the praetorian guard. These days, he would have no other bodyguard than those soldiers sworn to loyalty to his person alone. He remained within, refusing to expose himself to the mob of reveling travelers. Since the fires and the purges, he had trusted no one but Genesius, half a dozen picked troops, and Martius the centurion. He had lived an agony of fear during the absence of both Martius and Genesius but had been unwilling to send the young actor on the journey to Didyma without the protection of an officer of proven loyalty. Two cohorts of troops, numbering in total about nine hundred men, had gone ahead the day before to clear bandits from the route.

CHAPTER 21

Genesius looked back in wonder. Asia lay three miles behind him across a narrow strip of seawater. He had survived the crossing in a small boat and had now come out of Asia; Europe stretched westward from his feet. It was a thought to confuse the mind.

He had never been on the sea before. The ferry had moved under his feet, rolling on the swell that surged through the Bosporus past the once-noble city of Byzantium. His stomach was still unsettled from the unaccustomed movements, his head still swirling, when he felt a commanding hand on his shoulder. He whirled in alarm, his nerves strung too tightly for slower movement. The hands of the sea captain he had met in Ephesus steadied him.

"A touch of seasickness?" he said.

Genesius nodded, holding the sickness back with clenched teeth.

"Let's walk a bit," the captain said. "You'll have your land legs back in a little while." Still holding Genesius by the arm, as if the actor were blind and needed guidance, he led him away from the confused herd of travelers beached on the shore of Europe into a grove of trees at the base of one of the seven hills of Byzantium. It was the end of the second day of Diocletian's journey from Nicomedia to Rome.

Byzantium was a small city, incapable of accommodating the train that went with the emperor. It had been conquered and reconquered through the ages, but always with difficulty. There was only one approach by land; its conquerors had all been sea powers. It was an attractive prize because its promontories commanded the gateway between Europe and Asia.

The travelers planned to camp out for the night. In the morning they would set out along the Via Egnatia, the great road that led westward across the Greek peninsula. For the moment they were at relative liberty.

Within the grove it was already night. "I am trying to locate Lactantius, the rhetor," the captain said as soon as they were alone. "Where is he?"

Genesius had his own question. "Where is the girl?"

"What girl?"

"In Ephesus—the dark-haired girl who read from your scriptures. I have to find her."

"She's not for you, lad. God has got her."

"Will he share?" Genesius asked.

The captain raised his outsized hand as if to strike Genesius but stopped the blow before it landed. Genesius slipped the captain's grasp and retreated to the opposite side of the tiny clearing. He was out of reach but only barely.

"Do all Christians resort to force so quickly?"

The captain stopped in mid-lunge, nearly toppling to the ground. The sailor's balance was so tenuously held that Genesius stepped in and steadied him; the captain's arms went around the actor, and they danced spasmodically around the little clearing. Genesius looked into the captain's face as they struggled for stability and saw a twinkle of amusement. He giggled; the captain laughed in response, and they fell to the ground, dissolved in mirth.

"I'm sorry," the captain gasped.

"So am I," Genesius laughed. "I'll never say that to someone your size again."

"What you said was irreverent."

"I am irreverent. It's my job," Genesius said. "Where is she?"

"Not here."

"You already said that."

"If you are supposed to find her, you will," the captain replied.

"Why are you Christians always saying things like that?" Genesius said.

"Like what?"

"'If you're supposed to find her, you will.' Things like that." Genesius folded his arms and waited.

"It's obvious, isn't it?" the captain said.

"Not to me."

The captain was incredulous. "God loves you—" he began what promised to be a long explanation but suddenly stood up.

"Someone's coming."

"Who?" Genesius clambered to his feet just as two muffled figures entered the darkness of the little clearing.

"My lord," the sailor said, bowing. He elbowed Genesius, who also bowed, although he did not know to whom.

"Is this the one?" The voice was familiar.

"This is the actor. I have not found the historian as yet," the captain said.

"Never mind. We have already spoken with him." The voice teased at Genesius' memory. The second person did not speak. "You may go."

"As you wish." Again bowing, the captain left the clearing. The two masked people separated and walked to either side of the actor. The one whose voice he had heard before wore a dagger; both wore fine clothing. The second was a woman, a Roman matron.

"So this is his son," she said.

The man's voice was comforting. "Look at your daughter. What would have happened to a legitimate male child?"

"Under Galerius?" she said. "It's not even worth the asking. It's better this way, but still—"

"The longing is there."

She touched her breast. "Here."

Genesius knew who they were. "Augusta, who might have been my mother." He knelt in front of Prisca.

She stepped back convulsively. "Don't touch me!"

Genesius maintained his position. "Have you told him?"

Prisca retreated from him, until she backed up against the gnarled trunk of one of the ancient trees that surrounded the trio.

"The last thing we want is your death," the man said.

"I wouldn't mind," Prisca whispered.

"No!" Constantine insisted. "He may be part of the solution."

Genesius, still on his knees, realized that he was caught up in something more than he wanted. If others knew of his parentage, more would soon find out. He regretted ever having mentioned it to Lactantius. The rhetor's confidence was worth what he had given to ensure it—nothing. The gods alone knew how many others knew and how long the news would take to reach Galerius. Everyone knew how long Galerius would hesitate to eliminate someone who might stand between himself and the purple, no matter how unlikely an obstacle. He was risking everything; they were in Galerius' territory now, and Constantine, once held hostage for the good behavior of his father in Britain, having escaped, remained in the danger zone.

"Why are you here?" Genesius asked.

"Don't ask," he replied. "It is better that you don't know."

"It was better," Genesius said, getting to his feet, "that no one knew about me. But I have been compromised by the man I trusted. And by you. Let me see your face."

"So far, you have not seen me."

"Do you think I see only with my eyes? I hear the command in your voice, I feel the expectation of obedience you radiate in all directions, as if you were aflame with authority. I can barely bring myself to speak to you, except that you threaten me and that I want to know the truth. What do you want from me, Lord Constantine?"

"You have your father's grasp of politics," Constantine said.

"I live at the court. An understanding of power is a survival trait."

"So it is." Constantine hesitated.

"Tell him!" Prisca hissed. "Why do you waste time?"

"Time is our ally," Constantine said. "If I must, I will wait ten, twenty years. I will not be rushed into events beyond my control."

"Your father is not well," she insisted.

"If not in my father's time," Constantine said, "then in mine. When the time is ripe, we will act." The prince turned to Genesius. "In some ways, the Augusta is right. You cannot act effectively in ignorance. But we might as well sit down. It is not a short story."

"I've heard enough," Genesius said. He turned to go. The two made no attempt to stop him, and he was perversely disappointed by their inaction, until he blundered noisily through the brush into the arms of an armed and armored soldier. The man was short and heavily muscled. He did not draw his sword on Genesius, but neither did he let the actor pass.

"I'm afraid you cannot get by, sir." His accent was foreign, though his meaning was clear enough. "You'll have to hear him out."

Genesius turned to try another route. Shadowy forms barred his way through the trees. Silhouetted by the campfires on the plain beyond the grove, he could see the figures of the entourage, eating, drinking, arguing, talking. He could even hear their voices and the clatter of the supper dishes, and, from somewhere to his left, a singer.

"Please don't call out, sir," the trooper whispered. "I'd be sad to have to silence you. Why don't you just accept what has to be?" Genesius nodded. There was no escape from the grove. He returned to Constantine and Prisca.

Constantine picked up the thread of the conversation as if Genesius had never tried to leave.

"I am troubled by dreams and visions," he said. "I have no taste for what your father is doing. It will destroy the empire if it goes on unchecked. There are too many Christians to be eliminated, and I am afraid that their god is too active in the world to let the persecution continue indefinitely. I am myself a son of one of the Pharaoh's lieutenants, and the plagues are nearly upon us. Like Pilate's wife, I have dreams—nightmares of what is coming. Diocletian can give forth decrees on the advice of Galerius, but still the comets fly their courses, the moon waxes and wanes, and the nature of the people changes according to some law not made by human minds. That change, which has been centuries in coming, is here. Diocletian resists passively, Galerius in panicky terror. They both might as well command the tides to stop their ebb and flow.

"I have been a student of history," Constantine went on, "and history has a tidal rhythm. The Greeks once put colonies in the Latin heartland; now Athens itself is a client of Rome and has been for most of its existence. Alexander crossed this strait"—he waved his hand vaguely eastward—"to conquer the Persians and even India. Where are they now? Diocletian and Galerius are both wrong; they share a delusion that it can all be put back 'right,' whatever that means. But time doesn't work that way. Once you dam a stream, the water backs up, deeper and deeper, until it threatens to overflow the dam. So the engineer must build the dam higher, and the process is repeated. The engineer may be talented, perhaps even a genius, and conscientious workers may build his dam well, but the flow continues, filling in all the low places with the water of time, drowning trees and farms and villages, even great cities. Sooner or later, the dam is bound to break. The original engineer dies and a lesser craftsman takes his place. Or one of the workers gets sick, and does his job haphazardly, leaving a flaw, a weakness in the dam's structure. Or an earthquake loosens the dam from its moorings at the choke point. It doesn't matter what; something gives way. Everything downstream is swept to rubble. An empire vanishes; another takes its place.

"But a man can ease the pressure behind the dam, open a sluice gate, and let the water out a little at a time. Perhaps, with luck and care, he can prevent the catastrophe of a flood. I don't know whether the Christians' god is what they say he is. But the dam that Diocletian and Galerius have built cannot hold. Something is making the people change throughout the world, and the pressure is building. I think that this new god is at the center of the change. Nero, Domitian, and Decius tried to exterminate him and failed."

Constantine fell silent, his argument finished.

"You too would betray him," Genesius said. "And you want my help."

"It's not a betrayal we want," Constantine argued. "Convince him. Change his mind. You have access. He trusts you."

"Because I ask nothing of him."

"You have saved his life," Prisca said. "He is not ungrateful. He might listen to you."

Genesius knew otherwise. Diocletian had based his reign on achieving his own goals, not those of others. Such a man was not easily manipulated, even in his old age. His distrust had grown since the beginning of the persecution; he trusted no one except Genesius, and that trust existed only because the actor had thus far demanded nothing of the emperor. Diocletian would take any request from Genesius as the betrayal.

The old man's love was fragile. Genesius said as much.

"We have it from your friend Lactantius that you are very close to becoming a Christian yourself," Prisca urged. "How can you ignore the suffering of your brethren?"

"Then my 'friend' has it wrong," Genesius exploded. "I am not a Christian; I am an actor. Nothing else."

Genesius heard distant voices raised in alarm. Constantine and Prisca either ignored or failed to hear them.

"Don't you care?" Prisca said.

"It's not a question of caring," Genesius said. "I have no influence over him."

"But you perform those awful plays," Prisca countered, "and they make the people hate the Christians. They incite them to the persecutions."

"I poke fun at the stupidities of the Christians, yes," Genesius answered. "None of what I do incites harm. Others mock the pagan gods—Diana, Venus, Mars, even Jupiter himself. What I do is what entertains. It so happens that there are many stupidities in your Christian belief. How could anyone with an ounce of brains believe that a virgin could give birth? What kind of sense does it make for forgiveness to be offered to someone's evil deeds when he saves them all up until he is at the point of death, and then—and only then—decides that it's time to be good?"

"Now see here—" Constantine began. But whatever he was going to say was lost. The sailor crashed into the clearing.

"Someone saw you, my lord, and reported it to the praetorian guard. The alarm will sound at any moment. You must escape—now, while you have the chance! And you, Augusta, must return to your tent unseen. The soldiers are already searching."

"You say that a general alarm has not been given?"

"Not yet," the captain said.

"What can we do?" Constantine asked.

"Your disguise is inadequate," Genesius said. He did not want to help them so much as he felt the actor's need to tinker with a scenario badly conceived. Talented politicians Constantine and Prisca might be. As actors, even amateurs, they had a claim on his assistance. "Amateurish. It looks like a disguise."

"That's what it is."

"You come here with a squad of soldiers surrounding you. No disguise can work under those circumstances."

Genesius peered through the brush into the camp. There was more movement. From the tents and campfires came a murmur of anxiety. Something was wrong in the camp; everyone in the imperial entourage was experienced in the ways of the court, capable of reading the change in rhythms caused by the most discreet action of the emperor and his guard. No change in the general situation would pass unnoticed. The only factor on the side of Constantine and Prisca was darkness.

"Take off your clothes," Genesius ordered Constantine.

"What?" Constantine had not been given a peremptory order in years.

"Strip," Genesius said. "We're going to turn you into a madman. If you are naked, everyone will look at your private parts; no one will see your face."

"But it's cold!" Constantine objected.

"It's colder in the grave," the captain offered. "I think the actor is right. Send your guards on ahead; they'll only draw attention to you. Have them meet you somewhere outside the camp perimeter."

Constantine hesitated. "Everything?"

"Down to the skin," Genesius said. "The one thing no one will expect is a naked prince."

Constantine whistled three warbling notes; the commander of his guard appeared through the trees. Constantine took him aside to confer. While they argued, Genesius turned to Prisca.

"If you think I will go naked through the camp, think again," she said.

"Nevertheless, lady, you are in a dangerous position," the captain said. He moved into the trees to keep a lookout.

"Your clothing is too fine," Genesius said, "and too clean. A prostitute might have been given fine clothing by one of her customers, but she wouldn't wear it like an empress. Difficult as it is, my lady, you must be made repulsive." Without waiting for consent, he disheveled her hair and her dress, making her look as if she had hurriedly covered herself after a scene of debauchery.

"I must be a mess," Prisca complained.

"Quite, but we're not finished yet." Genesius spat into his hands and gathered a handful of soil to make a small mudpie.

"What are you doing?" she wailed.

"Making you invisible. Hold still." Immobilizing her head with one hand, Genesius drew on his art to create a portrait of an old courtesan, using mud as makeup, his fingers as brushes. The empress of Rome stood transformed.

"There!" Genesius said. "Your own mother would cross the street to avoid you."

Constantine finally had to order his soldiers away from the little grove. He turned to see Prisca and laughed.

"I'm glad you appreciate my work," Genesius said. "Get out of your clothes." Prisca turned her back. While Constantine stripped, Genesius explained his plan.

"Prince, you and this courtesan have been dallying here in the wood. Her 'employer' pulled the badger game on you. You escaped, but just barely. The experience has been so humiliating that you are, temporarily, insane with shame. You won't tell anyone who you are—you'll simply shriek something along these lines: 'O Venus, how you have trapped me!' Some kind of lament. Make it loud, make it absurd, and keep moving to your rendezvous. When you get outside the perimeter, keep up the role—there may be patrols beyond the camp."

Genesius turned to Prisca. Her face was set in a grimace of revulsion.

"I can imagine what I must look like," she said.

"Good!" Genesius answered. "That will help." He took her hands in his. "I beseech you, put aside your anger with me. You must not be found here. Remember what you must look like: a mud-daubed whore, turned out by your customer who threw your fee into a mud puddle. You're angry, you're disgusted, but you have your fee, and you'll eat well for a few days. People will laugh at you, but you will hold your head high and go about your business."

"How am I to get back to my tent?"

"The same way you got out—without being seen," Genesius said. "How is your problem."

The captain emerged from the brush. "They're coming this way, like beaters during a hunt. They're flushing everything in their path."

Genesius regarded the two characters he had created. "Don't run away from them. That's how they'll identify you. Blunder into the line. Stay in character—Go!"

The empress and the prince stepped out into the moonlight.

"They are taking a great risk," the captain observed.

"They take a bigger risk staying," Genesius said, "as do we. We need a reason for being here." The beaters were moving closer. The reason had to be sufficient to explain their presence without raising suspicion among the searchers.

"Sit!" Genesius ordered, doing so himself, "at my side."

The captain bridled at the suggestion. "That's insane!"

"I know. That's what will make it work." The beaters' noise was in the grove now, but they were slowed by the underbrush.

"I am not afraid," the captain said in a whisper. "They can torture me if they want to."

Genesius had no time for argument. He scissored his legs and brought the sea captain down hard. As the sailor fell Genesius met his jaw with his fist. The captain hit the ground unconscious. By the time the beaters arrived the captain was apparently asleep, Genesius sitting cross-legged at his side.

A handful of soldiers burst into the clearing, swords at the ready. Behind them came the imperial chamberlain.

"What have we here?" Publius Labius sneered. The troops joined in his laughter at Genesius and the sea captain.

Genesius smiled, as if he were keeping a secret.

"I'll see you later, little friend," Publius Labius said. "Be sure of it." Then he was gone, catlike through the brush.

CHAPTER 22

Genesius patted the captain's face, who gradually woke up to see Genesius' visage looming above his eyes. As consciousness returned, he realized where he lay and leaped to his feet.

"What are you doing?" the captain cried.

"There was no time to argue. They were right here. Now we have to get moving ourselves. How do you feel?"

The captain wiggled his jaw. "So, actors can fight?"

"When there's no alternative," Genesius said. He stood up and brushed the dirt off his clothing. "Another costume shot. Diarius will be furious, as usual."

"What do we do now?" The captain had passed leadership to Genesius.

"I don't know about you," Genesius said, "but I shall go and find something to eat." He started into the brush.

"Wait," the captain said. "We still have to—"

"We have nothing left to do. You're lucky I didn't turn you in to the soldiers. You have involved me in an act of treason, and all I want is to be rid of you." Genesius again turned to go.

"Her name is Lydia," the captain said. Genesius halted, waiting.

"She is in Philippi," the captain said. "Against all sense, she is waiting for you."

"Why?" Genesius' voice was hoarse, his throat suddenly tight.

"God knows," the sailor said in exasperation. "You're so pig-headed you can't admit what the rest of us see clearly. So take my warning: Lydia is a Christian. She has formed some perverse fascination for you, God knows why, and it is tearing her apart. She's young; when she's older, she'll know better, but who can talk to a young girl? She loves you, fool."

Genesius found it impossible to speak. Love meant betrayal, abandonment. His tongue pressed against his palate. Love meant imprisonment. His jaws clenched against each other so that his teeth ached. Love was an impossibility. He could not speak.

"It tears at her because you will not admit to yourself that you must confess that you are a Christian. And because she is one, she must not love you. You are a persecutor of the brethren. To love you is to betray her other love." The captain grew angrier as he explained. "She has told me that when she goes to the prisons where the saints are kept for trial, to encourage them and help them remain steadfast, she sees your face and thinks of you. Then she is tortured by guilt, because she ignores the suffering of those who are caught. The inquisitor's face becomes your face, and it is you she sees ordering the deaths of the martyrs, you she sees releasing the lions from their cages, you who hone the sword, incite the mob to cry for the blood of the innocent. Get out of my sight!"

Genesius slipped from the grove of trees, back into the illusive normality of the emperor's camp. All around him were shadows.

✦ ✦ ✦

On the next night's stop Genesius explained the baptismal rite to the rest of the actors. At Diarius' insistence he had called the first rehearsal even though he had not yet finished the script. Three days of travel had left the actors irritable and testy. On the third night, somewhere between Byzantium and Perinthus on the coast of

Thrace, Riotamus drove the actors' wagon away from the main encampment to a place where they could enjoy privacy for their rehearsal. Even Publius Labius was there, although he grumbled half-heartedly about being kept away from his official duties.

"There's no help for it, sir," Diarius pleaded. "You knew that we would rehearse on the road when you took the role. We absolutely must have the production ready when we reach Rome."

"Those were your own orders," Hysteria sniffed.

"Can we get on with this?" Janus asked. It was to be his only contribution to the rehearsal. Riotamus, the apprentice, sat wide-eyed at Hysteria's side; she kept a protective arm around him, glaring fiercely at Publius Labius whenever his gaze rested on the youth.

"Baptism is the Christian initiation ritual," Genesius began. "In it, a priest either sprinkles the new Christian, or catechumen, with water or dunks him into it."

"Sounds like drowning," Publius Labius interjected. "Did you know that when a man is hanged, he—"

"Must you?" Hysteria said.

Publius Labius smiled at Genesius, his eyes glittering. "I wonder if anything like that happens when one drowns?"

"Baptism is only administered," Genesius said, "after a three-year period of preparation, unless the candidate is near death. In that case, the usual restrictions can be waived so that he doesn't die in what the Christians call a 'state of sin,' that is, with all his misdeeds still unforgiven by Christ. During those three years, the other Christians watch his behavior and instruct him in what they call orthodoxy, or 'right belief.'"

It was not only Publius Labius' palpable lust that unsettled Genesius, but also the odor of danger that hung in the air around the chamberlain. His thrill, Genesius sensed, came from hurt, corruption, and degradation.

"The essential formula for baptism demands the use of water and the words 'I baptize you in the name of the Father, and the Son, and the Holy Spirit.' Oddly enough, it can be given, in dire emergency, by a non-Christian, if the candidate is in mortal danger and sincerely desires baptism."

"Do you mean to say," Publius Labius leered, "that if I came across you lying on the ground, bleeding to death, I could perform a baptism?"

Genesius chose not to take the bait. "Yes. And in the eyes of the church, it would be valid, as long as the intent was sincere on both sides."

"How delicious!"

Diarius, seeing the direction the discussion was taking, jumped in to sidetrack the growing animosity. "Well, there's our play then—deathbed conversion! That is what you had in mind—isn't it, Genesius?—and we need to get on with it."

"Yes, of course," Genesius said.

"Well, then," Diarius said, "I think we've done all we can do tonight. Riotamus, let's go back to camp."

The company clambered aboard the wagon, with the exception of Genesius.

"I think I'll walk back," Genesius said. "I can use a little fresh air."

Publius Labius met his eyes.

"I think I'll join you." He slipped to the ground. "I need some exercise myself."

Riotamus took up the reins, a smile spreading over his features. Publius Labius slapped the near horse smartly. The wagon moved off, the light of its lantern growing swiftly smaller in the growing darkness. In moments, they were alone.

"If you leave me unmarked," Publius Labius said, "I will do the same for you."

Just before the waning moon vanished into the clouds, Genesius saw its light reflected in a gleam of steel.

✦ ✦ ✦

I believed, Genesius thought later, *that I was invulnerable to evil.* Alone under the stars, he wept.

✦ ✦ ✦

Improvisation was the most exciting game there was. Never knowing how the action might twist and turn, dependent on the other players but holding absolute freedom in one's hands, the improvisational actor could do anything that presented itself. As the mime went forward some avenues closed as others opened. It was in a sense the purest form of poetry, for the actors could no more go back and correct a line or a piece of business than Menander, dead six centuries, could alter his own works. It had the spice of danger because the audience must always be pleased. It was a circus dance along a rope stretched across an arena filled with wild beasts.

It was the best fun in the world, and it kept Genesius' mind occupied. Onstage, he was the master, the emperor of the space bounded by the audience of Philippians and imperial travelers. Before each performance of any kind, especially an improvised show, the actors begged and received the forgiveness of the emperor and all the spectators in advance for any offense they might give. They had, therefore, license to take on any subject, any personality. When, centuries ago, Aristophanes had satirized even Socrates in *The Clouds,* the philosopher stood up in his seat, so that the crowd might see how accurate the imitation was.

Of course, Genesius thought as he waited for the show to begin, one had to remember what finally happened to Socrates. Hemlock was a bitter drink.

Diocletian sought distraction from the rigors of the journey; it was rumored that Publius Labius kept the emperor so overwhelmed with details concerning the administration and the arrangements for the coming triumph in Rome that Diocletian was only getting a few hours of sleep daily. Genesius had not seen Diocletian since the day before they set out on this despicable journey, and he longed for the simple directness of the emperor's company. But each time he attempted to see Diocletian, he was turned away by the army of Publius Labius' assistants.

The chamberlain must have labored like a devil in order to keep up the administrative pressures on the emperor and to try to seduce the actor.

Genesius thought he knew what was happening. In the daylight hours he viewed his relationship with Publius Labius with sunlit clarity. At dusk he felt himself tempted to outwit the serpent, to wrap himself in the snake's coils and yet slide free when he had seen enough.

But it was daylight now, and he was called on to perform.

The freedom of the stage beckoned him. Until he found himself in front of the audience, he had no idea what he would say or do. He stepped out of the patient shadows into the sunlit arena of Philippi's theater.

He was on.

The Philippians did not know him, of course, but the emperor's train recognized him at once and greeted him with cheers, which turned to laughter as in three steps he adopted the mincing walk of Publius Labius. He carried an imaginary wax tablet and an imaginary stylus as he patrolled the aisles, taking inventory of the audience.

He worked his way through the local priesthood, checking them against a list that no one could make sense of.

"Apollo has a quota of four," he lisped to the keepers of the local shrine. "We already meet that requirement. Sorry, you're out."

He moved to another section. "Mars, Mars, Mars, Mars, Mars," he said. "Nope. Can't have you either. The army is full up. Besides," he nudged one priest in his ample belly, "you're out of shape." His hand moved lower. "But not in that department. See me later."

That brought a moderate laugh from the crowd. Publius Labius countered by standing in the royal box, at the side of Diocletian, and turning so that all the spectators could see him.

"Another Socrates!" Genesius bowed and waved. Publius Labius bowed in acknowledgment.

Genesius abandoned the priests and moved higher into the audience. He gradually edged his way toward the imperial box, but he could not move in a beeline; his purpose would be too obvious. The crowd, while warming up to him, would need a little more development before it would accept what he wanted to get across.

He wished that he had a better script; he had no idea what would come next.

"It's a good thing this town was named for Philip. Otherwise you would be Alexandrians," he shouted, "and have to move to Egypt!"

The audience groaned at the pun; the joke was old when Julius Caesar was in swaddling clothes.

"I'm sorry for that," Genesius said. "The devil made me do it. I am beset by evil spirits. Where in all of Philippi is there someone who can save me? I am tormented by devils!" He spied a local matron, surrounded by slaves and sycophants.

"The aura!" he proclaimed. "I see the aura!" The crowd laughed; they had all seen the antics of visionaries going into their trances. Genesius stared at a spot just above the matron's head and toddled unsteadily into her entourage, bumping her followers right and left. They fended him off with distaste to the background of the audience's nervous laughter.

Why nervous? Genesius wondered. The answer came hissing from one of the slaves. "If you knew anything at all you wouldn't make fun of the wife of the provincial governor."

"I can't stop now," Genesius whispered. Then he raised his voice: "The governor's wife? No, no! Don't make me!" He danced into a spin, dervishing around her, scattering her train and even forcing the youthful lover to escape her grip on him. "Will you play, madam?"

he whispered. "Will your dignity allow it?"

She was quick on the uptake. "You're stuck, aren't you?"

"As you see, madam," Genesius whispered. "And there is no time for the amenities."

"I'll play along," she whispered, "but you won't know how far. Will you take the risk?"

"You have a noble soul, madam," Genesius shouted. "Surely you can save me from these malicious demons who possess me!" With that, Genesius went into a full-fledged fit. He threw his arms wide, windmilling furiously. Spittle foamed in his mouth and plopped to the ground. He whipped his head back and forth and from side to side. The slaves tried to grab him, but his spastic antics made it impossible for any of them to get a grip. Seemingly by accident, he punched one on the point of the jaw. The man went down as if felled by an ax. The crowd loved it.

"When I fall down, catch me," Genesius whispered through clenched jaws, "and scream. That's the cue."

"O great-souled one," he shrieked aloud, "I seek salvation in your arms! Give me safe haven!" He encircled the matron, as far as he was able, with his arms, locking her tightly in his grasp. From the folds of her embrace, he whispered directions to her.

"Scream."

She obeyed, with notable projection.

"Beautiful," he said. There was no danger of anyone's hearing his spoken directions. "Is there anyone onstage yet?"

Before she could answer, a cry rang out from below. "Let the possessed man be brought to me!" Diarius was dressed in the robes and miter of a Christian bishop, one of Aristarchus' new costumes for the baptism play.

Genesius felt the matron's slaves detach him from the matron and carry him back to the stage. They laid him at the feet of Diarius and backed away.

"Stay, friends," Diarius ordered. "I need your help." The slaves looked at each other in confusion. The senior slave turned to his matron, who waved her hand and nodded graciously. They remained.

Diarius prayed loudly over Genesius, who fell into a seizure. He flung gobs of spittle through the air with the contortions of his limbs. Diarius moved in a little too closely. Genesius' foot caught him in the belly; he doubled over to the accompaniment of the audience's laughter.

"I'm going to exorcise you," Diarius whispered.

"Let's do it," Genesius said. "Thanks for coming out. I was stuck."
Again his foot lashed out, but Diarius was ready this time and caught
it handily, twisting to pin Genesius facedown to the earth of the
orchestra floor, as if they were wrestlers.

"O evil spirit!" Diarius cried. "Release this man from your despicable clutches."

Genesius shouted an obscenity, his mouth filling with dirt.

"Truly a horrible spirit," Diarius said, "to hurl such foul words at
a servant of the Lord. Depart!" He gave Genesius' leg what appeared
to be a vicious wrench. Genesius honked like a goose and writhed
out of Diarius' grasp.

"Grab him, friends," Diarius called to the slaves. "Lay hold of him."
Again, their leader looked to the matron, who signaled her consent.
The group of four men circled to surround Genesius. At a signal from
Diarius they each grabbed a limb of the younger actor, holding him
immobile three feet above the ground. He struggled, but to no avail;
he had nothing to push against. The watching crowd laughed at his
dilemma, but the laughter was formal—more out of politeness than
mirth.

Diarius approached. "Let's get this over with," Genesius whispered. "We're dying out here."

Diarius gave the slaves a series of orders. They began to move
Genesius' limbs rhythmically. Diarius called cadence to the involun-
tary calisthenics. Genesius screamed and writhed. When the slaves
had the rhythm going regularly, Diarius threw off his bishop's miter,
stepped in front of the imperial box, and called to the crowd.

"You know what the Christians do to people who have fits, don't
you?" he asked the audience. The slaves continued their manipula-
tions of Genesius.

"They *exorcise* them!" Diarius cried. A drum from backstage
sounded: ta-tat—*tum!* The audience groaned at the pun, and Diarius
led the slaves, still carrying Genesius, at a run backstage as the sound
of applause echoed through the theater. The two actors brought the
slaves out for a quick bow and sent them back to their matron in
the stands. She stood to acknowledge her part in the playlet, and the
audience gave her a brief patter of applause. Genesius and Diarius
darted back into the stage house. Another act took their place.

As they rested one of the matron's slaves tapped at the entrance
to the dressing room. Genesius motioned him inside. "You did well
out there."

"Thank you, sir," the slave answered. "Everyone was wondering how you would get out of that situation."

"So was I," Genesius said.

"It was dangerous, if you don't mind my saying so."

"You're telling me," Genesius said. A small silence followed. The slave did not leave. "What do you want?"

"My lady wants to see you."

"We shall be happy to oblige," Diarius said. "Show her in."

The slave coughed politely. "I beg your pardon, but my lady said only the actor Genesius, sir."

"What?"

"She was quite specific," the slave said. He addressed Genesius: "She also asked that you bring with you the rhetor, Lactantius. Can this be arranged?"

"It will have to be soon. The journey continues tomorrow morning," Genesius said.

"Would now be a good time?"

"As good as any, if I can find Lactantius," Genesius said.

"I will wait outside," the slave offered and left. Genesius toweled off the sweat from the performance. Diarius was unhappy. "What does the old biddy want? Do you know her?"

"I never saw her before in my life," Genesius answered.

"And why does she want you and Lactantius?"

"I don't know. See if you can find him, will you?"

Diarius was nonplussed. "I will not! You can run your own errands." He stomped from the dressing room. Genesius left to find Lactantius himself, unwilling to face the questions that clamored in his mind for answers.

✦ ✦ ✦

Genesius came to me in my tent at our camp at the north side of the city, just within the walls. At each town we visited, invitations arrived to offer temporary lodgings with the local dignitaries. Diocletian had ordered all such invitations refused with appropriate ceremony to avoid spreading his train through the confusion of each city. Regrouping for the next leg of travel would take too long if all the travelers dispersed. At the more important towns like Philippi we stayed perhaps two days.

Genesius made the slave wait outside.

"The Augusta," he began without even a greeting. "How is she? I have not seen her since Byzantium."

Prisca, now without her daughter Valeria for companion, had sunk into sadness; the only thing that eased her mind was to recount the story of her short career as a seeming prostitute in her escape from Galerius' soldiers after crossing the Bosphorus.

"She is well and unhurt by her adventure," I told Genesius. "She sends her thanks to you and appreciates your quick thinking."

Outside my tent, the slave coughed. Genesius explained his errand, and I hurried to comply. We walked, the press of people too intense to ride a cart through the city streets. Genesius fell silent; he spoke only enough to be minimally polite. We had not met for days, and I wondered what had caused the change in him, but the presence of the matron's servant inhibited conversation.

We were passing with some difficulty through the crowded agora, or marketplace, when the shrill cries of a young girl fell upon us.

"There's one!" she shrieked. An unkempt slave girl in her early teens, she was standing on a raised platform used by orators. She had black stringy hair, plastered to her face and scalp by sweat and filth. Around her head was a wreath of long-dead laurel, the few remaining leaves brown with age. Half-healed scabs pocked her face and arms. One eye was sunken into her skull, while the other glittered with madness.

Her worst feature, however, was the snake that draped itself in coils around her. She must have been extraordinarily strong to carry its weight, for uncoiled it must have measured nearly fifteen feet. I recognized its reticulations from my reading as those of an Indian python. Its saliva dripped from its mouth and covered her arms and legs with a silvery sheen.

She leaped from the platform and landed in front of Genesius. "This one!" she cried. "This actor is an enemy of the state! This actor is a Christian!"

She repeated her accusation over and over again, until she had gathered a crowd around us. The matron's slave melted into the mob and vanished from sight. I initially felt a thrill of fear for myself, but the demon within her only saw Genesius. I was ignored completely, for which I must admit I was grateful.

The python girl let go of the snake's head. It uncoiled itself and slithered across the ground toward Genesius. The crowd muttered threats at him. As yet he had said nothing in response to the python girl's denunciation. As the snake began to curl around his leg, he stood stone-still, his eyes focused on the seeress, his face a mask, emotionless, unmoving.

The python gleamed in the sunlight as it moved up Genesius' still body. Not even a tremble of revulsion escaped him. A well-dressed Greek, wearing the emblem of Apollo, emerged from the crowd surrounding Genesius and prodded the snake with a switch.

"That's the way," the snake girl cried suddenly to her serpent. "Take him! Take him now!"

She passed into disjointed speech, drooling and spitting at Genesius in fury. He remained impassive, displaying a control I had not thought possible. I know that had the python crawled over my own flesh, I could not have maintained his discipline. The Greek poked again at the snake, which turned its head to and fro, trying to find the source of its irritation. The snake girl was screaming now, meaningless angry sounds that seemed as if they should make sense but did not. She spun about in frustration, her limbs windmilling, as the snake, distracted by the torment of its owner, coiled its way down Genesius' legs and tried to vanish into the crowd. The people who awaited Genesius' denunciation were frightened by the serpent, now out of control, and moved to avoid its path.

The prosperous Greek took his switch to the girl. At that Genesius finally moved, stepping forward and holding the Greek's upraised arm in a grip that must have rivaled that of the python, for the Greek's face turned red with effort, then white with pain as Genesius tightened his fingers around the man's wrist. The python girl cowered, silent and hopeless, waiting for the blow to fall. The Greek cried out; the switch fell from his fingers as the bone snapped. Genesius let go. The Greek fell to the ground, nursing the fracture and whimpering. Genesius flexed the fingers of his hand and started to walk away.

"What about me?" the snake girl called. Genesius turned to look at her, still silent.

"He'll beat me because of you," she said. Genesius did not move or speak. "Maybe kill me. And it'll be your fault!" Genesius again turned to go.

The snake girl scrambled to her feet. "Wait!" She dashed into the crowd, searching for her pet. After a moment, she found the serpent and draped it about her slight form.

"Now I'm ready."

Genesius set off in the direction in which the slave had been leading us. The snake girl followed behind him, and I followed her. After a few blocks the slave reappeared. He led us through the twistings and turnings of the Philippian streets, doubling us back several times to search for followers, never explaining his actions.

The snake girl dropped behind, as if trying to slow us and thereby make pursuit easier. Genesius took the serpent from her over her protests and gently laid it over his own shoulders. She dogged our steps after that, and we made good time. No one was on our trail when we arrived at the house of the matron.

The slave led us through the atrium, past the rain pool, and through the entire house to the colonnaded garden, where a group of people awaited our arrival. As we entered the garden the entire assembled company turned to watch. The snake girl recoiled, but Genesius snatched her wrist before she could escape.

The crowd shrank away from him, and many glanced around the garden's walls, looking for a means to escape. But the matron stepped forward.

"Truly this actor has conquered the serpent," she told them. "It is a sign that he will soon be with us in spirit as he is now with us in the body. He will not betray us."

"What about the girl?" one of her guests asked.

"We will heal her," the matron answered. "Lydia, take her inside and clean her up, please."

"Yes, madam," Lydia said, stepping from among the group toward the girl still held in Genesius' grip.

"You're alive!" Genesius said.

"And so are you," Lydia answered.

"Come, child, I asked you a favor," the matron reminded her. "You two can talk later."

Genesius released his grip on the snake girl, and Lydia led her back into the house. His eyes followed her.

"Now, Lactantius," the matron said, "we were told to expect you. What do you have to say to us?"

I did not know until that moment that I had a message for them. It was as if someone else spoke through me.

"That the persecution is serious, worse than those of Nero or Decius. That some are fated to glory, and others to mere survival. That the church will endure, beyond Diocletian, beyond Galerius, beyond even Constantine.

"That it must all be remembered, even to the end of time. As you remember the passion of Christ, remember the passions of His saints. Write it down. Let the pagans know that something new is happening, that you are not ruled by fear, but by love. And remember: the blood of the martyrs nourishes the seed of the faith. As Jesus said, 'I am with you always, even to the end of time.'"

Then I told them of Dorotheus, of Euethius, of Anthimus—how each of them held fast to God even to the end of his life, how each traveled a different way to the gate of the same heaven. Dorotheus was a servant to the secular power yet held fast to the faith when faced with evil. Euethius was impulsive and afraid, yet he too found the strength to face death bravely in the name of Christ. Anthimus the bishop knew that death awaited him and met it with resolution, depending on God alone. I told them these things because the time would soon come when they would face their own trial, and they needed forewarning. It was not that their faith was weak; for all I knew, it was stronger than mine.

I told them how the persecution had begun. Our God is a God of history, not of myth, and to know Him, they needed to know what had actually happened. The pagans know that their gods are not God, only personifications of human need—for love, for power, for fleetness, for conflict—for all of the sins that the flesh is heir to. What is Eros, but lust, or Jupiter, but dominion? The legend of Jupiter's descent to earth is only legend; no one in his right mind claims to be a witness to his dalliance with Leda.

But people saw Jesus the Christ. They touched Him, even after His death and resurrection. A cloud of witnesses surrounds His every action. He was known to be dead. Then, later, He was known to be alive and even to eat with His friends. Who has eaten with Aphrodite, or touched the torn flesh of Dionysius?

The gods are dead, but God lives.

God lives within the human ken: in the experience of Peter, in the sight of the martyrs, in the touch of Thomas the apostle, in the tears of Magdalene.

This is the crucial fact. His word became flesh. He takes part in history. And so, knowing what happened is important. We believe in Christ because He exists.

When I was through, when they understood anew the history that would climax their lives, I fell silent. In the quiet recognition of what was to come, a high, pure voice sang the words of a psalm. Lydia had returned from cleaning up the snake girl.

The fool said in his heart,
"There is no god."
Their deeds are corrupt and vile,
There is not one good man left.
God is looking down

At the sons of man,
To see a single man, one man,
If a single man is seeking God.

Genesius knew he was both subject and object of Lydia's song. He backed away from her and fell into the pool surrounding the garden's fountain. The matron's slaves pulled him, sputtering, from the water and took him inside to dry off.

CHAPTER 23

The snake girl let Genesius keep her serpent, and it traveled with him all the way to Thessalonika. The girl's former owners had spent more money for her creature than for her. And against all reasonable expectation, the beast took what passed for a liking for the actor. However, such was not the case for the chamberlain. At the first meeting of the snake and the chamberlain, the animal spat and convulsed around Genesius.

"An amusing creature," Publius Labius said. "I wonder why it hates me so."

"It probably knows what you are," Genesius muttered.

"And what am I, do you think?"

"I don't know," Genesius said. "A sorcerer, perhaps. Perhaps one of those demons the Christians are always talking about."

"Be careful, friend," the chamberlain said, "of associating with them. People are beginning to wonder about you. People in high places."

"You mean yourself."

Publius Labius smiled and walked away. The serpent relaxed into a gentle coil around Genesius' trunk.

It was near dawn, and the wagons were drawn up, the camp in the throes of breaking for the day's travel.

Thessalonika was the next stopping place. Diarius was at the reins of the actors' wagon, peering about anxiously for Genesius.

"There you are!" he said. "We almost had to leave without you."

"I'm here. You needn't worry." Genesius rode to the back of the wagon, tied his horse to it, lifted the snake, and climbed in himself, ready to settle down for a long morning nap. The others ignored his arrival, merely shifting in their still sleepy resentment to make room for him among the props and costumes. The wagon gave a jerk as Diarius pulled it into line, and the day's trek began.

"We have been invited to perform," Diarius called from the driver's seat.

"It's not ready," Genesius muttered, unwilling to open his eyes.

"Well, if it's not, we have to do something. It'll have to be the virgin play again." Diarius was making an effort not to sound accusatory, but Genesius recognized the tone of the remark and realized that he was being a "difficult" actor. That is, he, who had always prided himself on his professionalism concerning anything to do with the theater, was allowing his personal shortcomings to interfere with the work. Diarius was letting him know that he was aware that Genesius was laboring under a hardship, but the work was still waiting to be done. In a few days, if Genesius did not straighten out and complete the task of scripting the baptism play, it would come to an outright confrontation. Diarius would have the support of the other actors against him, for their reputations and livelihoods were at stake. For the moment there was time for Genesius to pull himself together, but not much. Genesius roused himself from his reverie enough to speak.

"Where do we perform?"

"In the theater in Thessalonika," Diarius said.

"Who's the audience?"

"The show is for the citizens."

The sleeping actors grumbled at being disturbed. Genesius clambered over them into the driver's seat beside Diarius. The actor-manager gave him a glance as he sat down, then returned his attention to maintaining the distance between their own wagon and the one in front.

"Got yourself in some trouble, eh?" he said.

"Too deep," Genesius answered.

"You think too much."

"But not clearly," Genesius said.

"It's what comes of mixing yourself with the higher people. You ought to stick to your own. Stay with what you know."

Genesius stared at the back of the preceding wagon. "I can't. I'm missing something."

"What?"

"I don't know."

"Look, boy," Diarius said, "I don't know much, but I know the business. You're as good as they come, for your age, and you have a great future if you can keep yourself alive. But that isn't going to be easy. I've seen a couple like you. They flash, and then they're gone, like a shooting star. What you do as a matter of instinct, I had to work forty years to learn. I came up the hard way, but you had it all handed to you."

"Sure I did," Genesius said.

"Ah, maybe you were poor and an orphan," Diarius countered, "but the talent comes easy for you. And that's the problem. You don't have to struggle to learn to act. Maybe you learned it in the womb." He flicked the reins; the horses were dawdling on an upgrade. "What you need is to learn how to get along with people. You ask too many questions. You always want things your way. That makes you a good performer, but you have to learn to ease up a little offstage. Get Atalanta into your bed. Relax a little. Take my advice. I'm right, you'll see."

Genesius had no answer. The horses plodded along without thought, responding now and then to Diarius' flick of the reins, putting one foot down, lifting another up, step after step, mile after mile. The clop-clop of their hooves against the cobbles of the road, the creaking of the wagon, and the growing warmth of the sun slipped Genesius into a reverie in which his father recognized him, understood him, held him to his breast, and consoled him for all the hurts of living, made up for the years of loneliness, and protected him from the nights of evil and the days of confusion. The illusion of comfort in his father's arms lulled him, and he rested content within it.

The next thing he knew, Janus was shaking him. Genesius looked ahead. The train was passing through the Arch of Galerius; Thessalonika was the capital of his domain. Like Galerius, the arch was disproportioned. It was too tall, too wide, so that its overall effect was repulsive at first sight. The arch was appropriate for its namesake—oversized, maldesigned, and far stronger than its needs.

The arch celebrated Galerius' victory over the Persians, which occurred on his second attempt at fighting the eastern enemy. His first had ended in a rout. On his return he was in such disgrace with Diocletian that he had camped outside the palace walls for months before the emperor would allow him into his presence to beg another expedition against the Persians.

The second attempt was wildly successful. Galerius even captured the harem of King Narses. His triumphant return from the second campaign against the Persians almost made up for the humiliation incurred in the first, but Galerius never forgot how he had had to grovel to Diocletian. The memory ate at his vitals and went far to explain his attempts to humble the Augustus.

The arch was squatty—no other word could describe it. Even though it towered over the street, its two pillars were so massive and so crowded with scenes from the second campaign, stacked one atop the other, that to Genesius the arch seemed to resemble in outline if not in intent, the hindquarters of an elephant squatting to relieve itself.

The serpent roused itself with Genesius, looked up at the arch of Galerius, hissed, and spat. The python secretes a slimy saliva when it ingests its prey. When it spits, its target gets wet.

✦ ✦ ✦

When the chamberlain took his customary ride around the camp during the evening, Genesius was leaving camp with me.

Publius Labius, on horseback, caught up to us as we walked out of the camp.

"Where are you going?"

"To stretch our legs after the day's travel," I answered.

"And visit whom?"

"Visit?" Genesius asked. "I have never been here before. Thessalonika is a capital. I want to see the sights."

Publius Labius' horse snorted and wheeled. With difficulty he controlled it.

"When will you be back?"

"When we've seen them, I suppose," Genesius said. The serpent coiled itself more tightly around his breast and arms, baring its teeth at Publius Labius. It had no poison fangs; its teeth were made for holding on until its victim died from asphyxiation. It was quite large enough to kill a man, although it would be unable to devour him afterward.

"You perform tomorrow," Publius Labius said. "Don't be late. Diocletian would be displeased." He rode away without waiting for an answer.

"That man is after your soul," I said. Genesius watched the chamberlain ride away. Already the sweat was springing from his palms. He wiped them on his tunic and grinned nervously at me.

"First, he has to find it," he said. "Where are we going? Will she be there?"

"Lydia? I doubt it."

"Who then? Anyone who knows her?"

"Possibly."

"What are we waiting for?"

"Darkness," I said. "This is Galerius' city. For the moment we are merely tourists, working out the kinks of travel."

"Then let's get unkinked," Genesius said. "A town this size must have a bathhouse or two."

We made our way to the baths. The camp was above the city proper. We had approached from Philippi, to the northeast. Stretching below the sloping streets of Thessalonika was the blue water of the Thermaic Gulf, an arm of the Aegean Sea. Somewhere far to the south was Athens, where the beginnings of Genesius' art first touched the hearts of men. Even further away, to the west, Rome awaited our arrival. There, preparations were already long underway to greet the Emperor Diocletian and his court.

In every city we had reached thus far, there had been massive welcomes given to Diocletian and the higher officials of the imperial bureaucracy. Local dignitaries scheduled feast after feast, entertainment after entertainment, for the delectation of the emperor. Meetings were held to discuss matters of imperial policy and defense, problems of local importance, and, of course, taxation and the rising persecution of the Christians. Each stop on the journey brought trouble for local followers of the church because each civic official was anxious to show loyalty to Diocletian, who came to welcome the journeys between cities as a hard-earned rest between rounds of diplomatic showmanship.

But as lower caste members of Diocletian's train, Genesius and I had time on our hands and few official duties.

Genesius tenderly set the snake on the floor beside the pool. The dust of the road muddied the rinse water. Having cleaned ourselves, Genesius and I lowered our bodies into the steaming waters of the caldarium pool. At this hour we nearly had the place to ourselves. Most of the inhabitants of Thessalonika were too busy with the imperial visit to linger in the baths. Through the steam I noticed a powerfully built man enter the caldarium.

"May I join you?" It was the sea captain from Ephesus.

"Of course," I said.

"You do get around," Genesius observed.

"A hazard of my trade, I'm afraid," the captain said. "You know, you're being followed."

"That's why I was waiting until dark. It will be easier to lose a tail."

The sea captain stretched underwater. "Not necessarily. With darkness they will expect some kind of trick. Right now, there is only one man. Later, there will be more. I suggest that we leave now. I will accompany you. The actor can trail behind the one who is trailing us. The poor fellow will be thoroughly confused."

"What's to prevent me from giving you away to the follower?" Genesius asked.

"Nothing, if that is what you decide to do," the captain said. "God will take care of things. What He wants is what will happen in any case."

We raised ourselves from the pool as the attendant came in with towels. As we dried off the captain explained his plan.

"Lactantius and I will go out first. Wait until you see a dark-haired man, a Greek Jew, start after us. He will probably be confused, since he saw Lactantius come in with you. Just wait until he follows us. Then follow him. Keep your eyes open for another tail; sometimes they work in pairs."

Genesius bent to let the snake wrap itself around his body. "Leave the serpent," the captain said. "It attracts too much attention."

"You give orders well, Captain," Genesius said. "But the beast is mine. I will decide what happens to it."

The captain turned to me. "Can you do anything with him?"

"God presented him with the snake in Philippi," I said. "As you said a moment ago, He will take care of things."

✦ ✦ ✦

The two older men left the baths first, and Genesius noted the Philippian Jew's ostentatious nonchalance as he picked up their trail. The actor waited a few moments before setting off behind the follower, watching from the shadows of the baths' entrance for others who showed too much interest in the direction he had taken. Finding no one else, he fell into line.

✦ ✦ ✦

The sea captain cross-examined me about Genesius as we walked. "Where did he come from? Who is he? Can he be trusted?"

"He came from the gutter," I answered, "and he is a child of God, a battleground between Christ and the devil. As for trust I doubt that an archangel could make him break his word." I was thinking of the scroll.

The sea captain hurried on. "We will not have long to talk. We are almost at our destination." We walked a few steps in silence.

"I have, for whatever reasons, been sent to guard the girl. She has conceived an affection for this actor, regardless of the fact that he is not one of us. He troubles me."

I laughed out loud. "He troubles everyone he meets. He is a walking outrage, but he is also one on whom much will turn." I thought a moment. "Tell me about the girl. As you are her guardian I fancy myself his."

"Lydia is named for one who helped Paul early in the life of the faith. She was found on the streets herself, although she was born the daughter of a respectable family of Ephesus. She was thin, dirty, and wounded. A family of believers took her in, secretly, to save her from a father who—well, the less said, the better, if you understand me. She still bears the scars of her early life, although you would not think so. She took the faith of her adopted family, in gratitude at first, then with sincerity. She serves now as a messenger, much as you do, keeping the faithful in contact with each other across the empire. She is vulnerable to gentleness, and I would not have her hurt."

✦ ✦ ✦

The little procession wound its way through the narrow streets of

Philip's town. The captain had us stop at every stall and storefront, meandering through the streets without direction, several times circling back the way we had come. The man who followed us spent half his time ducking into doorways to avoid being seen, and Genesius had to do likewise to avoid being seen by him. The weight of the snake pressed heavily across his shoulders.

The captain pulled me into a shadow and motioned for silence.

The dark man stopped in mid-stride. His quarry had vanished from his sight. He whirled about, searching, and his eyes caught Genesius, recognizable because of the serpent. The eyes bore into his own; the snake, sensing danger, hissed in warning, its tongue flicking the air. The dark man advanced on Genesius.

Genesius was suddenly changed from hunter to quarry; he was alone. The dark man came closer.

"Where did they go?"

Genesius lowered the python to the ground.

"Keep that thing away from me!" the dark man said. He drew a knife from beneath his robes. The dagger gleamed in the afternoon sun. The snake lay between them. The dark man thrust his knife toward the serpent, his grip weakened by the sweat of fear. Genesius kicked at the steel, and the blade arced into the air, twirling through the light. The dark man looked from Genesius to the snake and ran away.

"Not bad," the sea captain said from behind Genesius. "This is our destination. Come in."

Genesius gathered the snake in his arms and followed the captain into the house. It was like all the other houses on the street.

Inside, the meeting was much like the one held in Philippi. Christians of all shapes, sizes, and social classes crowded the home of a respectable, wealthy citizen. They welcomed me and tolerated Genesius. Lydia was nowhere to be seen, and it was folly to have expected her, in any case. I passed on the same message as I had in Philippi, bringing encouragement to the Thessalonikan Christians.

Afterward there was singing and prayers. Genesius seemed confused. He wanted someone to explain how there sometimes seemed to be one Christian deity, sometimes two or three. One of the guests, a converted Jew, tried to explain it to him.

"I am a Hebrew by birth and by inclination," the man said. He still wore the Jewish dress, even though converted to Christianity. "The Trinity was a sticking point for me. After all, we are taught that the Lord our God is one, perfect and whole. The idea of three gods in one is difficult for Jews; it goes against all our teachings. But think of the three persons of God as one actor wearing three different masks. Our experience of God as Father, Son, or Spirit depends on the circumstances in which we encounter Him. As Father, He is creator of the universe, the maker of all things. As the Son, He is God on earth, sharing our human nature. When He wears His mask as the Spirit, He is touching our minds and hearts, fulfilling His promise to be with us always."

But Genesius threw up his hands and exclaimed, "It's a mystery to me!"

"Exactly!" the guest said. "That's it!"

"What's it?" Genesius said.

"A mystery."

He was moving away from the convert, in apparent disgust, when the doors of the prosperous house crashed open, admitting a flood of troops from the local garrison. Genesius pulled his cloak over his face. Mixed in with the troops—guiding them—were civilians, members of the local Jewish community, recognizable by their yarmulkes. Each "adviser" located one of the local Christians, called out his or her name, and pinned his victim until a soldier roped the prisoner's wrists. The civilians saved their greatest fury for the Jewish convert who had been speaking to Genesius. The apostate was nearly beaten to death before the troopers could rescue him from his accusers.

In the confusion the sea captain lifted me bodily into the air and put me on top of the wall that encircled the garden at the rear of the house. Genesius let the snake, excited by the melee, down to the floor to create what havoc it could, which was substantial. The local troops were largely barbarian mercenaries, fair-skinned and blonde, from the northern reaches of Europe. They had no experience of exotic serpents, and the feel of the python slithering against their legs defeated what little discipline they had. Their centurion drew his sword and aimed a blow at the snake, but Genesius kicked at the man's feet and brought him down heavily. With their leader unconscious the soldiers had no heart for their task. They abandoned their civilian accomplices, who were left screaming for attention. Genesius, still hiding his face, and the sea captain detached the Jewish accusers from their intended sacrifices and, one by one, shoved them out the door and on their way. When they were gone, Genesius retrieved the serpent.

The captain jumped up onto a table and addressed the group.

"Go home," he said, "before they can regroup and come back for us. Who is the host?"

A man raised his hand.

"You are in the gravest danger. Is there someone who will hide you?"

A dozen people offered.

"Fine," the captain said. "Go with one of them. Stay out of sight for a few days. Soon, the emperor will be gone. It's possible that things will quiet down once he leaves. Now, don't waste time—get going!" He leaped down from the table and followed his own advice. Genesius followed him. Once outside, the captain circled around to the back of the house. I was waiting, crouching on the wall above.

"Help me down," I said. "I'm too old to be jumping around like this." Genesius and the captain eased me to the ground, and we set off, walking away from the house.

"Someone knew about that meeting," I said.

"Obviously," the captain replied.

"I sent the spy packing who was following you," Genesius said. "He was alone; I'd bet on it."

"It doesn't mean that there weren't others," the captain said. "Any one of those people could have been followed there. But the point remains that there was a man following us. We have been identified. And if you want to bet on something, actor, bet that the man you dealt with will tell his story about a young man who carries a snake to someone who would like to know it. Do you have any enemies?"

"Just a few," Genesius said. Publius Labius would have been informed already.

"Do you want to escape?"

"I have a show tomorrow," Genesius said.

"You would risk your life for a show?"

"It's what I do," Genesius answered. "You risk your life for a cargo, do you not?"

The captain turned his attention to me. "What about you? It may be that you are the focus of all this attention."

"I, too, have a task to perform," Lactantius said. "I can't perform it hidden away in a catacomb."

Without another word the sea captain vanished into the darkness.

✦ ✦ ✦

The next morning's command performance of the virgin play for the dignitaries and citizens of Thessalonika went well—too well, in fact. The crowd's laughter was vicious and demanding, like the mobs that slavered over the gladiatorial combats. They wanted blood more than comedy.

Blood was what they had in the end. As the actors took their final bows a disturbance started in the stands. A man—I recognized him from the previous night's meeting—stood up in his seat, and with a voice that would have done credit to any actor, denounced the players and all the spectators as blasphemers, the play as an abomination, and the old gods as demonic impostors who kept people from a knowledge of the Father, Son, and Holy Spirit. Declaring himself a Christian, he was dragged from the stands down into the orchestra's half-circle. Two citizens tied ropes around his wrists and held him with arms outstretched, keeping themselves at a safe distance from the stones and bad fruit thrown at him by the mob.

When he was dead, another Christian stood up in the *cavea* and announced himself. He, too, was taken to the orchestra, stretched, and stoned. Yet again, a Christian revealed himself; he suffered. The rush was on. The Christians formed an orderly line, waiting to martyr themselves to the fury of the pagan crowd.

A part of the crowd was less patient than the hopeful martyrs. It stormed the line of Christians who hoped for violent death and satisfied their wishes. Knives were used—also rocks torn from the orchestra floor, timbers from the stage supports, the cords that gathered their colorful tunics in graceful folds, hair pins, bare hands; and the limbs torn from some of the dead were used as clubs to beat the living.

From the royal box, surrounded by nervous members of the elite praetorian guard, Diocletian watched, his inmost feelings hooded by an expressionless face, with Publius Labius smiling by his side. The emperor spoke briefly to one of the soldiers, who left the stands at a run, sword drawn, armor clanking, feet thudding on the stone.

Afterward Genesius told me what I had done during the frenzy. I have no memory of events after I saw the trooper run from the stands.

During the frenzy, Genesius searched the stands for me, afraid that I would be caught up in the intoxication of godliness. I was standing at the edge of the orchestra, he said, leaning forward over the low stone rail that separated spectator from performer, my eyes locked on the carnage before me. Genesius raced across the intervening space and reached me just as I began to climb over the stones into the arena. The actor tackled me; both of us fell hard to the stones below.

I struggled with Genesius, who had the breath knocked out of him, and nearly broke away to join the dying. Gasping for air, Genesius launched himself again at me and managed to grab my wrist. He twisted my arm up behind my shoulder blades. Lifting me nearly off my feet, Genesius half-carried, half-pushed me ahead of himself back into the stands and toward one of the tunnels that led under the cavea to the safety of the street outside.

✦ ✦ ✦

Genesius woke up in the cell with me. The blow had been heavy; his face and clothing were soaked with the blood that had flowed from his scalp. Fortunately, the soldier had recognized him at the last moment. While it was too late to stop the blow, the trooper had been able to turn his sword so that only the flat of the blade had landed on Genesius' forehead.

If the soldier had not been able to withstand the momentum of the troops behind him, Genesius and I would not have found ourselves in jail. Instead, Martius had flung us into a small niche in the tunnel wall to save our being trampled. The rear guard had found us, and not knowing our positions in the court, had ordered our arrest along with everyone else's. I expected it to be sorted out before long.

"Are you all right?" I asked Genesius.

Before he could answer, the cell door flew open. Waving a sprig of aromatic herbs to fend off the fetid stench of the prison, Publius Labius, the emperor's chamberlain, came in.

"Lactantius, Genesius!" he cried. "A mistake has been made! I do hope you'll forgive me. They should never have arrested you. I can't imagine what made them."

Genesius crouched in the far corner of the cell, away from the chamberlain. Publius Labius knelt in front of him and put forth his hand to examine Genesius' wound. Genesius slapped the hand away.

"Keep away from me," Genesius warned.

"You're upset. You'll feel better later." Publius Labius stood up and brushed at the dirt on his clothing. "Maybe this will help. Besides coming to get you out of jail, I also bring the congratulations of the emperor on your performance today. The results were most gratifying, and he wants to see you. Frankly, I advised against it, because he was upset by the disorder, but when he understood what actually happened, he changed his mind and was most insistent. He really does want to see you. And even I have to admit, you did well."

Genesius rose sullenly. Publius Labius put his arm around the lad; Genesius shook it off.

✦ ✦ ✦

Genesius rode in the imperial wagon with Diocletian. They acted like strangers with each other, not having spoken since before the journey began, back in Nicomedia.

He had left the snake in the actors' wagon with Atalanta, who had developed an affection for it. It was safe with her and seemed to know it.

West of Thessalonika, the countryside rose gently along with the great highway, the Via Egnatia. Diocletian had ordered that there be no more stops in the cities until they reached Illyria. He had no wish to deal with more provincial officials, nor to witness another riot as he had done in Thessalonika. Twenty years of rule had insulated him from mass bloodshed. Not that he had a weak stomach; it was not the blood, but the disorder that had been terrifying. During the riot in the theater, Diocletian had a vision of what lay ahead for the empire. The stability of Rome, to which he had given his life, was falling away. Whether or not he tried to subdue the Christians, the result would be the same—the challenge of their god to the traditional ways would tear at the fabric of his domain, already weakened by inflation, regional jealousies, external attack, and the in-fighting of those whom he had chosen with such care to work together to maintain the status quo.

He fought a rear-guard action against change, yet change seemed inevitable. It had been building for centuries, as if history came in tidal waves, the waves themselves the effect of earthquakes in the minds of the whatever gods in fact ruled the universe. How could any man—even the incarnation of Jupiter, he thought wryly—stand against such a wave?

Genesius saw Diocletian's smile and returned it tentatively. His mind was uncertain, his emotions tangled. It was a relief to be with Diocletian again; it had been a long time, and their silence as the procession moved through the afternoon sunlight was companionable, if uncommunicative.

"I'm happy to see you smile, lord," Genesius ventured. "It has been too long."

Diocletian made a noise half laugh, half grunt. "It's not happiness,

I'm afraid." He examined the face of the actor. It was more mature than he remembered, with a degree of anguish he had not seen before in Genesius. "Something is troubling you."

Genesius turned his face toward the road ahead.

"What is it?" Diocletian asked. "Is it something I can help you with?"

Still Genesius maintained his silence.

"I'm not used to being ignored," Diocletian said. "I would like an answer."

Genesius again faced Diocletian. "Your chamberlain—"

"I have heard the rumors," Diocletian said. "I am not entirely ignorant, even if I am the emperor of all Rome."

"He is evil, sir." Once the words started, Genesius found himself unable to stanch their flow. "I don't mean ambitious or treasonous or anything like that—though he may be all of those things. I mean that he is *evil.* Whatever he comes near is made corrupt and decayed. He is a death-bringer. He serves some dark force, and he takes pleasure in its exercise. I have known actors like him who delight in appealing to the worst instincts in the audience, whose work makes the people worse than they already are." Genesius paused for breath.

Diocletian was looking away. "This is a serious charge you make."

"And I cannot prove a bit of it," Genesius said. "But you have been close to him, have you not? You have had a chance to see the effects of his presence."

Diocletian closed his eyes, not willing to look at Genesius as he said, "Publius Labius warns me that you may become a Christian."

For Genesius to keep silence would be an admission of guilt.

"Does he?" he said. "That would be the final ploy to isolate you from everyone but himself. How many other people do you see? Everyone is someone's agent, but you and I are friends. If he can poison that, and he will try, he alone will have your ear. And then you can kiss everyone else good-bye. You will hear only the opinions of Publius Labius."

"It has already happened," Diocletian whispered. He opened his eyes and turned them toward Genesius. "I know that my chamberlain is in the pay of Galerius, and he does his job well. He corrupts my opinion of others. There is no one left for me to trust. I have killed them all, and I am alone. I had to fight with him even to be able to see you, boy."

The emperor's eyes filled with tears but did not overflow. The rigid emotional control that had characterized his life as a soldier and a ruler stayed with him now, but it was a measure of the depth of his feeling that the tears appeared at all. He was as alone as Genesius felt, the actor thought. With all the power of the earth at his command, Diocletian was lonely. Genesius held his emperor's hand in silence as the journey continued.

Diocletian berated Publius Labius. During the diatribe, the emperor seemed a young man again, full of vigor, a strong, virile centurion bawling out one of his troops for a monumental act of stupidity. His voice echoed along the line of march as it must have done when he led his troops through the mountains of Dalmatia searching out barbarian guerrilla fighters. The transformation was such that Genesius forgot to enjoy the discomfiture of Publius Labius in his admiration for Diocletian's newfound energy. The chamberlain was properly chastened, and the emperor strengthened by the confrontation.

The royal progression followed the old Via Egnatia through the mountains of Macedonia, having passed by the cities of Edessa and Heraclea, Lyncestis and Lychnidus, climbing all the while along the ancient highway, especially—and hurriedly—repaired for Diocletian's passage. West of Lake Lychnites they began the downhill portion of their journey. They turned on the northwest fork of the road, which would lead them to the city of Epidamnus.

Genesius faced the problem of his script. With the serpent coiled around him, he kept away from everyone except Diocletian and labored over the plot and characters of the baptism play. The script, the culmination of his work for the sake of the emperor, would be the touchstone of his career in the theater. The script would be the proof he needed for Diocletian and for himself that his loyalty to his unknowing father was ironclad. He rode in Diocletian's wagon during the day to avoid the distractions of his fellow actors. While the emperor conferred with his officials, Genesius scratched words into the wax surface.

Diarius acted as his copyist, taking the wax tablets that Genesius covered with words and fair-copying them for the actors. There were roles for each of the principal players; extras would have to be hired in Rome to fill some of the smaller parts and to dress the stage with warm bodies. The Roman audience would accept nothing less than a full-scale production. There would be little doubling. The jobs of the extras were simple—stand where they were told when they were told and troop on and off at the right moments. The principals had lines to learn, blocking to practice, and timing to get down. Like all comedy, the baptism play depended on getting each moment precisely right. Approximation would not do.

Thus, while the actors' days were reasonably free to suffer the discomforts of travel, the evenings after supper were spent in rehearsal. Even Publius Labius entered properly into the spirit of the rehearsals. The chamberlain seemed to have undergone a radical change. He treated everyone with courtesy and respect, including Genesius. It was as if he had unilaterally declared himself a member of society. There was no hint of his former predatory nature, no reference made to what had passed between himself and Genesius, who was puzzled by the change, but accepted it under the pressure of his work. Diarius gave everyone their movements and arbitrated problems of interpretation and timing, occasionally consulting with Genesius. Publius Labius behaved admirably, for an actor; he was always ready to work at the appointed time, learned his speeches accurately and quickly, performed with zest and flair, and was gracious when overruled on a question of interpretation.

While onstage, Genesius let his serpent hunt. If it had fed recently, the snake draped itself from their wagon and seemed to watch the actors' work with a skeptical eye.

The imperial entourage left Macedonia and the Via Egnatia at Epidamnus. Their route was now to the northwest, aiming up the eastern coast of Dalmatia, sometimes called Illyria, still in Galerius' territory. With the Adriatic to their left and the Dalmatian Alps over their right shoulders, they followed the Roman road that paralleled the seacoast. Genesius was left in relative peace, avoiding all unnecessary contact with his fellow travelers while he labored over the script.

Their destination was Aspalathos, a suburb of the provincial capital, Salonae. By the time they reached Aspalathos, Genesius was exhausted from his frenzied writing during the day and rehearsals at night. But the job was finished, the play well along in rehearsal.

Aspalathos was the birthplace of Diocletian. Years before, he had begun a palace there, which contained his tomb. Part of the reason for this side trip was to check on its progress. He was journeying to Rome to celebrate the milestone of his twentieth year in power; it was only natural that he should turn his thoughts to retirement.

Genesius maintained the habit of riding with Diocletian, even after the script was essentially complete. As they approached Aspalathos, Diocletian gave way to sentimental recollection. He pointed to the palace, visible in the distance.

"I started that five years ago," he said. "It should be nearly finished, if the builders haven't been sleeping."

Even at a distance, the palace seemed huge, more fortress than retreat. They had gone through Salonae without stopping to receive the homage of the people, who had been forced to run alongside, panting their praises to the emperor. Diocletian had kept moving, acknowledging the crowd with a wave of the imperial hand. With the haven of his palace within sight there had been no stopping him. The people were disappointed, being deprived of their show, but it made him no difference.

"They," he said, meaning his officials, "think that I ought to stop in every hamlet and burg to let the people worship me. And perhaps I should. But we'd never get anywhere—this train would still be waiting to cross the Bosporus."

His eyes never moved from the vision of his palace waiting by the sea. The road approached from the northeast, skirting the older town's harbor. Diocletian, impatient with the slow pace, called to his driver to go faster, but the man was unable because of the plodding of the men and horses in front of him.

"You see how the government traps me!" Diocletian growled. "I can't even set the pace at which I travel." He grinned at Genesius. "Look at me—I am like a small child again, excited to be coming home."

As the procession wound along the track, off the main highway now by miles, Diocletian pointed to a forest grove. "That is where I lost my virginity," he said. "What was her name? I was thirteen and promised that I would never forget. I remember that, but not who she was." He looked at the grove as if his gaze would pierce the thick stand of trees, bent almost double by the constant sea wind from the west, their tops flaming with yellow and red, leaves blowing from them in the winds of autumn.

The grove fell behind them and out of sight beyond a small hill. "This was where my father brought me to teach me how to fight," Diocletian said. "The lessons he taught me! I still remember the bruises I had at the end of each session. Even with me—his own son—he was not gentle in the field. He was a member of the Thirteenth Gemina and a centurion at his retirement."

Each foot of earth seemed to awaken memories in him. "He was a veteran, retired from the legion, then, of course. It was always assumed that I, the oldest son, would follow him and be a soldier. He died, of course, but I wish he could have known."

Diocletian drew a deep breath. "I always find myself talking differently with you than with anyone else. Have you noticed?"

Again, he inhaled deeply. "By all the gods it smells better here than in Asia. There's less corruption in the air. The earth is younger here, and so am I. This would be a good place to plant a garden and live out my days. It smells right."

Genesius sniffed the air companionably. Diocletian was right; there was a difference, a warm, fertile scent of soil combined with the tang of the sea.

"I don't tell other people these things," Diocletian said. "Not my servants, not my wife. They don't understand or even want to. To them, my every utterance must be analyzed until the political meaning is teased out of it, even if there is no meaning greater than the fact that I like the smell. I have not even seen them since we left Nicomedia, but they're back there somewhere"—he nodded to the rear of the procession—"hatching one kind of intrigue or another to make me change my mind."

While the two talked, the wagon passed through Aspalathos, a little hamlet of thatch-roofed huts.

"But I am like that!" He pointed to the fortress, which stood out in stone solidity against the sudden horizon of the sea. All around it, circling the palace like a crown, grew the thorn bushes that gave the village of Aspalathos its name. Cut like a sculptor's chisel, the road straightened out as it approached the palace through the thorny avenue.

The palace was a fortress massive enough to withstand any assault that could conceivably be mounted. From the land side its walls stretched straight up for thirty feet of blank stone. The only interruptions in the north wall were square bastions that gave a commanding field of fire against any who dared approach along the ground. In the center of the wall—five hundred feet long—was a doubled gate. Anyone gaining entrance through the first door could be trapped, if unfriendly, and killed.

The master builder met the procession at the north gate. After paying royal honors to Diocletian he begged permission to lead the emperor on a tour. Diocletian dismissed the normal retinue of servants, who tried to follow his divine presence everywhere he went. "This is for myself," he muttered as they slowly and unwillingly dispersed. "I must have something for myself."

The chamberlain was shouting commands to the arriving wagons. They came to a halt in line on the narrow road, hemmed in by the thorn bushes that surrounded the palace. Diocletian called Publius Labius to his side and gave orders for camp to be set up outside the walls.

"Outside?" Publius Labius asked.

"Outside," Diocletian repeated.

"But my lord—"

"The emperor has spoken," Genesius interjected, grinning. "Do you question his word?"

"No, of course not," Publius Labius said. "But I thought—we all thought, surely, that after so long a journey—"

Genesius was enjoying the chamberlain's discomfiture. Somehow he would have to make the wagons back up along the single-tracked road. The dense and prickly underbrush left no possibility of turning the wagons around.

"You are paid an unwholesome amount of money to anticipate my wishes," Diocletian said, "not to obstruct them."

Publius Labius drew himself together in what little remained of his dignity. "As you say, my lord." He bowed low, turned, and went about his duties. As he berated the wagon drivers for their stupidity Diocletian grinned at Genesius.

The master builder had been standing to one side while Diocletian dealt with Publius Labius. Now he came forward. The servile smile dancing across his features vanished when he saw the serpent draped around Genesius. The snake tongued the air the builder passed through, searching for his scent, and the man jumped away in panic.

"It won't hurt you," Genesius assured him. "It's quite tame."

But the snake was not behaving tamely. It waved its head around, tongue flicking wildly through the air. Genesius tried to comfort it. Something seemed to be making it nervous, but there was no sign of what that might be. Genesius murmured to the snake and stroked it. It stopped its movements but kept tasting the air.

"It doesn't look tame to me, begging your pardon, sir," the builder said.

"Just show us around," Diocletian ordered. "I want to see what you've accomplished."

The builder, keeping an eye on Genesius and the serpent, led them through the doubled gate into the palace. The gateway itself was five times the height of a man but narrow. One mounted soldier might pass through without scraping his knees, but only one. Overhead, an iron grid allowed a defender to drop missiles. There was an interlocking mechanism, which could be disabled from inside the palace, which, when activated, would force the outer door to shut before the inner door could be opened. Diocletian seemed fascinated with the mechanism.

Once past the north gate, they found themselves in an unroofed colonnade that stretched over two hundred feet to the south before being crossed by another.

"On either side, my lord, you have your bedrooms and offices and suchlike, for the officials and guests," the builder said as they strolled between the ranks of columns. "I don't imagine that you're too interested in those, so I planned—"

"No, I want to see them," Diocletian said. If he had any failure as a leader, perhaps it lay in paying too much attention to detail. The builder led them between a pair of columns and into the work area. The offices were only empty rooms, scheduled to be filled later with the scores of functionaries who kept the bureaucracy working. After a few moments of wandering through unused rooms, the builder led them into the eastern end of the main east-west corridor. The afternoon sun nearly blinded the three men as they made their way

to the main intersection nearly two hundred feet away. Diocletian
and the builder were chatting amiably about construction techniques,
as Genesius followed a few paces behind. The serpent was giving him
trouble again; its muscles rippled down its length, a rapid tightening
and loosening around the actor's body. Again, its tongue flashed
through the air, in and out, tasting. The contractions of the snake
became more violent as they approached the crossing point of the
two colonnades. Diocletian and the builder had already turned to the
south when the snake's convulsions threw Genesius to the floor at
the exact point where the two corridors met. The snake seemed to
hold Genesius' head pointed at the exact center of the palace floor.
Diocletian and the builder turned back and tried to tear the serpent
from Genesius. She raised her head and hissed at them, as if in
warning. The sound made Genesius stop struggling against her
strength, which far outmatched his own. She seemed content merely
to hold him in place; as long as his head was pointed toward the floor
she relaxed her muscles, but as soon as he tried to shift his position
she tightened around him again.

Eventually he got the point and looked at the central stone in the
floor. Chiseled into the granite was the sign of the fish, and it
contained the letters I-C-T-H-Y-S.

Genesius bit back a scream.

"What's the matter?" Diocletian cried. He pulled at the snake, and
the serpent released Genesius and slithered along the floor. Genesius
pointed at the inscription with a trembling hand. Diocletian and the
builder knelt to look.

"I didn't put it there!" the builder said. "I didn't know. It wasn't
there this morning, I swear it wasn't. I inspected the whole palace
today—it wasn't there." He quivered in terror; the emperor's rages
were famous. Word had quickly spread about the deaths of his
servants who publicly embraced the Christian faith. "I didn't know."

"Have it removed," Diocletian said. "Today. Now." The builder
scurried to find a stonemason to erase the offensive carving.

"My serpent," Genesius said, "forced me to look at the inscription—
against my will."

"That's impossible," Diocletian said.

"I know," answered Genesius. "That's what bothers me."

Diocletian began to speak, then shut his open mouth with an
audible click. Their eyes met, their expressions puzzled and more
than a little worried.

The snake, having moved southward into the peristyle, paused in front of an arched doorway, and stared back at them.

Waiting.

Genesius shrugged. Diocletian nodded uncertainly. They followed.

The serpent entered the temple of Jupiter built to celebrate the divinity of Diocletian. The actor and the emperor followed, slowly, cautiously.

They plunged into darkness. Where the colonnaded avenues of the palace had been bright with afternoon sun, the temple's roof cut out almost all natural light. Beyond the weak glow from the eastern doorway, only a few candles relieved the towering blackness. The two men were blinded by the gloom. The serpent was out of sight.

"It's magnificent," Diocletian said, his voice hoarse with emotion.

"It frightens me," Genesius said.

"Yes, exactly," Diocletian said. "I know Jupiter. I have known him for years, but only now do I finally stand in his presence."

"It's a statue," Genesius said.

"It is the god." Diocletian led the way, still whispering, in a circuit around the massive granite idol. "The sculptor has captured us in stone—myself and the god. Now I can see myself as I am, man and god, looking up at myself, looking down at myself, seeing myself." He whirled on Genesius. "Have you ever done this?"

Genesius' eyes by now were adjusted to the gloom. By the candle's flickering, uncertain light, he saw Diocletian's face. The emperor was happy, even joyful—justified. The worry lines that wove a net around his eyes and furrowed his brow were relaxed. The shadows moved across Diocletian's face. *Perhaps,* Genesius thought, *it is a trick of the candles' dim light.* Diocletian turned him to look up at the massive idol.

"It is Jupiter. The skeptics are proved wrong. The atheists are proved wrong. The Mithraists are proved wrong. The Christians are proved wrong."

The idol cowed the actor. It loomed over him and seemed to move in the quivering light and shade thrown by the candles. Its outstretched arm hung twenty feet above his head in benediction—or was it anger? The massive hand at one moment seemed to bless, at the next, to deny. Was it opened or closed in an angry fist?

"And I will prove to them that they are wrong!" Diocletian shouted. His parade-ground voice bounced against the unyielding walls and poured back over the two men, encompassing them, and growing stronger through some acoustical idiosyncrasy of the architecture.

Diocletian fed the waterfall of sound, renewing his challenge against his opponents.

"Roman Jupiter!" he screamed, "I shall bring you home!"

His added words cascaded against the walls and thundered back at them tenfold strong, a hundredfold. The floor moved against their feet in waves, throwing them to the floor. Stone cracked over their heads. Genesius saw what the result must be. The quake had thrown him against the wall, where there was some safety from its structural strength. But Diocletian lay on his back, transfixed under the hand of Jupiter.

The serpent struck out of the darkness. Her unvenomed teeth snatched at Diocletian's flesh. The pain galvanized the older man into movement. She kept after him, biting furiously.

Instinctively he dodged her. She chased him from his place under Jupiter's outstretched arm. The unnatural effort exhausted her. She lay helpless on the stone floor as the armature gave way.

The hand of Jupiter dropped down and crushed the life from her.

T he earthquake brought Diocletian's guards running into the palace. When they arrived, they found Genesius helping the emperor out of the temple. Diocletian was bruised but conscious, bearing the wounds of the serpent's bite. Genesius was unmarked, and the guardsmen drew their conclusions accordingly. Several of them arrested him, while the others removed Diocletian to the camp outside. Publius Labius was with them.

"Take the assassin outside," he ordered. "If he tries to escape, kill him."

Diocletian tried to protest, but he was disoriented and confused from terror and pain. The soldiers carried him to his tent and the ministrations of the court physicians. The smaller group roughly hurried Genesius out as well. They bound him with cords to a tree that stood among the thorn bushes and placed a guard on him. A small stream ran nearby.

The soldiers had removed his clothing, and he crouched naked, his back rubbing raw against the tree's bark. Under his bare feet, they piled branches from the thorn bushes. When he allowed himself to sag forward, the thongs pulled his arms upward behind him; when he tried to stand erect, his bonds only allowed him to straighten his knees partway. When he sagged against the bonds, his limbs went to sleep. When he tried to stand erect, the pain of returning feeling made every restricted movement agonizing. No matter what he tried, the thorns clawed at his naked soles.

They had tied him so that the setting sun shone in his face. Since the soldiers were from the praetorian guard, their weapons and their armor were polished to mirror brightness as a matter of course. They amused themselves by reflecting the sun's light into Genesius' eyes, forcing him, at least at first, to twist and turn against his bonds to try to protect his eyes. Mercifully, the sun soon slipped below the horizon.

Shortly after dusk, Publius Labius appeared and dismissed the guards.

"Genesius," he whispered. The actor raised his head. "I haven't forgotten you."

Genesius tried to speak, but his throat was parched.

"Do you need water?" Publius Labius asked. Genesius nodded weakly. The chamberlain cupped his hands into the stream and held them to Genesius' lips. The actor struggled to drink, then coughed explosively. The water was brackish from the nearby sea. Nevertheless, it moistened his throat, although the salt stung the soft membranes.

"Can you speak now?" Publius Labius asked.

"Yes," Genesius croaked.

"You have been arrested on a charge of treason. You have endangered the life of the Augustus with your serpent, which I am happy to say is dead. Tomorrow you will be examined in front of the entire court, and you will confess your crimes. If all goes according to plan, you will be beheaded. If not, you will be tortured until the plan is carried out satisfactorily. Do you understand me?"

"But Diocletian knows—"

"The emperor knows nothing," Publius Labius said. "He has been given poppy juice, to ease the pain of his wounds, and he is asleep. The dosage was such that he will probably sleep out the night and well into the day."

"That's too much," Genesius protested. "You could kill him."

"I doubt it. He's a tough old bird," Publius Labius said.

"Think about what I said. An easy death or a hard one, but a death in either case." He turned to go, a satisfied smile flirting with his lips. "Have a good night."

He disappeared into the gathering darkness. Genesius was left alone. He did not even bother to struggle against his bonds; surely the guards would return soon. But as the night deepened, and the torches began to be lighted along the walls of the palace and in the camp, Genesius was still alone. It was unaccountable, unless Publius Labius wanted to terrorize him with night fears. But Genesius had spent too much time cold, hungry, and lonely in his youth to succumb easily. He fought against his bonds. As the temperature dropped the leather tightened and hardened against his flesh, biting even more deeply.

An animal rustled in the brush. Genesius tried to see into the darkness, helpless if the beast were predatory. It passed, and he willed himself to relax. The pain was becoming a companion he understood—not pleasant, but familiar, predictable. He let it guide his thoughts about the morning to come, when he would face the choice presented by Publius Labius. Death was common to young and old, even though a mystery. He had no longing for it, but his bonds were tightly secure; he lacked the strength to escape them. Injustice was as common as death, but he could not reconcile himself to the wrongness of it. He seemed to hear Lydia's voice: "Blessed are you when men revile you and persecute you—" He could not remember the rest.

✦ ✦ ✦

With the darkness came the night's chill. He began to shiver. The movement hurt, and he cried out involuntarily.

"Ssh," I warned. He started violently. I clamped a hand over his mouth, and he held in the agony of his scream, forcing the pain back down his throat. He slumped unconscious. I untied his bonds.

When he came to, I was kneeling beside him. A package with a few days' food was by his side.

"You scared the devil out of me," Genesius said weakly.

"I hope so," I said.

"What time is it?" Genesius lay weak from shock and fear. He had no idea how long he had been unconscious.

"Late."

"They'll be coming for me at dawn."

"There is time."

I pressed the package of rations into the actor's hand. My own hand trembled.

"The charge is treason."

"I know."

"You must go away," I said. "Can you walk?"

Genesius gathered himself to stand. First he raised himself on his elbows, with my arm for support, until he reached a sitting position. The scabs on his back had dried. They cracked open as he sat up; blood trickled down his back. With help he got his feet under him and slowly stood erect. The gravel underfoot dug into the tears in his feet, and tears filled his eyes.

"Which way?" he asked.

"I'll take you out," I said. "There are some people I can take you to—people we can trust."

"Christians?"

"Yes."

"I am not a Christian," Genesius insisted. "I don't want your help."

I put my arm around the young man and started to walk along the path. Genesius had no choice but to go along slowly, hobbling with stiffness and pain.

"Where else can you turn?" I asked. Genesius was too busy making his legs work to answer. He concentrated on putting distance between himself and the tree to which he had been bound. Haltingly at first, then more rapidly as he grew accustomed to the tendrils of pain that shot upward through his feet, he walked.

"What about you?" Genesius asked.

"I have done what I can," I answered. "My time at the court is finished."

We moved up a small hill and stopped to rest a moment. Spread out below and a mile behind us, all along the narrow road that led from Aspalathos to the palace, lay the wagons of Diocletian's train. Lantern light danced around each vehicle. Distant sounds drifted up to their hilltop refuge—the clash of metal on metal as the guards walked their posts, the snorting and snuffling of the horses, the low rumble of the travelers' snoring and breathing, and the lone notes of a pan flute floating high above the other sounds.

"You have never finished the story of how you came to be a

Christian," Genesius said. "I've heard bits and pieces but never the conclusion."

"We will be plenty of time for that when we are safely away from here," I said.

"What do you mean, 'we'?" Genesius said.

"I'm going with you."

"No." Genesius disengaged himself from my supporting arm. "I am strong enough to go the rest of the way myself." He fought against dizziness as he pushed away from me. "I was just stiff before, but I'm all right now. I don't need your help."

I watched the young man struggling to stand on his own without showing the weakness that made his legs tremble with effort. I turned my gaze away to hide the tears gathering in my eyes. I felt the pain of a father rejected by his child, a pain which I am now ashamed to own. But if he was determined to find his own way, there was little I could do to change him. Genesius was young, I told myself, but the tears did not stop.

"You have told me," Genesius said, "of the purpose you have found in your life—to record what happens to your fellow Christians, so that others will know of it in later times. Are you ready to abandon that purpose, just to help me get away?"

"Yes." The tears flowed freely, silently, now that I made no attempt to hold them back.

"I never married, never had a son," I said. "Until—"

"Nor I a father," Genesius whispered. "I thought I could make him see me—but it is not possible; it was never possible. I looked to him, when all along I could have looked to you." He knelt by me, still stiff and sore no matter what he claimed. He took my hands in his own. "I have been with you and used you badly, always thinking of myself. But whenever I needed you, you were ready. You are more father to me than he could ever be. Will you forgive me?"

I wiped the tears from my eyes. "Forgive you?" I laughed. "You? It is you who should forgive me! Yes, of course I do." Under the cloudless night sky we hugged each other on the top of the hill. We laughed out loud, shushing each other so that the guards down below would not hear our laughter and come to take it from us.

Exhausted, sprawled on the gravel, Genesius stared up into the sky, fruitlessly trying to count the stars that glittered against the velvet dome of night. I watched the lad's youthful wonder.

"I know what you want to say."

"Do you?" Genesius said softly.

"You haven't changed your mind. You still want to go alone out there."

"I don't want to go anywhere alone," Genesius said, "but either I go or I die. And there's nowhere else to go."

The boy's face was streaked with dirt, blood, and spittle, but it was unbroken. It was lined more than it had been when he first joined the acting company but still retained the nobility and arrogance of youth.

"Before you go—alone, I won't try to follow—I owe you the rest of my story," I said. "You are going off to escape Diocletian; more important, God is out there, waiting for you like a serpent. He may strike any time—or not strike. You may walk past Him, never knowing how close you've come. But He is there, and you, I think, are the perfect bait for God."

"I know," Genesius said, "something is waiting, impatiently. I can feel it out there. It's time to go."

"Nothing I do can prepare you, I'm afraid," I said, "but sometimes young men can learn from the experiences of their elders."

Genesius took my hand and grinned at me through the predawn darkness, and I finished the story of my conversion.

✦ ✦ ✦

The Christians in Patmos told me to see a priest named Anthimus when I reached Bithynia, that he had things to say that I ought to hear. After leaving the ship and her crew at the quay I wandered through the streets of Nicomedia. This, remember, was during the days of toleration, before the killing began again.

Philosophers were everywhere—street corners, private houses, the baths, the markets, the law courts, the temples—even hanging from the trees, I thought. And each one had his own idiosyncratic key to the secrets of the universe.

For that is what we philosophers thought them to be—secrets which could only be read by a special talent or knowledge. We have learned better but only at the cost of many of our fellow seekers' lives.

The secret is that there is no secret. You do not need to be one of the initiates of the mystery cults; you do not need to be a scholar or intellectual to be capable of understanding the way the universe works; you do not need to have a special key available only to some select group.

The secret is that there is no secret.

Anthimus pointed this out to me over and over again. "Come all of you that are heavy laden, and I will give you rest." I found him preaching in his church, the same building burned down by Diocletian's soldiers. Over and over he explained the obvious—God built the world in such a way that we are important to Him; the proof of that importance is the fact that He sent us His son; the proof that He is God's son is that He was murdered and came back to life; and, once you accept that fact, the things God's son has to say to you take on a certain importance. You take on a certain importance, because God in His infinite wisdom finds you worth speaking to.

God finds you and shows you to yourself. When God first found me, I wanted to convert the emperor. That was obviously my task, because God placed me in a position to do so.

Anthimus was appalled; he would not allow me even to try. If it were God's will that Diocletian should embrace the faith, he argued, God would be able to find a way without my help. If God had a task for me, he said, it would become obvious.

The way he explained that point—that God Himself would show me what He planned for me—was what solidified my faith; it made such sense that it became an intellectually attractive proposition. First, it implied that God indeed had a place for me in whatever plan He had. Second, it said that God had a plan, that the whole world and everything in it has direction. But the real attraction was that God had a way of letting me know where I belonged. He gave me, either from birth or through training, certain abilities and characteristics, certain strengths and weaknesses. As these traits come into play in the course of my life, I can, if I pay attention, see how they are to be used. Things will happen to me, and I learn, for instance, that my ability to use words has the power to harm or to heal another person. Something else happens, and I learn that my tolerance for physical pain is very low. God pushes and pulls and kneads the clay of my self until I am sculpted into my unique shape. Or I am like a piece of granite that the sculptor works with, chipping away the excess stone until the form within the stone emerges into view. But there is a difference. Stone is far less animate than a human being; we resist the sculptor's chisel with far more vigor and intransigence than does stupid stone. We twist and turn away from the sharp edge and the cracking impact of God's tools, and so, twisting when the chisel strikes, we sometimes splinter under the blow. If the stone does not trust the sculptor, what other result can there be?

But Jesus comes to say, "Stand still! Be quiet! Nothing that I do will harm you," and He steadies us under God's chisel. We can trust Him because He has been through all of this before us and shown us that there is a life beyond.

And if we stand still and let the sculptor work on us, instead of falling into fragments at the chisel's touch, we grow stronger as our form more nearly comes to be what God intends. This is what Anthimus, who, before he knew Christ, earned his living as a sculptor, told me.

God only asks of you what you can give.

Sometimes He asks everything.

✦ ✦ ✦

Genesius left Lactantius behind on the hilltop an hour before dawn.

The air was chill against the actor's skin with a dampness from the nearby sea that made his tongue taste salt around his lips. The breeze was toward the shore; it seemed to help him climb away from the seacoast toward the foothills, through the small farms that littered the coastal lowlands.

Genesius climbed with more strength than he had thought possible. The early chill braced him, and the food that Lactantius had brought gave him fuel for travel. He wondered what kind of figure he cut, striding through the fields of Illyria in his parti-colored motley, feet soaked with dew. What would the pagan farmer in the sod house below think when he saw the citified actor tramping through his fields? More than likely, he would think that Genesius was some sort of demon and offer an extra sacrifice to the lares and penates, the gods of his hearth, if he didn't charge Genesius with a pitchfork for trampling his crop. The pagans were an unpredictable lot.

A sudden shout sounded behind him. Genesius whirled, surprised more by the fact that he was not alone than by the noise itself. He had felt as if he were the first man in the world and all of creation was his alone. Now there was someone else. It was one of the farmers he had been thinking about. The man gave a friendly wave and bent to his work again. Genesius, silhouetted on the ridge with the rising sun behind him, waved back, then ducked down the western slope. There was no point in advertising his presence any more than he already had. This was not a recreational stroll. People were after him.

A viper lay coiled under a flat rock, now warming as the sun touched its surface and making the animal active again after the torpor of the night's cold. Tendrils of warmth penetrated through the thin rock; the pulse of the snake's heart picked up, and her breathing became more rapid.

Genesius wondered whether Publius Labius would send the troops after him, or would his absence be enough to satisfy the chamberlain. In any case, he would do better to keep moving.

He did not understand his mood. Why was he cheerful? He was leaving behind everything that he had ever managed to gather—recognition, fame, money, a steady diet, friends—and following a will-o'-the-wisp into the wilderness. And as he walked he even sang, the lunch sack on his back bouncing companionably, if painfully. It was completely unaccountable and great fun.

He had not thought that being on the run would be so pleasant. His legs stretched as his feet trod the rocky path, parallel to the sea but out of its sight, as the sun's rays penetrated into the shallow valley. Thoughts of gods and persecutions were far from his mind as he skylarked ahead.

The viper was approaching what passed for consciousness in its tiny reptilian brain. There were only a few urges that it knew—eat, rest, nest, and protect.

The rhythmic pounding in the earth was faint at first and the viper torpid from the night. But as it warmed the pounding sounded louder and louder, an insistent rhythm that shook the very structure of the world the snake inhabited. Gravel—small bits of the sheltering rock—began to spatter the viper's coils as Genesius neared. In the warming darkness the snake felt his approach with rising fury and a mother's rage. Her nest was freshly laid, and though exhausted from the effort, she was roused to its defense by a pattern of behavior older than any living thing.

The walker's approach was deafening underground, a cascade of thunder heard with every cell of the ancient reptilian skin, each scale weighed down by sound and its meaning for the creature, a reenactment of the pattern of attack and defense. Every footfall terrified the quaking viper, making her cower below the ground, unable to stop the power from harming her eggs. Every vibration pumped more venom into her already-dripping fangs. Every pause between footsteps let her edge closer to the hole through which light entered her hiding nook. The vibrations became overpowering, but her concentration never wavered from the light-filled gap.

When shadow fell across her eyes, she struck. Genesius screamed. The attack was so unexpected that the pain found expression without the least inhibition.

The skin resisted at first, but she was too strong; the points of the fangs delved below the surface of his shin, where they struck bone. Genesius grabbed at the snake's lashing body and ripped it from its hold on his flesh. As the broken fangs came free, poison squirted from her mouth. Genesius swung her overhead, thrashing the tree trunks with her long body. Her lungs collapsed. Her fangs were broken off. Her spine shattered. Her heart burst. Having given everything for the sake of her eggs, she died.

Genesius fell to the ground, whimpering still at the shock of the attack. He clutched at his torn leg.

"You're a fool!" The voice slapped at him as the shadow blocked out the sunshine.

The stranger knelt beside him. Genesius would have shrunk away when the stranger brought out his knife, if he had not been so shocked. As it was he only watched as the man cut a cross in each puncture and bent to suck out the venom.

The man sucked the poison into his own mouth, along with Genesius' blood, then spat the mixture to the side. Genesius could feel the poison—or at least much of it—being drawn backward through his veins, which resisted as if they themselves would help to kill him. But the man's strength was too much for his rebellious body, and much of the poison retreated back through vessels and tissue to the stranger's insistent mouth.

"Get up!" the hermit said. Genesius stared, stupid with pain and fear.

"Get up!" he ordered again. A calloused foot prodded Genesius' kidney with no trace of gentleness.

"Get up!" The foot kicked. Genesius hopped to his feet, trying to get a good look at his tormentor, but the man was hooded.

"March!" he ordered. Genesius limped slowly in the direction indicated.

Discoloration spread from the wound—yellow, purple, and red lines radiating from the site of the bite. Every step sent a shooting pain through the leg; every step's pain was stronger than the one before. The stranger poked and prodded at Genesius whenever he showed signs of slowing down. The actor knew that he needed to minimize movement to have any chance of surviving the snakebite, but the stranger made it clear that if Genesius did not maximize his movement, he would not move at all.

His pulse was pounding. Sweat popped out of his skin and dried there, leaving him cold and clammy. Nausea rooted around inside his belly, and dizziness began to spin his head. He was ready to collapse and accept whatever punishment if only he could rest, when the stranger halted him on a small hilltop. Genesius fell down.

"Wrestle with me," the angel said. Genesius wondered how he knew that the man was an angel.

"Because I told you so," he claimed. Genesius did not remember speaking out loud but decided that he must have; after all, the angel answered.

"Angels can do that."

The one-sided dialogue was too strange for Genesius to understand. He decided to put his side of it into words.

"What else can angels do?"

"This!"

The angel swept up his hand, and the two of them leaped into the air, rushing upward so rapidly that the wind of their passing chilled Genesius. But the vision below was worse. All the world that Genesius had ever heard of was below them, and some parts that no one had ever mentioned before. Genesius and the angel-hermit-stranger (a random, parenthetical thought: no one he had ever met had been stranger than this) were sucked up into the heavens. At first, Genesius saw the hilltop dwindle away below them, then the path on which he had been traveling when the snake struck came into view. Now they were gathering speed, and he could see Aspalathos again and the sea. To the northwest, he saw the Alps, westward the boot of Italy came into view.

Genesius stuck his head between his legs to see Greece appear over one curving horizon and beneath the other.

"Are you impressed?"

Genesius nodded, mouth drooping open in awe. "This is because of the snakebite, right?"

"Wait and see," the hermit said.

"You're a hallucination, a vision."

"One or the other," the angel agreed. "Like what you see?" He waved his hand again; he was, it appeared, given to making grand gestures, like an actor who may not know what's going on but surely knows how to put himself across.

When the hermit waved his hand, though, things changed. They flew westward, swooping in a magnificent descending turn around the rock of Gibraltar and up the coasts of Spain and Gaul. Dover's cliffs rose up in front of them, and Genesius screamed involuntarily.

At the last moment they swerved up and over the chalky buttresses.

The view took his breath away.

"That usually gets them," the angel said, a smile of self-satisfaction playing on his face. "Hold on, now!"

They climbed like young hawks, filled with strength and with desire for the airy heights. Ahead, on the northern horizon, a jewel glowed with a light to match the sun's. They arched ahead, like arrows launched from a bow at the shining target.

"Is this what angels do?" Genesius yelled.

"It's what I do," the hermit said, now flying in the shape of a falcon.

"I want to do this forever!" Genesius cried. The bird of prey smiled through his beak, eyes glinting with the northern target's light.

"This is what I want for you too," he said. The shadow covered them an instant before the attack came.

The eagle struck from above, but its shadow had given the smaller bird warning, and it had rolled to fly on its back, its smaller talons raking the eagle's breast even as the great bird's claws sank into the falcon's throat, killing it.

Genesius fell into a coracle, drifting on a frozen sea. His feathers molted, leaving him naked, alone, and once more human.

Human, he was cold, colder than the salty waves that washed across his little boat.

Publius Labius swam up to the side of his boat. "Help me get in," he said. His teeth were chattering with cold.

"This is my vision," Genesius said. "What are you doing here?"

"Everybody has to be somewhere. Are you going to help me in? It really is cold."

"It's no better here," Genesius said, but he reached over the side to help Publius Labius into the coracle. The added weight made the little boat ride lower than it should; water poured over the sides, rapidly filling the little boat.

"You can't stay," Genesius said. "You're swamping us."

"But I have no boat," Publius Labius said.

"What happened to yours?"

"I lost it, a long time ago."

"There's only room for one in this boat," Genesius said.

"Would you throw me out to drown," Publius Labius asked. "Would you be so cruel?"

"You were swimming well enough to get here," Genesius said.

"But I'm tired of swimming."

Genesius gave up talking. The only solution was to throw Publius

Labius into the water, but the coracle was an unstable craft at best; swamped, it gave no protection at all from the waves.

Genesius tried to stand; he needed leverage to remove the chamberlain from the boat. Each of Genesius' movements made the coracle tip alarmingly. Publius Labius made matters worse; he mirrored Genesius' actions, making the craft pitch and tilt even more. Naturally, it spilled both of them into the black, cold water. Salt stung at Genesius' eyes and his wounds and the double crosses carved into his shin. Publius Labius was laughing at him from below.

"If I can't have a boat, then no one can have a boat," he cried, "least of all, you!"

Genesius struggled to get back into the coracle, but it was impossible. When he tried to put his weight on the side to hoist himself in, the little boat turned upside down and smacked him in the head. He tried over and over, until, exhaustion setting in, he let himself drift down below the surface of the frozen sea, a trail of bubbles escaping his lips. Publius Labius swam alongside, grinning, seemingly not needing to breathe.

Where the dolphin came from, Genesius never saw, but clearly Publius Labius saw its arrival. He paddled backward under the sea, frantically trying to distance himself from the approaching form. It ignored him and slid up under Genesius. Using the pressure of the water to hold him in place, it carried Genesius gently back to the surface. Fresh air revived Genesius, and he was able to jump from the dolphin's back to the relative safety of the coracle.

Safe in the tiny boat, Genesius gasped for air. Before the fish that rescued him vanished back under the sea, he saw that engraved on the dolphin's back, like a brand burned into flesh, were the letters ICTHYS, and he wondered what was real, what hallucination.

Publius Labius surfaced, his body that of a seal. He barked twice, then he vanished below the waves.

"Hallucination," Genesius said out loud. "It has to be." But his near-drowning had seemed real enough to him.

The wind had been substantial when he was flying into these freezing Arctic regions. It seemed to Genesius that all of it would almost make sense, if only he could have time to think, to connect all the parts of the puzzle. He recognized the sensation from his dreams, which had always been vivid and colorful. But in dreams, to ask was to answer. Now, he could ask the question and have no sure sense of what the answer might be. Everything was open to question.

He picked up the coracle's oar and began to paddle, but he had no sense of direction, and the flat-bottomed little craft would only turn in circles no matter how he tried to steer it.

With all the transition of the dream state Genesius found himself scraping at the sand of the desert. The coracle and the paddle were gone. Instead of the frigid cold he had been suffering, now he sweated salty pints onto the desert floor. His skin was sticky with dusty sweat. A hand dragged across his throbbing forehead and left a trail of mud, which, in rivulets, dripped down into his eyes to sting and to blind him. The stinging was unpleasant but somehow expected; the blindness was a relief from the searing sky's light but brought its own danger. He could see nothing of the things that he knew were waiting to attack him.

Part of their attack was the waiting. Anticipation of pain is at least part of the act of suffering. Genesius knew that he had been through this before in outline if not in absolute detail; he knew that to make the waiting as terrifying as it was, he had to know approximately what would follow. He could not recall the details, but some of the sensations to be felt drifted into his consciousness no matter how hard he tried to keep them at bay.

"Make it stop!" he screamed into the brightness. "If you don't, I'll kill myself!"

Go ahead, a voice whispered inside his skull. *Try.* The voice's intimacy startled him. He whirled to look behind, forgetting that he was blinded.

"Where are you?" he cried.

With you.

Genesius stood very still, conscious of the grit of sand between his bare toes, the heat, the sweat.

"What do you want?"

I want what you want.

"What?"

You and I are one. What you feel, I feel. And the other way around.

"Why can't I see you?"

You are blind.

The vision shifted again; the waiting was over; the assault began. Lances of the purest pain slid between the surfaces of facing bones, the very joints themselves scraped raw by the invading shards. Genesius recoiled from the first only to back into the next, over and over again, until he was gibbering in panic, flinging his arms and legs in all directions, striking hopelessly against the streaming agony.

Why do you kick against the prickings?

"You again!" Genesius said.

Always. But you have not answered me.

"Why should I?" Genesius said, dodging, too late, a pinprick.
"Ow!"

The voice seemed to sigh with infinite sadness. "That is not a friendly noise," Genesius said. It echoed inside him, making him forget the pains and the sweat. He heard the sighing of God and knew it for what it was. The sadness was so great that he disappeared into it, was lost in its infinity, not even knowing himself lost, not knowing himself at all, just . . . gone. He would have remained gone but for a gentle touch that recovered him from emptiness and put him back inside himself, breathed breath back into his empty spirit, and set him conscious on the hilltop where the old man had brought him. He opened his eyes. The old man was watching.

"I thought you were dead," the hermit said.

"I think I was," Genesius answered. "I think I am. You are no angel."

"On the contrary," the old man said, "that's exactly what I am—a messenger of God. Just because you do not like the message is no reason to demean my calling."

He manipulated Genesius' body until the actor was pinned to the ground.

"I'm in no shape to fight with you," Genesius protested.

"It is not a question of convenience," the old man said.

"But I don't want to fight!"

For reply the hermit tightened his left arm around Genesius' belly and yanked on the actor's right wrist. Weakened by the snakebite and his ordeals in the ocean and the desert, Genesius fell without resistance to the mat. The hermit was furious.

"Why don't you fight with me?" he screamed. Genesius tried to shrug, but his collarbones were dislocated from the fall. His face distorted in pain. The hermit, seeing his pain, sat on his back, twisted his arms up behind him and rocked to and fro with his knee in the small of Genesius' back,

"You are alone," the hermit said. "There is no one to help you. Not your mother, not your father, not your friend, not your lover—no one to help you, for ever and ever, world without end, amen." His litany, once completed, began again, an endless repetition of despair. Genesius' face was forced against the mat of the gymnasium. As if projected on its surface, an image appeared before his eyes. It was of Jesus the Christ, lying supine on his cross, surrounded by Roman soldiers. One raised a hammer well overhead. Genesius watched it flash heavily downward and imagined the ring of steel on steel as it struck the crucifying spike into the Christ's left hand. He saw the body writhe soundlessly, trying helplessly and fruitlessly to ease the awful invasion of his person, the pain that was orders of magnitude worse than he might ever imagine. Genesius fell silent in awe.

Lost in admiration of his vision, he barely noticed when the pressure in his back eased suddenly. He was helped to face upwards but struggled against losing the vision of the crucifixion that fascinated him in its graphic detail. The actor in him noted details—how the body responds to the unspeakable agony of penetration, how the muscles cringe in a desperate effort to release the tension, to yield to the pain, to the hardness of the spike. The soldiers drag the twisted frame back into position to receive the second spike, but his muscles have contracted spasmodically and will not be stretched. Tendons and flesh tear in the left wrist as the executioners do their work. When the second spike is driven through the right wrist's bones, Genesius faints in sympathy.

Genesius awakes to find Lactantius looking down at him. "I thought you stayed behind."

"I did," the new vision says. "I am another vision. I saved you from the old man."

Genesius nodded, although he did not understand. His visions—hallucinations—came in waves, and this seemed to be another.

"The adversary was pinning you down," Lactantius said. "We thought you needed some help."

"We?" Genesius asked.

"Father, Son, and Spirit."

Genesius swallowed hard.

"You don't mean—"

"Go ahead," the vision said, "say it."

"Jesus Christ!" Genesius breathed.

"The one and only."

In spite of himself, Genesius was impressed. "No choirs of angels? Flaming chariots? That sort of thing?"

"We thought that you would respond better to the direct approach," Jesus said. "Nothing flashy, but—"

"And the visions, the snakebite, all of that—"

"Softening up, you might call it," Jesus said. "Preparation."

It was the final lie.

"No!" Genesius screamed, the sound tearing at his throat. He cursed the face before him.

Genesius trembled at his temerity. The face of Lactantius melted into that of Publius Labius, who hissed at him and vanished in a puff of sulfuric smoke. There was a ruddy flash, then Genesius was lying on his back, the body of the snake crushed between his fingers, the stones of the path digging painfully into his back, the light fading from the sky into evening.

"I have been almost a Christian all my life," he whispered.

The laughter began deep inside him; it took a moment or two to find its way to the surface, but once it did, he could no more deny it than he could deny himself breath. The realization of the obvious—it was what he had dealt in all his life—and here it had happened to him.

The word, the truth, and the life—it was so demandingly simple that no one could see it. Everyone searched for complication, but it was as simple as his old teacher had told him in trying to teach him to act: the truth is the tool of the artist and the weapon that the common man lacks and will pay to see used. And here was Christ, offering truth so simply, so easily, that none—or few—could accept it and make it their own.

He wanted to shout from the rooftops—Genesius the actor is a Christian!—but there were no roofs, no houses in the wilderness. Even Diocletian could appreciate the insight, the knowledge, the gift of Christ. Genesius understood now the inability of the tongue-tied mystics to explain what they had been through on their mountain-tops. He would be a fool for this Christ, who came to him not as a tale told by a wandering preacher, not as a pale memory ten genera-tions old, but as a living presence, as a breath of life-giving air. He foresaw a future when the presence of Christ would be as familiar to him as the inside of his clothing, as comfortable as an old shoe. And he knew that when he felt safe, when he thought he knew what to expect from the Word of God, the Word would turn him inside out. He laughed out loud, alone, when he understood that there would be no dullness, which is what he had feared most, that God would not be boring after all.

It was a great relief.

But he was still, he noticed, alone. His epiphany was strangely solitary. He had thought, when he realized the truth, that his percep-tion of the world would somehow change. The colors ought to be brighter, the world filled with symbol, his being transformed by his newfound Christianity.

But it was not so. Now that he knew, there were no signs of angels hovering overhead. The air smelled the same. The dead snake crushed between his fingers was as slimy as ever. Corruption was still part of the world.

So was weather. He had no idea how long he had been in this particular spot. It was beginning to get cold. Genesius wondered, briefly, how he would manage alone in the autumn night. He began to throw the snake's corpse away, then realized that it would make a nourishing, if small, meal. Thought of the snake reminded him of the wound. He lifted the hem of his tunic to examine his leg.

The paired holes were still there, although the discoloration had lessened. Centered on each puncture was a thin cross cut into his flesh. He probed cautiously with his finger; the pain was small, nothing to what it had been.

The poison had been leeched from his body. If he had wanted a miracle, he could have this one. It was there for the taking. All he had to do was accept it, but he did not know how. What trick was it that had healed him surgically while alone in the wilderness? Had he, somehow, while hallucinating, worked on himself? He drew his dagger; there was a bloody residue left on the blade. But what did that tell him?

A primitive part of his mind bent his knees before the power of the God. Whatever Its name, reasoned the old brain, it was stronger than he. It was left to Genesius' reason to name the power that had healed him.

He was a city-dweller, a sophisticated man, well-versed in the trickery of appearances. He knew how to deceive the senses. He could make no decision, reach no understanding, about what had happened to him along the trail.

Genesius looked back the way he had come. Behind him lay the East—the empire, Nicomedia, all he once was. Ahead lay the West, though his trek would force a northerly detour at first; ahead lay whatever he would become.

Kneeling, he bit into the raw flesh of the viper. He would need his strength for the journey to come.

CHAPTER 26

Genesius whistled. He hummed. He chuckled to himself. He sang a few snatches of song from some of the plays he had been in, until he heard himself mouth the lyrics, and, understanding obscenity a little more than he once had, he stopped, sheepishly wondering if he had been heard.

He wondered whether the theme of his song was lost to him forever now that he was a Christian, or would there be a place for sexuality in Christian-ness? It was a question worth considering. He had heard that many of the Christians eschewed marriage, let alone whoring; he would hate to have to give up everything.

The road to Rome was long. Until he reached Aquileia, at the top of the Adriatic Sea, he had avoided cities and towns, trusting his luck to stealing farmers' grain and whatever wildlife he could capture. But after a few days of hunger (he was an actor, after all, without experience as an outlaw), he needed food and rest.

He wandered into a village outside of Aquileia, apparently aimlessly, until he came across the sign of the fish: Jesus Christ, God, Man, Savior. He was not an idiot; he recognized a sort of operational necessity. He drew the sign of the fish absent-mindedly in the dirt with his toe, next to the original, and an arrow pointing to the patio of an inn, where he sat down and ordered a drink, prepared to wait as long as it took for some member of the local church to notice his presence.

"I'll see the color of your money, first," the innkeeper said. Genesius opened the purse Lactantius had prepared for him and removed the silver coin bearing the image of Diocletian.

"Is that good enough for you?" he demanded. He was afraid, thirsty, hot, and irritable.

The innkeeper eyed the silver piece like a hungry boar, peering around the folds of fat that covered his cheeks.

"What will you have?"

"I want the tallest, coldest, driest wine you have," Genesius said. "And bread to eat with it."

"Anything else?"

"No," Genesius said, keeping his eye on the street where he had inscribed the sign of the fish.

"Bread and wine it is, sir," the innkeeper declared. "It will only be a moment."

Genesius felt exposed as the innkeeper left his table. The sun beat fiercely down, and everything was covered by a thin film of dust, including all the membranes of his mouth and throat. He was impatient for the wine to cut through the layers of earth collected on his lips and tongue.

It would be difficult to enter the network that the Christians must have, Genesius thought. Their security—smiling, he corrected himself. The Christians were no longer "they" to him. As soon as he could prove himself, "they" would become "we." Our security must be stringent, or else it would long ago have been penetrated by imperial agents. In the countryside there were as yet few Christians; it was an urban phenomenon. The country people—the *pagani*—were notoriously conservative, but the cities were honeycombed with novelty. Aquileia was a port town; there were Christians here.

Genesius was hungry for the company of others who had experienced something similar to what he had. Christ could be so distant when He wasn't hammering away at you, and Genesius was beginning to doubt the reality, if there was any, of what he had been through. At first, he had enjoyed being alone with his newfound revelation—he sang to Jesus, had long talks with Him during their walk up the coast of Illyria. But the freshness had faded after the first few ecstatic days. What he had left was the memory of revelation, a pale shadow of revelation itself.

The innkeeper brought the wine in a bottle sweating from the unseasonable heat. He thumped it inhospitably down on Genesius' table and waddled off. Genesius wiped the bottle where the greasy innkeeper had held it. At least it was cold. He poured it into the goblet, mixed in a little water to ease the bite, and drank. After tasting it, he added more water; the wine was as rough and new as could be. He tore off a chunk of the fine bread the Italians made and sank his teeth into it. The bread soaked up the wine in his mouth and calmed the sting it left.

The coin with which he had paid for his meal was his last. Lactantius had made him leave with some money in his purse, but what little there had been was now gone. At least Genesius was on Roman soil, now. He had often been afraid while tracing his way through Illyria that an alarm had traveled ahead of him, a warning from the imperial procession that there was a traitor loose in Illyria. Diocletian was extraordinarily popular in the region, being a native. But Genesius had made it to Italy. Now, broke, tired, and hungry, he devoured the last of his resources and waited for the Christians to come to his aid. Idly, he traced the fish in the rings his wine bottle left on the table.

Jesus, where are You now that I need You? he thought to himself. He dunked another chunk of bread into the wine and chewed morosely on the crust. A hand tapped his shoulder.

"Come with me."

Genesius leaped to his feet, and turning, saw who beckoned him.

"What do you want?" he demanded.

"Are you coming or not?"

Genesius stared into the stupid, porcine eyes of the barman, past the greasy sweat that glistened on his pocked cheeks, the forelock of damp hair that hung from a forehead wrinkled with impatience.

"Are you coming?" The innkeeper walked away, not seeming to care whether Genesius followed him or not. He was disappearing into the house when Genesius was finally able to make himself follow.

When he reached the interior, the innkeeper had vanished. The room was empty but for a girl who stood with her back to the door.

"Excuse me," Genesius ventured. The girl seemed to stand up a little straighter. "I—I don't quite know what—"

She turned to face him, and he floundered into silence. It was Lydia.

"You have come," she said.

"You're alive," he breathed.

"Ssshh." She put a finger to her lips. "Don't speak. Just let me look at you for a moment. I have been hoping so long." She stared at Genesius until he became uncomfortable under her scrutiny. All the while, though, he could scarcely contain himself. She remembered him. She loved him. And he was now a Christian, and there was no bar between them. He stepped forward to take her in his arms.

She retreated.

He advanced.

She retreated again, a look of such pain in her eyes that Genesius stopped almost against his will.

"What's the matter?" he asked.

"You are," a male voice behind him said, "and you don't even know it." The sea captain stood over Genesius.

Genesius nearly screamed in frustration.

"Did you bring the book?" Lydia asked.

Genesius turned back in confusion.

"What book?"

"Paul's letter," the captain said, "entrusted to you by Anthimus."

"I left it," Genesius said. "I didn't know it was important." The captain gave no sign of having heard him. "I had to leave in rather a hurry."

"Oh, don't make jokes now, please," Lydia said. To the captain, she ordered, "If he doesn't have it, he doesn't have it. There is nothing we can do about that."

"What is so important about a book?" Genesius wanted to know.

"From his own hand?"

"Jesus'?"

"Paul's."

"Don't you have other copies?"

"Yes, but that's not the point," the captain said. "Paul himself held that one in his own hands, wrote those words himself."

"Are those words any better because they are from Paul's hand?"

"It's not magic, if that's what you're thinking." Lydia broke into the discussion. "That would be idolatrous, and we are cautioned against that. But if we held the pages actually written by Paul in our hands, we would be that much closer to the earliest days, when the faith was pure and uncorrupted. Relics like that give me a feeling of connection. It would be like having a souvenir made from a piece of the cross itself—a constant reminder that it is all real."

"Do you mean that you have doubts too?" Genesius asked. The revelation shocked him. Lydia was all that was ideal in his world. Was she flawed?

"No, not really." She blushed. "Not now." She reached for his hand.

"We must be going," the captain said.

"Where?"

"Rome," Lydia answered. "Where the emperor is going."

✦ ✦ ✦

The emperor raged in the bedroom of his new palace. Publius Labius took the brunt of his fury but remained calm. I watched from a corner of the room, present but almost invisible to the participants in the discussion.

"You will come to see, divine one, that the actor is a traitor to you, to Rome, and to all of us," he said. "He tried to kill you."

"I was there," Diocletian said. "I should know what happened. Genesius did not do what you accuse him of."

The chamberlain moved carefully across the room in front of the emperor's bed. "Your grace will understand that the physicians have dosed you with poppy and that you might therefore have dreams that seem like reality. We all know of your affection for the actor Genesius. And given that affection, it is certainly no wonder that your mind would try to deny what it manifestly knows—that Genesius betrayed and tried to assassinate you."

"So you say," Diocletian muttered from his bed.

"So I know." Publius Labius had somehow lost his lisp. The voice that issued from his lips now was still pitched high, but it came from him with a strength and harshness that he had heretofore kept hidden. "Someone released him. Someone showed him a way to escape. Someone gave him food and money for the journey, and, thanks to someone, he is on his way northward. There is no doubt, my lord, that he is a traitor. And, he is not alone. The Christians are helping him."

"I don't believe it."

"Whether you believe or not," Publius Labius gloated, "he has left you."

✦ ✦ ✦

They moved from city to city, sometimes walking in the open, the sea breeze teasing at their hair, sometimes hidden in the night, unable to see, only hearing the anti-Christian rioters parading through the streets.

Lydia taught Genesius to talk to God—Father, Son, and Holy Ghost. She taught him the basics, not attempting the subtleties of the faith, because her own belief was immediate in its literal sense—nothing stood between her and her God. She taught Genesius her kind of belief. He listened to her voice, but he learned as much from the changing colors of her hair in the varieties of light that fell from the Italian sky.

She learned from him, as well. He told her the stories of his life, for the first time holding back nothing, telling all, from the smallest hurt to the greatest triumph.

The sea captain was no fool. He saw that Lydia and Genesius walked side by side during the day and lay side by side at night, but he could only take her aside at brief intervals by day and attempt to counsel her against involving herself with the actor.

"It is as if I were to fall in love with a whore!" he complained to Lydia while Genesius was in the bushes, relieving himself. "What will people say?"

She flared into luminous anger. "Who appointed you the guardian of my morals? You are no better than the pagans, who class actors with whores. We are supposed to be different!"

Genesius came back to join them. The sea captain lengthened his stride and pulled ahead of Lydia and Genesius. Soon, they were alone on the road.

✦ ✦ ✦

The emperor's people took ship in the harbor at Aspalathos to travel across the sea to Italy. It was the second sea crossing of the long journey, and in accordance with the wishes of Diocletian and the detailed plans of Publius Labius, the ships arrived in the evening at the harbor built into the side of the palace. They came in strict order of precedence from the sea, into the little harbor mouth, along the far shore, then up to the quay by the palace's side, where the wharf was jammed with wagons and travelers waiting to board.

Diocletian was already on the water. A small boat was leaving his ship of state. Aboard it was the centurion Martius, who had just finished delivering his report to Diocletian concerning the fires which had destroyed the palace at Nicomedia. Martius' report left no doubt who was to the blame for the conflagrations.

The sight of the retirement palace, another site of betrayal, was unbearable to Diocletian. He waited at sea, alone insofar as he could be alone, buried in details of state politics, occupied with the trivialities of ruling a world, having lost the love of his friend, for Galerius was due on board the ship which Diocletian had taken from Aspalathos. Diocletian knew that Publius Labius had arranged the meeting at the behest of the caesar: another betrayal.

"My lord," Galerius said as they met in the ship's cabin, where Diocletian had retreated from the view of Aspalathos. "Greetings."

Diocletian was silent; Galerius seemed not to notice but went right on.

"Your daughter, my wife, sends her greetings and her filial love through me to you," he said. "She also begged me to greet her mother for her."

"I'll pass the word."

"Of course," Galerius said. "How goes the campaign in the East?"

"Campaign?"

"Against the Christians."

"I am not so sure that it was the best thing to do. You know the doubts I had then. They have come to plague me now. I have killed or driven away the best men I had around me, and I am left with sorry creatures like that chamberlain you've saddled me with."

"I, my lord?"

"Don't be coy, Galerius," Diocletian said. "I have been around a long time. Don't presume that because I haven't opposed you, that I agree with you. Don't confuse powerlessness with stupidity."

"I beg your pardon."

"As you should." Diocletian flung the words at his adopted son. "You have manipulated me shamelessly, and you are safe behind the savagery of your legions. You know I will not oppose you on the field because I fear civil war even more than you fear the Christians. But you were to be a son to me. Instead, you foment treason. I have lost my daughter to you. I mean to have her back."

There was again a silence between the two men, one rising in power, within sight of power, within reach of power, the other disgusted with its sight, its reach, its weaknesses.

"Very well," the coward said. "You may have her. I do not need her any longer. When will you abdicate?"

"When I have her," Diocletian said. "When I have peace, when the danger to my country is removed. After my vicennalia, when things return to normal."

✦ ✦ ✦

Lydia pushed his hand away but held the rest of him close to her. There was a past tumbling through her that Genesius knew nothing of. To him, she knew, she was still a mysterious object of love, perhaps even a sign from God. But she did not want to be a sign for anyone; she wanted to find God in her own way.

Her plan for her life had been to maintain her celibacy, making it a gift to the Spirit. It was for her an easier gift than for most. Her Christian teachers had interpreted the events of her life to be signposts on the way to a monkish existence. She had a long-standing admiration for the monks of the desert and for the virgins who had committed suicide rather than submit to rape.

When she was a child, her father had used her badly. All she knew of human love was pain.

When the opportunity arose, she escaped her family and found refuge in the arms of Mother Church. Now, at seventeen, she had little memory of the events and no experience at all in dealing with matters of real affection between the sexes. Genesius' arms around her felt warm and comforting, but he wanted to do more than hold her companionably.

Her teachers confirmed the sense of wrongness she felt concerning love. They encouraged her acquired tendency toward celibacy. The love of another human being, they said, was the snare of Satan, the means used by the enemy to entrap the souls of the saints and draw their minds away from the contemplation of the pure spirit that was God.

The body is evil, she repeated to herself as Genesius touched her hair. As long as his caresses remained innocent, she enjoyed—more than enjoyed, she reveled in—what was happening. But when his kisses became insistent and his hands moved demandingly toward parts of her body she tried not to look at, something happened inside of her.

Her skin flushed and sweat broke out over her body. Her nerves stretched taut until she felt as jumpy as a drop of water on a hot skillet. Nausea stabbed deep in her belly. Genesius felt her stiffen under his touch and mistakenly believed that she was becoming as aroused as he was.

"Stop!" she ordered.

"I'm sorry," he whispered into her ear. "We'll go slower."

"We're not going anywhere at all," Lydia said.

"But I thought—"

"It's not your fault," she said, "but I'd rather stop now." Genesius disengaged from her.

"I see."

"It doesn't mean I don't like you. We could still—"

"What?"

"Never mind," she said. "Rome is a long way away." She led the way from the glen. Genesius followed reluctantly. Lydia seemed not to notice his discomfort; it was impossible that she could understand it.

✦ ✦ ✦

Diarius was in a state of mortal terror. His principal player was accused of treason and of attempting to assassinate the emperor.

The praetorian guard was grilling each member of the acting company. One by one, the troopers had taken each of them for interrogation. Diarius' turn had arrived.

The soldiers led him into a cabin deep in the hold of the ship that was carrying them to Italy. Their ship was a trireme, with three banks of oars as well as a sail for propulsion. The two troopers led the actor-manager down a narrow flight of stairs into a little room that groaned with the sweep of the oars, where they left him with Publius Labius.

With each sweep of the oars, the ship plowed forward. Its progress was a series of lunges through the sea.

Publius Labius sat at a small table, using the only chair in the cabin.

"What has befallen us?" the chamberlain asked. Diarius decided not to answer.

"We have lost our best actor," Publius Labius went on smoothly, "to treason. Yet he left us the scenario he was to write. Have you examined it?"

Diarius nodded, afraid to use his voice, knowing that it would betray him as surely as Genesius had betrayed them. He was tormented with the knowledge that the man he himself had chosen for the emperor's service had tried to kill the sovereign. He had held the lad in fatherly affection, impressed as much by his audacity as for his ability. Now, that very characteristic had led him into—

"Treason!" Publius Labius cried. "No matter how you sugar-coat the act, it was treason. Only the influence of Jupiter himself prevented Genesius from killing Diocletian. Had it been attempted in a place less holy, I don't know what would have happened."

Publius Labius noticed that Diarius still did not speak.

"This place," he said, "has a particular virtue—privacy. There is no need to whisper; the sound of the oars masks almost anything one might say. No one can even listen at the door—the coxswain doesn't take well to strangers visiting his territory. As far as anyone else is concerned, you and I are just invisible—and inaudible." He paused for breath. "And there is so much I want to know."

Unfortunately for Diarius, there was little that he could tell the chamberlain.

CHAPTER 27

Every word was a lesson, every caress an example. Lydia was determined that Genesius understand the love of God in all its dimensions. He was formally made a catechumen, a "seeker" in Christian parlance.

He had never been in school before. He found his lessons—and his primary teacher—exciting but frustrating. Both the lessons and the caresses always seemed to stop short of completion.

Genesius found the sea captain's smugness, once the latter realized that Lydia's chastity remained unbreached, thoroughly unchristian. And chastity—not engaging in sexual relations seemed to be its definition—was, insofar as Genesius could tell from the Christians visited along the way, one of the main signs of Christianity.

"Why do you hate the body so?" he demanded of Lydia. They were in Atria at the time, staying with a family of hidden Christians who wanted to hear all the news from the East, where the persecution was in full swing. Here in the West conditions were easier, but many, out of fear, remained quiet about their faith.

"It is a distraction," their host, a man named Lucius, said. He sat at the feasting table surrounded by his wife, his nine children, Genesius, and the sea captain. "Believe me, it is much harder to keep one's mind on God when it is inflamed with lust."

Genesius leaned forward, taking another cup of the wine that had been served following the meal. It was evening. Soon, they would all retire for the night, and he had hopes of retiring with Lydia but was unwilling to risk another scene and did not want to force himself on her. Besides, the sea captain would kill him without stopping to consider the morality of the act if she so much as raised her voice in protest. But she was becoming an obsession with him. Somehow, he had to break through her fear.

"Jesus may come at any moment," Lucius said. "Certainly, no one wants to face the judgment while wrapped in the coils of sin."

Lucius' wife, Octavia, lowered her eyes, smiling. Genesius caught the blush that reddened her face. "Are you, also, a Christian, madam?" he asked.

"Of course," Lucius answered. Octavia nodded, still blushing. Genesius looked over the nine children, ranging in age from a baby of one year, sitting in Octavia's lap, to a girl of twelve who waited upon the gathering as if she were a family servant.

"If you don't mind my asking," Genesius said, "when did you decide to become Christians? Was it just recently?"

Lucius bridled. "No, indeed. We are from a long line of believers. Our ancestors have been Christians since Peter first came to Rome. We were born into the faith, both of us, and our children raised in it."

"Aha!" Genesius said. "Then the faith is more—how should I say it?— more subtle than I have been led to believe."

Octavia laughed out loud. She enjoyed seeing her husband caught out. Lydia was embarrassed.

"Thank you for your hospitality." The sea captain stood up, stretching ostentatiously. "It's time we were asleep. We continue our journey tomorrow, early."

"I'll show you to your rooms," Octavia said. Genesius, it turned out, shared a bed with the sea captain, while Lydia would sleep with the twelve-year-old girl.

Genesius did not sleep well.

✦ ✦ ✦

Constantius, father of the prince Constantine and the caesar who ruled the western reaches of the empire—Britain, Gaul, and Spain— and Maximian, the junior augustus who ruled Italy and most of Africa, greeted Diocletian and Galerius at the pier when they arrived at Ariminum. The ceremony was exhausting, the first of many that would delay the imperial passage through the Roman homeland. The city had on its finery. Banners fluttered through the broad main street that began the Via Flaminia, on which the emperors would travel to the eternal city itself.

Ariminum was Rome in little. I was one of the speakers scheduled to present a formal ode on the occasion. From the speakers' plat- form, the three-thousand-foot long stretch of cobbles beckoned the visitor's attention to the triumphal arch erected in honor of Julius Caesar, the first of the emperors, centuries before. Such thoughts were appropriate, for the purpose of the entire journey was to confirm the continuity of the imperial government.

Constantius warmly greeted Diocletian, who was by now exhausted with the journey itself, the machinations of his curia, and the disap- pearance of his young friend. The circles under his eyes were deeper than I had ever seen them before. To Galerius, Maximian was warm enough, but Constantius performed only the minimal necessities of courtesy. His nickname Chlorus, the pale one, was well deserved on this sunny day. His skin was transparent. Beneath it, blue veins pulsed, pumping some unknown illness through his frame.

The crowd that gathered in the piazza was demanding entertain- ment. It was a single organism, collected of many parts, now hungry for its proper food of pomp, color, noise, ceremony, and tribute—es- pecially tribute. It rumbled its impatience like thunder out of a bright summer sky.

The time came in the ceremony for the ritual embrace of the four saviors of the empire. The event—choreographed to the last detail by a mixture of precedent and by each leader's chamberlain—was full of ceremony, as each of the three juniors—the lesser Augustus, Maxim- ian, and the two caesars, Galerius and Constantius—demonstrated their solidarity with the senior emperor.

Diocletian, robed in purple at his entrance, enfolded each of his juniors in a robe of the imperial color on receiving the obeisance due him. In full view of the waiting crowd the four rulers embraced, each dressed like the other, each crowned, each armored, each armed with the sword of the Roman legionary, each turning a watchful eye to the outside, each guarded by the three others. As chamberlain to the senior member of the tetrarchy, Publius Labius flung wide his hands to signal the completion of the tableau. The crowd cheered with real, if fickle, enthusiasm.

On cue the soldiers guarding the tableau each tossed a handful of coins into the crowd. By tradition the coins should have been gold, but Diocletian hated the mob and would only agree to silver. When the coins were first thrown to them, the crowd cheered again. But as the coins were caught and examined, the cheers turned to mutters of discontent.

The city had raised a triumphal arch in record time to mark the occasion. It was barely finished; wooden scaffolding still surrounded the gleaming white marble. The mob, unable to vent its dissatisfaction on the well-guarded emperors, turned to their symbol of stability. With a roar that sounded like the groaning of the earth in movement, the mob rushed the arch. The more adventurous members stormed the scaffolding. The stone of the arch resisted their attempts to pull it down, but failure only infuriated the rioters. Servants were ordered to bring the chamber pots from the houses of rich and poor alike. As if the monument were on fire, the citizens of Ariminum formed a bucket brigade, passing their night's excretions from hand to hand, smearing the triumphal arch with excrement, urine, and blood. Children, catching the madness of their elders, squatted to relieve themselves in the street. Members of the lower classes followed their example.

The soldiers were helpless to prevent the desecration. Their duty remained to protect the imperial court. Only their weapons and their discipline prevented the mob from turning on the aristocrats and the emperors themselves.

The captain of the praetorian guard led the ceremonial grouping with a flying wedge from the dockside, down the imperial avenue, and onto the Via Flaminia, away from the city which was to have been the first on Italian soil to welcome Diocletian.

All of us, whether Christian or not, were terrified that the mob's violence would be turned on us.

✦ ✦ ✦

Genesius found that he had to study. There were doctrines to learn, language with specific meaning, attitudes he had held all his life that demanded changing in light of his newfound belief. Lydia and the sea captain, who finally became willing to reveal his name, Sextus, taught him during each day's trek.

Sextus recited stories from both the Hebrew Scripture and from the tales of Jesus that had been handed down by word of mouth and in writing from the days when He walked the earth with men and women. But Genesius had questions. Rather than ask the big sea captain, who tended to become angry when questioned, Genesius waited until he could be alone with Lydia after the formal sessions of instruction.

"How do you know that what you feel and believe and trust is true," Genesius asked, "and not just what you want to believe?"

Always lurking near his faith was doubt, like the serpent in the garden, waiting for his faith to lessen, for a question, like a small ache or pain, to distract him from the work of believing.

"What if we are wrong?" Lydia asked. Her liquid eyes regarded him with a compassion that he nearly rejected. "It's possible. It really is. The story sounds so fantastic, so unlikely, that it is hard to 'take on faith' the way we do. But let me turn it around. What brought you here, to this point in time, asking me this question?"

Genesius lay with his head in her lap. Her fragrance surrounded him like grace.

✦ ✦ ✦

On another occasion Genesius asked Sextus, "Why do you come with me? Lydia loves me, I know, but why do you tag along?"

"Everyone has to be somewhere," the captain said. "I find myself most often with her. And I go where God sends me. It is a constant surprise, a constant adventure. Sometimes, I think I am like her guardian angel—and I mean no disrespect in saying so—and it is my purpose to be with her when she needs me. Sometimes, this means being there when she doesn't need me—now, for instance, while she has you."

Lydia was away from them, tending to herself, doing the things that women do alone. Their feet had grown callused from their walking.

"But she will need me again, sometime," the captain said, "and I will be ready."

✦ ✦ ✦

"Hold me," she said in the darkness. She had looked ahead to Rome and seen the loss which was to come. "Hold me."

Sextus, the sea captain, waited until she would need him again.

✦ ✦ ✦

"Is there word of him yet?"

"None, my lord."

"You have searched well?"

"Everywhere your legions can search," Martius said, "they have done so, from Aspalathos to Aquileia, from Aquileia to Rome. We cannot find him."

"Keep looking," Diocletian ordered.

He could not yet put Publius Labius away from him, but he could undermine the chamberlain's orders to his household and ensure the search for Genesius. Diocletian knew, no matter what Publius Labius claimed or some of his soldiers believed, that Genesius had indeed saved his life, and he missed the actor's brash honesty. There was an empty space in him, Diocletian found, where the memory of Genesius fit perfectly.

This space was the old, still jagged memory of his early days with his wife and infant daughter, then the middle-aged days with companion Prisca and young woman Valeria, both now estranged. He had tried to heal some of the pain between them but could only feel awkward and shamed in their presence. But with Genesius he felt no shame or had felt none until now, when he had been unable to prevent the chamberlain from accusing the boy of treason.

✦ ✦ ✦

Without quite knowing why, Genesius hurried the trio on toward Rome. A tide of people surged toward the eternal city for the vicennalia; Genesius, Lydia, and Sextus were flotsam riding the wave's crest. The swell led them on, quickly and surely, following now, after Ariminum, in the wake of Diocletian, Maximian, Constantius, and Galerius.

After the imperials passed the local people, inflamed by the pious rhetoric of the paganists, treated their local Christians badly. Christians known to the public were dragged from their homes, pelted with horse dung, ridiculed, beaten, tortured, interrogated, and even killed. Genesius, Lydia, and Sextus witnessed the so-called trial of one Christian.

The mob's victim, a woman of good family, in fact the daughter of one of the city officials, was called Felicitas by her Christian friends. She was not yet a baptized Christian, but a catechumen, a seeker after Christ, still in her three-year period of probation before she would be admitted to the full communion of the faith. Felicitas tempted the mob; after the emperor and his entourage passed through the city she took the place in the agora, or market place, and denounced the tetrarchy and its policies against the fledgling church. Her father, Sempronius, tried to drag her from public view, but he could do nothing with her, and she continued her indictment of the imperium and all who cooperated with it.

Sempronius stayed for a day and a half, arguing with Felicitas and trying to convince her to moderate her views. He appealed to his paternal authority, but she rejected it, saying, "My true Father rules over heaven and earth, and His will only will I obey."

"If you have no regard for my authority," Sempronius said, "then at least take pity on my old age. Look at my gray hair. Think of the care and love that your mother and I have spent on you. Think of your sister, who may never be able to marry because you will have died in disgrace."

Felicitas remained obstinate.

Speaking through his tears, Sempronius disowned her on the spot and turned her over to his second cousin, the magistrate.

"Do what you want with her," Sempronius said. "She is no child of mine."

The trial took place right away, as soon as the *catasta*, the raised platform used for trial and torture, could be erected in the amphitheater. Felicitas was hauled in unnecessary chains before the magistrate.

"Cousin," the magistrate began, "let's get this farce over with. Burn a pinch of incense for the emperor and go home to your father."

But Felicitas intended to die. She saw the heavens split, and a ladder came down and touched the earth at her feet. A voice called to her, "Come home, daughter." And she knew it was the voice of her true Father in heaven.

The ladder was narrow, and on either side there were knives, axes, and swords, so that if she strayed either to left or right, she would be torn to pieces.

Suddenly, she found herself on the rungs of the ladder. She paused to look down. Below her, waiting for her to slip, lay a dragon coiled around the base, its mouth open, and venom dripping from its fangs. In her vision she scooted up the ladder and reached the safety of heaven. There, a man was tending a flock of sheep. Around him were many others wearing white robes. But the shepherd looked up from his work, handed her a little piece of cheese, and said "Welcome, daughter." She took the morsel and ate it, and all the white-robed people shouted, "Amen!"

When she came back to herself in the prison, she awoke with a smile and told the others about her visions. All the prisoners rejoiced with her.

When finally she was brought back before the magistrate, in the seats of the arena were many Christians, as well as those who came for the sport. The Christian brothers and sisters came to witness the agony of the witnesses for God.

To shame Felicitas, the authorities decreed that she should wear the garments of a priestess of Ceres as she was brought forth for her passion, but she refused to give even this honor to a false goddess.

"Let her go naked, then," the magistrate, her cousin, ordered.

Felicitas wore her skin as proudly as Eve must have done before she learned shame. Felicitas walked naked and alone into the arena and climbed the steps that led to the *catasta*, where she was to receive her sentence. Even this far into the persecution, the authorities failed to understand the motives of the martyrs, failed to understand that there was a greater good than avoiding execution, failed to understand that pain and death were not the worst things that a human being could face. Felicitas wore her nudity as a jewel which ornamented her trust in God. She mounted the *catasta* in serenity, a faint smile playing across her lips, as if she knew that her struggles were nearly ended, that there would be only a little more to undergo before she found her welcome in the arms of her Shepherd.

The magistrate called her out of herself.

"Felicitas!"

She looked down from her platform at the official, then at the crowd of people in the stands. She smiled at them, and her eyes seemed to rest for a moment on Genesius. She nodded to him, and her smile widened, as she recognized one of her fellows. Lydia saw the look, as did Sextus, as did Genesius himself; and all three took it for an omen.

"Will you sacrifice for the well-being of the emperor?" the magistrate demanded.

"I will pray for his health and wisdom," Felicitas said, "but I will not sacrifice in his name."

"Think of your father's suffering," the magistrate whispered, now close to Felicitas and speaking under his breath. "All you have to do is throw a little incense in the fire. That's all!"

Felicitas shook her head.

"Are you a Christian?" the magistrate asked out loud.

"I am a Christian," Felicitas answered, and her voice trembled with what Genesius could only feel as joy, as she stood before the world and repeated over and over, almost singing the words: *Christiana sum!*

The brothers and sisters in the arena picked up the chant; Felicitas was not the only martyr to be called out on that day. While she stood on the scaffold, the others, below her in the dust of the arena, lifted their voices, until the earth trembled with their massed declarations.

"Chris-ti-an-us sum!"

The magistrate felt the chant spread from Felicitas' lips to those of the other prisoners and thence to many in the audience come to watch the executions. It was not a majority of the spectators that took up the chant; but the size of the minority frightened the magistrate. Later, after the killing was over for the day, he sent a letter to Maximian, explaining his anxiety over the heretofore unrealized spread of the cult of Christ and asking for instructions. As the persecution grew in fury similar letters poured in to the courts of each of the members of the tetrarchy, each testifying that there seemed to be more of these Christians than anyone had suspected. The answers that each official received depended on which ruler he obeyed.

Just before the magistrate sent his troops into the stands to silence the chanting and try to prevent a riot between the Christians and the pagans, Felicitas raised her hands for silence.

"Your time is coming," she reminded the spectators. "It is our time, now." She looked the magistrate squarely in the eye. "Cousin, I am ready to die. Are you ready to kill me?"

She climbed down the stairs and knelt before the magistrate. She held her hair away from her neck, so that his sword might strike cleanly.

"Please, cousin," Felicitas said, "do what you have come here to do."

"Forgive me," the magistrate whispered.

"I forgive you."

The magistrate drew his sword. Its short length seemed to take an eternity to emerge from the gilded scabbard. Felicitas' lips moved silently in prayer as the magistrate raised his sword over the naked woman curled before him. The crowd grew silent; not even a whisper disturbed the tableau. The sword glittered in the evening sun, catching its last rays as the magistrate held it high over his head.

The down stroke was off by a few inches. A trembling in her cousin's hand fouled the blow. Instead of dying cleanly, Felicitas suffered a terrible blow to the head. Her scalp was torn behind her ear, and her skull shone whitely even down to the point where her spinal column emerged from it.

"Thanks be to God!" she screamed.

The magistrate raised his sword and hacked at her until it was over. It took him five more blows before Felicitas was released. The rest of the executions were delayed. The mob departed, aroused, trembling, and unfulfilled.

✦ ✦ ✦

Rome loomed on Diocletian's horizon. The Via Flaminia led inexorably from Ariminum southeast, across Italy, to the eternal city.

Diocletian was embarrassed by his own reaction to Rome. It was huge, larger than he had ever imagined, even though he had pored over the manifests of the ships that traveled almost constantly from Egypt bearing hull after hull of grain for the nonproducing capital. Even knowing how much grain Rome devoured in a single day, he was unprepared for the scale of what faced him across the Milvian Bridge. The mob, standing forty and fifty deep, lined the Flaminian Way to the very gates of the city, where they were held back by the soldiers, and towered over Diocletian; the thousands of them peering down from the walls overlooked the tetrarchy as its members entered the city. Maximian already knew; Rome was within his rule, and, while he avoided it, preferring to govern from Milan or Ravenna, he had seen it often before. But Diocletian was appalled.

"Why are they silent?" Diocletian asked Maximian. "We are their gods. Should they not cheer us?"

Just then, as if to answer his question, a mother broke through the cordon of soldiers keeping the crowd from being trampled underfoot by the procession. She thrust her infant high in her arms to receive the favor of the passing divinities. Two troopers from the second line struck her down from behind. Her infant fell under the wheels of Diocletian's wagon. The mob stopped its cheering while the woman dazedly shook her head, kneeling on all fours in the street, and the wagon rolled over the child. When the wagon had passed, the baby was still alive. When a soldier picked it up and presented it to its mother, escorting her back into the crowd, a cheer rang out. Diocletian knew that it was not for him but for the soldier. He wished that he had worn military regalia rather than following the advice of his chamberlain, who had acted as his valet this morning and placed him in the raiment of a petty Eastern king. Galerius, in the wagon behind the two augusti with Constantius, was garbed in the armor of a legionary, and Diocletian could hear the crowd respond to him.

Maximian leaned across the seat. "That beggar was well paid for that trick, I would wager."

"No doubt." Because of the noise Diocletian could speak in a normal voice without being overheard.

"Has he pressured you?" Maximian smiled broadly and waved to the crowd.

"To do what? He pressures me every day."

"To abdicate." Maximian's smile was through clenched teeth. The lips were stretched almost to the point of splitting. "To leave the thrones to him and to Constantius."

Diocletian waved automatically. What cheers the augusti received were only from the old, who remembered the years of chaos, the year of the thirty emperors. The young, and even the middle-aged, saved their praises for the caesars, for Galerius especially.

"They would cheer more if you paid more," Maximian said. "It is the custom, you know, old friend. They have looked forward to your visit for years."

"I buy no man's love." Diocletian's jaw was clenched in anger and in understanding.

He was silent for the rest of the journey along the Flaminian Way, through the crowds of Romans, whom he regarded as little better than animals. Their stench troubled his nostrils, accustomed as they were to the clear air of the countryside. The marble marvels of the city passed into and out of his sight as if they were daydreams—the mausoleum of Augustus, the temples of Hadrian and of Isis, the forum itself, even the temple of Jupiter Capitolinus where Diocletian received the ritual homage of the city. He only got through the ceremony with difficulty. The priests were disgruntled, but what priest would dare to criticize the god who employed him?

With the official ceremony of welcome finished, the procession wound through the forum to the Alta Semita, or High Street, which led past the baths, that Diocletian had paid for, to the camp of the praetorian guard, where he would stay during his visit. The army's camp was the only conceivable place within the walls of Rome where Diocletian might feel secure. Rome was foreign to the Illyrian soldier. He could not act the tourist but must allow himself to be held up to public display; must allow the Romans, parasites on the body of the empire, to examine him, look for his warts and imperfections; must give himself over to their scrutiny, seek their approval for his long twenty years of work on their behalf. It was insupportable.

Diocletian was weary and beginning to realize it. He would have had, if the accident had not occurred with the Jovian statue, a few days of peace in his palace at Aspalathos. He and Genesius might have taken time to relax and recover the ease with each other that they had enjoyed earlier. He had disposed of Publius Labius just that morning.

"You," Diocletian told him, "may still keep your office as chamberlain; I owe that to your patron, Galerius. But you will avoid my person at all costs. I do not wish to see you. I do not wish to be reminded that you exist. I do not want to hear you. I do not even want to smell your artificial aroma as I walk through the halls of my palace or the avenues of the camp in Rome. I will dress myself, wash myself, feed myself, and think for myself! Stay out of my way, or I will kill you."

Diocletian had picked up the nearest thing to hand, a goblet full of wine, and thrown it at the uncomprehending chamberlain. The wine missed him and fell on the floor. It hissed against the stone; a thin smoke rose from it as it sank into the granite, etching the place where it spilled with the shape of its passing. Publius Labius ran away.

✦ ✦ ✦

"How do they know that they are called to be martyrs?" Genesius asked. He and Lydia were resting after the day's trek toward Rome. He felt ready to give everything, including his life, for his Christ if asked. But he knew that what he might perceive as what his fellow-Christians knew as a call might be no more than a hidden desire of his own. He had been through enough to know not to trust his senses or even his understanding without some means of confirmation.

Suddenly, he comprehended something more about the story of Christ's temptation in the desert. It was a question of voices, and what one could do to distinguish between the false and the true. If it was possible to hear God, it was also possible to hear something else which only acted God's role for its own purposes. He shuddered at what that might be, for the agency he had in mind was worse than human, and the evil of its purposes must rival the sanctity of God's.

Genesius refused theology. But he knew struggle; he knew evil. Evil was the killer of the spirit, the poisoning of the breath, the destroyer of love. Evil's hands were at the throats of his new friends and his old friends. Evil lived to destroy them. And with his knowledge of evil—gained at court, on the journey, on the stage—he knew where he would find his combat. His battle awaited him in Rome in the court of his father. Only by joining it could he find his salvation.

He finally understood the word. He rolled it aloud in his mouth. "Salvation."

"What did you say?" Lydia's voice was soft, her body warm with sleep. She had drifted off in the straw of the barn, comforted with the late autumn's last golden warmth.

"It's nothing," Genesius said. "Go back to sleep." She rolled closer to him, taking soft comfort in his presence, as he did from hers. She was his penultimate gift, his solace and a source of strength before he returned to the world he had come from, returned with his hope to Diocletian, to Diarius and Hysteria and Atalanta, even to Riotamus and Janus. His last temptation was to remain as he was, listening to his elders in the faith, taking comfort from the promise of goodness in the world, avoiding the final conflict, if it waited for him.

The great temptation of the Christian was the apparent safety of the saved.

He knew that pull, as well as a chunk of lodestone knew the pull of the north. The people who had opened their homes to him, to Lydia, and to Sextus on their journey south risked their lives to help them on their way. The fish sign, scratched into their door frames or drawn in the dust of their thresholds, could bring each of them a painful death. It had happened, was happening.

Some played it safe, coming to the worship secretly, darkly, claiming their salvation as a personal right, unwilling to take in the stranger who might be their betrayer, afraid to take the final step in imitation of the Savior but demanding His salvation nonetheless. Their salvation eluded them, as Genesius' would remain unreachable were he to stop where he was. He must accept not only the glory but the cross as well.

He hoped—and prayed—that he was not again being deceived.

Then he nudged Lydia into wakefulness.

"What is it?" she muttered through her veil of sleep.

"It's time to go," Genesius said.

"So soon?" Lydia was awake instantly. "I knew it was coming. Are you certain?"

"As certain as I know that I love you," Genesius said. Her arms encircled him, wanting to hold him in stasis forever, never to let the last moment pass into eternity. Then, with a strength that she had not known she owned, she released her hold on him.

"Will Sextus come along?"

"He knows Rome. I will need a guide through the city."

CHAPTER 28

The mob waited like wolves outside the camp of the praetorians, where Diocletian had taken refuge. The field of the praetorians, where the pack lay in wait, was between the camp and the baths of Diocletian, in the far northeastern section of the city. Diocletian had placed himself as far from the center of Rome as he could and still remain within it. But Rome had his back to the wall.

He hated Rome, the filthy whore at the heart of the empire. Everything that he had spent his life opposing lay within her walls. Rome drew to herself all the forces bent on her destruction. Barbarians walked the streets unmolested. Blue-painted Gauls wandered her alleys side by side with Persian religious fanatics, while trousered Germans and circumcised Jews paraded her avenues.

The native Romans were weak and corrupt, afraid of the interlopers who owned more and more of the ancient imperial city. Rome's degradation was nearly complete.

The ancient senatorial class still believed that it ruled the empire.

But if the senators could see themselves, decked out like barbarians and oriental princes, aping the very aliens who sought to destroy them, they might realize that they were—and had been for centuries— extinct as a ruling class. That was why Diocletian was needed; Rome could no longer govern herself. But the old fantasy lived on. The senate still met to argue old arguments, a debating society infected with perpetual talk, an engine powered by hot air, doing nothing useful. The emperor ruled, and the once-proud citizens of Rome were now and would be forever subject to their former subjects.

The mob, though, was dangerous. The field of the praetorians, measuring some fifteen hundred by two thousand feet, was filled, and the pack bayed for its prey. Whores plied their trade within sight of the camp's walls, mixed in with charlatans and gamblers and proselytizers and actors and tumblers. Entire families camped, some under tents, waiting for the emperor's gold. Food vendors hawked their wares, and wine sellers urged the mob to drink. A constant stream of wagons brought new people, supplies, and distractions to the crowd.

They waited, less and less patiently as time dragged on, for what they considered their due. Their emperor had to pay for their presence, to buy their assent to his being among them. Many carried weapons. Some were soldiers. Some were children. They waited for Diocletian to appear at the gates to appease them.

Inside, in the quarters of the prefect of Rome, Diocletian was trying to outwait the wolf pack outside. I waited with him. The troops were at full alert, anxious to keep the wolves at bay.

Maximian, Diocletian's co-emperor, Constantius, his caesar, and Galerius surrounded Diocletian. Each of the three lieutenants argued his own point of view. Maximian spoke first.

"I know these people," he said, "and I know how fast they can turn on you. There must be tens of thousands of them out there. Already their mood is sullen and hostile. We have to act soon, whatever it is you decide. Eventually, they'll do something. All it takes is someone with a grudge against us and a little bit of organization."

Diocletian looked into the face of his old battle companion. It was no longer the young, ugly face that came to mind when he remembered the early days, the days in which he and Maximian had been centurions together in the Danube. Their commands had been together, a special unit in the frontier army. At the head of two hundred hardened troops he had ridden with Maximian through the Carpathian mountains, joyful in the shared danger and thrill of battle, searching out the small bands of guerilla fighters on their own terms and bringing the might of the imperium to bear on the enemies of Rome. They had been, then, full of youth and ambition, an endless time stretching before the two young fighters in which anything had been possible.

Now, in his friend's lined and leathery face, he saw only a chronicle of weariness and anxiety. Did his own face, Diocletian wondered, thus mirror his own inner state? Was this the beginning of the end for the two young men who, once, in ages past, believed that they would never die?

He smiled at the anxious face of Maximian.

"Do you remember the early years together?"

"In Carpathia?"

"In Carpathia."

"Yes, lord," Maximian said. "With longing. Our enemies were different, then."

"Easier to identify, at any rate," Diocletian said. He walked to the window, staring outside pensively. "What I wouldn't give to be at the head of a cohort, raining steel down on barbarian tribesmen! Now, I have to rain down gold, and from the look of that crowd, half of them are the kind of barbarians we used to fight."

He turned and examined the faces of the three men with him. Constantius was pale, as always. He always looked as if he were in the grip of mortal fear; "Bleach-faced" his men called him. But he won his battles, no matter what his appearance. With his son Constantine now safe in Britain, he would back Diocletian only as long as it was to his own advantage.

Maximian would always be predictable, but he was as dependable as the rising of the sun in the east.

Galerius was the puzzle among the three. Nearest to Diocletian, he was the most anxious to overthrow him, to snatch the purple robe for himself.

Diocletian was getting older. Twenty years of rule had, inevitably, taken their toll on the first emperor. But he was not ready or willing yet to give it up. He still had plans to bring the Romans back to their hereditary glory. It could still be done—even with the dregs represented by the mob outside. If he, Diocletian, a peasant by birth and a simple soldier by experience, could see the glory that had once been Rome, the heterodox mob outside could be brought to see it.

Made to see it. Made to want it.

There was glory waiting for Rome again. He knew. And with that remembering, he regained his sense of purpose.

"Tell the people that there are better things in store for them than bread and circuses. Tell them that the substance of the state will not be wasted on empty pleasures. They have a destiny which, though it awaits them, they do not yet see. But the day is coming when they will know it, and when they will live it."

He turned back to the window to watch the mountebanks and whores and their giddy victims.

"Tell them."

I looked to the other three members. Each was locked in thought, silent, not willing to share the contents of his mind. I looked again to Diocletian. He saw my hesitation.

"Tell them!"

I left their conference and arranged for the proclamation to be made. What happened among them thereafter I do not know.

✦ ✦ ✦

Genesius was now in the mob, having made his way from the slums in the trans-Tiber, where the Christian community had its stronghold.

Throngs of subjects had come in from the countryside for the vicennalia. The prospect of wild entertainments in the theaters, the circus, and the Colosseum; the money gifts expected of a celebrating emperor; the chance for an interruption in the tedium of work had brought them. Instead of following the city streets, which were packed with crowds, he had, with the help of Sextus, crossed the Tiber near the Theater of Marcellus, then south past the Aemelian and Sublician bridges to a sewer that opened into the Tiber just below the Sublician bridge.

The sewer ran full.

Genesius stopped when he realized that Sextus meant for them to wade through the sewer. They were above its outflow on the northern bank; the Tiber flowed sluggishly on their right, discolored by the flow from the sewer.

"Must we?" the actor asked.

"You saw the crowds around the Theater of Marcellus," Sextus said. "The Circus Maximus is just across this little stream; the crowds will be even worse there. The Forum is jammed with visiting dignitaries. You wouldn't stand a chance of making your way past them. This little brook will get you across the Forum. Take it or leave it. But if you're going to change your mind, change it now. I don't want to go through all of this for nothing."

"It smells," Genesius said.

The guide was silent, waiting for the actor to make his decision. Genesius had no choice. He knew that if he were gone from Diocletian much longer, he would never be able to see the man, the emperor, his father, again. Imperial favor was the most mutable quality in a changeable world. Genesius took a final breath of relatively clean air and lowered himself into the sewer.

Chest-deep in the current, which was swollen with the effluence of the thousands of extra people in the city for the celebration, Genesius vomited again and again until his stomach was empty of the rich breakfast Lydia had fed him. It left him lightheaded, watching the remains of the meal swirl in the current and join the common excreta of the city.

They moved on.

The sewer led them along the base of the Capitoline hill, between the forum of Nerva and the temple of Peace. The stonework was rough and ancient but coated with the deposits of centuries of Rome's excretions. Algae smoothed the cobbles underfoot and made walking treacherous. The walls above the water level were overgrown with soft, dark moss. Above the two sojourners, the open sky tempted them with a promise of warmth.

By the time they reached the sewer's beginning, at the intersection of the Vicus Longus and Alta Semita on the eastern side of the Forum, the two men were soaked in Roman filth. They emerged from the sewer stinking and foul. Their smell and their appearance made it relatively easy for them to pass through the mobs unharmed. People pressed away from them into the crowd as the two approached, giving them a wide berth.

"Is this how Moses parted the Red Sea?" Genesius asked Sextus, who merely grunted and pressed on. The smell was ferocious, but it enabled them to push through the mob by the Forum and begin the climb up the Quirinal hill along the Alta Semita.

The Alta Semita, or High Path, followed the crest of the Quirinal, one of the seven hills. Initially it ran northerly, until it reached the temple of Serapis. After a turn westward near the temple it bore in a straight line northeast to the baths of Diocletian and the praetorian camp.

Sextus stopped in front of the temple.

"You can find your own way from here," he said. "I still don't understand why you want to go back to him. The offer stands. You can stay with us."

Genesius was tempted.

"Get thee behind me," he joked, though that was the last place he wanted a devil to be. "I have to do this."

Sextus was unmoved.

"He is our enemy, I know," Genesius said, "but aren't we told to love our enemy?"

Sextus shifted uncomfortably on his feet. "Yes, but he is trying to kill us all!"

"I can't help it," Genesius said. "I love him. He is my father and I love him."

"Didn't our Lord tell us that he who loves his father and mother more than he loves the Lord will die?"

Genesius sighed and looked down the long, straight street. "We can trade quotations from the Scriptures all day long, but it won't change my need to go on or your need to return. Jesus went where He needed to go, even into Pilate's hands. As long as there is a chance that I can slow down the persecution, how can I remain in the safety of the catacombs? Diocletian is my friend. Shall I abandon him because he is blind? He is still a man. He has a soul."

"I think you're a fool."

"I know I am," Genesius said. "It's my trade and my calling. Good-bye."

"God go with you."

"And with you."

The two men embraced, forgetful of the stench that clung to both of them.

"Take good care of her," Genesius said, "if I don't return. But give me a little while before you start." He grinned mischievously into Sextus' eyes. "You never know—I might be back!"

Then Sextus stood watching as Genesius began the mile-long walk to Diocletian's camp. Even at this distance, he clearly heard the rumble of the huge crowd that awaited the emperor's largess in the field of the praetorians. As he progressed the street filled with people, all heading in the same direction. By the time he reached the baths of Diocletian three-quarters of the way to his goal, the road was nearly impassable because of the crush. But his aroma preceded him, and the crowd opened before him. People fell away in disgust, holding cloths to their noses. Some actually collapsed, retching.

Genesius was conscious of the smell, but the hours he had spent with it already, and the emptiness of his stomach, had left him immune to his own stink.

Here I am, he thought, *a walking heap of night-soil, on my way to see the emperor, the Augustus of Rome. I am now everything that he hates. Why should he see me? How will I pass the guards that surround him? I am the protagonist in a fantasy of my own devising. The best I can expect is that some centurion will beat me—and not too severely, I hope.*

Shouting interrupted his reverie. He was well past the baths now, and to his right was the field of the praetorians, filled to bursting with a swelling sea of humanity. This near to the imperial presence, not even his stench could ward off the mob. He was pressed on all sides and carried by the swell into the field opposite the camp.

Ripples of emotion passed through the human sea, as rumors swept from one end of the mob to another, sometimes crossing like waves on an irregular shoreline. In a quiet trough he could hear nothing, then suddenly he was swept up to the crest like driftwood, with as much volition. He moved through the mob as human flotsam, tossed this way and that by some unknown tidal force.

Troops poured from the gate of the praetorian camp. The crowd surged away, leaving a bare patch of ground as the sea does when a wave is gathering force to batter against the shore.

The sea of people spat Genesius, stinking and alone, into the bare patch between the sea of the Roman mob and the sea wall of the praetorian guard. The wave backed up against the old rampart that separated the baths from the field of the praetorians. The wave foamed bodies over the wall, curling, preparing to break on the field. Genesius stood alone between the towering breaker and the iron shore of the praetorian guard.

He swung one hand up toward the mob and fixed them with his gaze. When, unaccountably, the crowd fell silent and still, he lowered his hand slowly, still watching them sternly. Then he shifted his gaze to the troopers, searching for a face he knew. He found Martius, the centurion, and walked slowly to him.

"Do you recognize me?" Genesius asked.

"The actor, Genesius," Martius said. "You're a mess."

"Can you get me inside? Diocletian will want to see me."

"You'll be lucky if he doesn't kill you," Martius said. "He has gotten tired of asking about you."

"And you'll be even luckier if they don't kill you." Genesius nodded back at the mob, still poised to break over the contingent of soldiers. "I had some business that needed attending to. I'm going to talk to them now, if you will take me inside to see him."

Martius looked past Genesius at the mob. "I'll take you. But watch what you promise them. He's in no mood to let them have anything."

Genesius turned his back on the centurion and strode to the middle of the open field.

"People of Rome!" he cried, using his best theatrical voice. "You wish for recognition from your emperor?"

The crowd snarled wordlessly in reply but stayed in position.

"Four legions are in the city. Each man of those four legions has sworn an oath of fealty to the emperor. If you attack his troops, they will destroy you, your homes, your families, and your shrines. Rome will be as Troy—sacked and burned until not one stone stands on another."

The mob lost its poise; individuals began to argue with those near them. At the edges some people drifted away, looking over their shoulders for pursuit, every movement tempered by suspicion.

"People of Rome!" Genesius cried again. "I know your hopes and your needs. You came to celebrate twenty years of stability and peace. The emperor ended the thirty years of civil war! He made it safe for you to live as Romans! He defended your rights as citizens! Will you let me speak to your emperor for you? Tell him of your honor for him, your trust in him, and your love for him? For I will report it truly." He paused for breath, then resumed.

"Give me your reply!"

The roar shook the earth of the praetorian field. The wave that had been poised to break over the few hundred soldiers disintegrated as Genesius turned to the troops and led the way to the gate of the praetorian camp. The troops were turned from a pitiful force facing an onslaught into an honor guard for a hero.

Martius caught up with Genesius to walk by his side. "How did you do that?" he asked. "They were after blood. They might have settled for gold. But you gave them nothing but a few words. And you stopped a riot."

"I didn't have anything else," Genesius said. "Let's get inside before they figure out what's happened."

"Don't run," Martius said, "whatever you do. They'll sense your fear."

Genesius laughed. "I'm not afraid of them. Not now. Now I have to see Diocletian."

Diocletian, along with most of his civilian entourage, watched Genesius halt the mob's intended storming of the praetorian camp. He called Diarius to his side.

"What is he doing?"

"Giving the performance of his life, my lord," Diarius said. Diocletian watched in rapt attention as Genesius led the soldiers back into the relative safety of the camp. The sentries threw open the gates for Genesius and the troops, then hurriedly closed them again in fear of the mob.

Once inside, Martius resumed his authority. Two soldiers clamped their hands on Genesius' arms and marched him to face Diocletian. Or rather, they began to; on touching him, they recoiled from the stench of the sewer that clung still to the actor's flesh and clothing.

Martius berated the soldiers. He had served with Galerius in Persia and knew when to observe the social amenities and when to ignore them.

"Are you soldiers or aesthetes?" he snarled. "You've smelled worse in the field."

"Not often," one of them murmured loudly enough to be heard.

There were chuckles in the crowd that had gathered. The two chosen soldiers, faces rigid in their effort to avoid disgracing themselves in the emperor's presence, guided Genesius to the dais where Diocletian sat. As they reached him the troopers tried to kneel; it was, after all, a public occasion; proper behavior was expected. But Genesius, in spite of the soldiers' weight dragging at him on both sides, remained standing. At most, almost imperceptibly, he nodded to Diocletian.

Martius strode forward to add his strength at Genesius' shoulder. Still the actor failed to bend his knees to Diocletian. Martius grew angry. He slammed his shield into Genesius' back and sent him sprawling at Diocletian's feet.

Diocletian thundered to his feet.

"Is this how you treat the man who saved your life, Martius?" He knelt by Genesius and lifted him up. Martius stood open-mouthed as Diocletian, heedless of the stench, led Genesius to a couch by his own and laid him on it. As Genesius settled, dazed, onto the couch, the two soldiers backed away from the imperial wrath, leaving their officer to face it alone.

"Bring water, food, and drink," Diocletian ordered him. The emperor turned to his friend. Martius backed away, uncomprehending. Behind him, a servant scuttled to obey. A huge hand clamped onto Martius' shoulder, and a coarse voice sounded in his ear.

"Come with me," Galerius whispered. "We—you and I—will take care of this actor later." The grip tightened, until Martius almost cried out in pain.

"Come."

With a last glance at the actor whose behavior had humiliated him before the entire court, Martius followed Galerius to his tent. Diocletian, his attention focused on Genesius, never saw them leave.

"Are you all right?" Diocletian asked.

"Yes, sire," Genesius said. "Though Martius nearly broke my back."

"He will be dealt with."

"Don't bother," Genesius said. "He was only doing his job."

"You are more generous than you ought to be," Diocletian warned. "You have an enemy now. He has influential friends."

"So do I."

"So you do," Diocletian laughed. "By all the gods it's good to see you again. That was a rather spectacular entrance you made. What did you promise that mob in my name?"

"If you had listened, not much. Just that I would talk to you. But you'll have to give them something. All I really did was to buy you some time. They want their bread and circuses."

Diocletian wrinkled his nose. "You stink, my friend, and so do your ideas. Have you gone Christian on me?"

"We are in the midst of your entire court," Genesius said. "I would like to get cleaned up. I had to come through the sewers to get here."

Diocletian waved at the court. Bowing to him, they left the area. He helped Genesius up from the couch and into his own tent, which stood nearby.

"You went through the—"

"The Cloaca Maxima, I think it's called." Diocletian swallowed back a spurt of bile.

"That is the largest, oldest sewer in the city."

"Well, it seemed like the biggest while we were in it."

"We?"

"I had a guide."

"What kind of man would guide you into the sewers?" Diocletian asked.

Genesius had no chance to answer. Publius Labius led in a group of three slaves. Two carried a tub of hot water and placed it in the far corner of the tent, away from the entrance. The chamberlain carried towels and the harsh soap used by the legions. The third servant carried bread, wine, and cheese on a golden tray, which he placed carefully on a small table.

"Your costume is ruined," Diocletian observed as Genesius hurriedly stripped for his bath.

"There is another." He held the reeking garment out to Publius Labius, who produced a pair of tongs with which to accept the fouled garment.

"Burn that," Genesius said, stepping into the copper tub. The chamberlain held the stinking motley at arm's length as he left the tent. While Diocletian's attention was on Publius Labius, Genesius broke the chain that held the coin of Jupiter around his neck and dropped the medallion into the bath water.

Genesius' body, Diocletian noticed, was leaner than it had been. The flesh that the actor had put on during his luxurious life in the court had melted away during the weeks of his absence. He had returned to the wiry form of his youth. And he seemed older, wiser.

"At least you haven't been circumcised in your absence," Diocletian observed.

"Never that, my lord," Genesius said from the tub. "This feels wonderful. I haven't had a bath since leaving Salonae."

Diocletian turned away from his friend.

"Why did you leave me?"

"I came back," Genesius said, "to be with you again."

"You left me when I needed you most."

"You seem to have survived."

"You left me!" Diocletian shouted. "Without permission!" Genesius was uncowed by the emperor's anger. He seemed strangely calm to Diocletian, strangely unafraid.

"I was not aware that you owned me," Genesius said. "If you want me to be your slave, I will be."

"You know that's not what I have ever wanted. But you left me alone. I had no one." Diocletian slumped into his chair. "Why do you do this to me? Why didn't you tell me you were leaving? I was worried about you."

Genesius paused in his washing. "Would you have allowed me to go, if I had told you in advance?"

"Yes, of course. Why not?"

"Dismiss the servants."

Diocletian waved a hand and the two slaves left the tent. "They are gone."

"Is anyone listening?"

"The way you smell?" Diocletian laughed. "They won't come within yards of this tent. I may have to have it burned along with your costume."

Genesius laughed with him. "You may be right. I will just have to take the chance."

"What chance?" Diocletian grew serious. Genesius reached down into the water, now scummed with the filth from his trip through the sewer. He searched for the medallion, heart hammering against his chest until his hand closed around it.

"Do you remember a woman, years ago, when you were but a general, who was kind to you," Genesius asked carefully, "who among all was unimpressed with all the trappings of your dignity, who never presumed upon her relationship with you, asked nothing of you, but simply gave herself to you?"

Diocletian remained silent for a long moment, sunk within himself. At last he looked up.

"Sarah," he said, tonelessly. "She died."

"Loving you," Genesius said.

"Yes," Diocletian said. "I know."

Genesius watched in silence as memory, long hidden from its owner, washed over Diocletian's features. For a long moment the two men sat in silence. Finally, it was broken.

"'I remember," Diocletian said.

"You treated her well," Genesius told him.

"It could have been better."

"She never complained."

"She wouldn't." Diocletian suddenly stirred, his reverie broken by the realization. "How could you know these things? The men who helped me are dead. She is dead.

"Sarah!" he whispered.

Genesius stood and stepped from his bath. The water had grown tepid and foul. He took a towel and dried himself. Diocletian watched in silence.

"She never took another man, after you," Genesius said. "I am her child, the only child she ever had."

Diocletian was shaken. His eyes sought something to fasten on, anything but the youth who stood before him, naked, claiming to be his only son. But the young body was a magnet for his vision, and at last his eyes came to rest upon it.

"How can I trust you? What do you want from me?"

Genesius stood in silence, having no answer. The two men were suspended, lost in a time when everything between them had changed and left them no place to plant their feet. Genesius knew, as he had known since discovering the fact of his sonship, that to presume upon the relationship, to interfere in Diocletian's rule would be to destroy what was between them. If he were to ask for what he wanted, Diocletian would at best deny it, and the trust between them would be broken forever. And what he must ask was the end of the persecution.

Diocletian would see the request as an attempt to manipulate the relationship. He would refuse.

Genesius opened his hand. "It is not proof, sire, but it is truly one of the coins in the purse you had sent to Sarah. When she died, she placed it in my hand."

"She told you?" Diocletian demanded. "I don't believe it."

"Never," Genesius said. "She told me only that my father's name was Diocles—never what he became."

Diocletian relaxed visibly. "She never could have survived in the court, you know. She was too innocent. I would say too good, but goodness was not a characteristic she tried to cultivate. She accepted. She was at peace. No one here—not even you—is at peace. But she could make me feel a part of her peace. I miss her, even now."

Naked before his father, Genesius waited. The servant returned, saw the two men looking at each other, placed the fresh costume on a chair, and left without speaking. Genesius picked up the garment.

"Am I a fool for telling you?"

"I think so," Diocletian said. "You must never ask me for anything now. Every request would seem an attempt to use your position."

"Even from me?"

"Especially from you." Diocletian rubbed his nose. His voice was hoarse. "Who else have you told of this?"

"Lactantius, the rhetorician."

"Has he told anyone?"

"He told me to keep it to myself," Genesius said, "to tell no one, not even you."

"You should have listened to him. We would both be better off not knowing." Diocletian sat rigidly in the chair that had held Genesius' costume, distant and cold. "Get dressed. I am not so decadent that I enjoy the sight of your body."

Genesius jumped into his clothing.

"Since you have returned," Diocletian said, "we will celebrate the event. You will perform, and I will watch. And I will take your advice. I will give the mob their bread and their circus. You will be the major attraction. Along with entertainment, they will receive from you instruction in the duplicity of the Christians. You will perform your play of baptism. It should go down well with the mob. And I will watch."

"I would rather—"

"You may ask nothing of me," Diocletian said. "We will erect a stage in the field of the praetorians, and you will perform as soon as it is ready."

Genesius moved to the tent's entrance. At the doorway he stopped and turned.

"You may ask nothing." Diocletian's voice was a monotone. Genesius left.

Outside, Diarius was waiting for him.

"I heard the news!" the little man crowed. "Where the devil have you been?"

"I had to have time to think," Genesius said. The two men embraced. "He wants the baptism play."

"It's about time!" Diarius said. "When? Where? We could go to the Theater of Marcellus, but it's all the way across town. The crowds are terrible and—"

"Here. Or rather, in the field, outside, among the mob."

Diarius whitened. "But there must be thousands of them out there!"

"I know," Genesius said, "but those are his orders. He wants a stage erected. He's going to watch too. You'd better see to it."

"He's insane," Diarius said.

"But he is the emperor. Talk to the praetorian captain. Arrange for a heavy guard and for the stage and a dais to be put together. It should take several hours to get everything ready."

"What are you going to do?"

"Get ready myself," Genesius said.

"It's not the best way to handle a premiere," Diarius said. "Can't you talk him out of it? Ask him for a delay?"

"I can ask him for nothing, now."

✦ ✦ ✦

Genesius found me in my tent and explained what had happened between himself and Diocletian. He had rushed through the camp to speak with me, and he was still breathless.

"What do I do?" he asked.

It was the same question I had been asking myself. Someone had to survive to tell what happened during the persecution.

Genesius now believed. He told me of his time in the wilderness, of the serpent's bite and the visions that followed. He told me of his love for his father and his father's suspicion.

I had no answer for him.

The church had given me a commission to commit the martyrs' acts to paper and memorialize their sacrifice. Genesius knew that to perform the play would be an act of treason to his Lord. But I could not advise him to refuse because refusal would mean his death. He was not yet a baptized Christian, but only a catechumen; he would not be violating his baptismal vows if he performed as he was ordered. I reminded him of the commandment of Jesus Himself to render unto Caesar the things that are Caesar's.

It was legalistic casuistry. I knew; Genesius knew. There was a right action to be taken. He was about to speak when Diarius appeared at the entrance to my tent.

"So there you are!" he cried. "Everything is ready. I have your mask."

"Give it to me," Genesius said. He took the half mask and dangled it from his hand. "How long?"

"Ten minutes until the emperor begins his procession. The stage is set up in the middle of the field. Diocletian will proceed from the gate to a dais, ringed by a cohort of praetorians."

"He hates the mob," Genesius said. "It's out of character." None of us had a response.

"You'll be ready then?" Diarius asked.

"I will be ready," Genesius said.

Diarius left, hurrying to attend to the details he imagined to be important. Genesius stood unmoving, eyes downcast, the mask dangling from his hand.

"So you've decided to perform," I said, less in question than in confirmation.

"I can decide nothing, Lactantius," he said. "Not yet. Or maybe it was all decided at the beginning of time."

CHAPTER 30

T

he procession was a ceremony designed to awe the mob into good behavior. As a member of the entourage of the emperor, I was a part of it. After Genesius left my tent, a messenger from the chamberlain ordered me into my finest robes and told me to present myself at the praetorian gate instantly.

Like all events organized by the army, there was great hustle and bustle to get everyone ready in plenty of time to wait for at least an hour before it actually began. In the army of the Lord at the last trumpet, I expect that some officious archangel will have everyone in ranks two eons before Armageddon actually begins.

At the head of the procession was a troop of light cavalry, all mounted on black horses. The animals were nervous, being all crowded together within the narrow confines of the gate area. The cavalry would ride out first, to push the mob away from the entrance to the camp.

Next in the line was a cohort of the praetorian guard. Its nominal strength was six hundred men, but in practice it totaled only five hundred soldiers. The foot soldiers carried the standard of the cohort and the imperial eagle.

The third element was a procession within a procession—the priests of Jupiter-Diocletian and of Maximian-Mercury and of all the pantheon of the gods of Rome. Each priest in each group had at least half a dozen attendants. All were dressed in their ceremonial robes, wearing or carrying their symbols of office.

The fourth element was the household of the emperor, including myself, along with the court officials, members of the personal staffs of Diocletian, Galerius, Maximian, and Constantius. The last had claimed new fighting by remnants of Carausius' rebels as an excuse to keep his son Constantine far away from the celebration in Britain. Prisca, the empress, joined the procession. She looked ill but carried herself with her accustomed dignity. The household slaves and servants made up the balance of the party.

The soldiers in front were present merely as a demonstration of the emperor's power; we were there to demonstrate the emperor's "security" among the people of Rome.

Most of us went armed.

When all were assembled, the order was finally given to move out from the safety of the praetorian camp into the wilderness of the crowd. The huge gates were thrown open. The mob outside roared with anticipation and began to pour toward us.

The cavalry troop charged at a gallop into the crowd, meeting its anarchy with discipline and momentum. The force of the charge threw the mob back against itself, leaving a cleared space between the crowd and the gate. The infantry quickly moved to fill the vacuum, establishing a perimeter into which first the priests and then the household entered. While the infantry held the perimeter, the cavalry regrouped and circled the island of priests and courtiers, using their horses' weight and height to keep the crowd at bay. Gradually, we moved toward the center of the field of the praetorians. For the moment we were safe.

One of the priests of Jupiter stepped onto the stage. He drew off his headgear and the mob fell silent.

Diocletian himself stood among them.

"People of Rome!" he thundered. And for a moment he seemed to be an incarnation of the god. His face was set like marble, his voice reverberated above the cries of the mob. I understood at least one of the reasons why he had become the emperor of Rome—he commanded.

"Do you know me?"

The multitude murmured in response. Diocletian surveyed the field passionlessly, his expression unchanged. He signaled the guardsmen at the perimeter. Five hundred soldiers opened their purses and threw gold coins into the crowd. Each coin bore the portrait of Diocletian.

"Now do you know me?"

This time he was answered by a wordless scream.

"Who makes the gold you crave?" he called.

"Diocletian!"

"Who gives you grain to eat?"

"Diocletian!"

"Who makes your borders secure?"

"Diocletian!"

"Who gives you life?"

The roar shook the very earth of the field where we stood. He waited for the cheering to die down. Then he walked around the outer edge of the stage, looking into the faces of the people in the crowd.

"The actor has spoken to me of you," he said. "He tells me that you need something from me. And he is right.

"You have food—bread and meat and grain enough. I know. I send it to you from Egypt by the boat-load.

"You have money—from my hands into yours. You have life—my troops have seen to it, fighting against the Britons, against the Persians, against the barbarians who press against us from all sides.

"But look at yourselves! I stand here among you, and I do not recognize you as the sons of Aeneas, of Cincinnatus, of Cicero, of Augustus. I do not recognize you as the sons of Rome! You are a mongrel dog, descended from a dozen noble breeds yet heir to none.

"Where is the Rome that was?

"I see the national costume of the Gallic tribes, the soft gowns of the Persian fakir. I hear the chants to a thousand gods foreign to the heritage of Rome. I smell the stink of Persian incense, the blood of Christian orgies!"

Diocletian held them spellbound with the power of his oratory.

Although I had heard of his abilities, I had never seen him in action. He hated to expose himself in this way, always limiting his audiences to a few people chosen with great care, administering the far-flung empire from behind a wall of functionaries. This version of Diocletian was dangerous.

"Purify yourselves!" he ordered them. "Cast out the irrational, the exotic, the foreign from your midst!"

I had not thought it possible, but his voice whirled over the crowd's wordless cries. He had them. They would go anywhere, do anything at this moment for his sake.

He stretched out his arms, hands clenched in determination, raising them above his head.

"Purify yourselves!" he cried. "Purify Rome!" He stood rigid for a moment, then slowly lowered his arms to his sides. His fists remained tightly clenched, the tension knotting the muscles of his arms. From the ground below him I could hear his teeth grinding even through the crowd's cheers, as he waited for them to subside.

"You believe," he said into the comparative silence that followed, "that my gift to you is money. And you expect me to entertain you as well. Bread and circuses, the old cry. You will have what you ask of me, never fear. But embedded in your circus, like a ruby shining in the mud, is a treasure beyond what you hope for. It will entertain you, I promise that.

"Horace—a *Roman* poet—tells us that the aim and goal of poetry is to delight and to instruct. Be delighted, therefore, with what you are about to see, but be instructed also. Let it also remind you how to think about who you are.

"Here is the circus that I give you."

Diocletian, as he finished, resumed the headdress of Jupiter; not a soul in the audience missed the significance of the gesture. With all the dignity that twenty years on the Roman throne could give a man, he descended from the stage and took his seat.

Genesius wandered out of the crowd and up onto the stage, accompanied by Atalanta. Both wore the togas of the Roman senatorial class.

"What a speech!" Genesius exclaimed. "What a speech! I hope you paid attention."

"I did, dear," Atalanta simpered. "But I didn't understand that part about mongrels. Did he mean to say that I'm—"

"I knew you would misunderstand."

"I didn't! I understood perfectly well. Only, well, I don't know that it will be socially correct to 'purify' everything. I mean, what about the Marcuses, who live next door? They're a good family, even if they did let their son marry that Egyptian hussy. Honestly, I can't stand the way she dresses, all rouged and kohled with nothing on but a dozen veils just to go down the street to the well to fetch water. It's a disgrace!"

"Don't gossip," Genesius ordered.

"It's not gossip!" Atalanta was incensed. "I've seen her myself. I wouldn't mind purifying her, I'll tell you."

"That is not what our noble emperor had in mind."

"And I suppose you can read his mind?" Atalanta said. She stretched her arms out in a gesture meant to mimic a Persian fortune-teller. "Ahura-Mazda sees all, knows all, tells all. I, the priestess of Zoroaster, look into your mind and know your inmost secrets."

Genesius stopped in his tracks. "Stop that!" he cried.

"You will fall into a fit—"

"That's not funny—"

"—a fit of great foaming and moaning—"

"Stop it!"

"You will lie on the ground and shake your limbs. Gouts of spittle will sprinkle—"

Genesius swayed. "You know what—"

"—sprinkle the flowers by the roadside, and they will wither and die."

Genesius trembled, speechless. Atalanta continued her incantation.

"You will fall first to your knees."

Genesius, eyes staring helplessly, fell to his knees.

"You will teeter from side to side."

He teetered.

"You will fall to your left side."

He fell.

"I mean," Atalanta said, "your right side."

Genesius looked up at her, a question in his eyes.

"Your right!" Atalanta insisted, kicking him in the ribs. Genesius rolled over onto his right side.

"That's better," Atlanta said. "Now, drool a little for the people."

Genesius did as she commanded.

"Come on, you can do better than that!"

He tried.

"More!" Atalanta ordered. Genesius did his best to obey. She drew away from him, careful to avoid soiling her gown.

"Now shake yourself!" she cried.

Genesius' limbs shook, each moving, by some supreme effort of concentration, to a different rhythm. The crowd applauded in their admiration of his craft, while they laughed at his ridiculous position. He had rolled on his back. His left leg was pointing straight up. His right leg extended and retracted spasmodically. His arms windmilled in opposite directions. His head bounced against the wooden planking of the stage to the seeming accompaniment of an invisible drum. The fingers of his left hand clenched and unclenched, while those on the right enacted the first five gestures of Quintilian's *Rhetoric* over and over again.

While all this was going on, Atalanta leaned out over the audience, displaying herself in the process, and called to her lover.

From the crowd appeared a youth, Riotamus. He was wrapped in a cloth which covered him from head to toe. When he reached the stage, Atalanta took one end of his swaddling clothes by the hand, gave it a yank, and spun him around, unwrapping him and revealing him as a boy who looked to be no older than twelve. I wanted to leave the ugly spectacle, but the press of the crowd prevented me. The boy's body was shining with oil. Strapped at his private parts was a theatrical phallus, the traditional emblem of comedy, dating all the way back to the earliest Greeks, which likewise shone in the sun. Atalanta draped the boy's clothing over the still-seizing form of Genesius. She grasped the boy by his false member and drew him off the stage and out of sight. After a moment of silence she moaned loudly and lasciviously.

The crowd roared its approval.

Genesius was still having a fit on the stage. Eventually, being the only thing to see, he drew their attention back to himself. If anything, his shaking and foaming increased. Through some feat of acrobatics he rolled to his hands and knees, never stopping his fit, and bounced across the stage.

The audience applauded his dexterity.

Mercifully, at this point Hysteria entered upon the scene, accompanied by several of the extras hired for the performance. In the role of his mother, she had Genesius carried off stage.

There was scarcely a pause while several slaves tossed some furnishings up to the stage for the next scene, which opened with Genesius lying propped up on several pillows in his bed, surrounded by his friends and family.

Hysteria, kneeling at one side, wailed inconsolably.

"My son, my son! My son is dying! Ohhhh!"

Genesius sat bolt upright in bed.

"What did she say?"

"My son, my son! My son is dying! Ohhhh!"

"Dying?" Genesius said.

"Dyyyyyiiiiinnnnnggggg!" Hysteria wailed.

"Dying," moaned the friends and neighbors.

"Never to hold his hand in mine," Hysteria cried.

"Dying," moaned the friends.

"Never to see his face again," Hysteria sobbed.

"Dying," moaned the friends.

"Never to hear his happy voice," Hysteria complained.

"Dying," moaned the friends.

"Never to—"

Genesius shouted, "I get the point! Which is the doctor?"

"If it please you, sir," said the physician, "I am he."

"Cure me," Genesius ordered.

"Alas, sir, I cannot," the doctor said. "Your fit has damaged your brain beyond any hope of recovery."

"Beyond any hope?" Genesius whispered.

"Beyond any hope," the doctor confirmed.

"Never to smell his honeyed breath," Hysteria wailed anew.

"Dying," moaned the friends.

"Stop that!" Genesius screamed. "It's in terrible taste. How long do I have, doctor?"

"Before the sun goes down . . ."

"So soon?"

"So soon."

Genesius swallowed hard. The gulp could be heard across the whole field.

"He was a perfect son!" Hysteria declared.

"Dyi—" the friends began to moan.

"I'm not dead yet!" Genesius cut them off. Suddenly he gasped for air. Another fit was beginning.

"Send for a priest of the Christians," he choked. "There isn't much time."

"The Christians?" Hysteria turned down her mouth as if she had tasted something bitter. "And you talk about bad taste!"

"I am heavily laden with sin," Genesius said. "I want to lighten my burden before I die."

The friends, all in one movement, jumped back from him.

"How can you be made lighter?" one of them asked. "Shall we cut off your fingers and toes? Will that be enough? Or should we go all the way and take off your arms and legs too?"

At this purposeful misunderstanding of the gospel the audience howled with laughter. Personally, I failed to see the humor, but the crowd was fully involved with the action. The actors went with the mob's response. I believe the term the actors use is "milking the laugh."

"Are we carpenters then," one said, referring to the honest, though humble trade of our Lord, "that we can cut a chunk off you?" Led by the actors, the audience again dissolved in laughter.

Genesius cut the laughing short. I don't know how he did it; perhaps it was some trick or technique of his craft. It was something that I, as a rhetorician, should have known how to do but never could. Or maybe it was something greater.

"Fools!" he cried, and waited in his comic dignity until silence reigned over the stage and the field of the praetorians. "Fools!" he whispered into the quiet.

"I want to die a Christian."

Sensing an unexpected change in the rehearsed rhythms of the scene, one of the mourners knelt hesitantly by his bedside.

"Why?" he asked.

"So that," Genesius said, "on the day of my death I may be found in God's heart."

While music played, a sad and lonely flute, the actors cleared the stage, leaving Genesius alone in his bed, and no one spoke. The tune melted into a rousing walking rhythm. From the gate of the praetorian camp, through the mob, Diarius, dressed as a Christian bishop, rode an ass to the stage. He was accompanied by a deacon and an exorcist. They carried a tin tub between them, beating a march rhythm on its sides with scrolls meant to represent the holy Scriptures.

The ass ascended the stage awkwardly. Still in his bed, Genesius tried, without success, to bow. Diarius dismounted and the ass split in two, revealing a priest and an acolyte, representatives of the other two offices in the church.

"At last, you've come!" Genesius cried.

"What is it you seek of Holy Mother Church?" Diarius boomed.

"Holy baptism," Genesius said.

"Take off your clothes," ordered the deacon, setting down the burden he shared with the exorcist. The two of them placed it beside Genesius' bed.

"My clothes?"

"Your clothes." Diarius, as the "bishop," was firm, although his voice quavered and his wrist was limp.

"As it is written," the deacon explained, "'You must be born again.' Whoever heard of anyone being born fully dressed?"

"I'm shy," Genesius said.

Diarius knitted his brow in anger. "Will you be shy when you come before the glory of the lord, and he asks why you refused to be baptized, and you answer: 'I was too shy'?"

Of course, the audience laughed at this perversion. Genesius started to answer, but the exorcist interrupted.

"The question was rhetorical."

"I'm sorry," Genesius said.

"Don't be too sure about that," the priest warned. "Is this your deathbed?"

"Not yet," said Genesius.

"Take off your clothes."

Genesius hesitated still.

"Very well," Diarius said. "To prove that we mean no harm, we will remove our clothing, because all men are equal in the sight of the lord. Then you will have no reason for your wicked modesty."

Diarius the bishop, the acolyte, the priest, and the exorcist all threw off their robes and stood naked on the stage. Each had a phallus over his private parts. Each was different; each was grotesque.

"Your turn," the exorcist told Genesius. The baptismal candidate stood up in his bed and removed his robe, thereby exposing his own nakedness. The phallus he wore was shriveled and small. Seeing this, the wretched audience, the refuse of the Roman city, howled in obscene laughter.

With Genesius standing in his bed, the four clerics formed a circle around him. Each poured water from a secret place in his costume, out of the audience's sight. What else they performed while reciting a horribly twisted version of the baptismal rite can well be imagined. I would not write of it, out of a regard for the proprieties, except to demonstrate the lengths to which many have gone to humiliate the Christian hope and to denigrate the faithful. You know that the theater is a temple to the idols. The Greeks dedicated it to Dionysius, we to Venus. Is it any wonder that debauchery and obscenity should rule, and that the name of Christ should therein be mocked? It was hard to watch this act, knowing that I should rise and, like a prophet of old, denounce it as a sin before God. It was harder still to keep silence, allowing the old gods' sway. But I held my peace there among the crowd. Suffice it to say that the obscenity of the actors made the angels in heaven blush with shame.

You may imagine what I saw but will not speak of.

The deacon then leaned over to whisper to Genesius *sotto voce*, "Get in the tub." Genesius stared, disbelieving, at the man. He repeated the order.

Genesius stepped down from his bed and entered the tub. The acolyte, the deacon, the priest, and the bishop stood over him.

"I baptize you," the bishop began. The acolyte dipped his hands into the fluid and held it over Genesius' head.

"In the name of the Father . . . " The acolyte spilled the liquid on Genesius.

"And of the Son . . . " The exorcist mimicked the acolyte.

"And of the Holy Ghost . . . " The priest followed suit.

"Amen."

From the distance there came the sound of shouting. Hurriedly the four clerics picked up their robes and put them on. The priest and the acolyte again became the ass. The bishop mounted the ass's back, and the little procession returned from where it had come, leaving Genesius alone on the stage.

"Now what?" he called after them.

"You'll see," the ass called back. It galloped off, bearing the bishop, and the exorcist and the deacon ran after it. Their escape was made just in time, for from the opposite direction arrived a handful of soldiers, who pulled Genesius roughly from his baptismal tub.

"What are you doing?" Genesius cried. "I haven't done anything!"

"You're under arrest," the officer said.

"What for?"

"Treason!" said the officer and handed Genesius over to his men. "To the magistrate with this fool!" They dragged Genesius off the stage.

The mob laughed cruelly during the intermission, while the stage was reset for the final scene. From the tent came an extra, bearing a tripod containing incense. Flanking him were two priests, one in the array of Jupiter, the other of Mercury, his servant. Clearly, they were meant to represent the divine aspect of Diocletian and Maximian, who nodded approvingly from his place on the imperial dais.

A second, smaller tripod was brought on. In the first, the priest of Jupiter kindled the sacred flame of sacrifice, out of olive branches and beeswax. At last, the magistrate, played by Publius Labius, entered, wearing a mask that gave him the appearance of Diocletian himself, the chief magistrate of the empire.

When all was in readiness, a pair of soldiers brought Genesius out and forced him to kneel in front of the magistrate.

"Your friends have accused you of treason," the magistrate said, "because you have accepted the atheism of the Christians and denied the gods of Rome. What do you have to say for yourself?"

Genesius was silent.

"Come on," said the magistrate, "this is your chance to clear yourself. You can disprove the accusation by making the sacrifice."

Genesius was silent. This time, the actors around him traded uncomfortable glances. Had Genesius missed a line?

The magistrate cleared his throat. "I said, this is your chance to clear yourself. You can disprove the accusation by making the sacrifice." His voice had an urgency that seemed to add meaning to the words, a meaning they had not had a moment before when he had been secure in the performance. Something was out of kilter.

Genesius remained silent, his face an expressionless mask. The tension on the stage increased. The play was going wrong in front of thousands. Genesius was, everyone now knew, missing his cues.

"What's the matter with you?" Publius Labius demanded. "Are you so frightened that you cannot speak?"

"I can speak," Genesius said.

"Then go on!" the magistrate said, leaning forward. Genesius looked the chamberlain in the face, then turned his gaze to scan the multitude watching him. Finally, his eyes rested on Diocletian, whose face was drawn and pale. The emperor knew what was coming.

"Sire," Genesius said, "I have served you faithfully for many months. I have been your true friend, and you have been like a father to me."

The other actors were lost in confusion. They listened to Genesius open-mouthed, stunned as he abandoned the script entirely.

"I mean no disrespect, no disloyalty. But I am a Christian, and I will make no sacrifice."

The crowd exploded in laughter and applause. They cheered for Genesius' audacity and inventiveness. The other actors, seeing the mob's response, broke into confused grins and began to take their bows.

But between Genesius and Diocletian there was no laughter, no smile to put everything right again. Across the gulf between the actor and his imperial spectator, their eyes were locked in mutual understanding. As the applause gradually faded into silence, still the actor and the emperor searched each other's faces. When the crowd was again quiet, Genesius repeated his words.

"I am a Christian, and I will make no sacrifice."

Galerius leaped to his feet and shouted, "Arrest that man!"

Diocletian reached up with a restraining hand on Galerius' arm. "He will not escape. Restrain your soldiers."

Galerius looked down at the emperor and saw the sense of betrayal in his face. He waved a hand, and his troops relaxed.

"As you say, my lord," Galerius agreed, resuming his seat. A wolfish smile began to play on his face.

The other actors had already begun to draw away from Genesius, leaving him alone on the part of the stage nearest the emperor. Atalanta and Hysteria, along with several extras, emerged from the dressing tent, having heard the change in the rhythm and tenor of the performance. Diocletian turned to me.

"Come, Lactantius," he said. "I will serve as magistrate in this case, you as my secretary. We will try him now."

I scurried to keep up with Diocletian as he left the dais and strode to the stage. We mounted the steps where the "bishop" had ascended. The imperial guard closed in around the platform, keeping the mob at bay. We were surrounded by armed men.

"Have you gone insane?" Diocletian asked. "You force me to try you publicly."

Genesius was silent, the expression on his face one of calm. He stood without moving, merely looking out over the heads of the guards at the crowd around him.

"If you resume the play," Diocletian said, "we can pass all this off as a joke that went too far." He too watched the crowd, trying to gauge its changing mood. The Roman mob, knowing Diocletian's distaste, was waiting, enjoying his discomfiture, to see how he would respond to the challenge from the young actor. It was as if the whole world was watching him to see what he would finally decide to do.

"Please, stop, father," Genesius said. "Stop the killing. I hate to stand against you—"

"Then don't."

"I was not given a choice. I must do this thing."

"Why?"

"Standing here, I learned that for this I came into the world," Genesius said. "I looked out at this sea of people, with you sitting in their midst like an island, and I knew that everything I have done, everything I have been, was to make me ready for this moment."

"A moment of betrayal," Diocletian said.

"Of truth between us," Genesius answered.

"What is the truth, then?"

"That you will lose everything you have made. That against your will your whole life has been given over to the purposes of God. That even when you are at the height of your power, you are helpless against Him. That you are the emperor of nothing. That I cannot save you from yourself." Tears rolled down Genesius' cheeks. "That my father will kill me and it will kill him to do so."

"I don't have to kill you," Diocletian said. "Recant. Announce to them that you were only joking." His face was rigid, his jaw clenched. "It doesn't have to be this way."

"If I choose your way," Genesius said, "we will lose each other. If I choose your way, we both will die forever. Give it up. Abdicate. Arrest Galerius. Make Maximian abdicate with you. Leave the throne and together we will learn what other thing Jesus might have in store for us. There are only two choices now: End the persecution, or kill me."

Diocletian looked out at Galerius and Maximian. Each was securely surrounded by his own picked troops. He looked to his illegitimate son. There was a strength of purpose in his face, his stance, his bearing, that allowed no middle way.

Diocletian wept.

Weeping, he backed away from Genesius, to the edge of the stage.

"Will nothing change your mind?" he screamed. Genesius did not answer. He sank slowly to his knees, eyes raised to the sky.

"Answer me!" Diocletian demanded.

As Diocletian reached the edge of the stage the soldier there reached out a hand to steady him. At the touch of the trooper's hand Diocletian whirled and bent down, removing the soldier's sword from its scabbard. He stood, facing Genesius, and began to walk toward him, his face contorted in pain. He reached Genesius and stood over him.

"This man is my friend," Diocletian shouted to the mob. "This man is a Christian. This man is a traitor—to you, to me, and to Rome."

He raised the sword in both hands.

Genesius looked.

He crossed himself.

He winked at me. Then his eyes lifted to the heavens. What he saw there, I do not know, but it caused him to smile, as if grace itself were poured out upon him. He bowed his head to the sword. It fell, and Genesius died, his head, like that of the bishop Anthimus, bouncing from his shoulders to come to rest, face up, at the feet of Diocletian and myself, baptized in his own blood, smiling, full of grace.

After Genesius died, Diocletian marched back into the camp of the praetorians, surrounded by his soldiers, but alone. The short journey back to the camp was made in silence.

As soon as he was away from the stage individual members of the congregation came forward and formed a guard of honor around the body. These were the Christians among the mob. Their pagan adversaries, who might have otherwise destroyed the corpse to prevent its being kept as a relic, allowed them to come forward.

Lydia cradled the head against her breast, alternately laughing and weeping. The sea captain, Sextus, found her and led her from the field to one of the houses used for Christian worship. There, just a short distance from the praetorian camp, was also carried the body of Genesius. With head and body reunited, Genesius was buried and a shrine was erected to the memory of his passion. In the time since then, stories of miracles performed by Genesius gained currency. These I can neither confirm nor deny because for a time I stayed with

Diocletian.

He was never the same afterward. He left Rome almost im-mediately, traveling in a closed wagon with only a small group of soldiers and servants. I was still, somehow, among the latter. We made our way out of Rome at night, in a driving winter rainstorm. He was already suffering from a melancholy following the death of Genesius. The rain lashed at every crack and gap in his wagon. He took a chill, from which he only slightly recovered; the illness trou-bled him ever after. We went to Ravenna, where he feebly took the honors due him on the acceptance of his consulship. He was dispir-ited. Honors meant little.

After Ravenna our little group traveled by land, slowly retracing Genesius' path through Aquileia, back to Aspalathos. We finished out the winter in the echoing vaults of Diocletian's retirement palace. He spoke to no one beyond expressing his elementary physical needs. No one listened to the murmurs of his heart. He kept all at arm's length.

One hopeful sign appeared. Publius Labius was, of course, among the party that traveled from Rome with the hopeless emperor. The chamberlain was almost as quiet as his master, speaking only to give the orders necessary for the comfort and safety of his charge. This job, in fact, he performed with more zeal now than he had earlier, as if his whole attention were focused on the needs of Diocletian.

And, finally, Publius Labius came to me.

"I know you for what you are," he said.

"I could say the same of you." My answer was short, I am afraid. Too many times had I watched the man twist meanings to his own advantage.

"I want to talk to one of your priests."

"You?"

"If you knew what it has cost me to come to you," he said, "you would be more kind." His affectation was gone. He acted more like a dog who had been beaten than like a man.

"How do I know that you won't betray the man I send you to?"

"I can give you no proof. Diocletian himself would leave the Christians alone now, if he could. But I will say and do whatever is necessary to expunge the thoughts that refuse to leave me. Day and night, I think about what I have done, and my thoughts will not leave me in peace. I need resolution. I need an end to my memories. If your God can give me that, I will give myself to your God."

So it turns out that the devil himself may be saved. Publius Labius eventually joined us. His entire being seemed to be transformed. He became celibate, avoiding all excesses of the flesh. He learned humility, allowing to others all pride of place and making himself a true servant. He learned discretion; none of the brothers whom he met was betrayed to the authorities.

One thing he would not change. He continued to serve as Diocletian's chamberlain, although the office was much reduced by the Augustus' decision to withdraw from active participation in the government. What passed between Publius Labius and his emperor I cannot say, for it remained, as always, privileged communication.

Eventually, we set out for Nicomedia to return to the imperial seat. The journey was long, with many stops to accommodate Diocletian's chronic illness.

We had not been there long when Galerius reappeared. If anything, he had grown physically as well as politically. He seemed a Goliath standing next to the shrunken form of Diocletian. The old man listened as Galerius explained the necessity for a new edict of persecution that would go much further than the earlier ones.

"I visited my own city," he explained to an uncaring Diocletian, "my own city, mind you, where everyone knows me. And there—even there—nearly half of the people refused to sacrifice to your godhead. What is it like where Constantius rules, in Britain and Gaul, where their church has nearly complete freedom?"

Diocletian seemed not to hear him. In my sight Galerius took the old man's hand in his own and made it move to sign the new edict. His purpose accomplished, he departed Nicomedia for his own capital, from which he ruled both Diocletian's territory and his own. There also he fostered his plans for dominion over all.

Do not think that I am trying to absolve the supreme emperor of his guilt for his dealings with the church. Through all of what passed, he had the power to intervene—even to eliminate Galerius if need be. But he chose instead to oversee the great tribulation.

The new edict was worse than what had gone before. Now, it was made illegal for all people to be Christians, no matter what their age, their gender, their rank in society. In essence it was merely the codification of what had passed before. Perhaps that is why Diocletian allowed his hand to be guided. Or perhaps his thoughts were elsewhere and not on what went on around him, as they often were after he killed Genesius.

Some say he was mad. I say he was broken. Sometimes in the small garden of the palace, which he had taken to watering and tending himself, I heard him talking aloud, alone. The person to whom he spoke was Genesius. Diocletian would, apparently, hold long conversations with the actor, as if he were alive, discussing when to prune a decorative bush or how deep to plant the seeds of a summer flower. More than once, Diocletian asked forgiveness of Genesius, who, if he had been there, would willingly have granted it. Diocletian seemed so certain that these conversations were real that once I took him to task on their account. He chided me, saying that he knew I was a believer in Christ and that, therefore, I must believe in Christ's promise of eternal life.

"But the dead don't talk to us," I argued. "You have to give up this fantasy."

"Genesius tells me that he's not dead," Diocletian said. A melancholy smile played at the corner of his mouth, almost as if he were wishing that what he said could be true. He cocked his head as if listening to a faint voice. "He should know."

Then it seemed as if the voice failed him. Tears welled in his eyes and crossed slowly down the worn cheeks.

"I killed him, didn't I?"

I had no answer for him. To insist that Genesius was alive in heaven was to feed his folly. To confirm that he had murdered his son was a cruelty.

Then he seemed to brighten a little.

"I often wondered, when I was younger, how a child between myself and Sarah would have turned out. She knew so well how to love.

"Is that what your Christianity is, Lactantius—a cross between Jewish and Gentile, neither wholly one nor wholly the other?

"Do you know what a risk your God takes?" He was sitting on a bench in the garden and looked up at me, as if I knew the answer to his question. "He depends on human beings to carry out his work. What amazes me is that he finds them. I have heard that even my chamberlain has become one of you. Is it true?"

I nodded, afraid to speak.

"I have been abandoned by Jupiter. Galerius now guides my hand, and will not let me write the laws I ought. Tell me about your God. I don't promise to believe you, but at least they will be new lies. I have had enough of the old ones."

As I have written before, even the devil may be saved.

✦ ✦ ✦

The augustus was too old, too weakened by his illness to resist any longer. While Diocletian lay at Nicomedia, Galerius gathered up the reins of power that the former had let fall from his inattentive hands. The final confrontation was brief.

There had been a sudden flare of fighting between troops belonging to Galerius and to Maximian. Civil war seemed a possibility, and it was this fear that made Diocletian willing to listen to Galerius.

The caesar was friendly at first, concerned with Diocletian's health and age, which was now advanced past the beginning of his sixth decade.

"You have been at work on this ill-behaved empire for over twenty years now," Galerius said. "Surely you can use a rest."

Diocletian was adamant. "If I rest, I die."

"Anyone can retire," Galerius said. "There are many pursuits you can follow."

"Not die of boredom," Diocletian explained. "Of intrigue. I have made enemies by doing my job. Do you think that if I were powerless they would hesitate to take their revenge?"

"I will protect you."

Diocletian stared at the younger man for a long moment. The emperor clenched his jaws against the laughter that welled up inside his weakened frame, but there was no holding back. It burst from him and, standing nearby, I had to go and steady him against its effects.

It was not the end of Diocletian's bitterness at the thought of being supplanted, but it was the end of his physical strength, without which he could not resist. He knew—we all in his court knew—that he could not lead an army in a civil war, which Galerius promised to begin if he were not made augustus without delay.

The old man's strength was gone.

✦ ✦ ✦

I stayed with Diocletian until after the ceremony of abdication. No one quite knew how it was to be done, since a reigning ruler had never given up his power while still alive. With persuasion Maximian agreed to abdicate at the same time.

It was a foregone conclusion that Galerius would take over from

Diocletian. It seemed as certain that Constantine would be named caesar and heir to his father, Constantius Chlorus, who now assumed the purple.

Constantine was present at the ceremony, but Maximian turned away from him and brought forth an unknown, Daia, to fill the place Constantine had expected for himself.

When he removed the purple from his own shoulders and placed it on those of Daia, Diocletian became Diocles again. Shortly thereafter, he departed Nicomedia for Aspalathos, and Publius Labius and I went with him. Diocles, as he wanted to be called, rose early every morning to tend to his vegetable patch, enjoying the smooth same-ness of each morning's discoveries. The afternoons we spent review-ing the history of his reign, writing together the memoirs through which he would try to explain himself to the world that followed him. And secretly, as far as the outside world was concerned, when he was lucid and not stricken too badly with attacks of memory, he would ask either myself or Publius Labius, "Read me that section on 'justification.'" And then one of us would recite the words of Paul from memory, being too deeply in our own sins to pretend that it applied more to Diocles than to us.

"'For all have sinned, and come short of the glory of God; being justified freely by his grace through the redemption that is in Christ Jesus: whom God has set forth to be a propitiation through faith in his blood, to declare his righteousness for the forgiveness of sins that are past through the forbearance of God. . . .'"

The last time I read the passage for Diocles, he complained of the difficulty of the language. "Why can't your Saint Paul just come out and say what he wants to say?"

✦ ✦ ✦

It was some years later when I last visited the old man.

He recalled Genesius. "I still remember," he said, "the first time I saw that obnoxious little son of mine."

It was at this moment that I discovered that Genesius had told the emperor of his birth.

"Funniest thing I ever saw before or since," Diocles went on, chuckling aloud. "I know it was blasphemous, but it was still funny." Tears, whether of laughter or of sadness, we could not know, formed in his eyes.

"He took that cross we had set out there to catch the Christians and—" A paroxysm of laughter turned to a cough. I heard the phlegm rattle in his throat.

"—he anointed it with wine! He outfoxed us all.

"What an actor he was . . ."

✦ ✦ ✦

My duty leaves me alive long past the time when I would have left life joyfully to join the ones that I have loved along the way. I am, I learn, to join the entourage of Constantine, who on the death of his father has assumed the purple on his own. He is one of us, and his coming victory will change everything. Very soon now, Donatus, you and Genesius and the other martyrs will have won your crowns not only in heaven, but on earth as well. Your sacrifice, though late in the battle, is as important as any other. When you see the devil coming after you with his sword or with his fire or with his wild beasts or his flying stones, remember the actor Genesius, as he remembered God's promise:

> *He said to me, These are they which came out of the great tribulation, and have washed their robes, and made them white in the blood of the Lamb. Therefore are they before the throne of God, and serve him day and night in his temple: and he that sitteth on the throne shall dwell among them. They shall hunger no more, neither thirst any more: neither shall the sun light on them, nor any heat. For the Lamb which is in the midst of the throne shall feed them, and shall lead them unto living fountains of waters: and God shall wipe away all tears from their eyes.*

Come, Lord Jesus!

F ew saints begin life holy. They start out like most of us, a churning mix of good and evil impulses, tormented by fears and failures, uncertain, alone, and afraid. Above all, saints are human beings, with all the frailties of the species.

Before his journey to Damascus, St. Paul was a persecutor of Christians. St. Mary Magdalene was a prostitute, St. Matthew a tax collector.

The stories of the saints' conversions are our stories. They show the way from self to God. And for a conversion story to make sense, it must describe the life prior to conversion.

For that is the difficulty when we read stories of the saints. How can we measure ourselves against those who have achieved holiness, if we do not know that before they gained the crown, they were like the rest of us? Without the before, a saint seems unapproachable. With that before, they share with us the road they have traveled.

The veneration of the saints began during the persecutions. At the site of the victim's martyrdom or grave Christians would meet on the anniversary of the death and celebrate the martyr's birth into eternal life. The saint was a hero, a "role model" in modern parlance.

A martyr is a witness, and the original saints were just that— witnesses to the Christian hope.

Early saints were not canonized by the church, which merely recognized the existence of the saint's cultus. Even now, the impetus for canonization must come from the people, not the church hierarchy.

The Roman theater, by the fourth century A.D., was in decline. Many of the criticisms leveled against it by the early Christian fathers were valid. It was often tasteless, even obscene. It mocked the pagan gods, as well as the God of the Christians. The descriptions of performances found here are considerably toned down.

Genesius probably existed. The ancient legend outlines only his act of martyrdom; what leads up to it in *The Final Bow* is fiction. He became the patron saint of actors, and a church in Rome is dedicated in his name.

Lactantius also existed, more certainly than Genesius. He was one of the early historians of the church and did indeed serve both Diocletian and Constantine. His best-known work, heavily used as a source for this story, is *On the Deaths of the Persecutors,* which he wrote after the great persecution ended.

Diocletian died in exile in his palace at Aspalathos, having seen his work of twenty years come to ruin. Civil war raged throughout the empire. The war of succession was bloody and long fought, ending only in A.D. 312 with the triumph of Constantine, who legitimized the Christian church in the eyes of the law.

Lactantius despised Galerius and celebrated his death more than that of any of the other persecutors. His description of Galerius' suffering is replete with gory detail; the reader is referred to Lactantius' writing, if curiosity demands.

Prisca and Valeria never declared themselves either for or against the faith. They seem to have declared only for each other, and history last finds them together in exile somewhere in Syria, then loses track of them entirely.

The other actors, Publius Labius, and most of the minor characters are fictitious. Dorotheus, Diocletian's chamberlain, lived and suffered martyrdom, as did the city official Euethius and the bishop Anthimus. The description of the martyrdom of Felicitas is taken from her *Life.*

The tension between Galerius and Diocletian, the two fires at the palace of Nicomedia, and Diocletian's abdication are taken from Lactantius. (For those interested in this fertile period of history, the following may be helpful: Eusebius, *Ecclesiastical History;* Lactantius, *On the Deaths of the Persecutors;* Giuseppe Ricciotti, *The Age of Martyrs: Christianity from Diocletian to Constantine.*)

The great persecution under Diocletian actually took place and was the last effective pagan opposition to the growing church, and, in essence, prepared the church to take its position in the world, as it soon began to do under Constantine.

But that's another story. . . .

Anthimus	AN-thi-mus
Aquileia	A-kwill-AY-a
Ariminum	Ar-i-MINN-um
Aspalathos	Ahs-pa-LAH-thos
Atalanta	At-a-LAN-ta
Branchidae	BRAN-kuh-day
Branchus	BRAN-kus
Bythynia	Bith-IN-i-a
Constantine	KON-stan-teen
Constantius	Kon-STAN-shus
Daia	DIE-ah
Diarius	Die-AHR-i-us
Diocletian	Die-oh-KLEE-tion
Dorotheus	DOR-oh-THEE-us
Ephesus	EFF-uh-sus
Euethius	You-EE-thee-us
Felicitas	Fa-LISS-i-tas
Galerius	Gah-LAIR-ee-us
Genesius	Jeh-NEEZ-ee-us
Lactantius	Lack-TAN-shus
Marius	MAR-i-us
Martius	MAR-shus
Maximian	Max-IM-i-an
Nicomedia	Nic-oh-MEED-i-a
Octavia	Ock-TAY-vi-a
Prisca	PRIS-cah
Publius Labius	POO-blee-us LAY-bee-us
Riotamus	Ree-AHT-i-mus
Romula	ROM-you-lah
Valeria	Vah-LAIR-i-a
Via Egnatia	VEE-a Eg-NAY-sha
Via Flaminia	VEE-a Fla-MIN-i-a

Alan Justice lives and writes in north Texas. He has worked as a grocery clerk, groundskeeper, garbage collector, housepainter, bookstore clerk, lab assistant, psychiatric aide, recreation leader, order picker, administrative assistant, security guard, teacher, actor, director, and graphic artist.

Justice holds a master's and a doctorate in theater and has taught acting, directing, and theater history. He is married and has one child. He is a member of St. Alban's Episcopal Church.